NOTE ON THE AUTHOR

Benjamin Myers was born in Durham. His novel *The Gallows Pole* received a Roger Deakin Award and won the Walter Scott Prize for historical fiction. *Beastings* won the Portico Prize for Literature and *Pig Iron* won the Gordon Burn Prize, while *Richard* was a *Sunday Times* Book of the Year. He has also published poetry, crime novels and short fiction, while his journalism has appeared in publications including, among others, the *Guardian*, *New Statesman*, *Caught by the River* and the *New Scientist*.

He lives in the Upper Calder Valley, West Yorkshire.

benmyers.com / @BenMyers1

Also by Benjamin Myers

FICTION
The Offing
These Darkening Days
Turning Blue
Beastings
Pig Iron
Richard

NON-FICTION
Under the Rock

POETRY
The Raven of Jórvíkshire
Heathcliff Adrift

THE GALLOWS POLE

Benjamin Myers

BLOOMSBURY PUBLISHING

LONDON · OXFORD · NEW YORK · NEW DELHI · SYDNEY

**For my sister Kathryn,
my brother Richard
and their families.**

BLOOMSBURY PUBLISHING
Bloomsbury Publishing Plc
50 Bedford Square, London, WC1B 3DP, UK
29 Earlsfort Terrace, Dublin 2, Ireland

BLOOMSBURY, BLOOMSBURY PUBLISHING and the Diana logo are
trademarks of Bloomsbury Publishing Plc

First published in Great Britain by Bluemoose Books 2017
This edition published in 2019

A catalogue record for this book is available from the British Library

ISBN: PB: 978-1-5266-1115-4; eBook: 978-1-5266-1114-7

8 10 9 7

Typeset by Short Run Press
Printed and bound in Great Britain by CPI Group (UK) Ltd,
Croydon CR0 4YY

To find out more about our authors and books visit
www.bloomsbury.com and sign up for our newsletters

This novel is inspired by real people and events that took place in and around the Upper Calder Valley, West Yorkshire, England in the late 18th century.

The True Story
of King David Hartley
and the Cragg Vale Coiners.

Ravens cawed from the rune-scored bluestones;
   God's stroffage deemed my coin debased.

The Battle of Brunanburh: Part XX
by Steve Ely, 2015.

Oh father, oh father, a little of your gold,
and likewise of your fee,
to keep my body from yonder grave,
and my neck from the gallows-tree.

'The Maid Freed From The Gallows'
(traditional)

Contents

Bean as it is the first and lassed confeshun of Daevid Hartly at the time of his capcher and inprisament he shall wryt down the thorts and werds and lyfes idears of a man what rows to greytness A man called King by them that no him and them that feer him and them folk not yet borne but who will in hunnerds of callender yers cum to no his name and say his name and raymember his name and speek his name And sing his name also and carrie it on ther lyps to tell theare suns and dorters all about the magicul tayl of the greyt King Dayvid Hartley A farther a husban a leeder a forger a moorman of the hills an a pote of werds an deeds an a proud clipper of coynes an jenruss naybur who lorks after his own kynde an is also a lejen.

An even if theyve to fish thees werds out from up his cole ded scul still his storey will lyve on.

Part I
Spring 1767
Mennomith

Soot and ash. Snot and spume.

Quag and sump and clotted moss.

Loam.

The boy left the river and the village behind him and he felt the valley narrow and tighten as he turned up the track and the trees curled in around him and over him. Pulled him in.

In to dell and dingle. Gulch and gully. Mulch and algae. England.

Winter had just released its frosted grip on the valley and the sky was heavy with clouds that dragged themselves across it like broken animals behind him.

The scent of smoke was in the air but there was none to be seen. Only the scud and moil of the clouds and the trees closing in. The rising columns and tangled limbs of birch and beech and ash and alder.

The soil soft beneath his clogged soles.

He remembered his master Duckett's words: keep on the river path upstream and if anyone asks you're apprenticed to a woolcomber and running errands from Sowerby. Then when you pass the black mass of trees pressed up against the sky in the distance high up to your left, and the two waters meet and there are houses and an alehouse called Barbary's, take the packhorse brig and cross the cobbles with the death stone looming so large now it blocks the sun and casts the meeting of the two streams in shadow.

The boy had navigated the running waters at that bridge and crossed those cobbles and drawn up close to that great jagged black slab of stone lunging out from the trees to pierce the clouds, and he had seen gulls and ravens circling the distant edge of the cliff and his master had been right – it had blocked the sun – and then he had moved through shadows onto the Cragg pass where he was told it was just a short climb up the sky to where the king lived.

Hoo Hole barn on your right: keep going. There – see it. A gap and a flinty track. Take it. Watch your back. You're on your own, boy.

As he walked he thought mainly of what he had seen at sunrise when he had first set out with his pouch and a headful of memorised instructions: his first dead body, swinging in chains from the gibbet high up on Beacon Hill. The white morning sun was still cold as it had split through the trees and split through the chains in a glorious sky-burst that framed the form that turned and creaked in the clear air of the breaking dawn, and already the image was seared upon his memory for life.

The day was fresh but the body was not.

There it hung in a suit of iron custom-crafted to hold its crow-pecked shape for months; the sallow flesh that had long since receded was now a sagging leathered parchment beneath clothes matted and ragged from rainfall and decay. A hanged man.

Nails – scores of nails – were driven into the gibbet post to deter people from climbing it to tamper with this grotesque suspension, as they had been known to. For these were the feckless felons that never made it to burial and their boots were there for the taking.

This man's name the boy did not know, but he believed that the body once belonged to he who had poached and butchered a nobleman's stag. It was said they caught him elbow-deep in steaming gizzards as he dressed it out back of his hill-top hovel, the cheeks already boiling in a pot and a haunch blackening in a makeshift smoke house.

Indeed they said it was the sweet smell of scorching meat that had given him away.

Hunger then it was that had led this poor soul to the gallows steps – a hunger for warm meat rather than cold-blooded murder. Not greed but necessity. A stag like that could see a starving family right through a season and then some. No part

4

would be wasted, every inch smoked and seared, sliced and boiled and salted.

The execution had taken place in the dead of night after Fax folk had lined the streets in protest at the grim parade that had been promised them: the dragging of the choked body. The fixing of the chains. The second suspension of a man already dead.

Killing him once was not enough.

Valley people they were, but blood-drunk heathens they were not. They were hungry only for food, and the chains were a bad advertisement for the town.

And the smell...

Even a hundred strides from the hill this morning – even up-wind – the boy had been able to smell the diabolical perfume of the stag-stealer's remains; the warming morning's rays readying the corpse for hatching a forthcoming summer's insects in the clefts and creases of socket and sore, and the retraction of skin and muscle and gums over the gaunt architecture of a desperate man already hastening the sickening sweetness of the bubble and foam and fizz of him.

He had seen that on one side the jaw had come away; what secrets this man had carried in life he kept with him now in death.

The boy had quickened his step, and he quickened it now too.

Grace Hartley was bent double, her feet shifting, as worn wooden soles chafed on worn wooden boards.

Her knees, filled with fluid, were pressed flat against the cold metal frame of the wrought bedstead as she held her swollen stomach heavy in one curled arm and her husband put himself in and out of her. He too swollen in another way.

The only sound was the slap and creak of him.

She gripped the bed post and felt a shifting inside of her – a kicking – and she looked down at her pink ankles barely recognisable as being connected to her feet and legs as they spilled over the stiff black hide of her house clogs.

From the moor she heard the throaty alarm of a lone raven in need of a mate rising up from the lip of the sunken wooded cirque.

Grace Hartley's husband fumbled for a full breast and weighed it; his other hand wove its way into hair that had worked its way loose from the tied rag she used to bun it, and still she cradled the swelling belly so heavy that it pulled the skin of her white back tight across the apex of her spine, and the whole parcel seemed impossibly large to ever squeeze out of her.

He pumped methodically behind her and bounced the breast and the raven called again – a distinct croak that searched the sky for one of its own, for like lustful men of the moors ravens do not like to be alone. She knew these black triangles coupled as they winnowed the air on the updraughts.

She saw a spider. Down there in the gathering dust by her foot. She saw its web too. Down there below the sad slump of the bed's blankets. She saw a parcel of its eggs suspended, a tightly woven tear-drop shape that contained the next season's fly catchers.

Grace Hartley awaited the final wordless thrust and then the pop and spit of his chissum and knew that any moment now in a thick voice barbed in the back of his throat her husband would say something flat about wetting the baby's head or greasing the ginnel or doing the daily milking round. As he withdrew and reached down for his britches that were gathered around strong ankles, the floorboards creaked and the spider's spun parcel swung pendulously with their movements – with the movements of the room – Grace Hartley held the weight of the body-within-a-body a few more seconds and felt the warm wetness already cooling as it ran and dripped, and then there was another strong kick. And she straightened.

That's the morning milking done, he said.

* * *

Slop and spill. Smoke and singe. Sear and blister.

Smut and moss. Sky and rock.

And thunder.

Just as was told the instructions were good and the boy followed them true with his terrier in tow.

With the scent of the coming season scratching at his nostrils and souring his growling stomach, the boy entered the tunnel and let the trees pull him. The boy felt the burn in his legs and the drawstring pouch hanging heavy. The boy felt the twine digging in and rubbing a raw line across his hairless chest. Beads pearled on his brow and sweat swelled from his lip and thirst played about his throat. He thought of water. He thought of well and spigot and when he found a runnel he stopped and scooped and the dog joined him to lap at it noisily with a coarse pink tongue.

It had been a long season last. A brutal time where snow had filled the valley for weeks and only shortly shrunk back slowly up the slopes in steepening retreat. It had been a struggle to stay warm and the wood piles of most folk were down to the rotten damp stumps not yet seasoned and the still-green cuttings of autumn since. Shards of bark got the fires started and the last snapped kindle sticks blazed bright enough but gave off little heat. In the wood stores the thin rats had no hiding place.

The boy had been glad of the burner in his master's back room; glad of the meat tea he boiled on the stove top from the guts and off-cuts, and which he seasoned with dried thyme; the fat they skimmed to spread on dried bread. Though the working days were long and he rarely saw daylight, and the blood was never washed from the creases of his palm lines and beneath his finger nails, his hands a permanent map, never had he been better fed in his short and exhausting life. Being a butcher's boy brought benefits.

And now the first spring sun was rising though not yet warming the tight skin of the earth. Instead it only softened the frost that was as hard as the gritstone bed that lay beneath it so that the boy's boots became clogged with the black weighted mud through which the upper moorlands drained their coppery waters.

On his hip the pouch felt heavier still. The metallic rattle advertised its contents and the dog ran on up ahead, its ears pricked and soft shining black nose reading unseen signals on the softest of breezes.

As he walked the boy remembered his master's words: never mind the sky – *mind where you put your bloody feet.*

The boy picked his way carefully over root and boulder. He followed a deer run through the first ragwort stalks and listened for the swish and rustle of the dog through the undergrowth. He felt the trees loom and tower and watched as the dog disappeared. Heard it barking in full throat.

And then it was as if the sky tore an inch or two like a stretch of cloth as something streaked above him. It sounded like an intake of breath, a flat throttled whistle just above his head followed by a distant clatter behind him. The sound of stone hitting wood, then stone on dirt.

He stopped and spun to follow the sound. There was nothing. He whistled for the dog but instead of returning to him he heard it bark again, further in the distance, a coarse and urgent echo up through the trees. The boy recognised that tone. It was an alarm call. His finger tips touched the pouch that hung on his hip and felt its contents there, then he followed the sound.

The dog appeared, backwards-stalking, barking and baying as a figure stepped out from the thicket before them.

You best call that bag of fleas back before I put a river stone in its eye.

The figure from the thicket was that of a boy. Older and bigger than him. He had in his hand a slingshot that he raised over one shoulder. His words were spoken in a newly broken voice that was deep and coarse but with a wavering tone that suggested uncertainty too.

The boy whistled and then whistled again and then a third time he whistled before the dog heeded his recall. It stood in the space between them and barked once and when the boy said get by it pressed itself flat to the ground, but kept its eyes fixed on this stranger.

He saw that the boy with the slingshot had a haunted angular face and shirt sleeves rolled to the elbow to show the tightly coiled cords of his arms. There was a layer of soft hair on his lip.

If that mutt so much as flinches I'll kick him from here to Halifax.

His voice cracked again as he spoke and the younger boy thought of the winter geese that landed down at Brearley river bank, and how his honk made him sound less threatening than he surely intended.

And where is that you reckon on going, said the older boy.

He kept quiet.

If you don't answer you get to go nowhere, the older boy continued. This here's my wood. Bell Hole belongs to *me*. No strangers pass without my word.

The younger boy squatted and scratched the dog behind its ears and said *shhh* in a gentle voice and then he stood and nodded up the hill.

Reckoned on going up there up top.

There's nothing for you up there up top but sky and you don't look like no bird to me.

Just after having a wander is all I am doing, said the younger boy.

He felt the string pulling across his chest tighter still, the pouch heavier than ever on his thin bruised hip. The older boy stepped forward. He took a step towards the dog. The dog growled. Its top lip curled back and the dog's gums were blue, his cavernous mouth a beautiful dark marbling of pink and black. Pointed terrier teeth like ivory pins sat evenly spaced and deep set, flanked by two curved canines that were ready to tear and tatter.

9

Then you can just turn back around and wander yourself back down yonder to the hole you came from.

The young boy squatted again and patted the dog and said get by and then he said get by again and then he said: I didn't come from no hole because I'm not a bleeding animal.

The bigger boy straightened and stiffened. Made himself big and then bigger still.

If you leave now it might be that I'll not pretend you're a squirrel ready for skinning and it might be that I'll let you be. But any more lip like that and it's not the crack of this slingshot pebble that you'll feel but a fist curling your teeth and these clogs kicking your tallywags up into your mouth to meet them.

Can't, said the boy. I can't do that.

Maybe you're not hearing me, said the older of the pair.

I can't leave now.

Then your lugs must be clogged with summat rotten because I'll not warn you again.

I've a message to run.

What message?

I've a man to see.

What man?

A man up top.

There's no men up top that you could see, said the older boy. These here woods run up to the moors and on the edge of those moors there are a handful of houses and in these houses are men you don't want to meet because these men live by their old ways and by their own rules, and they don't want no tyke stirring his snot nose in their business. There's secrets in these woods and there's secrets up top on them moors and there's secrets in the hearts of men and secrets they'll stay because past the houses and past the moors there's just the sky and that's only there because the sky can keep a secret and because the men have bade it so. Men like my father.

Who is your father?

None of your beeswax is my father. Give me your name first.

The younger boy shrugged.

Jack Bentley is my name, he said.

I don't know it.

Don't expect you would. What's your name?

The older boy ignored his question and answered with one of his own.

What's this message?

That's a secret like your name is a secret.

I swear I'll bloody throttle you.

The bigger boy lunged at him and the dog growled and coiled itself but the younger boy stepped back and said – Hartley. It's Hartley that I come to see. The one they call the king.

The bigger boy paused and Jack Bentley drew the dog back and the bigger boy spoke – Hartley? I don't know no Hartley – but there was a flicker of recognition in his eye as he said this and Jack Bentley saw this and the bigger boy saw that he had seen it too. A silent moment passed until the trance of the unmoving woodland was broken by the ruffled racket of a bird taking flight like a flung book.

King David Hartley is the man's name, said Jack Bentley. And if you don't know it then you can't run the woods like you say you do because everyone knows Bell Hole belongs to the Hartleys, and the moor above it and the sheep and cows that graze them moors and the Hartleys own the sky above it too, and the kestrel and the hawk that hunt there and the hares that box there, and the clouds and the moon and the sun and everything that passes overhead. You said it so yourself. If you don't know King David Hartley then you don't know nothing about anything and anything about nothing, and I should be on my way.

A hand pressed at Jack Bentley's chest.

Wilcox.

The fingers rested there. The dog growled.

William Wilcox is my name.

Jack Bentley looked in the older boy's face. He looked at the downy hair on his lip and the streak of sweat that had cleared a way through the caked patch of mud on one of his cheeks. A cheek pitted with pox scars. He could smell his breath too. Sour milk. Onions. Wild garlic.

Something shifted between them.

William Wilcox turned away, his back broad in last year's shirt.

I'll take you up there, he said. I'll take you up to Hartley's.

Miths like paths you see are made by the passing of tyme No true path is dug or layde it becums that way and no true man of mith is borne one day like a babba no way Miths are shayped like river stones or worn away like dorestepps they leave a trayle throo the ages like a stagheads run that pushes out through the wuddlands and into the gorzy purplin hethur.

Men of mith they do spring lyke seeds in the mowth of a playce Grow from the soyle of a playce Burrow deep and tayke root Mennomith live on the lipps of ther chilluns granchillun.

Ihink of the boggart or the wyvern or the wite werm or Tom Tit Tot or even the wite witch said to stork every bluddy copse or wudd from Berrick to Bristul These are all miths made by fireside gathrins and bedtime storees wich issent to say they arnt real becors I is one to tork Its just that time has made them big in the minds of those that have seen or heard tell of them.

Miths are the crags and the bowlders They are the olde owke tree benden to the brees and the stream that carves its way throo the valley bottom Becors miths cannot be hewen or crakt or felled or dammd No miths is bigger than that Miths is bigger than any fucken fissykil thynge and the man of mith bigger still A true man Feggsample a man like me Kinge David Hartlee.

13

They followed the length of a berm that crested and cambered around the rim of the great sunken woodland whose canopy sat in a vast half circle beneath the moor edge, where the land fell away.

The trees sat below them now. To Jack Bentley they seemed far less significant than when wandering in the middle of them. He felt as if he could take great steps across their surface; the boy letting him pass had emboldened him and now it was as if he were a giant who could flick chimney stacks from roof tops and use tree trunks to gouge stuck food from between his gat teeth.

Above and ahead a stout solitary house peeked over the brow. It slunk low in the soil, its stones blackened and rain-chipped, its architecture all shadows. Next to it was a barn, also squat and cowering, the weight of the sky pressing on its slates and bending to its bone angles.

That's Hartley's, said William Wilcox, half raising a grubby finger towards the house and Jack Bentley said where do you live? and William Wilcox dipped his head and said further on and Jack Bentley said where? I don't see any other houses, and William Wilcox said there's houses alright you just need to know where to look but that there is Bell House.

They walked on, coming at it from the rear, through sopping bogs of rainbow puddles and acrid methane fumes.

When they got closer and the house grew in size the boy saw a patch of back land tilled and turned and planted with rows of all sorts, and a hut for hens to lay their eggs in and a great big log store with the logs all chopped neatly to size and stacked edgeways, seasoning.

He saw that the man who lived up here had made this difficult soil work for him because in the vast tended patch there were the beginnings of rhubarb and the little leaves of new sprung raspberries and strawberries and goosegogs and logans, and he reckoned on there being spuds sprouting down there too, and perhaps onions and turnips and maybe even cabbages and lettuces to come up. Perhaps, thought the boy, this was how the king got his name: because he lived like one up here in his gloomy sky palace.

Their feet were on rock now, the slippy grit stones of the fells sliced thin like pages of a book torn and placed softly on the soil. Then the two boys were at the door. The dog panted by their side.

William Wilcox raised a hand and rapped with his knuckles and then rapped again. A voice came from inside. A woman.

Who is it?

It's me, Missus Hartley.

Who?

William Wilcox Missus Hartley.

There was silence for a long moment and then the door opened and there stood an attractive woman. She appeared to Jack Bentley as fine and healthy-looking as a foal, her face flushed and fresh.

She looked first at William Wilcox and then to the boy and then she said: well, what is it you want William Wilcox and who is this you've dragged ragged to my door?

William Wilcox looked coy.

I found him in the woods. Skulking about, like.

Was he now?

I wasn't skulking I was—

Wilcox cut him down.

He said he reckoned on being here to see Mr Hartley, so I thought I'd fetch him up for you.

Bell Hole don't need no guard dogs when we've got you about, isn't that right, William?

She smiled. Jack Bentley saw that her teeth were strong, and again he thought of beautiful horses. The older boy blushed at the compliment, but did not meet her eye.

15

What's his name? she said and then to the boy she said what's your name sunbeam?

It's Jack missus. Jack O' Matts Bentley they call us.

So your father's Matthew Bentley?

The boy looked back at her blankly.

I think so missus, he said.

She raised an eyebrow.

You think so or you know so?

Well, we call him Our Father but I have heard folk call him by that other name also.

I don't believe I know a Matthew Bentley, she said. Or at least there's no Bentleys in Erringden or Turvin or Cragg Vale.

That's because I've come up from the far end.

Far end of where, God's elbow?

He's come over from—

Grace Hartley interrupted William Wilcox.

The boy's proved he's got a mouth of his own so let him use it, William.

From the top end of the valley missus. From over the Sowerby side of Halifax.

She studied him for a moment.

Folk that come from over Fax don't make that walk to smell the bracken and pick the berries – it's because they want something, so what is it that you be wanting from me? What business do you have wandering Bell Hole?

Jack Bentley cleared his throat.

I've brought the king a bag of coins missus.

He has as well, said William Wilcox. I did see them. There's enough to tile a pantry floor, and then some.

The king?

Yes missus. King David Hartley of Bell House, leader of the Turvin Clippers who are also known around and about as the Cragg Vale Coiners.

The boy lifted the pouch of coins and then passed them over. Grace Hartley took it. She untied the drawstring and looked inside.

16

I don't know about no king, she said. You can come in but the hound can tarry.

He's a friendly dog, missus.

That's as maybe Jack O' Matts Bentley but no hound has been in here yet. The moors is for the animals.

She stepped aside.

And you best run along William Wilcox. Tell John Wilcox there's a fresh stopper to be popped from a jug of elderflower press next time he's passing for raising a lad with the eyes of an eagle and the ears of a deer. You're the best lookout there is.

William Wilcox smiled and blushed again.

And you be sure to knock on if you see anyone else skulking down in them trees.

I will, said William Wilcox before adding: I will, Queen missus Hartley.

A loom filled the room and a web of wool was strung across it as if it were the lair of a giant spider.

On a table to one side the boy saw that there were fustian shalloons folded and stacked ready for selling; three in all. He knew, as any valley boy did, that that pile of stiff cloth represented close on a month's worth of daylight hours spent threading and pulling and folding and tugging. The light fading. Neck and wrists and shoulders aching. Pain. They gave it a name: the weavers' curse. The curse was all those ailments that moved around the body, and took root in joints and muscles and senses alike. Often it was the eyes that went first. The strain on them was great. A weaver could get dizzy or half-mad from the eye ache. Feel the sickness take hold. The summer months weren't so bad; some days a weaver could be up with the birdsong to open the doors and windows and let the hills and meadows come pouring in.

But in the darker months it was strain and pain and fainting and sickness. And in time stiff fingers would curl never to be straightened again and eyes would go and the permanent mist would settle and what use is a purblind weaver who doesn't have a steady hand?

The boy was standing hunched in the corner and wiping the ladle of spring water from around his mouth with his cuff when the man entered. David Hartley. His wife followed.

This him Gracie?

That's him. He claims he's come from over the Sowerby side of the Fax and Jack O' Matts Bentley is his name. He's got a new one for you too: called you the king, he did. King David Hartley.

Hartley took in the small frame of the boy and nodded slowly. Mulled the title over. He was not a large man but the way his body hung upon itself made Jack Bentley take the back foot. David Hartley had dark hair, dark eyes and dark jaw. His shirt sleeves were rolled and Jack Bentley could see blood pumping through fat blue veins that looked like the streaked sinews that ran through the meat he butchered daily. David Hartley appeared of the earth, of the moors. A man of smoke and peat and heather and fire, his body built for the hills. Where one began the other ended.

Is that right? he said.

It's what my master calls you, your highness.

Hark at that, said Grace. Your highness it is now.

In jest?

No.

Because if he speaks my name in jest he'll only speak it again while spitting teeth.

No sir.

David Hartley considered it for a moment.

Well, 'King David' I can live with.

Ask him what he's brung you, said Grace Hartley.

I will, said her husband as he lowered himself onto a chair and considered the boy. But you best fetch the lad a nibble first.

When his wife left the room he said: so then young sprat, who is your master?

Samuel Duckett, sir.

Came up here alone did you?

No, said the boy.

Hartley sat with his legs apart.

No?

No. My hound came up too.

Outside is he, your dog?

Yes King David.

David Hartley looked at the boy and the boy felt his eyes pressing at the flesh of his chest.

Now – tell me. What's this king talk really about?

That's just what they reckon on calling you over Fax way.

David Hartley scratched at his forearm.

Good hound is he?

What? said the boy, thrown for a moment, then catching himself he said: yes, the best. A great little ratter already. He bagged a dozen last week at Bunsen's chicken sheds and, mind, they were big ones too. Egg-fed, they were, fat as hogs and slow, but still. My father docked his tail when he were born so the little buggers couldn't get a nip.

I fancy I might have him then.

Oh, he's not for sale Mr Hartley.

That's not for debating. And you're sure there's no-one else with you?

No.

Not followed up?

Only by that boy that brung us.

Which boy?

The boy in the wood.

Wilcox's lad?

I think so, sir.

And what weapon do you carry?

I've not got a weapon.

No weapon? Then you've got some nick-nacks on you walking these woods alone.

The boy sniffed and rubbed his wet nose with the back of a trembling hand and then held it behind his back out of sight. He gripped it steady, his thin fingers curling around his pale wrist where his heart played a quickening rhythm.

So you're Duckett's best boy are you?

No sir.

No?

I'm not his son.

I didn't say you were his son, said David Hartley. I said you're his best boy. I meant you're with him. You're for him.

I've been apprenticed with him for near enough half a year now.

A meat man like Duckett – that's what you want to be is it?

Yes sir. Butchering is what I hope to do, sir. That and the slaughtering.

Handy with the blade and cleaver I bet, said David Hartley. Which part of the butchering is it that you like best?

I've not thought about it, said the boy.

Well think about it now then because questions needs answers and only a fool doesn't know what it is he likes and doesn't like in this life.

The boy shifted his weight from one foot to the other. His wrist still in his hand held behind his britches.

I think I like stretching the swine carcasses best. There's this tool for prising the ribs apart, you see. Honestly – the noise they make.

Hartley leaned back in his chair and spread his legs even further apart.

So why is it you're getting mixed up in this then?

He gestured vaguely around the room.

I don't understand.

You've no business being here.

I have to do what it is that the old man Duckett asks of me. I've brung up his coins.

Listen Jack O' Matts Bentley – in this life you don't have to do nothing that no-one asks of you unless it's David Hartley or the devil himself that's doing the telling, and being as he hasn't showed his face up this hill yet I reckon it's only David Hartley you need worry yourself about.

The boy blinked back. He let his hands hang by his sides.

David Hartley shifted in his chair.

But seeing as you mention him, how is that corn-mouthed collop-bollocked jug-eared bastard?

Sir?

Old braeberry blue balls. Old bloody apron. Duckett, lad. Duckett.

He is well Mr Hartley.

Not so well he has to see children do his dirty business though.

The boy said nothing for a moment and then said: I'm not a child.

Hartley considered him for a moment.

Well at least it sounds like you've got a bit of vinegar in your waters.

The boy swallowed and drew up a question.

Do you know of my master?

I know of everyone, said David Hartley. I know what every sod is going to do before they've even thought it themselves. I know every breath and movement of all who live in this valley.

The boy said nothing.

Listen, lad. Man's work demands man's wages; I hope he's paying you squarely.

Still the boy said nothing.

Duckett is crooked or why else would he be bothering me with this so then you'll at least take an ale and some bait for the trouble, said David Hartley. You can slocken your thirst and fill your guts for it's a good six Roman miles homewards over the back way.

The boy nodded and without taking his eyes off him Hartley turned his head towards his shoulder an inch or two and called

out Missus and when there was no reply he called out again –
Missus – and a moment later Grace appeared.

Bring up a jug with the boy's bait will you.

Hartley held out an open palm. To the boy his hand appeared
impossibly big. It was more like a tool or a slate or an object
brought in from the moors. Something unearthed. Dug up.
A weapon or a milling stone. He saw callouses and blisters, a
blackened nail ballooning with blood. It was a hand that had
built things and broken things.

Give us then.

The boy lifted the drawstring pouch over his head and Hartley
took it from him and said: now listen. Your Samuel Duckett is
a sackless man who is lower than the flies that scatter from a
cow pat, and no amount of king-talk can change my mind about
him. You can tell him that for me and fetch him up here if he's
minded to have a problem with that.

I don't understand, said the boy.

There's nothing to understand. Duckett is a sot. He's nothing.

Jack Bentley protested.

But he's sent me up here with those coins for you to clip.
He speaks highly of you.

Yes. And clip them I will.

But if you hate him why do you take his coins?

David Hartley stared back.

Because metal is metal and hate is hate and the two are not
related. Any man's coins is as good as another's if it's going into
my pockets. He'll get his bit out of all this but it's me and my
lads that are doing the grind and graft. And now you are too.
And if either of the pair of you meat men don't like it I'll tie your
tongues with twine to a stag haunch and set it on with a slap.

Hartley leaned forward and stared at the boy.

Listen to what I tell you now: no man but your master must
never know you've been here because if they do I'll put you in
the soil while you're still breathing and they say that to drown
in the red dirt of Erringden Moor is worse than drowning

in the flood waters of the Calder. It fills your mouth and pulls you under and strips the meat from your bones until there's nothing left but the last lonely cry of the boy with the big mouth that they called Jack O' Matts Bentley.

He leaned back again and then added: and it'd not be the first time.

Behind him Grace appeared with a board on which there was cheese and bread and a jug.

The boy chewed at his lip and then in a voice higher than he intended he said:

Will you teach us to clip?

Grace laid the board on the table.

No, said Hartley. I will not.

I'm a good learner, but.

No.

They say there's good money in the yellow trade.

And there's good money in meat too, said David Hartley. Stick to what buggerlugs is learning you and you might just avoid the gibbet.

The boy lowered his voice and said but no man ever got wealthy off blood and offal.

Hartley looked at his wife and then back to the boy. He raised an eyebrow. He shook his head.

No, but he never got his neck snapped neither. Now fetch us that dog you're giving us.

Part II
Summer 1768
Buzzems

In the fyres of the forges in the Black Cuntry was where I first herd tell of coinin where I learnit a little about chippin and clippin swimmers where I learnit about the yeller trade and the work of them men that darest to.

It was down neer the citty they name Burningham for reasons that shud be clear that I was apprentissed to the smithy The smithy made anything A big place it was hot and noisy and deirty like nowt yood ever seen or herd or smelled and when the men there got to torkin it was a revvalayshin to me they mite as well have been speeking in tungs the way the werds come out But thats by the by what matters is what they done and what they done is smelt and pour and hammer and mould What they done is hoist and heft and scald and steam And what they done was learn us a new trayde a new way. A way that I brung back up to the hills to tell to my kith and kin so that we can all get back at the man and maybe live more freely and comfurtable on this littul shive of tough hevven This littul patch of land I calls a kyngdum.

I'm torken about the fine art of the coinin and the clippen Makine munny and fucken the man.

Made all sorts did that forge Made nails railins locks buckels wether vaynes made ever thing from bayonetts to chatterlains Made ackses all sorts of ackses Made beard ackses bordin ackses broad ackses spiked ackses Made candul lanterns made ship lanterns three sided lantans Made horse shoos made cloth boilers and tea urns and flint strykers and cross bars for yer dutch ovens and stew pots an buckerts Made sords an all – all sorts of sords – court sords an huntin sords an cuttoes with engraved handels showing deer seens and forests and valleys and stags that did remaind us of home Made spoons and whissles and mouth harps and whizzer toys Made forged metal balls batted flat and strung on chains for the littleuns to whizz Everythynge that coud be melted and mowlded we did mayke with fire and mussel.

Dozens of men there was down there in the darkness Down in the black country swinging mallets turnin tongs and porin metal so hot it went the culler of the sun and ran like springe worter down a gill and drippin so much sweat we was there was allus a cue at the piggin to drink the water and cool your head And the steem – and the steem an the soot – so black yed be trippin over your own feet in the dork and the noise The noise of clangin an hissin and bashin and screechin.

See when I struck out my brothers were but pups Issaik being seven years yunger than I and our Willyam a full nine year yunger and therefore both still hairless of the chin and not yet hardened to the world like I already was at sicksteen year or more Aye long dark thymes Davide Hartlee did spend down there Years I spent there Yers I werked all to one day become kynge of my own kyngdum And so it was And so it was And hear I yam.

And the base coin. The base coin is what else was made down in that place set close up the edges of Burningham I herd tell of it over tyme becors the secrets of the coinin is not sumthin a man tells another man just willy nilly even when he's in the drinke or cort at it No the clipper denighs every thin at orl thymes Its the code is that You dunt speek abart it to anywan but your own tried and trusstid Yor own blud if you can help it.

That's a lessing Kinge David has learnt is that Hear me tell it now so that hisstory lerns from its misstaykes My misstaykes The lessuns of King David king of the Coiners no mattur what happerns And so I will tell it And so I will tell it true as is.

Like crows to the first pickings of carrion after the snow melt, from the four corners they walked.

Up they came and over they came and through they came. Many men.

Isaac Dewhurst and Absolom Butts.

Thomas Clayton and Benjamin Sutcliffe.

Abraham Lumb and Aloysius Smith and Nathan Horsfall and Matthew Hepworth and Joseph Gelder and Jonathan Bolton.

John Wilcox and Jonas Eastwood.

Fathers and brothers and sons and uncles. Up they came. And others too.

From across the moors, from all horizons.

They walked through bogs dried and cracked; they came through whin and gorse and lakes of wild sedge hung heavy with gobs of cuckoo spittle. Through the rutted trenches of dried-out streams they drove. Through ghylls that ran so shallow some had become nothing but a series of still, stagnant pools.

Up they came and over they came and through they came. Men. Tough men.

Working men.

Poor men, proud men. Desperate souls of the valley.

They bore nicknames such as Young Frosty and Mad Blood and Foxface. Tom O' Freckles and John Coughing. Foul Peter. Double Stumps.

Men of stone and soil.

Benjamin Sutcliffe came from over Halifax. Still pimple-faced at sixty and an old brown wig upon his head.

Pox-pitted Nathan Horsfall from up Warley arrived with weaver William Clayton from Sowerby, the latter broad-set and flaxen-haired and wearing an auburn shag waistcoat.

Thin-faced Thomas Clayton brought his bones along from Turvin.

Isaac Dewhurst kissed his blind wife and left their dark

house by the shallow stream in Luddenden Dene, his black hair uncovered and cheeks and jaw dusted black with stubble too.

Cherry-cheeked and handsome, John Tatham downed tools and let his long strong legs lead him down the Wadsworth slopes. Crowther O' Badger came rasping from Sweet Oak.

Up through Bell Hole they strode, the woodland canopy covering them and disguising their intentions. Up through the steepest grass slopes of Bell Hole they came, climbing them hand over foot as if it were a ladder to the expansive sky.

John Wilcox took the short walk from his home at Keelham Farm just over the brow.

John Parker and James Green came up whistling together.

Jonas Eastwood from along the Erringden Moor.

Joseph Gelder was another from over Fax in a fair-coloured drab coat and waistcoat to match.

Red-haired Matthew Hepworth had set off early and walked all the way from Ovenden.

Others too.

James Crabtree and William Harpur and Joseph Hanson in a brown bob wig worn askance to obscure his hairless curd-white pate.

Past the mere-stones that marked their turf they strode, with grass stems between their teeth and dandelion seed heads in their hair, and barbed burrs clinging to shirts that stuck to their backs in circular patches of sweat salt.

The breeze blessed their hot brows and their matted hair and the copper-bottomed stream waters ran clear, for it was an unusually dry spring day and Yorkshire was unfolding around them. The winter had been mild and the tight cloughs through which they ambled were in bloom, the first snowdrops having already been and gone, nodding as if in reverence for this clandestine gathering. It had not rained for days and as the saying went the dale without rain was as rare as the lamb that doesn't like to leap. Soon it would come, of course. The rain. It always did.

But for now the valley was bursting in a violent flowering of flora and leaves unfurling and branches stretching and ragwort reaching and nettles – especially nettles – vying for the sky. Great dense patches of them grew, four and five and six feet deep, impenetrable swathes of dark green bracts that advertised their danger. Elsewhere lower meadows were flowing thick with the first buttercups, the fine white fuzz of drifting dandelion seeds and the silken slung threads of settled kiting spiders.

Clouds hung in billows like blankets of wool drying after the dye vat and there were new scents on the breeze: mint and thyme and woodsmoke, and the released perfume that swirls around boscage and thicket as it is trampled underfoot.

The smell of spread pig scat hung over the top fields too, fresh and strong and sweet and astringent. It was the busy spell after the first birthings, a time for growth and feeding. The season for nest-lining and house-building. A time of plenty for the insects and the lambs and rabbits, and the deer too, as they tentatively wandered down from the woodlands where they wintered, their nostrils decoding the messages in the ether.

And still they came, the men. Up and over and through. Some in pairs and some alone. They arrived an hour either side of the sun rising highest in the sky.

Jonathan Bolton.

Thommo Sunderland.

Others still. From the dells and dales and dingles. The four-house hamlets. From lone homesteads in the spinney and the dank smallholdings built where the waters ran by. From the windowless back rooms and cramped upstairs quarters of the beer inns. From the forges and farm and looms. From deep in the trees whose dark forming corridors they rarely left.

William Hailey and Peter Barker, better known as Foul Peter. His hair tied tight and hanging down his neck like a mole strung from a fence.

Jonas Tilotson, who rode a skittish horse in from Mixenden.

Israel Wilde arrived last, his ankle swollen and already berry-blue after cockling at the top of Hatherself Scout.

Up through Bell Hole they walked, stepping over moss-clogged runnels and fallen limbs half-submerged in the woodland soil. Bell Hole was the moor's footnote, its overflow and midden pit. Its ugly sibling. Its shadow clough.

Crispin Crowther.

Brian Dempsey.

Eli Hoyle and Eli Hill.

Ely Crossley.

Their soundtrack was birdsong: dozens of contrasting avian calls that resounded through the church-like stillness of the place. Some wove into harmonious patterns before disentangling. Others still – the crows were loudest – sang with the waggish volume of vagabonds stumbling out from an ale house.

John Pickles.

James Stansfield.

Paul Taylor.

Slipping and sliding. Gasping and striding. Men whose family names were as much a part of the terrain as the boundary marker stones that mapped the moors and fractioned their tight territories from the days of the old wapentake. These were family handles deep-rooted and double-tied to time and place, just as was the Hartleys', for that name was as much a part of the valley's foundation as the gritstone bed from which Bell House was gouged and sculpted.

Here on the moor edge the earth smelled like a basket of broken goose eggs, and patterns swirled on the surface of puddles that were fed only by droplets falling from the moss that tasselled the moor edge, millions of beaded specks like tiny interconnected green stars as if a manikin galaxy had sprung from the soil. Even during a drought time such as this the moor was rarely dry, a wet rag never fully wrung.

It took the stubborn scavengers and the stealthy to live up here. The cunning and the vicious. The solitary and the half-mad.

The buzzard and the raven. The polecat and the pine marten. The hare, the fox and the adder.

Here lived those wild and red in pointed tooth and curled claw, and alongside them were those that walked on two legs and lived in houses but still emulated many of the upland creatures' feral ways. Quarrymen and poachers. Tinkers and trappers and hermits. Men that did not want to be found. Men who made myths of their own mad delusions.

Here they gathered.

With them the men brought provisions, token offerings to their recently found figurehead. Gifts for a king who had assumed sovereignty over his own fiefdom.

Nathan Horsfall brought a flour sack of apples, each wrapped in rags since autumn past.

On unsteady legs Matthew Hepworth carried a jug that had nothing in it but the scent of ale drunk.

Joseph Gelder had a piece of salt pork scored and saved for King David Hartley himself.

John Tatham had a loaf. John Wilcox brought berries.

Foul Peter Barker carried a pheasant he had thrown his full weight on and idly plucked on the way, the light down feathers accidentally decorating his sleeveless waistcoat. William Hailey offered a tea cake. Abraham Lumb treacle.

They brought blades and shears and hammers. Stamps and dyes and tongs. Moulds and spelters.

And some – not many, a few – brought coins.

These they had taken from their hiding places in the woods and crags, from deep in the twisted roots and bouldered cracks to stow about their bodies, wrapped in rags and held under arms or lagged to bandy legs. Tucked into waistbands, slotted into false hems.

Then out from Bell House stepped Isaac Hartley and behind him his younger brother, William Hartley II. They walked among the men nodding and exchanging words and greetings.

The Duke of York they called Isaac Hartley, and his was the familiar face to most. His hair was a heap of waxy curls and his mouth held gat-teeth between which he – but only he – joked you could pass a bootlace.

The Duke of Edinburgh was the name given to his younger brother, though that had yet to properly take because William Hartley was quieter than Isaac Hartley and time had not let his recently acquired moniker settle. He had come up younger than many of them. But they did know that he was as handy with his fists, for even as a young man of perhaps only fourteen years they had seen him on the cobbles on more than one occasion. Once he had slipped and broken a leg while fighting two packhorse lime-trail navvies single-handedly – witnesses had sworn to hearing the bone snap like stiff treacle tablet – but had fought on regardless, and still licked the pair of them, though one of his eyes had looked in on his nose for weeks afterwards.

William Hartley was red of hair and quiet of temperament, and known to speak only when necessary. The men knew that the big loud boys were rarely the ones you had to watch.

Isaac Hartley stood on the big stone that jutted from the ground like a bone and whose surface was worn smooth from years of sitting, and he said: Now listen lads there's a fresh ferment done and there's more than enough to go round until your head's turned backwards. Grace's special mash, it is. There's toasted oats and a pot of honey that goes into it.

A murmur of approval ran through the men.

Ale fit for a king is that, added his brother Isaac Hartley, the middle of the three siblings. I've tried it myself. Three stiff jars and you'll think you've met with God.

There were smiles.

You can taste the moors on it, added William Hartley, more for effect rather than because he felt he had a particular opinion to share on the matter, but his words came out quiet so he cleared his throat and spoke more clearly: it's the bees you see, he said. They make the best of these moors just like we intend to.

As if it had been orchestrated, at that moment Grace Hartley came out from the house carrying a jug and a fistful of pots. She passed them round and poured the ale as eyes followed her. Sitting at the back, where the cropped and cultivated patch of grass turned wild as the moors ran off to greet the sky, James Broadbent grunted and whispered to Joe Gelder.

How it would please me to get my hands on that throddy birthing body, he said.

Joseph Gelder leaned towards him.

It's as good a way to lose your hands as any, my friend.

How's that? said James Broadbent. I fear no man.

Well you should fear this man.

What man?

You know which man.

Joseph Gelder discreetly gestured to the figure who was standing on the protruding stone in such a way it was as if he had been raised up on it from the underworld.

This man. Hartley. This man that's welcomed you to his house. He'd have them off with a scythe as soon as wipe his arse with docks.

Well, said James Broadbent. He'd have to catch me with that piece of his first.

And there's plenty of men here who'd be happy to swear witness, said Joseph Gelder. And not just his brothers. Trust me. This valley's full of sneaksbys and blabbers. Besides, you've got neither the stiff stem or stones to please that woman. You can tell by looking at her. And looking at you too, you daft big link of dung.

Broadbent sniffed.

If I can get it up some bracket-faced sow down at Old Rose's nugging house I'd be as hard as a happy horse with that one, don't you worry about that. Oh, but to spend an hour in her hot notch.

James Broadbent whistled through pursed lips as Joseph Gelder laughed.

An hour? Who goes at it for an hour?

I do on the second or third time round, said James Broadbent. I'm known for it.

Are you now.

That I am. They call me the stone hammer. Just fill me with a jug of fresh-brewed stingo and watch me go. In hay-rick and hooer room, I've had them all. There's a lass at Mixenden who walks with a limp and thanks me for it. Ask around.

I think I won't.

James Broadbent leered as Grace Hartley poured the ale.

He nodded.

Yes. She'd get it good and long and hard.

Why don't you say it a bit louder so's the Duke of York can hear you, you shithouse? He's looking this way.

Isaac Hartley was indeed watching the two men as he helped Grace with the ale. Most knew him to be the more approachable of the brothers and it was regarded that Isaac Hartley always stood a drink and suffered no fools, but he had a dash of humour with it too.

Any one Hartley brother was formidable but together the threesome were feared. Their name alone could cause children to scatter.

Everyone knew of old man Hartley too, as it was their father William Sr. who had rented Bell House up on the moor in the first place, back before his eldest had wrapped up his hammer and tongs and sent himself south to the Black Country down in the middle lands to become a man and learn a trade and much more besides in the forges there.

What the world had taught David Hartley was that life beyond the valley was a lot like life in the valley, and though they had laughed at his way of speaking down there with that fat flat tongue that rolled words around like river stones in the cheeks of the thirsty, he had thrived in the west of Birmingham.

From there David Hartley had brought back to the valley what he had learned some seasons back. Two cold winters had passed now since his return to the Upper Calder Valley and the house there, with a younger wife in tow, and fear in her eyes and a bairn in her belly and one on her back, and a third yet to be conceived, and this plan of his that had taken seed in the arid bed of necessity and desperation and wanting.

Here his enterprise had begun in earnest, and now the men had been summoned and the men sat and the men rested and the men drank. The men exchanged greetings.

William Hailey and Jonas Tilotson and Israel Wilde and Joseph Gelder.

Aloysius Smith and Nathan Horsfall and Matthew Hepworth and Abraham Lumb.

John Tatham and Jonathan Bolton and Peter Barker and William Folds and Isaac Dewhurst.

William Harpur and John Wilcox and Jonas Eastwood and Absolom Butts.

James Crabtree and Joseph Hanson and Thomas Clayton and Benjamin Sutcliffe.

Others. All men. Valley born. Valley bred.

Those they called the Coiners.

Returning to the land that birthed me the land that sporned me the land that mayde me Orl I reely wanted to do was wark the hills unherd and breeth gods own good cuntree ayre But one day wandrain this man stopps us and says no No he says No youcannut Dayvid whoah there.

This man sed this is companny land now and I sed this land this land here this land belongs to no men an all men This land belongs to the stag of the stubble an the growse and the fox an the rayvun an the rayn and the hale my frend But this man was no frend becors still the man says thats as maybe but it belongs to the companny now I have it down in riting its legully bindin is that and thurs no cort in the landull judje otherways And I don't like his demeaner.

So I says stuff yor riting and stuff your legully bindin stuff it rite up your tyte scullery and any ways wots so spaeshel about this land that you reccons is yours and what are your intenshuns with it and whos this companny An he sniffs an he seys its none of your bissness And I says it is my bluddy bissness you bluddy doylem and he seys hows that and I seys because ahm King Daevid of Cragg Vale and if youv not herd of me ask around becors its me and myne that run these hills an they leeve us too it An he seys not for long you dunt And I says how do you reccon that How do you reccon that like.

An he says the companny the companny is running things now and I says what fucken companny you fucken doss cunt.

An he says cotton man cotton And I says what about the fucken cotton and he seys merkingeyesayshun and I says eh what you on about now cumpunny cunt An he says mills and mill wheels an waterways and industry and great bildins like cathydrals bildins like yor tiny hill dwellin sheep fucken mynd cannot imagun So keep your eyes on the horeysunn sunshyne.

And I says are you getting cheeky wirrus now and he goes no King Dayvid of Cragg Vale orl I'm saying is a change is comin and cotton is its making And I says dunt tell me about cotton me and myne have got callerses on ower hands from jennerayshuns of workin the loom you lippy licker of dog dick and he seys the loom is dead And I seys dead An he seys the day of the hand loom is over mass produckshun is cumin wether you lyke it or not aye mass produckshun and organysed laber is what I'm talkin abowt and if youv got any sens about yer yerll embrayce the new ways.

And I says fuck tho now ways and fuck the compunny and fuck your fucken scut with a rusted nyfe if yor still thinken on telling King David of Cragg Vale wer it is he can or cannit wander you soppybolickt daft doylem fiddler of beests And that was that for a while at leest.

Name your Gods gentlemen.

Out from the back door of Bell House stepped David Hartley.

He brought with him a jar in one hand and an empty wooden ale crate in the other. As he threw the wooden crate down and sat on it the men hushed. A flicker of something crossed his eyes like dark clouds over a full moon. He spoke.

Name your Gods gentlemen, for they are all around you.

His voice was clear. Each word was thickened in his throat and then held in his mouth and sculpted on the way out. Each word was weighted. Valley formed.

Sycamore and silver birch, he said. Beech and goat willow. Oak and ash. And before them pine and hazel, aspen and sallow. Alder. Because this is our kingdom of Jórvíkshire and time was the whole island was like this once. It was coast to coast with trees, all the way up to these higher lands of ours. The wildwood they called it. We lived as clans then. Under the trees when the trees were worshipped as Gods. Under the great rustling canopy. Tribal, like. Maybe a few of us still do. It was the way of the land then. You protected you and yours. You still do.

He looked at the men and nodded. He let the words sink in.

Protection was our purpose. Protection from any incomers. That and the providing of food and fire, and seeding your women. You banded together close then and you hunted and you defended and you fought for your corner of England under the great green canopy. You lived proud and you celebrated your fathers that spawned you and honoured your mothers that birthed you; you kept their name alive whatever way you could. You passed it down in the hope that your name would one day be passed down also, so that you too would live on beyond death. Defeating death and cheating death. Life was short and life was hard in the endless woodlands of England.

Like in that song about Robyn of the Hode, said one of the men, Jonas Tilotson. Or like yon Yorkshire lad Dicky Turpin.

Isaac Hartley flashed him a look and said: all Dicky Turpin got himself was a broke neck and he was no Yorkshire boy, but David Hartley ignored them both.

And Mother Nature got a look in too, he continued. Never forget her. Because it was Mother Nature that created the Gods we call alder and oak and birch and poplar – and it was she who made the rabbits that sit on your turning spit and the hogs whose backs you'd strip and the cacklers that lay the cackling farts that sizzle in your skillet beside it. It was she who made the moors wild so that men like us could walk across them and pitch up homes and live in silence.

David Hartley paused and let the words hang.

So name your old Gods, lads. Honour them. Live amongst them. And always remember your place. Because England is changing. The wheels of industry turn ever onwards and the trees are falling still. Last week I did chance to meet a man right down there in Cragg Vale who told me that soon this valley is to be invaded. He spoke of chimneys and buildings and waterways and told of work for those that wanted it, but work that pays a pittance and keeps you enslaved to those that make the money. This man – he told me this land around us was soon no longer to be our land but that of those who want to reap and rape and bind those of us whose blood is in the sod. They're pulling it out from beneath our feet like a widow shaking out her clippy mat. He said he had it in writing. Said it was legally binding.

Mumbles ran amongst the men.

That's right, said David Hartley. You'd be minded to care because they're taking this patch that barely feeds us at it is; the land on which they'll not let us settle – land that will never be ours so long as there's boundary markers and excisemen and peppercorn rents. The bastards are coming for us but rest assured that even if they chop down the last tree and pull its stump up blackened and burnt from the soil, and set up new walls to keep us out, one name will live on round these parts. And – yes Jonas Tilotson – like the heroes of your childish ballads, generations will speak the name yet. The name of the man who stood against all that. The man who brought an army. Three words – that's all. You tell them our Isaac.

King fucking David, he said. David fucking Hartley.

His brother nodded.

David Hartley watched the men for a moment. He noticed that some eyes were on his young wife and then he said: drink well, drink long and deep and any eyes that linger on our lass any longer I'll scoop out with my thumb and put in the pickling jar with last season's onions.

At this Joseph Gelder nudged James Broadbent and smirked but James Broadbent ignored him and watched as Grace Hartley passed him a jar and he took it readily for he was thirsty, and even though he had only walked up the Bell Hole woods from Mytholmroyd where others had walked half the length of Calderdale, he welcomed any ale that he hadn't had to give coins for. Then when she turned and walked away he took a pull and said out of the side of his mouth yes – good and long and hard.

Hartley continued.

Too long now we have been scraping by clipping a coin here and there. Milling the edges and melting them down to make what? An extra coin per thirty? All that work and all that risk for what? One more coin. A coin that'll get you hung by rope until your neck snaps and your body jerks and don't they say you soil yourself when you're dangling from that gallows pole? Your good wives left at home with nothing but the memory of a man who gave his life for a coin with which to buy a loaf and a jar and scratch-all else.

Some of the men made vocal their agreement.

Treason, continued David Hartley. That's what they call this enterprise. The yellow trade. And that's why I've called you here – to speak of this thing we've made our own. This treasonous offence that they say is an affront to the very crown that rules this kingdom. And do you know what I say to that? Fuck the king because you can be sure the king is already fucking you.

There's only one king, said Isaac Hartley. And it's this man standing right here.

Another mumble of approval ran through the men. Some nodded and muttered, and scratched their heads and beards. Another yawned.

Organisation. Organisation is what we need. Organisation against the man that wants to bend you over the barrel and pull your breeches down. You think I joke Nathan Horsfall?

No, King David. I was just smirking at the image.

Pity the poor rabbit whose tail is targeted white, said David Hartley. It thinks it goes unnoticed but it sits in the fox's sight. Do you understand me?

I'm not sure I do, said Nathan Horsfall.

Well take out the spuds you're growing in your ears and listen to what I'm saying, said David Hartley. If we carry on the way we have – a bit of clipping here and bit of grinding there – we'll get caught, and if we get caught we're for the gibbet and the chains. Our flesh will reek the wind. Because up until now we've been the rabbits that think they can't be seen. But we can do better than that. We can be the fox. No – we can be the man that hunts the fox that kills the rabbit. We can rise to glory.

Listen to this man, said Isaac Hartley. Listen to your king.

I'm saying it's time to split the coins proper and make the money that's ours. It's time to clip a coin and fuck the crown. It's time to let the bastards know that the only law is our law. That him that crosses a Coiner digs his plot. That him what crosses the clipper loses his tongue. That valley men fight and valley men sing and valley men bow to none but their king.

At this the men smiled and nodded and drank and toasted, and drank so much that in time the sun itself disappeared in fearful retreat.

Now lissen now for I tell you sum thin importent sum thin secret now When a dug misbyhayves you ponk that dug on its neb and when it misby hayves again you rub its phyz in scat and if still that dug misbyhayves a third tyme then you are doon sum thin rong so then you beet it until sum thin goes in its ays like the last ember of a dyin fyre and the spirit of that creechure will be yors and then yool have no trubble from that dug and that dug will give his lyf for you for now it nose its playce that yule have mayde for it And it will feer you an love you an protec you An that is how you run a ragged crew of desprit men That is how you run a gang that sum corl the Turvin Clippers and that uthers corl the Cragg Vayle Coiners.

The rain fell like the filings of a milled guinea bit onto a folded page of paper. It smattered and sat there in small puddles. The small puddles reached out to one another and bridged the gaps until they decreased in number but grew in size. They filled pot-holes and blocked back tracks and pathways. They turned the sod of the woods to sponge, and down at the valley's flat base the river rose, its mood darkening.

The three brothers took to the upper fields where there was little shelter but where dug ditches drained away the water to keep the pastures clear for the few who kept cattle.

They had been waiting and watching the warren for half an hour or more when there was finally a muffled cough of excitement and the rabbit came out in an explosion of panic from one of the holes in the nettle patch that they knew had bred generations of rabbits before it.

Coney, said Isaac Hartley.

At another hole the terrier pulled itself out backwards and stood blinking for a moment, wide-eyed and red dusted. Dirt-rimmed. Confused. It was the young dog that had belonged to the Bentley boy; David Hartley had named it Moidore after the Portugese coin that brought good return when clipped anew. The cloying clay coated its maw and clogged its fell-leathered paws. Dirt-red barbs of fur crested its spine and its tail pointed straight up towards the day-time moon. It was beginning to learn the ways of the hunt.

Isaac Hartley said *geeit* and William Hartley unhooked the rope looped around the neck of the straining lurcher by his side and David Hartley said nothing.

The lurcher bolted.

Seeing the soft white scut of the rabbit bob across the sloping field the terrier darted after its quarry, but with one stride to the terrier's three the lurcher had already overtaken it, lean and true like an arrow fired from a newly strung bow of birch curved by time and river water. Its taut shoulder muscles rippled and a string of gluey phlegm swung from its mouth before sticking to its cheek as it leaned tight into the hillside and cut off the rabbit as it bounced full tilt to a hole dug in above the worn groove of a holloway that they called Slack's Lane, a little used run at the back of the sun above the sheer black rocks of Hathershelf Scout.

We'll have to watch that lot, said William Hartley. Them men's not to be trusted.

There's good men amongst them, said Isaac Hartley. Honest men.

Honest men would not be doing what it is that we are doing, said William Hartley.

He's right, said David Hartley. Honesty isn't worth a tinker's cuss so long as them knows to keep their traps snapped. And fear is the only thing that'll work on them. Fear and a few good tannings.

They fear you.

William Hartley said this.

Across the field the rabbit had gone to ground but the disturbance of the chase had put two more basking rabbits up and the lurcher quickly shortened the length between itself and the smaller of the pair. The young rabbit found itself caught out in the open. Exposed to predators from ground and sky alike, it was too far from any earthen sanctuary.

It's us three that makes this what it is, said David Hartley.

And our Father, said Isaac Hartley.

Our Father is a tiring man. He doesn't need to shoulder thirty or forty of the most desperate sods of the north. He's already burdened.

Burdened with what? said Isaac Hartley.

Burdened with the three most desperate, cut-throat, skulldugging, scallywag barbarian bastard sons of all of them.

At this the younger two brothers laughed.

Turning, the rabbit faltered then flipped and rolled and

the lurcher was upon it, then seconds behind it the terrier too, a streamlined blur of flexing young muscle. It clamped its jaw around its neck. The rabbit was much the same size and weight as the terrier but it locked on and lifted it, then shook it furiously. Whipped it until something gave. Across the field the brothers heard the flap and crack of breaking bones and the rabbit give a final desperate squeak before its head hung loose and its gaze froze forever in the aspect of smoke.

At this the dogs changed. Their stances relaxed and the terrier dropped the rabbit before gently nuzzling and licking its fur. It nibbled at it. The lurcher padded off with its tongue lolling in the direction of the other rabbit that it had seen.

William Hartley called it back with a shrill whistle.

Run things right and we'll be as rich as the fattest lord that bathes himself in goose fat, said Isaac Hartley. What will you spend all your coin on, our David?

Never mind all that, said his brother. Time is plenty for spending. Coin is coin – it keeps a while. Firstly we need to name our best men and keep them close; the rest can know only what it is they need to know and thems the ones we'll hang on the line if the storm clouds close in. And we need muscle and knuckle to persuade them that might think differently to us. There's a few folk in this valley – the churchly ones and them that bow to the crown or who think starvation is a virtue – who don't like it that we're showing a bit of enterprise. They'd rather see us shackled to the loom or picking pebbles from the coulter's path than have coin in our pocket and meat in our cold stores.

Those that speak against the Cragg Vale Coiners will be lambs to the abattoir cleaver, said Isaac Hartley.

Aye, said David Hartley. It'll be *their* fresh necks that will feel the rope-burn or nick of the blade if the lawman comes knocking up at Bell House. Not mine.

Secrets, said William Hartley. We need to know those that can keep them, and those whose tongues turn loose as soon as they're slaked with the ale.

47

There'll be no more fire-side sweating for us three, said David Hartley.

No?

No. I have a man in mind for the clipping of coins. And when this man is striking, these boys of ours can't be spending. No. This valley is too narrow for these things to go unnoticed but we'll be on our way to glory so long as we work it all rightly.

There are a few we can trust, said William Hartley. For years you were away, our David, but Isaac and me know the way things lie.

On your heads be it then.

Tom Spencer is one of them, said Isaac Hartley.

Yes. Thomas Spencer is one of us, agreed William Hartley. His blood runs close and he is good with the numbers also. Learned. His memory it has no holes. We can use a good man like him.

He paused to whistle and shout *geeit* again, and the terrier picked up the rabbit and trotted back between the tufts of whin and furze that dotted the field. It dropped it at their feet. Isaac Hartley picked the creature up by its hind legs and checked its eyes and teeth.

A good coney is that, he said. Good health.

John Wilcox too, said William Hartley. John Wilcox has always done us well. He speaks ill of no man – and that is a good sign. Already he has earned more coin than the others. James Jagger too we have known since birth.

Not I, said David Hartley.

James Jagger is true valley though, agreed Isaac Hartley. No two tracks about that. I agree with our William. He would kill a man that whispered a cross word about you. Loyal blood, is Jim Jagger.

Good then, said David Hartley. Thomas Clayton we know will do what is asked of him also. David Greenwood has shown himself to be a man with nutmegs of stone.

Nathan Horsfall is a worker.

William Hartley said this.

His face I do not like, said David Hartley.

His heart is good though.

And his face you do not have to see, said Isaac Hartley.

Fine.

Jonas Eastwood has brought us his share of bits and florins, said the youngest brother, his red hair slick against his faintly freckle-flecked brow. He has good connections over in Fax. His father-in-law is sympathetic. He asks for nothing but our protection.

Protection from who? said David Hartley.

From them that bother him.

Then they'll bother him no more. Who else can we trust?

Jonas Eastwood I trust also, said Isaac Hartley. And his brother too. Wiley like foxes are the Eastwoods.

I heard tell that Ben Sutcliffe has laid with all the bints from Field to Fax, said David Hartley.

What of it?

Does he not have a family to feed?

A wife and four sprats. One of them is tapped.

Well then, said David Hartley. The man that presses coins to the palms of fustilugged whores when his children are wearing rags cannot be a man of honour, no matter which side of the law he cares to step.

He's a worker, is Ben.

Then set him working. But he will never know the true nature of this business and he will never dine at my table. Never again will he be invited.

Now, said David Hartley. About this new clipping man I have in mind.

The wherefores and the howabouts of the serky stansums of how this magikal man of metal did fynd his way to us is a story unto itself Jaykob Tillysun it was who first raised his name to I after he did see this man from Bradford make a dog fly Yes yes I know wor yor thinkin Kinge Dayvid has been at the barrel of jaylers stingo or his mind has gone kittle after too menny days sat starrin at the worls of a sell so cold that the ice wetness does seep throo them and form ice shoggles on his cruckedd neb But no what I tell you Jaycub Tillysun did see with his owern peepers and Jaycub Tillison is one of the Kinges most trussed men One of the few left hoos werd is his bond and can still be taykin so And so when Jaycub Tilltson tells you that this alkemiss did rayse a sleepin dug three foot off the grownd weethowt wires or ropes or mirras or smoke then you be knowing that this be a man of speyshul magical powers A good fellow to hayve on your side because there's only the few who can muster majick.

At a harvest drinke up it was in the thwayte of Tryangul not but five myles from Bell Hole as the rayven goes when sum fellows Jaykob Tillyon inclooted did calle upon this majikal man to do wor it was he was allreddy nown for And so after some purswayshin and the promis of a haff duzzeen nyps of the finest harves fyment this alkemyist who only ever appeered when the werk it was dun and ther was nothink left to do but for the drinken and the eaten and the fucken of the valleys frootful vynes did corl up on the boys to put down their fidduls and tayke thur teeth out thur lassys titts for a moment and he did pray syluns and nod to the mangy dog – Boggit was its name – that was coiled up asleep in a skep that one of the wiffees yoosed for the sorting and carrying of her yarn borls And then he did mutta some werds the lykes of wich Jaykup Tillisen or no man there to bare witnes to had herd befor And with his eyes clowsed and fingers spread he did summin that wicker skep and the sleepin

dug to ryse up like a dorn mussrom Up it cayme off the growd
Both baskit and dug And up it cept cumin And that shut off any
laffta or the slocken slurps of the greedee baylers and reepers
who were neck deep in ale already for it had been a long season
I tell yoo Becors to see a floatin sleepin dug is to see the work of
god or the divil or hoo nose what And any man like that I can
use Any man like that must be a wizzid or an alchemisst or just
sumone youd sooner have on your side as not.

And thats how we cayme a cross the man wort tuck us from too
bit clippers to werld infoamy.

The Alchemist wore a hood and carried with him a blanket roll strapped across his back.

David Hartley watched him as he moved across the moor at a steady pace, a dark triangle like an unlit beacon awaiting the touch of a taper's flame. From this distance he appeared more of a man of the cloisters than the dark arts.

As he approached, he saw that the hooded figure wore a thin beard on his cheeks and chin.

They nodded in greeting and then David Hartley led him to an outbuilding. In it there was a fire burning and he said wait here. A moment later he returned with Isaac Hartley and William Hartley and their father William Hartley the elder.

This here is the man they say is the best at the melting, he said. He'll be doing our share now. No more burned fingers for us boys – what do you say to that, father?

William Hartley nodded and then spoke.

There's been bits of me dropping off and drying up for years, my lad, and I'll surely be glad to keep my fingers for a little longer yet.

His sons smiled at this.

They call this man the Alchemist, said David Hartley.

And how are we to trust him, our David? asked Isaac Hartley.

Because this man knows that we'll put him neck-deep in the moor alive and then after that we'll take his wife and his children and his children's children and all the children that will ever bear his family name if he so much as squeaks in the wrong direction. He comes from Bradford but if he proves himself you'll be seeing more of him. Much more.

The Alchemist looked from one man to the other and then unhitched his heavy parcel and squatted down to roll it out on the floor before them.

The blanket held a set of clipping scissors and files. There were bellows and two small three-cornered smelting pots.

Crucibles. There were rags and rubbing oil too. There was a knife and a cosh. Tongs and shears.

That's a better kit than ours, said William Hartley.

And he's going to show us how he uses it, said David Hartley.

The Alchemist squatted and began to assemble his effects.

Across two inverted V frames he placed a blackened metal crosspiece that hung above the dying flames and then he raked the heap of burning logs and tapped at them until they flaked into fragments. He broke the fire down into a neat flat bed of silent heat and then raked it once more.

You'll need fresh logs, said William Hartley. I'll fetch em.

Without taking his eyes from the fire the Alchemist raised a hand to halt the youngest brother. In the dark room the glow from the shards and cinders cast his skin in a sallow hue; he was a thin man. Taciturn, and with few teeth set in his mealy gums, his cheeks appeared to have sunken pathetically inwards in sympathy. That and the wispy beard made his age indeterminate. A decade either side of forty would still not necessarily be an accurate reading. He remained hooded.

The three-cornered crucible he hung low from the crossbow and then he re-shaped the bed of burning ash once again. He squared it off at the sides. Shortened it. Intensified its hazed glare in the direction of the pot.

The Alchemist took the bellows and cleared his throat and then he pumped them. Twice. Two short bursts. The stiff gusts of stale air brought the bed of fire alive. It pulsed with a new flameless intensity and his boots scraped across the dirt floor as he shifted around the fire pit, working the bellows again so that the briquettes of burning wood chocks raged.

The three-cornered pot appeared to tighten and groan. Inscribed in its side was a sigil, a crude rendering of what looked like a lightning fork. David Hartley noticed it.

What's that? he said.

The Alchemist followed his eyes.

That?

Yes. That. On the pot. What's it meant to be?

That, said the Alchemist. That represents the bladed branches of the stag.

His voice was dry in his mouth. His voice was fire-cracked and heat-worn.

Why, said David Hartley. Why?

Because the stag is the life force of the moors just as fire is the life of forging. I thought you'd know that.

I do know that, said David Hartley. I do know that.

Only then did the Alchemist look at the brothers and their father, and the glances that passed between them. In the latter he saw an aged man who had lived for six long decades of turf-digging and loom-mending, of flint-slitting and rock-breaking and pond-dredging and rabbit-trapping and slate-fixing, all with nothing to show for it but twisted fingers and a locked left knee, a squint and a crooked spine. He saw that the old man's dark eyes seemed to hold the seeds of fire too, and that his chin was pointed and one temple scarred with a white mess of flesh healed into a tight pattern like the fossilised form of flowering lichen across a wet valley rock. The mashed markings of a true coin smelter.

The Alchemist extended an arm. He held out a palm, requested alms.

David Hartley produced a pouch and poured half of it into the hand of the Alchemist who took the shears and clipped each coin in turn until he had a small pile of slivers.

With neat movements he circled the fire and roddled the coals and pumped the bellows.

The remaining coins he deftly stacked in a tower on the floor.

With his poker he tapped the pot and the four men leaned in to see that the guinea shards were changing shape. Softening and collapsing. They were gaining a liquid sheen.

The Alchemist signalled for the men to step back as he unwrapped another cloth and set down beside him a selection of moulds and dies of different sizes. He carefully arranged

54

them. He touched them once. He touched them twice, then with tongs he lifted the pot from the fire and poured its contents into four of the moulds. The pot he set aside.

Still squatting and stock still, the Alchemist muttered words to himself. The Hartleys could not determine what he was saying. His whispered words ran into one another. Strange incantations. He uttered a song without a melody. An inaudible spell for the casting of the metal. A twisting of the tongue.

Then in a sudden burst of movement the Alchemist snatched up a spelter stamp in one hand and hammer in the other. The stamp he pressed down onto the first mould and he twirled the hammer once and then twice over the back of his hand in a conjurer's display of showmanship before swinging it and bringing it down hard on the head of the stamp. He struck again and again, the shrill judder of metal on metal reverberating.

The stamp he cast aside before seizing the next one – this slightly larger – and swinging and striking in quick succession. Four times he did this, one after another; the stone space echoing with the hammer's call.

Then he laid his tools aside. There were beads of sweat on his brow now. They looked black. As black as the dew that settles on the coomb of a coalman's shovelled remnants.

The Alchemist turned the moulds upside down and tapped the bottom of each so that their contents fell into a bowl of water that steamed with each newly forged coin. Then he spoke. He said: the white hot hiss is a viscous liquid kiss from the lady of the fire who is softer than silver and swifter than light.

What's that? said Isaac Hartley. What's he saying?

The mottled dirty water he threw onto the hot coals and these too hissed and steamed and spat tiny gobbets of dead and dying embers in a cloud of smothering muffled smoke that had all the men but the Alchemist, who seemed impervious to it, hacking and rubbing at their eyes.

He rattled the bowl and swirled its contents then flicked the newly forged and stamped coins into his hand. From a pocket he produced a rag and a small snuff box of dark daubing into which he dipped a blackened digit and dabbed some of its contents onto each coin. With an economical flourish he buffed each disc.

He slowly stood and handed a coin in turn to young William Hartley and Isaac Hartley and the old man William Hartley the elder. At David Hartley he paused and held the coin aloft between thumb and forefinger and in the half-light it seemed to turn and spin of its own accord and he said come, come press a coin into my palm and I'll return you two like a curse reversed on a gypsy's tongue.

David Hartley took the coin.

He touched it. He studied it. It still held within it the warmth of the fire. He examined it further.

He said: this work is good.

The Alchemist said nothing.

Here, he's milled the rim, said William Hartley, and David Hartley studied the tiny writing that ran around the side of the coin.

Do you know what these words say? asked the Alchemist.

No, I do not, said David Hartley. They are not in any language that any right-minded man round these parts would know even if they were book learners.

That's because these words is Latin, said the Alchemist. *Decus Et Tutamen*. They say: An Ornament and a Safeguard. A hundred years or more this coin has carried these words and I'd wager it'll carry them for a hundred more.

What's all this Latin for?

Latin is the language that the crown favours, said William Hartley Sr. It's what they speak across foreign waters and it makes the king think he's better than common folk.

I'm not no fucking common folk, said David Hartley. I'm a king too; a king that's more respected amongst his own folk than these betterny-bodies who think their shit smells as sweet as pollen. And I'm a king that doesn't need no fucking foreign tongue from across no foreign waters to make him feel big about himself, nor a crown upon his napper. All I wear is the sky above me, and the only throne this man needs is that which sits above the shitting pit.

The detail is good, brother, said William Hartley. See the laurel upon my guinea. See the drapery on the neck. See the lions. This work is beyond even the best Coiner's capabilities.

This work is nothing, said the Alchemist. This I can do a thousand-fold.

Then a fold it is I have for you.

A fold?

Aye. Sheep fold. Away from here. Over the top dip. You'll use it.

The Alchemist looked at David Hartley blankly as the eldest brother spoke.

Once a week or two weeks or whenever it is that the valley has given up enough grubby coins to make it worth your while you will come and you will go to that fold where there is a roof and a pit and you will clip and smelt until the pile is doubled.

Still the Alchemist said nothing.

You will be watched and you will be protected, continued David Hartley. Looked after. There will be lads as lookouts checking the moor for nosey blow-ins and any man that wants to bring us down.

They will watch you too, said Isaac Hartley.

Why? said the Alchemist.

Isaac Hartley smirked.

Because the man who trusts others is the first to fall. We trust no fuckers, magic man or otherways.

Isaac Hartley cast aside his coin and said: good work counts for nothing if you cannot be trusted.

Can you be trusted? said David Hartley.

I ask myself the same question of you, said the Alchemist.

At this William Hartley snorted.

Shall I knock this man sparko, our David?

Let him speak.

Can I trust you to give this man – meaning me – his share and to keep him from Jack Ketch's rope? said the Alchemist.

You'll get your share, said David Hartley. Don't you worry about that. You'll get your share and more if you do right by us. But who is Jack Ketch?

Jack Ketch is the name of the hangman, said the Alchemist. Jack Ketch is the name of all men who do all the hanging. One name to fit all; just like his noose.

Your neck's protection I cannot guarantee any more than mine own, said David Hartley. But your name and whereabouts will go no further than these stone walls and no stranger will molest you to or from the moor. Do you trust me? Do you trust the Hartleys?

The Alchemist hesitated.

They say I should fear the Hartleys, he said.

Oh, you should. You should fear the Hartleys like you fear the reaper's scythe. Your tongue I'll take between these tongs and twist until your spells can be spoken no more if you durst betray a Hartley. I'll ask you once more: do you trust me?

No, said the Alchemist.

Good, said David Hartley. Many do, but more fool them. This then makes you of a stronger mind than most men. You are more like us than you realise. The only thing you should put your trust in is that fire will burn and metal will melt and the stag will always be a-rutting on these moor tops.

Men mite laff and men mite mock behind mine back but I seen what I seen an I recorl it now so many very yers later as cleer as if it were yestadaye.

Yes it was a dark nite with the wind raised up and whisslin round the chimernee stack and arattlin the tyles it was and the moore was darke darke darke an I was but a mite of a boy A meer pup of a thynge still hairless an not yet put owt to werk An it was becors of this wind and the arattlin of the tyles and the winders that I was wide awayke and trubbled Yes my sleep it was diysturbed by the sound of the moore tryin to get into my room an the sound of the moore tryin to get into my bed and the moore tryin to get into my mind becors it can do that can the moore and no man can sleep in that state no Not unless thur in a coffing.

So I was layin there starin out into the prickly blooness of it all when the room doore did open of its own accord I herd the latch lift and the hinges creak and I spoke then I said Farther I cannot sleepe but no voice came in reply so I said Mothere what gives but all I sor for a moment was darkness No thinge but the still blue darkness of the eternel Yokshyre nite But then.

But then there was movement Yes there was bodees entring the room an I could only just mayke out the forms of them the shapes of them for ther was severul of them I durst call them men and you shall see why in a moment becors then they stept out into the frayme of moon lite that did cut throe the nite and fell throo the winder an onto the flore A patch of it layde their on the florbords there was An what did I see but men Men yes But with the heads of grayte stags Yes stags With antlas and nostrils flared and steem risin from ther pelts and the black black eyes of the deere that do rome the moores and the wuds and the glaydes and the *vally edges But down below they were as I say men with mens bodees and the clothes of men and the boots an the legs and the hands of men and ther was menny of them mebbe four or fyve or six of them I recorl not.*

And it was then that they did start up a dance inna circul around my roome four or fyve or sixe of them ther was These great stag men of the moors And they did dance and move so sylentlee as if there was no wayt to them at all as if they were flotin like clowds Silempt but for the sound of there breathing like the anymuls that they was Anymils as I say for no man Ive ever known has a pelt and a snouwt and antlers and does a midnite dance in the bedrooms of boys what live in the shadder of the darke dark moor.

And I did wach as they dipped and swerled an I durst not move nor speek nor breath nor nothen And the moon lite cort them in her gays and the stagmen of the moors did dance in ther circle An I watched on from beeneeth my blankyts full of fear and wunder not daring to move nor breeth nor nothing an that nite I did not sleepe a wink Instead I just sat there full of that fear not moving an hardlee brethin until the men had left so silentlee still and morning came At last my old freind morning And the moore did leeve my room did leeve my bed then it did leeve me alone and I finally found the curridge to run downstairs to my Faether and my Mothere now dead may her sowel rest in peece and I says.

I says I seenum I seenum the stagmen of the moors And they says what is it yor blethring abowt now eh And I says the grate stag men of the moores I seen them dance in a circle in the patch of moonlyt An they did laff and say what rot you gab yung Daevid Hartley what rot you tork and what dreams you have and what an imaginayshun And I says no no but I seenum and then my Mothere did say to my Farther its that cheese whats been givin him the fritely nitemares is what it is and they went about ther

60

bisniss of cleenin the grate and yoking the ox and fetchin the eggs and porin the ale as if it were a normal daye.

But it was not a normal daye it was the day that changed me The day wot gave me fresh eyes and new beelefs and a sens of wonder and fear of what it is that this lande of mine can do and what it is that maykes these moores a place of magick and feer and what it is that goes on that we cannot understand up here and what it is that make rite minded folk stop away and keep these moors emptee and what is that maykes man and animal move as wan up heer where the land meets the sky and creechurs do dance and its all beyond boeth reesum and ecksplaynen.

Roots and radicles.

Cavities and corners. Caves and cromlechs.

Nooks and niches.

Stream heads and stream beds and rotting stumps.

Clefts and crannies. Cracks in the old cold wet rock.

Fissures and quarries. Gatepost holes. Dung traps.

Gravestone vases.

Old wasp's nests even – tucked away into perfectly papered lanterns submerged in the crusted soil.

The coins began to appear from the pockets of men who had garnered them, some with promises and others by threat, all to be hidden away. The soil accepted them. The walls and the trees and the woodlands accepted them. The hovels and the hay-ricks too. Soon new coins and old coins were stowed there. Coins worn away on their journey through the hands of the poor and the very poor. The ill and the injured. Dirty discs. Golden guineas. Shilling pieces and florins, and silver bits scuffed black through transactions. Coins won and coins lost on dog fights and cock fights. Coins earned and spent in cups and jugs. Coins tossed. Coins lost. Coins for clipping, coins for breeding and buying and multiplying.

It was boom time.

All found their way from butcher's aprons and baker's flour boxes and publican's pinafores; from draymen's pockets and hostler's handkerchiefs and hawker's hats and cobbler's waistcoats. From brogger's wallets and colporteur's coffers, into the hardened hands of the hardened hill men who had persuaded the traders of the valley to give up their gains for this great fraudulent venture, in exchange for a nice return and protection and discretion guaranteed.

Drawn like metal bits to a magnet, coins came in from foreign climes too. Lima shillings forged from Peruvian metal and Spanish pistoles and the Portugese moidores that had long circulated as legal tender in England, such was the imbalance of trade weighted in the English favour. Money was money. Metal metal. Coin coin. And soon the valley was flooding with the rattling rush of new money.

Into the hands of Eli Hoyle and William Hailey and Jonathan Bolton it went. Into the hands of John Pickles and Jonas Eastwood and Thomas Clayton. Into the hands of William Harpur and Joseph Hanson. John Tatham and William Folds.

Coins collected and collated and buffed and burnished, these ill-gotten gains were stashed in pouches and secreted at night – always at night, for the moon was in on the coining too – in places pre-arranged. The valley's bank they called it. The bank of hill-tops and hidden ravines; of forest and field, of coins stashed beneath boulders and cow troughs. By rats' nests under coops, shit-dripped and bird-pecked. In the seed of the pheasant feeder left by a gamekeeper in on another game. Squeezed flat beneath the chocks and hearting and copes of a dry-stone wall made drier still by another unexpected week of drought. In sike bottoms and clough clearings too.

Most in the valley gave up their coin readily, for the promise of getting half the value back again on top for their troubles was too good to refuse. There were those whose resistance was expected – the doctor and the book learner; the man of the cloth and the old maid who stumbled stooping to the same pew each day and twice on Sundays to hear his re-heated sermons. Those who refused to be part of the game. These received first a word of stern warning and then another visit from not one but two or three or more of David Hartley's men. The same men each time. Those with the fullest shadows and the fewest teeth. Those with the ebonised eyes and little to lose. Knuckle men. Muscle men. Not numbers men or head men. Not Hartleys but hired hands.

Keen men. Cruel men. Chief amongst them Absolom Butts and James Broadbent.

Brian Dempsey and Paul Taylor.

Young, mad, blood-drunk Aloysius Smith.

At night they always came when the candles were snuffed and the dogs made soft and slow by the glow of the moaning logs in the grate.

The gentle rap of a cudgel on a door frame or a pebble lobbed to a lonely unlit window or the mere sight of the huddle by the log-store on a moonless night was often enough to turn uncertain minds towards the coining cause.

But still a handful resisted, citing justice, God and morality as their reasons. Honour to the king and crown.

For these men there came back-ginnel beatings and stamped ankles. Daubings on their doors, their fattened family pigs slit and left bleeding in black pools, their store-rooms burnt. There were further nocturnal visitations too, their wives or daughters dragged and shoved and groped and poked and gang-fucked down darkened lanes by Coiners with corn sacks about their heads, their rancid breath reeking of beer and bacco and beef collop.

And soon, in time, these resisting men of principle and God and righteousness gave up their coins to the cause of a new king too. Through hands and from holes and hiding places their currency reached Isaac Hartley and William Hartley, because by now David Hartley barely saw nor touched this brilliant stream of cold metal that like a miracle from the big book itself flowed uphill all the way to the crest of this new kingdom he had constructed over just two summers or so.

The back end of the cart was piled high with flour sacks and in each there was a loaf and some cured meat, some tallow fat candles and vegetables freshly pulled from the Upper Calder Valley soil: parsnips and russet potatoes, carrots and leeks and mangelwurzels for those who kept livestock on their smallholdings. There was a plug of tobacco and some fat rascal cakes and wedged blocks of cheese and shives of pig fat and pickles and chutneys too. Beside the sack there were three barrels of ale, a jug and a bag of coins. Balls of butter bobbed in a bucket of cold milk.

The cart moved slowly crossways along Heights track from the tiny township of Midgely, the whole valley splayed out below. To the east, Sowerby Bridge and beyond it, hidden by hills, the town of Halifax. Then to the west Hebden Bridge and Heptonstall perched perilously above it on a spur of land between two densely wooded gorges on either side and the moor pressing up against its rear, its houses turned inwards like nested fledglings sheltering from a storm.

Below, the river moved like molten lead through Mytholmroyd and beyond it, where the houses ended and the hills became blurred through the wavering haze of the afternoon light, a narrowing streak of tapered woodlands darkened upwards to a tiny dot in the distance where the moors began, only visible to those who sought to see it: Bell House.

Other things sat behind the man that steered the cart and his companion who stepped down with a sack of gifted goods for every friend of the Coiners along the route: blankets and eyeglasses for the elderly, pairs of clogs old and new in different sizes, passed-down clothes cleaned and darned for a second wearing. Breeches and shirts and stockings. There were wigs. Clay pipes. Children's toys.

The front end of the cart was stacked with split logs, seasoned and ready for burning. It was the best wood that there was – a choice pick of ash and beech, hawthorn and horse chestnut.

A lone house loomed along the Heights track, that of half-blind Robert Howland who slept before a fire with a half dozen dogs around him.

The cart pulled up and the men climbed down. The first carried with him one of the sacks weighted with produce while the second began to roll logs down into the crook of his arms.

They knocked on the door and shouted Coiners coming Robert Howland, Coiners coming, and then they waited for the old man to answer.

* * *

Screens of shimmering smoke shot through with shades of umber and sepia rose in the far distance like the ragged backdrop of a tired troupe of travelling players unveiling the day's performance.

It was the turning time. It was the burning of the heather time.

These nebulous rectangles hung on the horizon like the flags of an unseen returning army, held in the haze a *fata morgana*, before dissipating into stray wisps and twists that were taken by a breeze. The scorched smoke of burned peat and the bone-dry pungent heather gave the breeze a shape and a purpose; draped in smoke it was made physical.

The best of the heather had already been clipped and picked for the making of besoms. The longest branches and thickest clusters had been cut to size and bundled around a stout pole – always willow – by those solitary bodgers and gamekeepers' wives who had gained the landowner's permission to do so, and who sang the same song as they worked at home with blade and cord, always to a melody that followed a descending glissando of notes:

> *Buy broom buzzems,*
> *Buy them when they're new,*
> *Fine heather bred uns,*
> *Better never grew.*

The heather's flowers too had been taken and set to boil in pots or hung to dry in clusters from mullions and over inglenooks, their mauve colourings turning darker with the darkening of shortened days bookended by nights that birthed new mythologies from old fears.

The remaining heather of the valley was burned at the behest of the few. Men unseen. Landowners who rarely walked the land they owned, let alone lived on. These were men from the cities, who spent their days away paving turnpikes and building mills. Sinking canals and striking deals. Buying and selling. Traders.

Sons of the empire, the aristocratic architects of England's new future. Men for whom too much was never enough.

Their estate work was done by land managers and it was these who took the heather plant and used it in brewing the ale that filled their master's bow-roofed cellars, while others used the cleared barren moorland spaces for housing hives for their honey-making. Sheep and deer grazed up there and grouse nested in it too, but mainly the heather was used for the dyeing of the wools, its branches for besom brooms.

The slow smoke drifted down now to settle on the houses of those weavers and land workers who lived in the hamlets and farmsteads that sat below the moor line. The scent of it was the latest subtle signal to mark autumn's tightening grip on the land.

The incoming season meant death and soon the trees were to become bone-like, and their leaves would gather in drifts down in the lanes, and the animals were already gorging themselves before the cold time announced itself in a famine of nothing but frost and fire and flickering candles.

Come April the pitch-coloured rectangles of burnt heather shadows would be dotted with the white fingers of new shoots peeping through, though as this summer past withered and died, slowly curling in on itself into crisp husks and falling tiny skeletons, the very thought of next spring's re-birth seemed beyond realisation for most in the valley, an impossibility, a wild, fanciful vision of the deluded.

Across the moor and through the drapes of smoke he came.

His red waistcoat marked him out; he knew as much.

Indeed he wanted the eyes of the hills to be on him, to note him. To be made aware of his presence.

He carried with him a bag and in the bag was fruit and bread and meat packed for him by his wife, and a pipe that he had recently taken to smoking, though his children disliked the smell of it on his breath when he kissed them goodnight. He also had with him a crudely drawn map with the named hamlets and farmsteads marked upon it, and beside each a list of known families and members. Against those he suspected of partaking in the yellow trade he had marked a red X. He had other items with him too: matches and a candle. A mirror. A knife.

A fine rain was coming in. William Deighton watched it comb the valley in waves.

He walked with the purpose of a man who considered the moors as much his as anyone's. This was his belief and these hills he felt were familiar to those of a childhood spent amongst moorlands and secret darkened tributary valleys so similar.

Things had been different then. He told his wife this often.

Five decades earlier the hills and moors and woods of youth had been William Deighton's playgrounds. Each holme and royd was there to be explored. Each thwaite and clough.

An inquisitive boy with strong lungs, he could walk for eighty furlongs through the landscape and learn much about life then. He remembered seeing secret gin stills and stone skep niches for the keeping of bees. He had crossed streams by slippery staup hoyles – the old name for the stepping rocks slick with spray and worn smooth by centuries of feet. He found hidden ponds rippling thick with pike so big they had been known to pull cats and dogs under, and in winter he saw waterfalls that had frozen solid into great glass shapes resembling strange creatures from tales of times now gone.

He witnessed strange things in quarries too. Oddness. He heard noises up top. Stalked deer. Watched foxes and brocks – and felt himself being watched too. He walked always with a sense of there being witnesses close by. Hidden but watching; and he heard further tales too of strange moortop doings.

But he had always been left alone, free to walk the valley unhindered, returning to town at night, stiff and spent and happy.

And now the valley was controlled by this insidious breed whose influence was killing the trade of the town, the Cragg

Vale Coiners, whose reputation had already spread to the Palace of Westminster.

It did not look good for him, William Deighton, sole representative of the crown, tax collector for Halifax and its surrounds, excise-man and upholder of the law in an increasingly lawless land. He had been warned: the authoritarian grip was weakening and this way outright anarchy beckoned. The responsibility to restore order fell upon his shoulders alone.

So he wanted to be watched. Wanted to be seen and marked and noted by these men they called the Cragg Vale Coiners because they needed to know that their trade could not go on unnoticed. Would not go on unpunished. He had sworn to the King and the King he would serve.

He turned his collar to the drizzle and walked towards the moors on which he knew these man-animals lived.

David Hartley called his brother Isaac Hartley in and when he came to the house he was wet with a fine rain that sat about his hair and shoulders, and swept across the moors behind him like a curtain being drawn across the memory of a summer whose harvest had been bountiful.

David Hartley passed his brother Isaac Hartley a rag with which to dry himself and then they sat before the fire, even though the fire was not lit and instead the hearth held nothing but grey spent ash in the shape of logs from yesterday's burn-up.

You look troubled, said Isaac Hartley.

Trouble is something that may be coming to our door, he replied.

Trouble, brother?

Yip.

I have seen about the place a man, said David Hartley. Twice I seen him across the moor. Once rising up through Bell Hole and another coming up over the back way through the bog patch as if Erringden Moor was his and his alone.

What use is having young lads with slingshots as lookouts if a man can get through those woods? replied Isaac Hartley. Those woods is our woods and no man gets through.

This one did. But we'll deal with that in time. For now this man gives me grief. I can feel it coming.

You always have had a way for feeling these things. Why is it you feel the grief this time?

Because he walks with purpose and his eyes take everything in, said David Hartley. You and I know that people do not come up here without reason. They do not enter the kingdom of King David unless it is to see King David but yet this man sets only a short while, watching from a distance, and then he walks on. He doesn't hunt or eat or roll with a girl or sleep a while in the grasses or any of the other reasons that a man might make the journey up from the valley floor to the moor top. It seems our reputation is not enough to prevent the visitations of this one.

The men paused for a moment and then David Hartley continued.

Yes, there can only be one purpose. This man is on law business. I'd wager all the coins stowed in every crevice and twisted root between here and Todmorden that his is excise duty. He's out to get us, Isaac. He's out for Coiners' scalps – I know it.

The younger brother nodded.

I think that I too have seen that man, brother, said Isaac Hartley. I have seen him over on the old horse track beyond Hathershelf. I too have watched him from a distance. You are right. This man is here for our coins – and our souls.

Yet you thought not to mention it?

I'm mentioning it now.

How do you know this is the same exciseman?

Because he is not one of us, brother, said Isaac Hartley.

In what way?

He does not look like a valley man. He does neither dress like us nor carry himself like us. His is an unfamiliar face.

How does he dress then?

The man I saw wears a wig, said Isaac Hartley. I have seen the breeze lift it. I have seen it snag on a bramble.

You have seen this?

With my own eyes.

The wig I did not notice as this man kept himself at a long distance from the house, said David Hartley. And did he see you?

He did not. I was out to take some pheasants and became concerned in my head that he might be the gamekeeper the way he skulked so I did give him a wide berth. Twice this has happened. The second time I nearly took that kindling hatchet to his head-top but then I did realise he might be a man doing crown's business and what trouble that would bring to us all.

Skulked? said David Hartley.

Yes. Like a prig-napper that's out to rustle a still-wet foal. Like Reynard sniffing the chicken coop on the breeze.

This is the one and same man then. What else did you watch?

I watched him wear a long brown coat down to here with britches of cord beneath, and a waistcoat made from the finest wool. He dresses like a man that's had first choice on the shalloon. Made of the best dye, it is. Red, it is. As red as oxen blood. Blood red, like. That's how I knew he wasn't one of us: no Cragg man could afford such a cut, nor would he flaunt his colours across this moorland of ours like that. It's that waistcoat that gave him away because in all other manners he moves like a moor man. On his head he wore a shovel hat.

David Hartley nodded and then spoke.

Was he mounted?

Once he was mounted but the second time he was on foot. That was why I was unsure as to whether he was gamekeeper or poacher or Coiner or what the devil may know.

I too saw him on foot, said David Hartley. They say that Deighton is this bastard lickspittle's name.

Deighton? I do not know the name, brother.

Well now you do, said David Hartley. And you'd be wise to remember it because this Deighton is the man who wants to end our enterprise. His first name I was not told but his last name is enough to know. He has the nose of a mole and the way of a weasel.

A pest then.

Worse than a pest, said David Hartley. He is poisonous. He is a predator. One word from him could bring down fifty men. Fifty men and their families. Our families.

Dangerous then.

A threat – yes. Surely. Undoubtedly.

So, said Isaac Hartley.

So, said David Hartley. So we do what any right man does to the fox that has his chickens or the mole that digs up his turf or the weasel that has his morning eggs.

Yes, brother.

We trap him or snare him or smoke him or burn him. We do whatever it is that needs to be done to remove him.

Yes, brother. This I understand.

We can't let one man of the crown rule over fifty poor men of the soil.

No we cannot.

It's just not right, said David Hartley. How could we sleep at night with this shadow cast over us? Too long in the past we have strived to make a living from the farming and weaving and look where it got us – nowhere but indebted to inferior men who now want to turn the soil for their own gain. They'll have us living with the hogs if we let them.

I can make this man disappear like the owl at daybreak, our David. You leave it be and think of other things. The next time he comes up through Bell Hole is the last time he'll come up through Bell Hole. You can trust me.

That I do, but for now we do nothing but put the hawk eyes of the valley upon him, said David Hartley. He is not yet worth risking our necks for. Our strength is in our numbers and we can make sure the hunter becomes the hunted. Not a single step he will take towards Cragg Vale without it being noted. Your job is to alert the men and make sure he gets nowhere near us. A man like this Deighton – he is out for glory. But the wrong kind of glory. He would rather persecute the poor and the needy to win favour with those that rule the land than leave them be in peace. I tell you this much: his loyalty and ambition will be his undoing. He'll rue the day he put his beady eye on a Hartley, will this cunt Deighton.

Amen brother. A cunt indeed.

Part III
Spring 1769
Chock-Chock

So what is it this time?

The exciseman William Deighton sidled up to Robert Parker through the crowd and stood shoulder to shoulder with the younger attorney.

Robert Parker turned to him and smiled. Not for the first time he observed the contrast between the man's town clothes and his slightly weather-worn face, the clear signs of one who leads a dual existence of paperwork and solitary hill-top wandering. Tailing illiterate tax-dodgers was an unenviable task, all told. William Deighton deserved a medal, or a rise at the very least.

Mr Deighton. I didn't expect to find you down here amongst the rabble.

It's where I do my best work – you know that. And I could say the same of you. I hear you're in with Mexborough. Chief steward of his estate and general affairs, they say.

New opportunities certainly seem to be presenting themselves.

You're well then?

Thriving, said Robert Parker. And how is that litter of yours?

They are well too. Thank you.

How many now?

I have eight children.

I don't know how you make the time.

Well, the older boys have left the house, said William Deighton. Elias is twenty-five now and works as a journeyman in the Midlands. Thomas has gone even further. He is in the East Indies. William is apprenticed to a candlestick maker and has two years to serve.

It's quite a job they've got you doing, said Robert Parker. An entire town's taxes and levies to collect and just the one man to do it. And not just the town either – they say your real office is those hill-top hinterlands that even Satan himself steers clear of.

William Deighton smiled wanly and looked up the street. He nodded towards the procession that was headed by a horse-drawn cart as it turned the corner.

What is it this time? he said again of the passing procession. Another moral victory for Parker & Sons?

I actually thought this fellow might be one of your hill-top evaders that I've been hearing so much of, countered Robert Parker. Those that dare to deface the coin of the realm. They can't be making things any easier for you.

No, said William Deighton with a deep frown.

He looked around at the bodies pressed tightly around him and said nothing further.

Robert Parker leaned in.

The town is flooded with their crude workings, he said.

Some I have seen are not crude.

All the more reason then for us—

William Deighton cut off the attorney with a glance.

Not here.

Robert Parker lowered his voice and continued.

Business is being affected. I've filed several bankruptcies this year alone. Those of honest men. Good men of long standing.

William Deighton concurred.

I know these men you speak of. Their taxes bills are growing and glowing red through no fault of their own. But we cannot speak of this here.

Around them there was murmuring and movement within the crowd that lined the streets as the cart drew nearer. There was a palpable tension.

The two men could see that tied to the cart tail was a man stripped bare to the hips. Behind him another brandished a whip. There were shouts from the crowd.

Leave him be.

Ellis Collis is an innocent man.

As he drew closer they saw that the tied man's back was split with lacerations. Behind the guard that held the whip were several large men who pushed away anyone who stepped out from the crowd – as several did – to try and halt this bizarre caravan.

Animals, shouted a voice close to William Deighton and the solicitor. That man's only crime was hunger.

Robert Parker tapped the protestor on the shoulder and said what is it that this man is accused of?

The protestor turned and looked at Robert Parker and William Deighton beside him. He looked them up and down. He saw a fine woollen waistcoat dyed a gaudy red and he saw top coats and hats that held their shape. In the strong distinguished features of Robert Parker he saw good even teeth without gaps or pegs or grey nubs dying in the bleeding beds, and when he looked down he noticed the polished leather shoes quite unlike the stiff clogs on his own feet.

They say he stole, he replied with disdain.

So hunger wasn't his *only* crime, said William Deighton.

The man shrugged.

Stole what exactly? asked Robert Parker.

The man looked at him again. Unsure of who these well-dressed men were and what powers they wielded he said: plates.

Plates?

The man nodded.

From whom?

The man shrugged again and turned back to the spectacle of flesh and blood and leather and horse dung that was passing them by. The shouting of the crowd increased as the cart's wheels creaked over the smooth flags of Nelson Street. Here the blinkered horse whinnied as steam rose from the fresh cuts of the tied man, and rose too from the muscular flexing flanks of the beast. The man was thin and his gaunt face unshaven. His flat stomach gave the impression of it caving in on itself, his ribs protruding, as if a form of living fossilisation was already taking place. One eye was blackened. He appeared spent.

Robert Parker looked at William Deighton and then tapped the man on the shoulder again.

I'll ask again: from whom did he steal?

The man turned back to the attorney.

What?

I said from whom did he steal?

They say he stole a plate of silver from the vestry up at Heptonstall church.

A thief then, said William Deighton as the crowd surged as one.

A hungry soul trying to feed his family, replied the man.

William Deighton snorted.

With silver?

They say God always provides.

William Deighton looked at Robert Parker then shook his head.

As the cart creaked away someone across the street whistled. The flogged man looked up to see an orange sailing through the air towards him. He instinctively reached out and caught it firmly and the crowd cheered but he wasn't finished. In a flash of showmanship the condemned man threw the fruit high up in the air again and all eyes from the throng followed it as it spun upwards in the Saturday morning sun and in that moment – that action – lay the hopes of much of the Halifax crowd; that one flung orange of a spent man dripping blood from open wounds in front of everyone who knew him, and plenty who didn't, carried one last trace of hope and defiance and humour too. And as it fell there was a fleeting moment's silence – a temporary suspension of the chatter and curse words and shouts and protestations – before the tied, flogged and bleeding focus of their attention reached up and without even looking caught the orange in the same hand and quickly took a big bite from it, peel and all. The crowd roared with laughter as he threw the fruit back to from where it came, responded with their ecstatic approval as Ellis Collis made his brief mark upon the town's history and shouts of encouragement rang down the street. In such moments local legends were born.

God bless Ellis Collis and smite the bastards that done this, shouted one voice.

Strength and glory to the man who feeds his family, called another.

May the rain wash the salt from your wounds, Ellis Collis.

Long live the king, shouted one voice.

King David of the Craggs, responded another.

Long live the Coiners, called several voices at once.

Robert Parker and William Deighton looked at one another. The latter nodded and then spoke.

I agree something needs to be done, he whispered. You're right. Times may be desperate for some but we cannot let these forgers bring us all down.

Yes.

But I can't do it all alone.

My influence and resources are at your disposal, whispered the solicitor. I have the ears of powerful men; those who long ago divided up Yorkshire and took a big chunk each. Men of initiative. Forward thinkers and empire builders. They will help us. Besides, would not your masters in London want you to protect the realm's own mint – the very foundation of this country's economy?

Of course, said William Deighton. And my work has already begun. But we cannot speak any more of it here.

No, said Robert Parker. Not here.

I serve only one king, said William Deighton.

And the other shall hang, said Robert Parker.

The tables of Barbary's corner snug were stacked with jugs and cups. Pie crumbs and bread crusts were scattered around beneath it and a fug of smoke drifted above the lolling heads of men. Some were with hats; others without. Some were with teeth; others without. But all had coins in their pockets and bulging bellies. Their veins coursing warm.

David Hartley was there and Isaac Hartley was there. John Wilcox and Jonas Eastwood and Nathan Horsfall were there. The boy Jack O' Matts Bentley was there and John Tatham was there and Matthew Hepworth and James Broadbent and John Coughing and Young Frosty and James Crabtree and Peter Barker. They were all there.

The men were spread across four tables, while in the front room of the inn there was a straggle of evening drinkers who preferred to give those men they knew to be Coiners a wide berth and free run of the place.

Barbara kept the jugs coming and no-one said a cross word or laid a finger on Barbara because she had fought men and she had beaten men but more than that Barbara knew the secrets of many and had a smile for everyone, and her cash-box rattled full with coins both matted and buffed and worn and bright and more than once she had stowed the stamps and dies and pouches of clippers at a moment's notice and at great threat to her liberty. Her lips were tight and her hips wide. Her word trusted. So Barbara was looked after. Barbary's was theirs.

As the jokes and songs faded the group of coining men fragmented to talk in slurred whispers. David Hartley raised his feet to a chair and leaned back. He closed his eyes. At a table behind him James Broadbent was talking loudly and rattling pebbles in his hand. *Click-clack. Click-clack.* David Hartley listened to him talk and rattle his pebbles for a while longer – *click-clack, click-clack* – and then without looking at him David Hartley said to James Broadbent:

Stop.

When James Broadbent did not hear the order one of the men nudged him.

What? he said.

That, said David Hartley. Stop.

What?

That.

This?

James Broadbent tossed the pebbles. *Click-clack.*

Aye.

Why?

Because.

This?

Again James Broadbent tossed the pebbles one more time. *Click-clack.* Thomas Clayton raised an eyebrow and went to stand but Isaac Hartley tapped his knee and shook his head.

Why? said James Broadbent.

Cunt, said David Hartley.

Who?

Thee.

Me?

Aye.

Cunt?

Aye.

Me?

Aye. You. Cunt. Deaf cunt. Daft cunt.

How? said James Broadbent.

Cause.

Cause what?

David Hartley shrugged.

Breeding I expect.

The men smiled and laughed, unsure as to the direction of the situation.

But—

David Hartley swung round in his chair and planted his feet on the floor. Cut him off. Cut James Broadbent's complaint right off.

What?

You—

What?

You're—

David Hartley looked at him. His eyes were clear. They held within them the flames of flickering candles.

Yes? he said.

Nowt.

Go on.

No.

Say it.

Don't matter.

I'm what? I dares you to say it.

No.

Go on.

No. I wasn't saying nothing.

Go on, said Thomas Clayton as he pushed his chair back. Call the king. Take his name in vain. I dares you. See what happens.

Broadbent dropped his head and muttered something into his chest.

What? said David Hartley.

Nowt.

Speak up, bog breath.

I said nowt.

You'll say nowt all right.

In one quick move David Hartley stood and lunged at James Broadbent with stealth and grabbed his wrist and squeezed it hard and James Broadbent's fingers unfurled and David Hartley took the pebbles from his palm and jerked James Broadbent's head back and before he could resist David Hartley shoved the pebbles into the bigger man's mouth and tapped it shut with his fist on his chin and then spread his hand across his face like a spider's web. The men roared with laughter. James Broadbent spluttered and tried to spit out the stones but David Hartley had his face in his hand and was squashing his nose as he pushed him backwards. At this the laughter of the men became even louder.

Look at his phyz, said Isaac Hartley. The man's a donkey, that one.

With one forceful push David Hartley let go and James Broadbent spat the stones out onto the flags of the floor. He coughed and gasped for air as a pendulous glot of hockle hung from his lip. His eyes were red. He wiped his mouth.

Scrofulous shit-rat cunt, said David Hartley as he returned to his chair and sat back with his boots raised. He closed his eyes and nodded off to the sound of more braying laughter that was as comforting to him as a mother's lullaby to her sleeping child.

A man with a gud wumman should not lay with another wumman unless that wumman is carrying his babbs in wich cays he can lay with uther wimmen for those three seasuns she is laden wich is how cums I've layed with Barbra on two occayshuns when in the drinke and I did feel that the sap it was arising And oh my she was a fine buttaborl with luvley rownd cheeks and goode teeth and a sweet fanny and bran faysed with frekils she was An a stronge mind too And besides Barbra is a widowd and tho not short of offers shees ofting lonley becors some of the men rownd the valley are not the tipes that even an auld harryden with a fays like a boggart and dugs like curd borls dripdryen in cloth sacks wud want to lay with even if she were orl dryed up like a hamlet well in drowt seesun nevermind Barbra a wuman what keeps a fine inn and maykes good munny on the sides from looken after King Daevid and his merry band of men they do call the Turvin clippers Sweet Barbra I will misser I will misser so.

The boy heard the stout *chock* sound of a hammer hitting stone. He walked towards it not because he was curious but because the dull noise came from down the sunken lane in the direction of which he was already heading.

He whistled a meandering melody to himself.

Brambles lined the lane but the previous year's bounty had long since withered and rotted on the vine now. The small bulbous fruits had turned grey and dusty and were consumed into the intricate architecture of the spider webs that were now strung all the way across it. A city of arachnids occupied this intricate entanglement, and it seemed to the boy that caught in their webs were more flies than there were stars in the sky.

Branches closed in above him and the *chock* sound of metal and stone came up the lane and then the branches pulled back again and the heavy sky was above him, and there was a bite to the air as the boy rounded the corner and saw the waller at work.

The man was fixing a tumbledown gap of about ten paces. He had with him a hammer and a mallet. Chisels and a spade. Also a bait bag and beside that a dog, its chin rested on its paws, eyes wet and watching. With a twinge of sadness the boy thought of the hound he had lost to Hartley, but then thought of all that he had gained. The king had seen him right.

Chock-chock.

Beyond the wall was an uncut field busy with thistles and dotted with tussocks. It held no animals. A light breeze lifted and the boy heard it rustle through the grasses.

Across the valley he saw the sloping funnelled cluster of Bell Hole woods and at the very top above it, where the land met the sky, he saw Bell House.

The waller was bent double and he looked over his shoulder when he heard the dog give a low, throaty growl and then he said now then and the boy pushed his hat back a-ways and replied with the same words. Now then.

He stopped and watched for a moment.

Are you after fixing that wall?

No I'm digging coffin holes for clog-poppers, said the waller. Of course I'm fixing this bloody wall.

Is it hard? said the boy. The wall fixing?

It is a skill to be long learnit.

The man lunged to one side and hefted a large stone. He rolled it along the ground and then lifted it. The dog kept his eyes on the boy.

Why, said the man. Are you interested in learning the ways of a waller?

The boy snorted.

This tickles you?

Not bloody likely, said the boy.

It's honest work. People will always need walls. Boundaries are what makes us civilised.

It's a wonder they stand up, said the boy.

These walls will be standing long after your children's childrens' have gone to the grass with their teeth upwards.

He bent and sifted through some smaller stones for middle filling. Those that did not fit he tossed aside.

The boy spoke.

I don't want children.

Don't want children?

The waller said this to the stones.

Everyone wants children, he said.

I don't.

The boy looked at the wall. He saw the sheep creep that the man had built into it down the hill, and the larger tie stones that ran through the wall.

Don't want to work as a waller. Don't want children. What is it you bloody want then?

Not lug stones all day, the boy said to the man's broad back.

The waller stood and fixed the boy with a puzzled look.

And how is it you're expecting to feed yourself then?

There are ways.

Are there now?

Yes, said the boy before falling silent.

What's your name, young sprat?

Bentley. And I'm no sprat.

Bentley who?

They call us Jack O' Matts Bentley.

I don't recognise that as a Royd name. Don't know no Matthew Bentley neither.

That's because I'm not from Royd. I'm from over Sowerby.

The waller sized the boy up.

And where is it you're off to today then? This lane leads nowhere but to the valley beyond. Up there is Bell Hole woods and thems not a place for lads like you I shouldn't wonder.

Why not?

Bell Hole is beyond the boundaries.

What boundaries?

The boundaries of the parish, said the waller. You've passed the stones.

What bloody stones?

The waller shook his head.

What bloody stones, he says. The boundary stones, lad – and mind your tongue.

The boy said nothing. He just shrugged. The waller continued.

The Cuckoo Stone and the Bueldy Stone and Churn Milk Joan. These are the markers and you'd be best to stick within them if it's Royd you're visiting. Else you're passing on the land of others and them might not be as friendly as I.

Who said I'm going to Royd? I never said that.

Where then? said the waller.

I go where I want.

Do you now?

Aye I do. And no-one bothers us neither.

Not yet, said the waller.

Not ever, said Jack Bentley.

That so?

Aye.

How can you be sure?

Because Bell House is where I'm going.

Here the waller paused. His face changed as he considered the boy anew. He did not say anything. Aware of the balance tipping in his favour the boy sniffed and then looked at the rocks scattered around and then he said: that's why I don't need to build no stupid walls to make my pie crust.

This time it was the waller who kept quiet.

There's coin going through my fingers like water down a waterfall, Jack Bentley continued. There's peck in the cupboard and bottles full to the stopper of barleybroth and there's plenty of bints to empty my nutmegs when it is they need emptying – which is often. A different piece every night if I want it.

The waller frowned.

And look, said the boy.

Here he held up his hands, palms out.

There's no bloody blisters or callouses on these hands.

He drew phlegm up from the back of his throat and held it there, just like he had seen David Hartley do. He rolled it around his mouth and then spoke through it.

I'd say that's good going for a *boy*.

The inn was empty save for one man asleep in the corner with his chin pressed to his chest, his shoes removed and drying by the fire, when the exciseman William Deighton drained his glass, threaded his arms into his coat sleeves and jerked it up onto his shoulders.

The ale had tasted watered down. He would have to look into it.

To the tender he touched his hat. He turned and left.

Already the days were darkening and the town would soon be wearing a new mask. It seemed to him to be two places, Halifax. A town of two faces. One of sunlight and another of shadows.

Autumn and winter would make secrets of the unlit corners. With the dying of the bright blue days of sun and insects and harvest song, the town and its people always turned inwards – collars up and curtains drawn. Conversations became clipped and hushed.

Crown Street, so busy and bustling on trading day, seemed to close in on itself too; just one more empty street in the maze of alleys that ran through the town, a labyrinth of bevelled stone.

The spaces between the street lamps seemed to be patiently awaiting new crimes to occur.

William Deighton passed the Old Assembly Rooms and the Talbot Inn – a hostelry he suspected was embroiled in the yellow trade – and turned into The Square. Built in the aspect of the broad and bold spaces in London, it was the town's most impressive corner. Robert Parker had done well for himself. Deighton had noted that the young attorney had expanded his business quickly upon his return from being articled at the chambers of one Matthew Coulthurst in Lincoln's Inn in the capital. Back in Halifax where competition was lean, he had soon taken the reins of a stagnant partnership with the widower John Baldwin and revitalised the firm. Robert Parker was pragmatic and diligent and fearless.

It was no secret that John Baldwin was connected to the Waterhouses and the Prescotts and the Rawsons and the Listers. Those families who ran the town. William Deighton knew all about them. Most did. At only twenty-two Robert Parker had married a Prescott, Ann, sixteen years his senior and the daughter of a surgeon. Their pairing had caused a minor scandal in some circles but not in the Fax where folk were not easily offended or simply didn't care.

William Deighton knew all about Robert Parker's rise too. How he had turned the partnership loss into a profit within two years and still in his twenties, and with the help of his wife's substantial legacies, had dissolved the partnership with the old man Baldwin to become the sole leading attorney in the town. His clients were the wealthiest and longest standing families of the Yorkshire Ridings.

And now in his thirties Robert Parker was already leading a more comfortable life than William Deighton was in a house that felt permanently cluttered with steaming pans and drying sheets, living on a far less substantial exciseman's wage. Yet for all its dangers, monitoring the business revenues of the more remote corners of the valley, it at least allowed him plenty of time to himself. The fells may have housed many foes full of hostility towards him but as a representative of the crown none would be so foolish as to do him physical damage. Threats and curses were the worst he heard. He walked the hills unharmed.

Robert Parker though. Robert Parker had a maid and a suite of offices and two articled clerks and a communal garden. He had a law library. He owned further properties.

He ate well. He was handsome. Well-tailored.

He cut quite a figure around the town.

And where others might be envious, William Deighton couldn't help but like the young attorney. He admired his fearlessness and fortitude, for it was people like Robert Parker – energised and educated young men – who would prevent the valley falling to the barbaric bandits and forgers entirely. Lawlessness must not prevail. Of that they were in agreement. An odd pairing nonetheless, thought Deighton. Me and he.

The six houses of The Square were well-lit and imposing. They were the first to be built in brick. One open side led up to the wooded slopes of Beacon Hill.

A sign at the gate-post marked out Robert Parker's house

and practice. William Deighton saw the attorney in the front room. William Deighton raised a hand but it was too dark outside for him to be seen.

He opened the gate. He closed the gate.

He smelled the subtle singed tones of autumn flavouring the night.

The rainfall sped and eased at will. It fell with force and then it withdrew to a light sprinkle before returning heavier and more persistent than ever. It plunged with volume. With aggression. It dug and dredged. Dissected. Dotted.

The day was not yet fully dark when a breathless James Broadbent banged on the door of Bell House. The dog barked in its kennel nearby and James Broadbent hissed *sherrup you*. The bark settled into a low, throaty growl.

Beads of sweat gathered on his brow and when she opened the door Grace Hartley saw that the visitor had a wild look about him. He leaned on the frame.

Is he here?

Even through the smell of fresh earth that the rain had summoned she could smell the drink about him. She rested a hand on her swollen stomach.

Is who here?

Him.

Who's him – the sexton's cousin?

You know who, missus. Them the rest call the king.

And what do you call him, James Broadbent?

I call that man by his name because that is all he is. A man. David fucking Hartley.

You'd be minded to watch your tongue when there's children about.

James Broadbent looked at Grace Hartley's bulging stomach. He sniffed then pointed to her stomach. He leered.

How did that get there then? he said.

Don't come that with me.

He held his finger there, nearly touching the strained cloth of her pinafore.

When does it drop?

It comes when it comes.

They say it's a messy business, he said. Things splitting and tearing this way and that. Time enough for a nice tumble yet though, I'd wager.

Grace Hartley stepped forward and closed the door slightly behind her. She lowered her voice.

You're a worthless bletherskite you are.

James Broadbent grinned.

Keep talking like that and you'll see what happens, she said. Now what is it that you want?

James Broadbent leaned in. His breath was stale with malt and tobacco.

I want what it is that he's got.

What's that then?

He leered again.

Everything, he said.

You'll find yourself killed.

I just want what's coming to me. A greater cut and a little bit of something extra fleshy for luck.

Grace Hartley drew back into the house and closed the door. There were hushed voices and then seconds later it swung open again and there was a rush of bodies. Suddenly there were hands grabbing at him. Pulling James Broadbent in and then pushing him out.

He stumbled. He tripped. Fell onto the stone flags. He was pulled back up again and then fists rained down upon him. He felt them to his face and stomach. Fists dug into his sides. He felt clogs kicking him. The wooden soles on his joints.

William Hartley and Isaac Hartley and Thomas Clayton and Thomas Spencer had him. Were pushing him. They harried him out into the dank evening and he tried to swat them away but more fists and kicks came.

They stamped and booted James Broadbent to a stone outbuilding with a burnt, blackened floor and a roof of worn wood, and where the smell of smoke was in the walls, and they pushed James Broadbent in there and then Isaac Hartley punched him hard in the face and he felt his nose crack. He tasted blood, thick and almost briny in the back of his throat.

The rain fell and it sounded like spigot water spitting into a bucket.

He was wiping the blood away with the back of his hand and feeling his lips swell when David Hartley strode into the room. David Hartley was buttoning up his shirt. His terrier was springing at his heel.

He stopped in front of James Broadbent and then he quickly and neatly rolled up his sleeves. He nodded to the others and William Hartley and Isaac Hartley and Thomas Clayton and Thomas Spencer all grabbed him again and David Hartley walked up close to James Broadbent and said you want to give my Grace something is that right? Is that what you said? You want what it is that I have? And she carrying my child? The wife of the fucking king?

I meant coin, said James Broadbent. I just meant I wanted more coin for my work.

I know what you meant, said David Hartley. My wife told me so and she does not lie.

He called over his shoulder: Grace get in here.

A moment later his wife appeared in the doorway as a silhouette and stood there. The stone dwelling became darker still as shadows crossed James Broadbent's face.

David Hartley pressed himself closer in. Between them Isaac Hartley and Thomas Clayton and Thomas Spencer held James Broadbent by his arms and had his neck in a lock while William Hartley stood to one side with a crooked smile on his face. Watching. The dog watched too. Excited, it circled.

Well, I shall tell you what I'll do, said David Hartley. I'll take your piggy little pizzle and keep it as a candle. I'll stick a wick in the slit and dip it in wax. I'll light you up and burn it all night long. Your screams will send the crows scattering from the trees.

Their faces were inches apart now.

Let's see what you've got that's so special, said David Hartley as he reached down and grabbed at the front of James Broadbent's trousers. He yanked at the buttons and one came off and then as Isaac Hartley laughed and Thomas Clayton laughed, David Hartley pulled down first James Broadbent's trousers and then his drawers. Pulled them all the way down to his ankles. He kicked James Broadbent's feet further apart.

The dog yapped and sprang from side to side until David Hartley turfed it with his foot.

He looked for a moment and then he grabbed James Broadbent down there. Took him in his hand and squeezed. James Broadbent flinched and tried to kick out but David Hartley sidestepped his wayward boot.

Look at that, lads, he laughed. It's like a normal one but so much smaller. God's put the poor fucker together all wrong. For such a big lummox I'd have been expecting more than a bairn's finger.

The men looked and laughed and leered. Feeling the energy of the pack, the dog barked.

You could stick it on a hook and go fishing with that, said Thomas Clayton.

David Hartley turned to his wife and still holding James Broadbent he said: look, Grace, it's not as good as mine is it? Neither as thick nor as long. He's like a donkey born with the prick of a shrew.

He turned back to James Broadbent.

Aye a poor man's pizzle is that, James Broadbent. It's no wonder the lassies give you a wide berth. You'd not touch the sides with that beard-splitter. Now I'd already warned you and your cunty ways but still you turn up here malted and mouthy.

Reckoning on me not being the king. Reckoning on you being something special.

He squeezed again and James Broadbent flinched, and then he writhed and kicked out again but Isaac Hartley and Thomas Clayton and Thomas Spencer held him fast. Tightened their lock. He tried to look away but an arm squeezed around his neck. Began to choke him out.

David Hartley laughed again. He laughed in James Broadbent's face and the dog circled and David Hartley growled *get by Moidore*, and the dog shrunk backwards.

I do believe James Broadbent is getting hard lads, he said. He looked down and then back at James Broadbent and he smiled.

Yes, he continued. I can definitely feel this sausage fattening in my fives. Perhaps this dearest member of our merry men is not the tough nut he thinks he is. Perhaps this James Broadbent is a Miss Molly.

He glanced downwards and then lowered his other hand.

And look: his tallywags are nothing to sing a song about either though I feel that they too are hardening.

James Broadbent tried to struggle one more time.

David Hartley stepped backwards but still had him in hand. He now started to move it back and forward.

Look, brothers – see how it is growing. My, but it's ugly though. Look, Grace, my dearest wife. Look at the little weapon this man did promise to give you. Granted it grows but it looks like a blind cobbler's thumb. And does he have the seed to go with it? Does James Broadbent have the seed that makes a baby just as I, King David Hartley of Cragg Vale, have made many?

A look of panic filled James Broadbent's eyes as Isaac Hartley and Thomas Clayton and Thomas Spencer leaned over his shoulder to watch as David Hartley tugged back and forward with a greater speed and determination. Without slowing he stepped aside so that Grace Hartley could get a better view and so that James Broadbent too could see the silhouette of

97

his wife standing beneath the wooden stanchion, still framed by the stone doorway.

Look, Grace, he's fain for it, said David Hartley. He knows a good woman when he sees one – he has taste, does this one. I'll give him that.

Grace Hartley said nothing. She just watched. In the half-light the men could not see the expression on her face. The dog was close by again. It paced the room with its tail wagging and ears pricked.

Go on then, said David Hartley to James Broadbent. Take a good look at what you could have had. What I get to have any time I like.

He tugged more vigorously. The man was completely erect now and the brace put on him by the men held him even tighter. One hand was clamped over his mouth. The men muttered words of approval and encouragement.

You're going to snap it off brother, laughed Isaac Hartley.

David Hartley stopped and spat on the palm of his hand and then grabbed James Broadbent and went at him even harder.

The others fell silent. All eyes were on David Hartley's hand now as it became a blur and James Broadbent's breathing became heavier and deeper.

Look at that Grace, said David Hartley. It's getting bigger but it's still not as big as mine, though but, is it?

Still not as big as mine he said again.

James Broadbent groaned.

Look, Gracie, said David Hartley. It's like a blood pudding.

Look, Gracie, he said. Picture this big lump on top of you.

Look, Gracie. Gracie, look.

James Broadbent tried to pull away one last time but he was held fast and he drew a long inward breath as he spurted two white strings onto the damp blackened floor of the stone room.

The men loosened their grip on James Broadbent then. He dared not meet the eyes of David Hartley and there was a moment of icy silence. He bent to pull up his trousers. The dog came forward and sniffed at the ground with interest. It extended a pink tongue and lapped.

You've all seen it now lads, said David Hartley. It turns out this man is as bent as a drunken weaver's spindle. He is a quean. He is not a real man; he can never be one of us.

What do you think to that then Gracie? he continued, but when he turned his wife had left and in her place was nothing but the moor beyond stretching for miles and the tightening of the sky and the screeching of birds somewhere down in the valley below.

Thers men no berra than beests here in ole York castle Men thall think naut of taken anutha man an taken him for a ride like his wifey and fillen him up with all what hes got until the otha man wud feel its his wont to were a dress and grow dugs on his chesst and cry hisself to sleep at nite But with these words I rite the truth to you that wot ever is said abaht King Daevid Hartley he was not wan of them kinds Not one of them sorts Yess he was hard and feers and crool but he was not the wan to do them things that they do at nite here in the sells No King Daevid is a King and when yoos king you still live bah reules and you stick to them reules.

So now you see somewan is twisten the trooth for I never did tug that Rat Jaymes Brordbend's parsnip I have never seen it never tuched it If it happund I was not there that day in the Alcemmyists clippin bildin up near my pallas Bell Howse And it maybe that sum of the boys ruffed the man up but it was surely nothen that the Rat Brordbent did not deserve as you will sea And in fact if I new then what it was he was going on to do I wud have taken his pizzel and I wud not have tugged it litely for fun No I would have twisted it and taken the burdizzo and the hot tongs and tar to his nackers like a herdsman does his bull and kept on skweezing till his screams split the sky and they popped off and then Id have stuffed them down his gullit and nipped his nose and made him dance a merry jig ower hot coles.

And that's the teruth of it is that The Godshonest teruth I swearit on my chilluns heads.

In the gloaming of the shrinking day David Hartley left Bell House where the smell of hops and oats and a weighted mouldy dampness sat heavy over everything, and he tramped across the moor.

He went beyond the top dip and round the bog patch that never dried, a place in which he had seen half a dozen sheep die over the years. It had simply taken them – their legs thrashing at the heavy sky and their bleats of panic turning into death wails as the soil swallowed them up. A horse or two also. A rope was always too far away to rescue the sinking creatures. The last one to get sucked under had belonged to a stocksman who lived at Norland by the name of George Wharton and it was a known fact that this George Wharton had on more than one occasion refused to donate currency when pressed about it, and had now found his herd diminishing ever since. Another of his flock was spotted garrotted, one found twisted and drowned at the bottom of a foss and a third split cleanly from scut to teeth.

To most the bog looked like any other patch of moor but David Hartley and those who lived close by knew it was deadly. The shallow slow-running groughs fed the hag with a trickle of coppery water. They brought with them fresh alluvial deposits and gave the thick mud a life of its own. In the wet seasons – which was all seasons – it became a silent malevolent force. Often David Hartley had said that in years to come they would find a pile of bones down there belonging to different creatures and as they tried to piece them together would wonder what hellish beast it was that had been eaten up by the copper-coloured soil.

Up at Bell House the belief was that George Wharton should have come in with the Coiners if he'd had any sense about him.

He walked toward the fold. He walked toward the thin strip of light that seemed planted in the moor like a cattle jobber's spiked tine. He walked toward the slowly rolling billow of smoke that was too heavy to drift upwards, and which instead sank to the fold's stone foundations where it lay like a strange grey bed of flowers forever reshaping itself.

Coiner coming, said David Hartley as he rapped on the wooden door kept ajar and then pushed it hard through the jarring morass of shale and stamped soil that was the dwelling's carpet. Through the smoke he saw the Alchemist swigging water from a cup and beside him on a rotting old lintel beam that had once held the roof in place, and was now set across two rocks, were thousands of coins stacked in a line, twinkling like the faraway stars of the crispest winter night.

He crouched to the fire and warmed his hands. The Alchemist finished the rest of his water and then pumped the fire with his bellows. He too squatted. His face was stained with soot. His face was strained too. It was darkened by more than soot. It was the look of someone troubled.

What message do you have for me today then old friend?

I see shadows, the Alchemist said quietly.

David Hartley hawked some phlegm and spat it onto the coals. It sizzled.

Well, he said. We live in a valley of shadows.

I see shadows stretching long.

We live in a valley of little sun.

These shadows are not like the shadows cast by scar or scarp.

David Hartley wiped his nose with the back of his hand.

What are they then?

They are crooked, said the Alchemist.

Go on.

Bent forms, they are.

What are you on about now?

Figures. They're figures.

Figures?

David Hartley squinted into the fire.

And where do you see these figures, he said. In the flames?

All round. The signs are there to be read.

You've been clipping too long, friend. You're tired. This smoke will send a man's head west.

I see sevens.

David Hartley turned to the Alchemist and looked at him long and hard.

You're a good worker. You work hard. You do as you're told and you keep your trapdoor closed. There's no complaints. But you're jawing in more riddles than ever. It's time you got back to Bradford to clear your blackened lungs.

Ignoring this, the Alchemist spoke quietly.

First came the shadows in the fire and then out from the smoke comes the sevens.

Shadows and sevens now is it?

Yes – thems two sevens to look like shadows.

David Hartley shook his head.

You're talking out your back hole you are.

They'll cover your eyes like cold coins, said the Alchemist in a hoarse whisper.

Well I can always use more coins.

The sevens will cover your eyes like shadows; they'll cover your eyes like coins, David Hartley. These forms.

Munch a chod, he snapped. What simpleton fuck talk is this? You're getting wrong in the brain-pan you are.

It's written, David Hartley. The stars speak of an ill fate. The calendar. Don't you see?

I see fuck all, silly clot. Mine eyes are full of coins and shadows and sevens remember?

You'd be wise to mind the calendar.

David Hartley grinned a crooked grimace.

Calendar? he said with scorn. The sun and the sky and the rain is my calendar, magic man. The berries and the bluebells and the birdsong tell me what time of year it is. My larder tells me so. I don't need it written down on some stupid scroll. It's me that reads the signs. The true signs of the Calder Valley.

It's the year, King David. It's the year that's coming. Don't you see? Two sevens.

Eh?

It's a portent. Seven and seven. It can only be the year 1770.

What of it?

1770 is soon.

And again what of it?

It is a year of great shadows for you, said the Alchemist. Inescapable shadows beyond your reckoning.

He blinked, his red rimmed eyes ringing the ovals of white that stared out from a face veiled in smoke markings.

Life is shadows, said David Hartley.

The Alchemist shook his head.

Shadows that cross your eyes until they see nothing but the blackness, he continued. I predict things of terror because when the two sevens join, an empire crumbles.

Which empire?

The Alchemist paused and stared deep into the orange pulse of the fire pit. The heat was torrid and suffocating. The stone room confined it; created an oven.

Thine empire.

David Hartley stood. He spoke quietly and as he did he jabbed a finger at the Alchemist who continued to stare into the fire.

You're shitting through your teeth. You're wrong in the nous-box if you believe sevens and shadows can fill a man's eyes. This is the talk of duckerers and charlatans.

You asked for my messages and I give you them.

The Alchemist's voice was steady as he continued.

Thine empire is under threat from offcumdens and men that want to pull you under. Men that will appear one day across the moorlands like straw malkins to the crows on an autumn morning. One day they'll be there. They'll be there and you will have no place to hide. Not in the woods or up here on the moors, and no man will harbour you. And then you will wish you had read the signs and seen the shadows and seen the sevens for what they are: a warning prophesised.

David Hartley stared at the hunched figure still entranced by the fire as he always seemed to be. But for once he said nothing.

Take my words as you see fit, said the Alchemist in a voice so small that David Hartley was unsure as to whether the man had spoken at all.

Over the tops of the trees smoke settled itself like the tangled dirty white shearings of a summer flock not yet dipped and combed and dyed. Like oil on water it hung there heavy. Too thick for the sky to contain its density, it cloaked the wood and muffled the sounds of the work that went on within it. Spirals of it twisted away in wisps, diminishing helices taken by the breeze.

All his life Joseph 'Belch' Broadbent had been shrouded in smoke. Years tending the charcoal clamp meant it flavoured not just his clothes and hair with the slow dampened burn of oak and willow and alder, nor merely tanned his skin with soot and blackened dirt, but was within him; it had smoked him from the inside out and left Belch Broadbent with rheumy lidded eyes and a hacking cough that rattled most violently in the early hours.

James Broadbent walked towards the distant rising plume that marked his father's position as if it were a swarm of wasps leaving its fissure of an arid woodland floor or curl of a crawling tree root.

He left the flat of the valley and cut away from the river. Headed uphill. Cleaved his way through damp grass. A skein of geese flew low overhead, honking in rhythmic response to their leader's guiding call.

For a fleeting moment he wished he had something to bring down one of those birds. Cold metal to reach from trigger to barrel to tiny beating heart.

Any bird would do. Not even a goose. Any damn one. A partridge or a woodcock would look just as good plucked and speared on a spit dripping fat onto the sibilant fire. And by God he'd savour every greasy morsel, every fatty string, for his landlord John Sutcliffe and his wife Old Woman Sutcliffe barely fed him. Cold plates of smashed turnip or bowls of stodgy bread pap, watery stews or the last heel of last week's loaf and the dirtiest slick of bacon fat was the best he got there. Oats and water of a morning. Fuck-all else.

He'd stuff a spuggie in each cheek and suck on their bones given half a chance, for James Broadbent was big and penniless and he was always hungry, and it made no sense to always be hungry while all around him men were getting wealthy from the clipping of guineas – the same guineas he forced out of hard-working valley folk at great risk to his own personal liberty. From the Hartleys downwards, the men were buying clothes for their bairns and new furniture for their houses and gewgaws for their women, and for themselves leather belts and brass buckles and knives of steel from Sheffield. They were filling their stores with sugar and the best brew and good meat and here he was renting a cold room in a miserly house that often flooded with the rainwater and sewage that ran down Hall Bank Lane.

Worse than the hunger was the growing bitterness. Bitterness could make a violent man even more so. It could make him desperate – and desperation was the midwife of rash acts like fetching up drunk at the Hartley place.

James Broadbent followed the smoke from his father's clearing. He saw it at a distance as he left Stocks Lane and took the Roger Gate track deep into the trees, passing the three weavers cottages of Burnt Stubb sitting low in a hollow, the end one of which he had spent several seasons in, bent double at the loom in light so poor that he had been struck by aches in his head and spells of dizziness that only ceased when he gave up that work to devote his time to clipping.

The lane dipped and steered him back into the trees where he saw his father tending to his old burner. James Broadbent stopped and pulled a grass blade from the ground. He chewed it for a moment while he watched the old man.

His father worked at half speed, his body ruined by toil. Years at the burner had made him part of the landscape.

The coarse mud that he carefully applied to the cracks that appeared in the earthen skin of the charcoal clamp as it burned for four or five days at a stretch was a part of him too. Not just under his fingernails or binding the matted layers of the same britches and shirt and hooded tunic that he wore all year round, but a part of his very pigmentation.

The earth was in his father's scalp and his stubble. It had become him. His body hosted smoke. It was stirred into his essence to dilute that which made him human so that he was now part of the landscape and part of the fire; he was made of the smoke that billowed and rolled and tumbled during the slow process that took felled timber through combustion to become the shards and clots of carbon that fuelled fires and furnaces the length and breadth of Calderdale. He was wood-smoke manifest; man as a settled miasma. A nebulous fellow, burnt brume in stout boots, with a clay pipe clicking between what remained of his teeth.

And as he hacked and coughed and stooped and shuffled James Broadbent saw just how much the process had ruined a man who could barely afford to buy a candle even though he had worked the burner since the age of nine.

He cast the chewed grass aside and crossed the clearing. He sat on one of the cross-cut stumps that his father used to rest his legs upon and he kicked at the dirt with his heel. Joseph Broadbent did not acknowledge his son at first but then after a minute had passed he turned and looked as if seeing him for the first time.

What's your trouble then? he said.

James Broadbent heeled the dirt again.

Nowt, he said. Nowt.

Your face argues otherwise.

James Broadbent shrugged in silence, though he was seething inside.

Now I don't reckon you're here to help an old man make dusty diamonds so something must be ailing you.

It's that cunt Hartley. The one they call the King.

Joseph Broadbent chafed the palms of his hands together and then reached in his pocket for a pipe which he packed and lit and puffed at until a blue smoke flumed from his nostrils like a bull's breath on a cold morning, and then he coughed for a long time. The cough rattled around him and drew up phlegm that he rolled around his mouth for a moment and then hawked into the undergrowth. He repeated the process and then sat on a stump.

The thing about kings is they never keep the crown forever, he remarked.

He said this in a low, husky voice. Almost a whisper. James Broadbent didn't say anything in reply. He heard his father's teeth clicking against his pipe as he puffed again and then coughed again. Hawked again. Spat again.

Seems that kings usually get toppled or offed, said Joseph Broadbent, once he had cleared his chest. That man I never liked. Him or his father.

What is it you're getting at?

David Hartley, said Joseph Broadbent.

What about him?

Does he sit on a throne?

No he does not.

Does he have a palace?

His house is dark and busy with dusty looms he no longer uses, said James Broadbent. Though rarely does he invite me in. It seems he does not deem me worthy.

So he lives like most others in the valley.

He is better fed.

Fine. So he eats well. On a good day a full belly could make a man think he were a king, but it does not mean he is a king no more than the burning of logs into charcoal makes me think I am the god of fire.

He is arrogant, father, said James Broadbent. David Hartley and his brothers think they are better than everyone else. They treat me like a donkey. They expect me to do their bidding and their strong-arming but they tell me nothing of their business and they pay me pennies despite the great risk involved. I have fought many men for them; there are those I have slashed and gouged just for taking David Hartley's name in vain. He knows this but still my reward is nothing but humiliation. They are greedy.

Often greed is a man's downfall. Will it be yours?

James Broadbent looked at his father.

Mine?

Yes. What is it you're after with all this talk?

James Broadbent looked at the ground and considered the question.

I just want my share.

Your share?

Yes. I have worked hard.

Three days of log burning is hard work, said Joseph Broadbent. Hauling two score sacks of charcoal to the merchants is hard work – what you do is different. You are a big lad; you use what you have.

I don't pretend to be anything I am not, said James Broadbent. Unlike that swell-headed bastard Hartley.

Joseph Broadbent was quiet for a moment. When he spoke it was from the depth of a memory still sharp where his body was failing him.

You know, I knew his father a young man. They are cut from the same cloth, those two. Once he beat me.

Beat you?

Him and his friends, said Joseph Broadbent. William Hartley.

109

James Broadbent interjected.

William Hartley is also the name of one of his sons. They call him the Duke of Edinburgh.

Yes, I know. Like father, so like the sons. They're no titled gentry. A long time ago this was, but I remember it well: for no good reason William the elder and his friends once set about me. We were but tykes – but still. Mob-handed and brass knuckled, they were. And then just recently I have heard his sons loud in the ale by the bridge of a night. Shouting at the moon they were. No. I have no love for a Hartley. I share your dislike.

I just want what's mine, said James Broadbent again. The valley flows with gold but barely a drop has come my way. And I want to see that bastard toppled. Too many times he has humiliated me.

They fell silent for a moment and then the elder Broadbent spoke.

What I am about to say to you might mark the end of your problems.

Go on.

Have you heard of the Tyburn ticket?

I've heard of the Tyburn gibbet.

All Coiners have, said Joseph Broadbent. No. The Tyburn ticket is something else. It is a brave man's way out of a situation that he no longer wants to be in.

I don't understand.

You want to make some money. An amount you feel you deserve.

Yes, said James Broadbent. That is what I have been saying.

And you want to bring Hartley down.

A peg or two at the very least.

What I am telling you now will bring David Hartley down more than a peg or two. It will bring him down all the way into this soil wearing a wooden overcoat. If you want rid of the King, then the Tyburn ticket is the way.

How do I get this ticket?

You don't, said Joseph Broadbent. You don't get a ticket. You talk to a man.

What man?

A man whose name I happen to know of.

Tell me his name.

Once you speak to this man you yourself will be in danger.

I live with danger all day and all night.

I'm talking about real danger, son. Deathly danger.

I do not fear death. I fear nothing.

Do you fear the Hartleys?

I fear nothing.

Then I will take you to this man.

A second tyme the stagmen did appeer and this was menny yers later and I was a man now and father of chillun myself an back on the red terf of home Back on the moore of Cragg Vayle This was not so long ago that memree had faded No this was kwite reesunt an I rember every moment of it now as cleer as day as cleer as yer owen hand befor yer owen fayse As cleer as a candul flayme in the nite and the waxy stink offit when you wayke in the morning.

I recorl it well becors that nite in cweschun it was a full moon that did rise over Bell Hole and I cud not sleep My hed it was awayke with thorts and plans for more munny maykin and more coinin and more clippin and revenge on them that tries to stoppus Aye I cud not sleepe so I rose from my blankets and left my goode wife Grace sleepin the sleep of the ded and I warkt throu this howse that is the stone pallas of the wun they corl King Dayvid.

And I warkt passed the dyin embas still glowen orunge in a cullapsed heap of birch and alder logs and I warkt rite out throu the door and out onto the moore barefoot like a man possessed like a man dreamun.

But I was not dreamun I was very much awayke.

And I warkt out across the flags and onto the sod and the hethur and the moon as I say was hi and I warkt until I came to a boggy slack and I do not no what it was that pulld me there but wen I rechit it I crouchet low in the grass and I did see some thynge that no man but this King himself would believe and that was Stagmen Again with the Stagmen The Stagmen again An I watched them in rapt wunder.

Stagmen dansin Dansin in a circul under the moon on the moor at nite and my hart was thumpen in my chest And I new it I new then that them to be real and how that ferst time I seenum before was not a dream or the silly creatings of a fevered child or all them uther things my father and mutha god rest her soul sed it were No the Stagmen were real just as I sed they was just as I sed See David Hartley does not lie he trusts his eyes and he nose what he sees rite He nose what he sees And what he seas that is grayt vishuns misstickell visherns.

It were the stagmen returnin to me the same Stagmen I saw as a chylde The stagmen of the Jorvikshyre moors and I was so close I could heer thur feet on the grass so close I could heer the swish sound of it and the rustling sound of it und thur feet trampin on the grownd and thur breathes deep and throaty Snortin they was Snortin and raspin and I swear on the bybel I could heer thur chesseds thumpin too just as yor chessed or my chessed thumps when yoov been digging turf or splitten logs or breaken bolders for the plowin or dammen a streem or after having been pluggin yor missus.

I durst not breeth myself so I pressed down into the moore Deep into the moore Deep an flat and as low us u man cud go Low as a rigglen werm And I watched the stagmen dance to a music that only they cud hear The moon an open eye unblinken The hollow a saycrud place Blud in the eers Hartbeets.

And then thur was only the sownd of thur feet and thur breth steamin and my hart beaten and my mind runnen away with more kweschuns than you have fingus The nite turned mad by these creechurs Swet and vishuns Majic.

They allus telt us the Moors was a speshul place and there alwuss was storees of stagmen and things unseen and boulders that move themselves when your back is turned An big dogs too

113

that wander up here Dogs bigger than yoove seen Some they say with two heads And green Boggarts what live under stones and the mouse as long as your arm that is as whyte as a ghost and bad luck to anywun who sees it And the nite whisslers The nite whisslers that make a whisslin sound in the aire And they sed that some cows that had been set to grays up there did produce blew milke And what of him they corl Leathery Coit the headless man who had driven a cart with headless horses They sed he had been seen up there on the moors two And the Wite Lady also And many are the storees of men that have gon missun up yon They allways telt us the moors was a spashul place and now I no it to bee true havun seen the grayt Stagmen dancing not as a chylde in dreems but as a grown man As King David Harterlay of Crag Vail He of sownd mind and strong bodee Yass I seenum I tell you I seenum The Stagmen of the Calder dayle moor I seenum in grayt vishuns becorse I am graytness itself Just as was told Just as was told.

They moved across the field as one, hacking at the last late crop of grass with their scythes and short-handed sickles. Behind them there followed women with their tines and baling forks and at the rear, children, clutching rolls of baling twine. Some carried catapults with which to sling pebbles at the fleeing rabbits that they put up.

There was a frenzy to their work as they raced against the season and the coming of the harvest moon that was marked to rise that very night. To toil beyond it was ill luck. After this day, when the celebrations had passed, the field would only feel the coulter blade of the lone ploughman – his thick head still muzzy from too much beer no doubt – and then once re-seeded would remain untouched for four years. Next summer would see the wild grass crop rotate to the adjacent field; feed for baling and mulching was all these dank valley's lower pastures were good for.

Every so often the men seemed to lock into a rhythm as their blades swung in unison all the way from the field-edge to the sloping centre, their arms swinging in perfect synchronicity for a few moments before falling away into their own patterns.

They said little as they worked.

Thomas Spencer was among them, as was John Tatham in his recognisable blue, white and scarlet draw-boy waistcoat. Ely Crossley was swinging a scythe and Thomas Murgatroyd the corn miller had come to offer a hand. Red-headed Matthew Hepworth lent his muscle too, as did Jonas Eastwood down from Erringden Moor and Isaac Dewhurst and Israel Wilde and Foul Peter Barker and Abraham Lumb and William Hartley, because although the field belonged to Richard Feather, the brother-in-law of Benjamin Sutcliffe – better known to all as Benjamin Nunco – and a man considered too humble and busy otherwise caring for a wife of feeble mind to partake in the clipping trade, it was nonetheless the role of all members of the community who could stand on two feet to help at harvest time, Coiner or not.

When the silver sun was at its highest yet giving off little heat, and the field patterned with sheaves bundled to the height of the tallest children, there was a whistle and a wave of arms from the corner. One by one the field workers stopped and laid aside their tools and walked over to a stack of hay bales harvested in a June that seemed so long ago now.

The bales were covered with a cloth upon which were placed a dozen plates sitting tall with mutton pieces and loaves and wedges of cheese and pots containing vinegar onions and vinegar cabbage, and dripping and chutneys and honey the colour of amber that was flavoured with the heather of the moors. There were pies thick with buttered crusts and potatoes in their black fire-cooked coats. There were two ducks, plucked and cooked and carved.

There was a suet marrow pudding too, still steaming in its cloth and beside that another bowl contained blackberries, bilberries and raspberries. At the end a sugar cake sat in a pool of cooling custard.

There were jugs of spring water and ale and fresh unwatered milk with globs of butter floating on the surface waiting to be fished out and spread.

And there beside this makeshift moveable feast stood David Hartley and Grace Hartley and Thomas Clayton.

Victuals, said David Hartley through a seldom-seen smile. Strap on your nosebags and tuck in my friends. This year the valley has been blessed with a bountiful harvest in all ways.

The men and women and children looked at the food and then at each other and they smiled because this was an unexpected meal like none they had ever seen.

God surely loves those that wish to take what's rightfully theirs, said a smiling Thomas Clayton as the men and their wives and children lined up with plates, first tentatively and then with an excited chatter.

As chapped and grass-nicked hands reached out for the food David Hartley moved amongst them solemnly pressing a golden guinea into each. The gasps of gratitude from the women and children could be heard from across the field as their words turned first into laughter and then singing, and the men nodded and smiled quietly as the silver harvest sun moved ever closer to the pink autumn moon.

James Broadbent and his father took the bottom valley path along the river that here and there ran alongside the old horse track linking Halifax to Mytholmroyd and then on to to Hebden Bridge and Todmorden hard against the border with Lancashire.

Tiny hamlets dotted the route. Luddendenfoot. Brearley. Burnt Stubb.

Small gatherings of squat stone buildings cowered in the shadows of the woods that lay behind them as the valley narrowed then broadened out then narrowed again. These places clung to the old track or else retreated up the slopes into secret clefts and tree-covered hidden valleys. They were dark places, with streams running through them and gathering drifts of talus. Places of honey and wool. Vegetable terraces. Wet smoke and suspicious eyes.

Mytholm. Eastwood. Jumble Hole Clough.

Charlestown. Sandbed.

Across the moors and over the tops offered a steeper, shorter route from James Broadbent's lodging at the Sutcliffe place to father and son's destination but it meant crossing the wide open interior of the moors out the back of Bell House where the Hartleys had their boys on watch, and the trust of their nearest neighbours who were dotted across the Erringden top slopes. That was a risk.

Things happened on the moors.

And that way also meant dropping over the other side to take the old rakes used for walking the cows down from the moors and then passing through hamlets where the Hartleys had other known friends and allies; more watchful eyes to track their route.

Places like Mankinholes. Lumbutts.

Callis.

So they stuck to the safe option of the main thoroughfare, that broad rutted track that ran the horses and carts and traders through the valley, and whose pot-holes were routinely filled with shale and stone to ensure no goods got damaged and the wives of visiting money men did not have their powdered posteriors unduly troubled.

As the footpath left the trees and joined the main route they saw, dotted ahead of them, workmen. Half a dozen in all. Men with rods and spools of rope. Joseph Broadbent approached the nearest of them as he leaned idly against his length of wood. His trousers were tucked into his socks and his wool cap dotted with holes.

What's all this?

Land survey, replied the man, who was Irish.

Land survey? said Joseph Broadbent.

That's what I said.

Well what for?

The turnpike.

Turnpike? What bloody turnpike?

The man shrugged.

We don't know nowt about a turnpike, said James Broadbent.

That's not my problem, friend, said the Irishman.

Well, what do we need a bloody turnpike for?

Again the man shrugged.

Why does anyone need a turnpike? So folk can get from one place to another.

Things are reasonable as it is with the track and the trees, said Joseph Broadbent. Why should you go and change it?

Look, mister, said the Irishman. I just stand here. I just hold the stick.

Well where's it going to?

This one here?

Yes.

Up there.

The Irishman pointed up ahead towards the smoke-blackened stone buildings of Hebden Bridge peeping above the trees.

From Halifax to yonder, he said.

Joseph Broadbent started coughing and kept coughing, the rasp thick and trapped in his chest. Something almost solid. When he stopped he wiped his lip.

But past there is nothing but moors, he said.

Then it'll be nothing but moors still but with a turnpike running through it.

Joseph Broadbent shook his head and then he and his son carried on walking.

They reached the White Hart in Todmorden in two hours and when they entered William Deighton bought them ale and hot soup and squares of cold butter crust chicken pie and then they sat.

Joseph Broadbent introduced the exciseman to his son. They drank and ate and then William Deighton said: well now, James Broadbent, your father says you are ready to talk about the Hartley gang.

Yes I am, came the reply.

So you know that you will be rewarded fully.

One hundred guineas was mentioned to me.

One hundred guineas is what I could pay you.

No less?

No less.

The boy is putting his neck on the block for you, Mr. Deighton, said Joseph Broadbent.

I understand that Mr. Broadbent, though is not his neck already on the block – or in the noose – for being involved in this forgery trade?

James Broadbent shifted awkwardly in his seat and looked at his father and then in a lowered voice said: all I know is

Hartley is a bastard and one hundred guineas is enough to get me away.

There are questions I'll need you to answer.

And you can protect us?

William Deighton leaned back. Raised his eyebrows.

Of course anything you tell me will be in the strictest confidence until these men are brought to task, whereupon you will receive your reward direct from the mint of the king of England himself. But after that, your liberty is yours alone. This valley is your valley. These people are your people. Not mine.

Hartleys aren't my people, said James Broadbent.

But you know them.

Yes.

And you work for them.

I work *with* them.

I'll need to know everything you know, said William Deighton. Starting with a lot more names. The whole valley talks of this one they call the king, but no man runs something so widespread without a lot of minions.

What's minions? said James Broadbent.

People like you. No games now. I'll need names. A lot of names.

Joseph Broadbent coughed and then drank some ale and coughed some more.

Listen to the man, he said to his son. Do right by Mr. Deighton and he'll do right by you.

William Deighton nodded in agreement.

A moment passed while James Broadbent stared deep into his drink. He raised his head and spoke, his voice deep and dry in his throat.

What will happen to Hartley if I yap?

When he has been brought to justice? said William Deighton.

Yes.

That man will hang.

James Broadbent nodded.

Then I'll give you names of the whole bloody lot of them as long as Hartley hangs and I get the ribband that's owed to me.

You'll get yours, said William Deighton. But you can start by giving me a name. Someone close to you. Someone who clips. As a show of faith. So I know you mean what you say.

I can give you dozens of names but for now you can have John Sutcliffe.

William Deighton finished his drink and said: John Sutcliffe? I don't know of him.

He's my landlord, said James Broadbent. And a tighter more miserable son of a whore you could not meet.

Show me.

What?

Show me where this man lives, said William Deighton. I'll arrest him this day.

Not bloody likely. I can't be seen with the man who vows to hang all Coiners.

Then you go with your father now and I will follow. I will wait. And if this man has about his person or in his possession the tools of his vile trade then you signal to me and I will do the rest. I will begin to bring the whole cursed lot of you down.

Not me though, said James Broadbent.

No, said William Deighton. Not you. It's with God that you will have to make your peace.

The nite In the nite it was It came I sor it A rat A rat like no uther rat As big as a cat it were Its clors on the flor is what wokeus The scratchin and scrapin of it An its tayle its tayle was as long an thick as a bootlays right thick it was and its wiskys were long and thick too Mynde if Ive seen wan rat ive seen twelf thousand rats and didunt we yoosed to go rattin as lads down by the brown worters of the calder or rownd the chicken sheds killen mebbes twenny or thirtee in wan go with the hounds but this rat mynde this rat were different becors this rat had the ieyes of a man I tell thee its troo The eyes of a man An tho it were dark here in the jale sell it wernt that dark becors this rat was scrattin about in me stror mattin and when I went to boot it it moved away and sat back and lucked at us with this luck on its fays and thas when I knew it were pussessd by a purson.

Thats when I knew hoo the rat really were That's when I knew the rat were the nugget pushin yeller rat bastid son of a guffy fucker Jaymse Brordben and I did leep up and went forrit an it hissed then an I went Brordbent yoo loose tunged yeller cunt its yoo that's gorrus done for now and I swear on the heads of my chillun there was this luck in this rats eyes an it were laffin arrus it were laffin at all of us coyners So I booted it I booted it hard So hard it hit the worl an I stamped on it I stamped on it so hard it burst open like a bludd pudding that's boilt dry in the pan and I reecht down I reecht in and I pult with my fingus at what it was I could see in there wich was guts and strings and coils and werms An I fownd wot I recken were its hart and I took that hart and I ate that hart an it popped in my marth Jaimse Brodbents hart popped in my marth like a goosegog and the filthee stinken lyin cowidlee blud of his ran down King Davidd's froat an into my stomack An I sed to the rat I sed to the moon I sed to the cold dark wet stone room I sed have that yoo cunt Then I sleept the sleep of the ded and then I woke up and wrote

this down with the tayst of that yeller basterds blud still on my
tung an dryed into my beard an orl down my shirt fronte like
the tears of tankard on a gennulmuns westcott after hes tied
a long wan on But when alls sed and dun I feel in fine fissicle
fettul with it an all Strange it is the things a man will do when
confined down here in the dark sellars of the cassel and he is
hungree lonelee and faysun the gallers desprit in his thorts and
visherns Aye strange lyfe and straindge deth acummun in too I
shudnt wonder.

After she had slopped out the pigs and upended a bucket of peelings and scraps that were already fermenting into an acrid puree for them to jostle over, and squatted beneath the cow and milked it and then put fresh straw and water in the byre – she noted that the beast's teats seemed crusted and unduly red and mottled with what appeared to be tiny white welts – Grace Hartley went to the hen hut and lifted each bird in turn and carefully collected the still-warm eggs, each a small creamy mushroom-coloured miracle, some freckled, some not, and as she did one or two of the chickens ruffled their feathers or shook the fleshy wattles of their throats in agitation or curiosity but when she opened the door and scattered a fine mix of grain and dried grass and bread crumbs and tea leaves across the pen they slowly left their hut and pecked at the ground around her swollen feet with a concentrated frenzy, and then Grace Hartley took the eggs into the kitchen and placed a pan on the range and heated some butter and cracked three eggs into the bubbling liquid and then when the yolks were colouring like the evening sun she tilted the eggs to one side of the pan and then added a dash of the milk and into this she scattered some field mushrooms which she slowly poached and she cut two slices of bread and poured the eggs and mushrooms and butter on the bread and set it on the table and called to her husband who appeared in the doorway with a strange, strained look on his face that she could not read and then she boiled a kettle to mash the tea, and he sat and silently ate while steam plumed from the kettle's spout until its whistle became a shrill shriek that he could not stand and she saw the storm clouds coming.

William Deighton gave James Broadbent and his father Joseph Broadbent time and space. He allowed them the protection of distance.

When the father and son had left he waited in the White Hart and slowly drank one more ale, careful not to take so much that his senses became dulled. He then had his horse fed and watered, and he tipped the stable boy.

The six mile clip back to Mytholmroyd would be nothing on horseback but on foot the old man would surely slow the pair down. On foot they would take two hours or more. He saw death in that man's yellowed eyes. He wore it about himself like a broken man. It hung from him. Pushed his shoulders down. Scratched at his lungs and throat.

Precipitancy was to be avoided but haste was nevertheless important. It was something he and Robert Parker had discussed at length: the gang needed to be brought down quickly before they spread and fled, never to be seen again. Parker's letters to and from London confirmed the crown was behind them. Treason would be the charge, William Deighton the man to deliver the many felons.

The old man was the key with which to unlock his son, who in turn knew enough to send several men to their graves. James Broadbent himself could not be trusted. James Broadbent was as bad as they come and stupid with it. James Broadbent was greedy and duplicitous and un-Godly and a liar and bully and a cheat. His playing for both teams brought a death sentence either way, as sure as the Calder flows and floods. Both he and Robert Parker knew that this was an untenable position, hence the need for alacrity and action.

William Deighton would take them on. Take them on himself. Take them on and bring them down. Bring them in. Let them swing. String them up. For all to see. He would write a message across the sky with their blood then let the crows at them. Let the gulls at them. The shrieking gulls far from the sea. Create carrion of them. Send a message. A message to the hill folk. That times were changing. The empire expanding. That men earned money not made it; that a country ran on rules. Rules for everyone. Call it society. Call it civilisation. From the crown all the way down. Rules. Laws. Restrictions. The dark days were over. New ways were coming. Big ideas. Ideas that would change the world. Call it economy. Call it industry. Call it England.

William Deighton caught them up at the far side of Hebden Bridge, and then hung back. He let the horse canter and then stroll. Let it stop from time to time. To idle in the long grass. To chew at it with its lips peeled back and oversized teeth tugging then grinding. Tugging then grinding.

He heard the old man's cough a half mile off. He had heard that rattle before in the chest of his own father; it was a cough of death then and it was a cough of death now, each breath a grain of sand slipping through the hourglass of the old man's smoke-wracked body. His son idled beside him; his body too big for his clothes. His head too big for his body. His hat too small for his head.

Long arms dangling.

Up ahead on the river track James Broadbent resembled, thought William Deighton, a side of pork dressed in shirt and trousers, jacket and leather clogs. He was useless for anything but might and violence. Intimidation. A bestial type, Broadbent. Animalistic really. Savage. He would get no reward for his part in all of this for he was a forger, an enforcer and a savage, was Broadbent – and now you could add turncoat to the litany of his dire achievements. That was all. He served no purpose in society and never would. He contributed nothing but pain and had neither the integrity nor the true commitment to a criminal cause like Hartley. He would get nothing but a lesson in life. William Deighton hated him on principle.

When the pair stopped he stopped. Gave them a chance. Retained a distance.

Eventually they left the trees and entered the village of Mytholmroyd. He crossed the rising waters of the Calder and saw whorls of scum-foam forming there in an eddy where the river was joined by a feeder stream. The water was shallow and the colour of copper. It was moor-top run-off, metallic to the taste but pure too. Often trout hung in the shadows of the bridge, held there by the oncoming current and an occasional tail-flick. But not today. Today there were none.

William Deighton tracked them to Hall Bank Lane where he heard the old man coughing into the incline. A coffin's cough, it was.

They reached the three-house dwelling of Hall Gate. The Sutcliffe place. James Broadbent's lodgings. Father and son stopped. They stood by the black quoin of the terrace to confer for a moment then looked down the track to William Deighton then conferred again. He urged them on. To stick to the plan. To enter the house and then leave the house and give the signal.

At the bottom of the bank he alighted his horse and secured it.

James Broadbent entered and then providence beckoned for he returned a moment later and William Deighton saw him beckoning him on. He strode up the bank and entered the house. He stepped into a scene just like a thousand he had previously imagined during long days and listless nights. It was precisely how he had envisioned. It was a form of perfection.

John Sutcliffe was at a table, by the fire, clipping. He had shears and coins in hand. He looked at the exciseman with surprise. Broadbent feigned dismay – badly. Broadbent feigned outrage – badly.

He overplayed it but that didn't matter now; that was on his head. William Deighton had other concerns.

John Sutcliffe set the shears aside and said Well now.

Marble. Crystal. Porcelain.

Back chairs and tripod tables. Statuettes. An ornate fireplace. Several ornate fireplaces. Furnished textiles. A pewter platter. A tea service. A decanter. Mirrors. Many mirrors reflecting James Broadbent's eyes as they darted around the room and struggled to take everything in.

He saw candlestick holders rendered in the style of classical columns. A piano scattered with sheet music. He saw wood panelled walls and painted skirting boards. And the paintings. Paintings of animals. Paintings of children at play. Paintings of a family. Of a meadow. A man. Several men. Portraits in oil. Framed and hung.

He had not been in a house like that belonging to Robert Parker. Everything clean. Everything scrubbed. Dusted. White. So white. A world unimaginable, were he not witnessing it now.

That someone could have so much space to move about – to fill and occupy and stretch out in – made James Broadbent marvel. That they might never need to stoop for doorways or sleep three to a loom loft was close to beyond his understanding.

He was used to banging his head and squeezing his bulk beneath pressing lintels in dwellings built for half-blind weavers and the very poorest of charcoal-burners, but the Parker place was high-ceilinged and wide-windowed. It made him feel lost. It distorted his proportions so that his limbs felt heavy and cumbersome. It was the house of a man who had chosen the right side of the law, the side he had now crossed over to.

He did not see the King of the Craggs living in such a house.

William Deighton was there already when James Broadbent arrived, and already there were cigars circulating. And books. Books everywhere. More books than a man would ever need if he could read.

Robert Parker clapped him on the back and said: John Sutcliffe lives in York gaol but mere hours after his detention and we have you to thank for that, Mr. Broadbent. And now we need another name.

James Broadbent moved his bulk from one foot to the other and found he could not look this confident solicitor in the eye.

Well now speak up, said William Deighton. Mr. Parker is pleased enough to receive you into his house but our good work is just beginning.

The money, said James Broadbent, his voice thin.

There's plenty of that to come, said Robert Parker, and then turning to William Deighton he said: it seems like this whole valley has a mania for money one way or another.

Turning back to James Broadbent he continued.

Rest assured you'll be rewarded. We're men of our word. Hard to believe we exist, I know, but understand this: John Sutcliffe is just one small cog in the machine. One tiny insignificant cog whose arrest will have little impact on the output of your friends. Do you understand how the machine of a functioning society works, Mr Broadbent – that all working parts are related?

Before he could answer, the solicitor continued.

You must be aware that your naming of your landlord was little more than an exercise in trust. It's Hartley who we really want. All the Hartleys, but first we'll chip away at his foundations. Mr. Deighton here will dismantle his network and raze his hill-top fortress. And for that we need to take more names.

Names? said James Broadbent. Uncomfortable in his surroundings, he seemed unable to keep his eyes fixed in one place.

More forgers. We need more forgers. Clippers – or whatever it is you call yourselves. We'll soon have Hartley running scared. We need him incapacitated. Frozen. Before he can do more damage. And before he cottons on.

Cottons on? said James Broadbent.

Robert Parker looked to William Deighton then back to James Broadbent.

Before he knows you're informing on him.

James Broadbent nodded.

Are you fearful? asked Robert Parker.

James Broadbent shook his head.

Good. I was told you were once a soldier.

And a good one at that. Many years I served.

And you left when?

Discharged some six year ago.

129

At what age?

James Broadbent shrugged and said six years younger than I am now.

Robert Parker continued.

You understand that without names we are left with nothing but hill-top rumours and valley bottom gossip. We have a failed economy being ruined by cold-hearted forgers and we have a town with a reputation for lawlessness that has spread all the way to the back rooms of Westminster – to the seat of our very parliament and to the throne of the King.

The King? said James Broadbent.

The *real* monarch, not some barbarous land labourer.

Will I get to meet his majesty?

Robert Parker raised an eyebrow to William Deighton.

That remains to be seen on how co-operative you are, he said, gently humouring the swarthy man whose odour had tainted his dwelling. But do be aware the King always rewards his loyal subjects.

Your name won't reach his ear unless you start giving up some Coiners but, said William Deighton.

The money, said James Broadbent again.

The money will come.

Robert Parker gestured to a chair.

Sit, lad.

James Broadbent lowered himself awkwardly onto the edge of the chair.

My throat it is scratching, he said.

Scratching? said Robert Parker.

From the walk over. Dry. Itchy, like.

Would you like some water?

No sir, I do not care for water. Never have.

Fine then.

But perhaps something to flavour it. Or something to loosen my words.

I think he means alcohol, said William Deighton.

I don't take it, replied Robert Parker. But I could send down for some whiskey. I have been gifted several bottles over the years.

Thank you sir.

But first a name.

David O' Johns O' Dicks O' Jacks is a name, said James Broadbent. He is known to clip.

Robert Parker looked puzzled.

David O' Johns O' Dicks O' Jacks?

Aye. That is what they call him.

It's the valley way of naming offspring, said William Deighton to the confused solicitor.

Do you happen to know his actual name?

Aye. David. The son of John who himself is the son of Dick. And he is the son of Jack. Names get passed on round our way.

So I see. But what is his full name?

I told you, said James Broadbent. David O' Johns O' Dicks O' Jacks.

William Deighton stepped towards him.

Buckle up, Broadbent – Mr Parker is a man of the law, as am I. Makes fools of us to our faces and you'll be joining John Sutcliffe in York Castle by sun-up.

John Tatham of Wadsworth I do not care for, said James Broadbent. Nor Isaac Dewhurst or the Pickles lot. Go to the Pickles place at Luddenden Dene and you'll catch them red-handed. They keep their works behind a loose stone to the left of their fireplace. There are your names.

We need more, said Robert Parker. We need someone closer to Hartley.

A neighbour, said William Deighton. We need someone from Cragg Vale. From the moor.

James Broadbent scratched at his chin and still he did not meet the eyes of the men.

There's Thomas Clayton, he said quietly.

Now this name I know, nodded William Deighton to Robert Parker, and then to James Broadbent he said: Clayton of Stannery End?

Yes.

Along from Bell House?

Aye. That's the one. Shifty as a stoat on a morning egg raid and as mean as a mousetrap, is Clayton. Oh, as mean as they come that one. They say he is Hartley's right hand. He'd slit my throat if he could see this here scene.

I don't doubt it, said Robert Parker. And for your information I am grateful.

He clips then, this Clayton? asked William Deighton.

He has been known to. But often they have a man.

A man?

James Broadbent nodded at the floor.

A man what comes and takes the coins and the clippings that the men have collected and he makes magic out of those clippings. He makes coins better than any man's.

Who is he? asked Robert Parker.

Magic? asked William Deighton.

James Broadbent shrugged.

What is his name? the exciseman asked again.

That I do not know. No-one knows.

Nonsense, said William Deighton.

He comes from Bradford. He is never seen with his cowl down. They say he knows things. Plays with fire. Summons dark forces.

Robert Parker laughed.

What rot.

James Broadbent looked up at him then.

It's not rot. If you spent time on them moors you'd know it's not rot. Things happen up there.

I'm up on those moors regularly, said William Deighton. One more time: who knows the name of this man?

Hartley knows, said James Broadbent. And Tom Spencer

knows. And Thomas Clayton knows. Them knows. They all know.

David Hartley tumbled into the room and his wife saw that he was full of drink. The long walk back from the inns of Mytholmroyd was usually enough to sand away the edges, or else he sometimes slept it off in one of his dug-outs in the woods – under the stone slab of an overhang perhaps, or in one of the hunting hides that he and his brothers built as boys and to which they added new branches every year – but he carried with him a jar of something uncorked and his flinty eyes were rolling around like marbles. His cheeks red, wild grass seeds in his hair and the scent of spring blooming about him. His other hand held a small sack that he swung down from his shoulder onto the floor, where it spilled coins across the stone flags.

Wife, we is of wider wealth than you could ever know.

He stood proud, swaying gently.

You've woken the child.

I'll waken the whole fucking valley with my boasts if I want to, for it is warranted.

I've just got him off.

Why is a crying baby your only concern when you have a king for a husband and liquid gold flowing around your fat ankles?

Because he's not slept proper for three nights now.

David Hartley dismissed her words with a sweep of the arm.

Winter is for sleeping. But it's spring now and spring is for drinking and roaming and coining and fucking, and it's the stagman.

Stagman? What daft talk.

It's not daft, said David Hartley.

You're full of Barbara's ale, you lump.

He took a step towards his wife.

Full of beer I may be, but I talk the truth so mind your tone when you're talking to me. The stagman of the moors has chosen to treat me favourably. That's what I'm telling you. All my life he and his kind have looked over me. As a boy they picked me out. Chose me.

You're as daft as a privy rat, you are.

Daft but not tapped.

Every time you're filled from your boots to the brim of your brow with beer you talk of this stagman, replied Grace Hartley. But you should be careful else they think you've turned lunatic and then it'll be off to Manchester asylum with all the broth-dribblers for you.

They'll never chain King David. All I'm saying is the stagman has blessed me with a wife and three children and balls big enough to embark on an enterprise that by the year's close will see us the richest family in Calderdale, mark my words, Grace. You'll want for nothing. You'll have everything.

I'd take a good night's sleep.

Give us a kiss and I'll tell you more about it.

As her husband reached out Grace Hartley took a step backwards, and he slipped on the coins but managed to maintain his balance.

Two days and nights you were gone, she said. Where have you been?

I've been kinging from Hell to Halifax and back again, he replied. And now I'm back in this piece of heaven I've created. There's a reason I chose to live so high up and that's because it puts us closer to paradise.

He took a swig from his jar and then pointed to the coins.

There's five hundred fresh milled bits there. That's enough money to start building us an even grander palace.

You'll be wanting a throne next.

David Hartley belched.

Don't need no throne unless the stagman deems it so.

From up under the rafters the baby was crying louder.

Grace Hartley stooped and began to gather the coins up.

Here, give us one of those.

David Hartley snatched a coin from the hand of his wife and went to the front door and flung it out into the darkness.

That's for the stagman, he said. That's my tribute for him seeing us right, and there's more to come. Give us another.

I won't.

The stagman wants paying.

Turning the coins in her hand, Grace Hartley looked at her husband but said nothing.

Shake your head all you like, wife, but it's because of a creature with the body of a man and the head and antlers of a stag that your cupboards are full and those babes sleep on the best blankets and you've new boots and two dozen hens and a set of china the likes of which this valley has never seen. And that's just the start of it, queen.

You're three sheets, she said.

I'm drunk tonight but tomorrow I'll still be blessed by the horned one.

He slumped into a chair and drained the jug but the jug was empty. He closed his eyes and appeared to be asleep immediately.

Grace Hartley scooped coins back into the sack, but some she slipped into her pinafore pocket.

I've got a hunger, he said from behind his eyelids, his voice slurring towards sleep.

Four hundred coins, you say? replied his wife.

David Hartley raised his slumped head and opened his eyes. What, woman?

You said the stagmen is responsible for you acquiring these four hundred coins.

That's what I said. And then I said I've got a hunger.

He closed his eyes again. Grace Hartley put more coins into the sack, and then some into her pocket.

There's mutton slices and a new loaf, she said. And there'll be fresh eggs.

Then fetch it here and put it in my gob. A man could die of

starvation if it was left to his wife's own initiative. Get the food in here, and a new jar, and then I'll lay you down right here on this bed of gold, and give you what it is that any woman in this valley dreams of. You can sit on it and spin on it like a bobbin. But first I'll be needing feeding. A man needs meat as a pencil needs lead.

Grace Hartley stood and set the sack on the side and said: I'll need to check the hen hut.

I'll take four, he said, from somewhere approaching sleep. And fetch four for the fucking stagman too.

Grace took a lamp and went out to the hen hut. She unhooked the gate and crawled in to where the birds were roosting in rows and at the back in the corner where the reek of bird shit was strong she parted the straw and found the loose board and she lifted it. She took the coins from her pocket and stacked them in her hand and then she reached down in the darkness and set the stack there with the rest of them, and then she replaced the board, and feathers were in her hair.

Part IV
Autumn 1769
Clett-Clett

Autumn arrived like a burning ghost ship on the landscape's tide to set the land alight. The fire of the trees' turning spread far across the flanks and the ravens took flight to the highest climes as leaves fell like flung bodies. September had long slipped away. It was a charred thing now. Gone.

The hills were ablaze with the colour of brilliant decay as the cycle of winter began with a fresh palette. Crows blown like black handkerchiefs from a funeral feast into the tangled tree tops exchanged shrill chatter there, a running commentary on all that was happening around them. Because everything was in vibrant flux. All was facing death.

William Deighton came in on over Hathershelf and aback of Scout Rock. He followed the field line where it fell away dramatically to a series of deadly cliffs and precipices above the thick woodland below that some believed was cursed or haunted; a place where things happened that could not be explained. In that small wood they said there were treasures buried – and bodies too. During his life-time more than one person had hurled themselves from the rocks to their death below. And William Deighton suspected that in the base of these sheer drops, where the scree met the soft soil of the woodland floor, and moss-covered boulders the size of small houses sat half buried, each cleaved away from the cliff face by the steady battering of the elements and underground springs that ran through the rock like woodworms through the trusses of a timber roof frame, lay hidden the tools of the Coiners' trade too.

Perhaps it was they, the local criminals, who had spread the stories about Scout Rock wood: tales of the white witch that stalked its tangled undergrowth, the hidden medieval mineshafts that sucked children down and the mulchy terraces that were known to shift underfoot. And the small caves there too, where human remains were said to have been found. Where better to

139

hide and plot and conspire – and stash a cache of contraband – than in the place no local dared set foot?

From up here beneath the darkening sky William Deighton could see right along the valley where the new turnpike was to follow the River Calder to Hebden Bridge, and beyond it the steep rake they called The Buttress up to Heptonstall high on the hill, where the locals barely left and lived in sordid domestic conditions, investing all their time and what spare money that they had in the new octagonal chapel built by this preacher, one John Wesley, whose words it seemed had captured the imaginations of so many in the valley. They said he shaped it eight-sided so that there were no corners in which the devil could hide. They said his name was known across the land, that he had the ear of God himself and that he saw sin in people just by looking at them, between blinks.

Only five or six miles from his Halifax home lay these other worlds.

William Deighton paused in the furrow of a field recently tilled and turned and shorn of the valued winter grass, and he looked back the other way from where he came, where the safety of town now sat unseen.

His destination was over the brow to the solitary farmstead of Stannery End, a straight crow's mile across from Bell House.

It was evening and Thomas Clayton's place appeared as a mirror image of the Hartley home. It may not have been quite as high up nor as remote but it was still a good half hour's walk down to the cluster of houses and stores of Mytholmroyd and, sitting in nothing but fields, equally difficult to approach. As with the Hartley home its occupation was tactical. It was an asset to those who harboured secrets. A strategic bolt-hole.

William Deigthon cleared the last field that bordered the precipitous drop of Scout Rock cliffs and crouched behind a wall. Stannery End was in sight. There was light in the upstairs window. There was a shadow. There were shadows. There were several shadows stretching and receding.

He squinted and then keeping low he frog-crawled his way closer. He saw a figure cross the flame of the candle, a definite elongation of darkness bent crooked across the wall of that upstairs room. William Deighton crouched and waited.

Then the light went out. Snuffed.

The light went out and it was as if it had never been there at all.

The house was cast in darkness and suddenly William Deighton felt exposed, even here behind the wall with nothing but cliffs and woods behind him and the autumn sky closing in above him; night here, he noticed, had a habit of collapsing across the land quickly.

He climbed over the wall and ran across the field towards the house of the Coiner Clayton. He ran across the field, stumbling in holes. Holes that dotted the field. The field that would lay fallow and frozen over the coming months. The months of a winter already coming in on the autumn breeze. A breeze that rustled the stubby clusters of grass. Grass that fed the cows that made the milk. The milk that weaned the children of the valley. The valley that they said ran rich with gold.

William Deighton ran straight for Stannery End. He abandoned any attempt to remain unseen, for if his suspicions were right it was his sighting that had snuffed that candle. Killed that light. Emptied that room.

Then he was there. Then he was banging on the front door. Banging on the door and turning the handle at the same time. And the door was opening and he was entering to nothing but darkness. Darkness and the smell of a fire doused in water. Damp ash and impostor smoke. And cutting through it, the scent of a pipe and something cooked, hot, of salt and flesh.

He saw hanging from the ceiling onions strung in garlands. He saw on the window sill a row of corn dollies. Below them a basket of washed sheep wool. A roe deer's skull mounted.

William Deighton bolted up crooked stairs. Here was one room containing three looms and baskets and trimmings and

141

combs. Half-spun wool was strung everywhere. It stretched from ceiling beams to hooks in the wall. There were reels and bobbins. Yarn cleats and knotted tangles.

And tucked into recesses in the walls where bricks had been removed for this very purpose, there sat dripping stubs of candles. He went to one and touched it. The wax was soft. He pinched the wick. Still warm.

He quickly walked downstairs to the back door. It was ajar. It was opened to the anthracite night into which Thomas Clayton and possibly other Coiners had fled.

William Deighton went back into the house. He looked in the dresser and under the bed. He checked the stores. Checked the drawers. He looked up the chimney and felt the radiating warmth of the dampened fire in its stone, then he put his fingers into every nook and cranny. Between every cold stone. He tested loose floorboards. Lifted sheepskins still stinking of flesh. Scoured a raggy mat stitched from dyed scraps. Rifled through tangles of wool. Upended furniture then carefully replaced it.

Nothing.

He found nothing.

Not a sliver of metal nor a set of shears.

Not a single coin. Not a stamp or a crucible or tongs or buffing rags.

There was nothing but the presence of people recently departed to the hill behind. To the hill to hide and bury. To bury their counterfeit coins. Coins to clothe and feed. Here they surely watched and waited as William Deighton left Stannery End and began the long walk home back across the fields to the low lights of Halifax in the far distance, that flickered as if the sky had fallen in defeat, and draped itself across the rise and fall of the bloodless, smothering land.

With this stump of lead and wat papyre it is I have wangled from the turnkey I have writ a poem that I corl the Song of the Crag Vayle Coiners and it goes like this it goes Hot yorkshyre blood an tough yorkshyre bones Stiff yorkshyre prick and stout yorkshyre stones Theres no man can map where it is a afeersum Cragg vale clipper goes

An thats real mans poetree is that.

Many more nights he stepped into darkness and darkness was all around him. He wore it like a comforting shawl. It felt a part of him; an extension of his physical form.

William Deighton made darkness an asset and an ally and his feet began to find their way through the deepest blue so that in time he did not need even a stump of a candle. Soon he began to know the camber of the track over the hump-back hills from Halifax. He gained a feel for the undulations of the moorland's edge and saw the moon turned silver in the puddles and sump holes that never seemed to dry up. His muscles gained memories and the memories guided him.

Occasionally he went on horseback but mainly William Deighton walked.

He felt his thighs fatten and took pleasure from the way his feet gained traction and his entire body responded. The hills registered in his bones and joints. He felt the pull of them in each tendon and sinew. Nature's gymnasium.

He was not a young man but the ten Roman miles or more he covered on his night wanderings made him feel as if his blood was bubbling anew, just as a fresh spring stream bubbles after a flash of rain. The repetition of one foot after another, the corset of cold sweat sticking him to his undershirt, the gratifying burning in his lungs and the matting together of hair and hat all created a coursing sense of energy, the likes of which could not be mustered, summoned or experienced when wandering the town streets. He was surprised to learn of his own heightened levels of stamina.

Half a dozen times or more Robert Parker had insisted he took with him a young bailiff for his own protection but the excise man William Deighton dismissed the idea outright. The hunter, he said, works best alone. Many times his wife, too, tried to persuade him to stay by the fire in the house, where his younger children filled the floor and letters home from their eldest three sons sat stacked on the mantelpiece, but after Stannery End he was more determined than ever.

Stannery End was an affront. He said as much to Robert Parker. Stannery End was a snub to all lawmen and a puzzle too, for he had yet to work out how it was that the house's tenant, Thomas Clayton, knew Deighton was coming for him; how it was he was able to flee with only seconds to spare.

Only when he had flattened out across his kitchen table a crude pen and ink map of the Upper Calder valley that marked the hamlets and larger hill-top farmsteads and messuages did the thought enter his head that it was possible that the Coiners were operating some sort of advance signalling system. From its elevated position Bell House sat a crow's mile across the Cragg valley from Stannery End, and forming a third corner equidistant from the two across Calderdale was the house at Wadsworth Banks, where it was known that one Thomas Greenwood – who the turncoat James Broadbent had informed him was also known, in typical gang-style, as Great Tom or Conjurer Tom – kept a home. Wadsworth Banks looked back directly across to the blackened cliffs and tree-lined basin of Scout Rock along which he himself had stalked. Together these three houses formed a triumvirate of eyes able to watch all the main roads and routes in and out the valley.

Could, he wondered, the men be signalling one another, with mirrors or flags perhaps? Or something even more sophisticated. It was a trick not beyond their capability, but one he did not raise with Robert Parker for fear of being ridiculed.

Robert Parker was a reasonable and learned man and to be outsmarted by these illiterate hill-dwellers was not something William Deighton wanted known.

He made a note to visit Wadsworth Banks. Thomas Greenwood would be receiving a visit. His was another name for the list.

For many nights he walked alone and soon these journeys gave him a deeper understanding of darkness. They gave him a greater understanding of place. Plunged into the night, William Deighton refined his senses and let sound and touch – the whistle of the wind and the scratching and snittering of animals; the creak of leather sole on grainy cart stone – guide him as the laminated layers of night peeled back to reveal a state of mind.

Through the valley he tigered as if in a dream and often he wondered if this was all indeed a dream for when he returned home in the early hours it was not sleep that greeted him but a strange limbo where day and night, dream, nightmare and reality overlapped. Coming home he brought the soft darkness with him. They were inside him now, these hinterlands. He carried the moor everywhere – or perhaps the moor carried him.

Each time he returned to town, to home, to lie in bed perfectly still beside his sleeping wife, his senses enlivened, William Deighton felt utterly exhausted, yet he was nevertheless imbued and infused with a sort of joyful drunkenness too, and increasingly a part of him was still out there, stalking the moor, a half-feral man whose very dreams were now scented by heather and lit by moonlight, crackling with the mute power of all things connected.

Wans in the forges wesst of Burmincham I did have to fite a man
A rite big lump of a bastid he were A man they did say hayled
from Scotlan from Glasger on the Clide I believe it was Now this
lump had tayken a dislyken to King Daevid for wot reason I no
not ecksept perhaps for me good lucks that sum have lycund to
the Gods of olde or maybe it was my natril witt and gile but
this big carrot topped bran faysed bastid did corner me wan day
down in the forjes and I swear he was the size of an ocks up on its
back legs As big as fucken beest of the feeld he was Bigger mebby.

And I sed I dunt want no trubble with you Jocky but he says oh
you will get it for that bigg head and cruel tung of yours Hartlee
and the daft bugger ript off his shirt and underneath he was
hard as teek and his brisket boddee had mussels on mussels and
I thort oh fuckerduck Hartlee you are in trubble now sunshyne
An the lads were all gathrin rownd then becors they loved a good
roar up as it was a nice brake from the werk and the manigers
leffed us to it and most of them were just glad it wassunt them
that were havven to duke it owt with the big boy And tho sum
were happy to see King Dayvid who of cors at this pointe was
not yet kynge get a rite rummelling this ginjer jock was known
to be a bullkybuck too and tho this was no even handed scware
straytunner somewan hayted was goan to be given a goan over
wich ever syde you were so inclyned to take so it were summat
to see It were sport.

An thats when this cunt comes chargen attes but I was one step
on him becors as he did I reached into my arse pocked and I
pullt out my snuff bocks an with a flick of the thum it was open
and before he could grabbus I did flinge the hole fucken lot in
the mans fayse and puff the browne powder was in his eyes and
his eatin hole and up his bigg brokain snozz the daft cunt Well
after that it was easy becores I booted him ones in the nutmegs

147

and ones more for luck An at that he toppuld like a felled tree falls at the last chop of the acks blayde in a woodland cleerin Fell wimpering he did Fell like a lass he did and wan more punch to the hed did nigh on finish him sparko cold Dun up like a split kipper reddy for thur smokehaus.

Well aftur that he had no spit in him to get back up neythur I meen that man was leffed pissen blud for dayse and not a werd he sed to me when we were back at the smeltin and the pourin and the hammerin Not a werd And no man did trubble me after that in the Black Countree becors I tell you what a seed was planted that day A seed that sed I was to become a leeder of men A seed that I new would grow into sumthin big and strong and speshul and hoos roots would reech deep into the soil of my land and wud stay there and my name wud be planted too and it wud grow to graytness and so it did.

And so it did.

Evening eyes followed William Deighton all the way down the sunken hollow of Stake Lane and across the valley floor towards the permanent eventide of Bell Hole.

Eyes. The eyes of Stannery End. The eyes of Thomas Clayton.

When William Deighton left the lane and headed out across the open fields it was still light so Thomas Clayton sent his best boy out to get a closer look for all the Coiners and their children knew the face of William Deighton. They knew his brown coat and cord breeches, the red waistcoat and the shovel hat pulled low over the brow.

This man does not give up, remarked Thomas Clayton from this window. But this time he has not given us a second glance. This time he has foregone us for the King's sky palace instead.

The boy ran back up the hill, past the rabbit warren that spanned a hundred or more burrowed feet, through the pasture where foxes wrestled and tumbled at dawn in the dew-soaked grass, and up toward the post where a buzzard had often been seen tearing apart its morning feed, the fur and feather and tiny bones of its prey littering the grass around it as if ritually placed to demarcate a sacred feeding circle, a testament to its routine.

He ran into the house and said it's him – it's the wretched William Deighton. Thomas Clayton stood and opened up the wooden box and scooped a spoon of the powder mix made from the leached ash of wood and leaves and sodium mineral salt and the special unnamed, unknown compound that King David Hartley himself had supplied him with and he said step back, step back, and he flung the mixture onto the fire where it crackled and spat and the flame burned a fierce blue for a few fleeting seconds before the smoke turned into a heavy green colour that slowly spiralled from the Stannery End chimney, twisting upwards in an astringent column.

He repeated the process one more time and the spiral grew taller and stronger and the gusting back-draught of green smoke filled the front room and had Thomas Clayton coughing and his wife coughing and his children coughing. All of them hacking as the dense and acrid smoke burned their chests and sent them running to the windows to gulp in the clean sharp air of a settling Yorkshire autumn evening. Up at Bell House and Wadsworth Banks the signal was read.

Night. He circled Bell House as the hawk circles a freshly cut field, awaiting the opportunity to swoop down upon its prey. He viewed Bell House from all angles until it became first a portentous looming presence and then an abstract thing, a crude shape, and then a ghostly light like the famed will-o'-the-wisps of the fenlands, something unanchored from its heather bed moorings, a Jack-o'-lantern sneering into a darkness so infinite and eternal it seemed as if daylight was a figment of his imagination, an impossibility forever out of reach. He felt first an excitement, and then an emptiness.

William Deighton saw Bell House as a vessel. A mask. A beacon. A torch.

Bell House was a lure, a pit, a cursed place.

A quarry, a foe, an insult. It was his.

Because viewed from afar night after night the solitary orange flame that burned tiny on the horizon had become for William Deighton a symbol for society's undoing. It represented lawlessness. England's downfall. The home of Hartley was a fertile bed for criminality and barbarism. Theft and forgery. Violence and mendacity. It was against progress. It was anti-empire, anti-monarchy, anti-government. No county or country could éver hope to flourish so long as people like Bell House's inhabitants and their many pin-eyed, low-browed, dirty-fingered acolytes continued to ply their illicit trade without redress.

He walked to the house and he rapped on the door and when the door opened onto the night it was David Hartley himself standing there, and he raised one arm up against the door frame and said William Deighton is it and William Deighton said yes it is and David Hartley said thought so and then there was an awkward lingering moment of silence as the two men examined each other at close quarters for the first time.

I suppose you'll be wanting to come in and take a look around then, said David Hartley.

His words – his invitation – threw William Deighton. It unsettled him further. The casualness of his demeanour did not quite match everything he had imagined and expected David Hartley to be. No surprise had registered with the man.

Because David Hartley had known that he was coming. Of that he was certain.

This man they called King was, William Deighton noted, smaller in height too, as if perhaps the distance from which he had only ever previously been viewed had given him stature. It was a strange reversal of perspective. And his own fertile mind had perhaps played its part too, for in the endless hours of plotting and planning and rumination, William Deighton had surely elevated his prey. Inflated him. He was guilty of flattering him with imaginary abnormal attributes and making a myth from a man, just as the valley folk mythologised this gang leader whose behaviour they saw no harm in, so long as there was food on their tables and logs in their log stores.

Yes, said William Deighton. I have a warrant.

You need no warrant here, taxman. Come.

David Hartley turned and William Deighton followed him into Bell House.

As he crossed the threshold he felt as if the house were taking him. Consuming him.

And as he entered, William Deighton felt himself enfolded within its walls and beams, its secrets and its history, as if he were entering a realm whose architecture was comprised entirely of smoke and shadows.

* * *

William Hartley and Isaac Hartley were fastening an iron shutter to the fireplace when David Hartley said brothers this is the taxman that's been out wandering the moors night after night like a lost sheep, and he gestured for William Deighton to step forward. William Hartley and Isaac Hartley looked over their shoulders and then turned back to the fireplace where the younger of the two brothers was turning some screws while the other held the new grate in place.

Will you have ale with us, taxman? said David Hartley and William Deighton shook his head and said no you know it's not an ale I'm after but a look round your abode, and David Hartley said you've been invited so now you're a guest, but I'll take it as an affront if you won't share a pot with me and my brothers here after you've been watching us for all these weeks and even just this night have walked all the way over from Bull Close in Halifax.

To this William Deighton said how is it you know where I live? and David Hartley said you have two eyes but the king has many and they do see everything, and William Deighton said is that a threat? and David Hartley laughed and said you must be the first person to receive the offer of the best ale in Calderdale as a threat.

Just as he had seen in Tom Clayton's vacated place at Stannery End, William Deighton found nothing incriminating in Bell House except the smirking soot-lined faces of the brothers Hartley, and the derisive whistle of the wind around the sharp stone corners of a dwelling that cowered beneath the ceiling of cloud.

Later, when their business was done, William Deighton stepped into the rectangle of dull lamplight that meekly lit across the back flags of Bell House and into the night. He had only taken a few paces when he heard the three splintering crashes of David Hartley breaking a chair down into a heap of kindling.

There are rats amongst us he heard David Hartley say to his brothers. One of them is known as the taxman and that rat must fall but there is another who has not yet shown his face. Fetch them all. Fetch them all. Bring them here, the rats. Tell them their king is calling.

Todaye a boy cum to me in the yard just a sprat of a thin and he says he says to me Are thoo David Hartley the king and I says wor of it and he says who do thoo feer and I says I feer no man never have feered a man and never will And with wyde eyes he says to me they say if thoo cuts King Daevid they say thoo bledes golde and thet thoo drinke moulten lead an eat ginees and sleepe on a duck fetha bed an be fucken all the wimmen and wherein a crown of silver an sittin on a thrown above they kindom An still with wide eyes he says is what they say all troo an I says Nay lad its fucken goose fucken fethas I sleep on an nowt fucken elsel do.

He walked down into the trees in the palest of diminishing light.

It was those earliest hours when the day has claws and still belongs to the creatures of tooth and feather and snout.

Soon he knew the steel soil underfoot would soften, and soon too the sky would wheel away its stars of winter.

Once wolves had inhabited these woods. David Hartley was sure of that. The old tales told of these noble animals sighted padding across clodded fields or circling shrinking copses. Stalking the choking carrs. Skulking in the vales. Bear and lynx too; their bones had been found. Deep in cold dark caves their remnants had lain untouched for centuries. Fireside stories told of the night calls of the wolf ensuring the moor was a place to be avoided; their ghosted howls were still said to be heard now by the fearful and lost.

And still now they spoke of wolves in corner snugs and kept them alive in song and paintings, though it had been three centuries since the last great wild dogs had been hunted off this island. Their skulls had been found. Their corpses flayed and pelts rack-stretched. Claws kept as mementos. Teeth scattered in rituals. Alive only in myth and superstition.

What it must have been to have shared this space with them, thought David Hartley. To see a wolf at day-break with hot breath droplets hanging from its matted snout like ruby jewels.

Alerted to his presence, a squirrel leapt from branch to branch. Another behind it.

David Hartley followed the stream to a hidden hollow where there was a fallen log by a clear pool. He knelt and scooped water into his mouth and then he washed his face, neck and hands. He patted his cheeks and brow. Slicked back his hair. Sat.

He closed his eyes and listened to the sound of Bell Hole awakening. He bathed in the shrill birdsong. He listened to the falling leaves. The crackle of insects unseen. The rustling of life.

155

He thought on William Deighton. He thought on him in this still place as he had always thought on those topics that troubled him. He listened to the sound of the water and the way it sang over the smoothed rocks of flint and grit. The way it danced down through the woods like a child.

In time the day arrived in a crescendo of chatter and warming sun and the problem of William Deighton faded from view until all that remained was a soft orange sensation behind David Hartley's eyes.

But then he was aware that he was not alone. He felt himself watched. Felt a gaze falling upon him.

David Hartley turned and looked to the trees. To the wall of green. He felt another heartbeat nearby. A heartbeat and blood. Hot blood. Close. The pulse of something living.

There was no movement but that of the silent inner workings of whatever it was that lurked there deep in the green cathedral of limbs and timber and branches and leaves that tilted and turned to the lifting breeze. Bell Hole was his domain.

David Hartley looked through the green wall and as he did something stepped out from the unknown within. It was a stag.

It arrived as if an apparition. No sound or movement heralded it – it was simply *there*, proud and curious. Alert. Its ears cocked. Nostrils searching for the scent of him – and finding it: strong and sour. The musk of a man dressed in the dirt of the land.

The stag's eyes were wet dark pools of brackish black water settled in moor hollows. Its young antlers were still in bloom, the bony fuzz set in a base of matted fur and brilliant velvet bone.

Never before had he seen antlers at such close range in day-light – not unless they were attached to a stag skull – scalp-stripped, sun-bleached and mounted on an inn wall for men to hang their hats and crooks from.

He knew that once the whole of old Erringden Moor was a deer park whose boundaries took in all of the old farmsteads.

Cragg Vale. Turvin.

Hollin Hey. Stoodley Clough.

Once it was a wooded, managed manorial place to be hunted all the way down to Mytholmroyd hamlet, where a fosse and a border fence met to create the old palisade. Once there were keepers and lodges and venison aplenty for whoever owned the manor some four or five centuries ago, and nothing but grief and punishment for any peasant that might dare to enter the hunting grounds.

The eyes of man and creature met and David Hartley did not move. He stored his breath in his chest and rationed it. He did not blink. The stag read the language of scent written in the air. It noted the message. It too knew that something was close. It searched the woods with its nose a moment longer and then it dipped, snorted and shook its head. It stepped forward.

David Hartley allowed himself the luxury of movement as his eyes glanced down at the creature's hooves. This tiniest flicker of movement caused the deer to pause again. Sniff at the air again. David Hartley saw that the stag's hooves were strangely small and elegant, two delicately cloven pivot points perfect in both form and function. They allowed traction and gave the stag poise.

He noticed the dewclaws too, small and useless, and so insignificant as to rarely register even in footprints.

Then he blinked and the deer was gone. Like that. Gone. As if lost in a lightning flash.

He walked to the spot where the deer had stood and he crouched. He studied the soil for footprints but he could not see any footprints, so then he got on his hands and his knees and he carefully scoured the dirt and the wet fallen leaves and the wet moss that held the weight of the fallen sky in them, and he looked more closely but still he could not see the mark of the deer. It left no print.

Sike an seede and sod is my song for theese are what the moore is bilton Sike and seede and sod I say Sike to worter the seede the seede that does growe in the sod and a biddy blasd of the suns rayes to bring up the grass whose tussocks russel thur in a shimrinn bundance These are the things of my song And synge them long and lowd and prowd I shooly will.

Aye sike and seede and sod and the sownd of the breese as it blows throo and the sun risin and the sun setten over it orl And some dayes it feels like sike an seede and sod is just eneuyf.

Butt wayte there is sum thayne ells Sum thayne ellls that does tred along the moors edge Yes the Stagmen The Stagman dose feel the sike an seede and sod under foot that is to saye under hoofe and on boggy wet days you can follow his run and you can get downe low and put yore ayes to the grownd and see his markings there See his sunken prins there Freshen wet And they are nyethur foot print or hoof hole but sumthynge in between And thur they sit in sod a messayge from this grayte creachur wich has followed mine for all mines lyfe Wached over me Proteckted me Gyded me Warked with me And still he waches now and so too he will be there when im drug up to that gallis pole that awaytes us Heel be thur I no it Waytin o me.

Heel be thir.

Yet still sumtymes I do feer for mine mind here in the prisum sells of yorke cassel.

Too longe it has bean sinse I warkt or werkt the mooer.

It not be rite to cayge a man so.

158

A man laike me no.

Not rite is that.

No.

It was raining as David Hartley returned to Bell House. It was falling in mist-like swirls; a light, playful rain deceptive in its ability to nevertheless soak to the skin. Soon his trousers stuck to his legs and his leather boots first creaked with damp and then became clodded with clumps of heavy red mud.

As he cut across to the house and avoided the back bogs David Hartley saw the arrival of the men. Men from across the moor. Coiners from all directions. Men up from Mytholmroyd and Cragg Vale old village; men who had taken the back way up Swine Market Lane and past the farm at Stony Royd. Men from over Stannery End and Sowerby Bridge. From Brearley and Boulder Clough.

Men blowing snot from their nostrils, their wet hair pulled back with thick fingers or hanging down in dripping ringlets. Above them a mosaic of crows fell to pieces.

Only those who could receive the message and be up at Bell House in half a day came; those who had got out of the mill or were free from the loom – or those who made enough from the clipped coins to afford the luxury of no longer having to weave a blanket a week or dig drainage runnels or burn charcoal for a living. True Coiners, they came.

The smell of the men filled Bell House. Turned it tight with the funk of the moorland. Sweet and sharp. A tang of leather and mud and smoke and wood.

Dusted in ash and grime, unused old looms dominated the room and the men crowded in there between them, some standing, their heads dipped and shoulders hunched to mind the crooked beams, others squatting with their damp backs against rough stone walls.

You know why I've gathered my best and meanest, said David Hartley when the men had settled down. Because it is clear now that the black devil Deighton is out to ruin us.

Words of recognition ran through the room.

Just last night this man dared to show his face at my door.

He continued:

From this I know two things. Firstly that this exciseman who is content to do the other king's dirty work for little pay does not fear the Cragg Vale Coiners enough. And secondly this interference cannot be allowed to continue.

He's a milksop, said Brian Dempsey.

No, said David Hartley. You are wrong. A milksop he is not. This man shows courage in taking us on. Don't you see that?

But he's not alone, said William Hartley.

No, said David Hartley. Deighton does not work alone.

I heard tell there is a lawman behind him, said Nathan Horsfall. A man of power who has a big house in the new square. A man with friends in that London.

His large frame squeezed into the corner of the room, James Broadbent said nothing. He just watched, nervous by the request for his presence.

And you would be right, Nathan Horsfall, said David Hartley. They call him Robert Parker and it seems half the money in Halifax is not enough for him. No bribes can buy this man, for it is not money that drives him or William Deighton to pursue us, but moral superiority. Do you know what that means, James Broadbent?

James Broadbent looked up.

What?

Moral superiority. Do you know what it means?

The eyes of the room turned to James Broadbent.

No I do not.

It means he thinks he's better than us, said David Hartley. This lawman thinks there is only one king worth recognising. But what does this man do for us and our families? What has he done for this valley but help carve it up and sell it off? What have any of them done? Because it is lawmen and money men like this Robert Parker and flunkies like this William Deighton who serve the wealthy bastards who for years now have staked a claim on these moorlands, these woods, these waterfalls. The same rich pheasant-fattened bastards who'll have us out on our ears when the cotton men come. And they are coming – mark my words. The machines and the mills are coming, but it'll not be enough for them to have us living in hedgerows and ditches like the cursed Diddakoi of the road. No. They won't even let us make a penny to put scran in our cupboards. They care nothing for the people of the valley like we do. Every brogger, every butcher, every milliner, every drayman and landlord that has given up their coin has made it back two-fold. We share our gains with our people because they are *our people*. We do not take our money and build castles to keep them out. We welcome them in for victuals. The young widow forced to scratch a life for herself and her children on two flooded acres of a marshy carr after her husband has fallen face to dirt in the king's name on some distant battlefield does not scratch alone. She has friendly faces at her back door, food to fill her pantry. Her children will never walk barefoot because they are children of the valley just as the purblind toll keeper should not be affrighted that he is going to be diddled by some passing vagabond because this is our valley and those who come and go do so by our rules. This I have proven through my actions, just as was promised this spring or two since.

David Hartley paused to let his words settle.

The men nodded and muttered in agreement.

Robert Parker and William Deighton won't be stopped until they see our wives and children starved and naked, and our bodies swinging on Beacon Hill.

Fuck the lawman and fuck them that try to kill our king, said John Tatham. His vocal declaration roused the men further.

It is true, said Jonas Eastwood. Down in town last week Samuel Duckett refused to give his monthly tithe. And Duckett is as hog-like greedy as they come. He's been got at. Warned. Must have. He is afraid.

I too had a clipped coin refused for ale in town, said James

Stansfield. This landlord would not take my guinea – and in front of people too. So this landlord will be fixed. I'll take his teeth out with my toe cap one of these nights.

And then all the men were talking at once. Their voices overlapped, their words worn and chipped down into vowels uneasy in the mouths of the men like stones. Stones that fell clattering to the stone cottage floor. A cottage on the crest built in a nest of shadows. Shadows that never ceased to stretch. They spoke at once.

I have seen him out there, the bastard William Deighton.

More than once he has watched me go about my business. That man has the eyesight of a hawk.

Clip a coin and fuck the crown.

No chains so strong, no cell so small, no noose so tight to kill us all.

Cross the Coiners and dig your plot.

Valley boys fight and valley boys sing, valley boys fight for none but their king.

Aye. No law but our law.

Above the melee of voices rose one louder than the others. It was that of Absolom Butts, a man usually known for his silence, his expressionless face and cold indifference to the many victims who had felt the force of his fists and feet. Absolom Butts was the man who most in the valley feared above all other Coiners. Very few had resisted his silent persuasions. None had seen him smile.

The moors are ours and the woods are ours, he said. And the marshes are ours and the sky is ours and the fire is ours and the forge is ours. The might is ours and the means are ours and the moulds are ours and the metal is ours and the coins are ours and the crags are ours and this grand life in the dark wet world is ours.

It was more words than most of them had heard him speak at any one time. Encouraged and cheered on by the men, Absolom Butts stood and addressed David Hartley.

King David, he said. You have shown me another way. In this short time you have made me rich in mind and heart.

Go on, our Absolom, shouted a voice. You tell him.

You have saved this valley from starvation in lean seasons. You have given my life purpose where there was none. Any man that wants to bring you down will have to go through me first.

The men cheered.

I would rather die fighting than live long and prosperous on my knees, he solemnly added.

No law but our law, shouted one of the men.

Cross the Coiners and dig your plot, shouted another.

And these mill men with their new machines, continued Absolom Butts, gaining confidence now. I will smash every one of them. And after that I will break every waterwheel, every spindle. I'll fill their foundations with rocks. I'll poison their ponds and burn their horses from fetlock to mane. I'll fuck their womenfolk and fuck them again. This valley is your valley, King David. And I will protect it from the bastard scheming offcumdens.

Again the men cheered and Absolom Butts was slapped on the back as he returned to squatting on the floor.

You are a loyal man, said David Hartley. I know of none better at splitting and breaking bones.

There was laughter at this.

And your loyalty will be tested because as well as this Deighton and Parker there is a greater threat. And it is closer than you know.

My brother is right, said Isaac Hartley, beside him. Too many times the bastard taxman has known our whereabouts. Too many times we have evaded him as closely as the cut-throat avoids the neck vein. But one day soon we will slip up.

Deighton has extra senses, chimed John Wilcox. He has extra eyes and ears, does that one. There is something of the stalking animal about him.

That he does, said David Hartley. And those eyes and ears surely belong to one of us.

One of us? said John Wilcox.

There is a turncoat, said Isaac Hartley. William Deighton has a valley man in his pocket – of that much we are certain.

Then the turncoat will die firstest and slowest, said Absolom Butts. And by my own hand.

The men nodded.

A rat walks amongst us, said David Hartley. One who would rather take the taxman's coin than give it back to his own. One who would sell a soul to the hangman's collection than live as a glorious Turvin Clipper.

Then this bastard will die by midnight, said Brian Dempsey.

Aye, said Absolom Butts. Death will be merciful when we are through with him.

I'll snap his neck like winter kindling, said James Broadbent from the corner.

David Hartley fixed him with a stare and spoke as if to him and him only.

A turncoat will be nothing without a lawman to turn to, he said. It is Deighton who has the power – and Robert Parker more power still. The turncoat is nothing but shit on my shoe. When the power is gone the turncoat will be left alone. We shall smoke him out, even if he sits in this room today. Know this though: William Deighton will be the first to fall.

A man came out of the woods and onto the moor with a pack on his back. Below it a blanket roll contained his tools: a selection of chisels, a bowl gouge, a spindle gouge, a round nose scraper, a skew chisel, a sharpening stone, a drawknife. The handles of an axe, an adze and a coarse saw protruded from one end. A leather strap sat across his chest and his hat was worn askance. He was a bodger.

It was nothing but ill timing that he chose this hour of this day to wander onto Erringden Moor above Cragg Vale. Ill timing and ill fortune. Iller still that as he straightened after catching the breath stolen from his lungs by the arduous incline up to Bell House, his feet slipping once again on the dank carpet of leaves that shifted underfoot like a widow's rug on a polished floor, he should be met by three black forms blocking the sun before him. The shapes of men. Moor men descending.

Absolom Butts. Brian Dempsey. Paul Taylor.

He shielded the heatless sun from his eye and squinted towards them.

Gentleman of the hills, he said breezily. He touched his hat and then took a side-step so as to let the men pass and get a better view of them.

And a fine day it is to view God's country, he added.

When the men said nothing he made to carry on upwards to the moor but Paul Taylor blocked his path.

What's the rush now, stranger?

No rush, gentlemen. No rush at all.

And where is it you are coming from?

Well now – that's a good question.

So flourish it with a answer then.

I'm not so sure there's an easy answer.

Try, said Paul Taylor

I come from here and there and go where the work is, said the bodger.

What work? What business do you have in these hills?

The man pushed his hat back on his head and wiped his brow with the back of his sleeve. Wiped his top lip. Wiped his neck.

Well now, in the summer I wander and offer my skills and services and in the winter I do much the same, only I make sure I'm never more than a half day's walk from a hearth and my good lady wife's warm white body. It's all a man needs on a cold night.

And what about this dead season when the leaves fall and the animals gather their stores and the birds line their nests, said Paul Taylor. What then?

The bodger shrugged.

That depends.

There's nothing up here on these moors for you – or anyone else.

He's a thieving no good tinker is what he is, said Brian Dempsey. He's a cursed gypsy, this one. He'll bring trouble.

The man shook his head. He vehemently protested.

No, he said. No sir. I'm no tinker, sir. No, no. A man of the road, yes. But a tinker I am not.

Well you look like one and you talk like one, said Paul Taylor.

And you smell like one, added Absolom Butts.

Curses in the Romany tongue and the shearing of the heather is not my business, replied the stranger. I'm something far superior than your common tinsmith and rag trader.

What are you then?

The stranger stood proud.

I am a bodger, sir. A bodger and boardwright. Tables and chairs are my main trade. Bowls and baskets too. Building and fixing. Rectifying and remedying.

The men stared back in silence. He cleared his throat.

I'm good with wood, he added.

Where did you apprentice?

Where? Right here in the woodlands of England, lads. Right here amongst the beech and the birch. The hawthorn and the hazel. The whitebeam and the willow. With these hands I can craft just about anything. The trees taught me every lesson I need to know.

And now we're going to teach you one more, said Brian Dempsey. These is the king's woods.

The king? said the bodger.

Aye. King David of the Craggs.

I know nothing of a King David.

Brian Dempsey laughed then Brian Dempsey spat. He spat at the feet of the bodger. Something green, flecked with red.

He says he knows nowt of the king and if he knows nowt of the king then he's not paid his dues to the king.

Everyone has heard of King David Hartley, said Paul Taylor. The man who says he hasn't is a liar. Tell us bodger – why are you really here skulking in these woods?

The stranger looked from one imposing man to the other. Each in turn.

As I said, I'm just passing through, lads. From one place to the next.

And where might that next place be?

Wherever these feet take me. An honest coin for honest work. That's all I'm after.

He mentions coins lads – and honest ones at that, said Paul Taylor.

Is there any other type? said Brian Dempsey.

Now, said Paul Taylor. Who really sent you? Was it the devil Deighton?

He stepped closer to the bodger as he said this. The bodger looked straight at Paul Taylor's Adam's apple, small and hard in his throat now.

He raised his hands in protest.

Lads, he said. I really don't know anything that you speak of.

The bodger turned back to the trees. The bodger turned back to Bell Hole. He made to go back the way he had come.

I think I best be upon my way.

I do believe this one is here to do the dog bastard Deighton's dirty work, said Brian Dempsey, clamping a hand on his shoulder. He's here to bring down the king.

The bodger fell as the fists and clogs came. A hail of them. He was stamped and kicked down into the trees. Down out of sight into the crisp dead leaves. Absolom Butts and Brian Dempsey and Paul Taylor said nothing as they thumped and pounded and worked and grunted and clumped and punched and slugged and sweated. With feet and knuckles. With fists and elbows. Then logs and rocks. The bodger said nothing either for his body soon went limp and his eyelids twitched and his fingers slowly curled in on themselves as if grasping some unseen implement but Absolom Butts and Brian Dempsey and Paul Taylor did not stop. Absolom Butts and Brian Dempsey and Paul Taylor carried on punching the man, an honest man who was good with wood, whose hands were flecked with nicks and splinters, and who had a wife and children relying on him at home.

Down into the trees. In the dirt.

The crisp dead leaves beneath him.

They kicked until the branches closed in overhead, the trees' lissom limbs intertwining to form a latticed ceiling as the men opened the bodger up and broke him down and he blossomed with rising blood that turned to bruising clots, and then his bones became crooked useless things and his face a hot swollen mask, his hair wrenched out in clumps that drifted away in the gentle breeze like the empty husks of insects that had hatched and shed their former selves.

The bodger was put in soil scraped out with fingers and nails. Left there in this ripe bed. Inhumed. The shallowest of lazy graves.

His tools were taken. Coins kept.

The dirt kicked back over.

He was not yet quite dead when he was buried in the Bell Hole soil but the spores and stems of tomorrow's dawn-rising mushrooms welcomed him all the same.

Now see this man I know nowt about Swear down nowt for I am not my brothars keeper nor can I ackownt for the things it is that other lads did or do Killen a man stone dayde is just wrong is that Playne wrong when he is not meddlin or stealin your coin or rustlin your lyfestock or fixen to get you eckseycuted or fucken your wifey behind your back or fucken your wifey and your wifeys sister behind your back and your wifeys back or none of that No if its just a worken man of the countrayside a good Jórvíkshire man just goan about his bisness a man with skills and sweat on his underputs and a wife of his own back home sweepen the harth for him and who knows mebbay there is chillum there too and all he has is the misfortune to come across the worst ones in the coinin gang thems we do call the knucklemen The very worst ones The ones that would slap the teeth out of there own mothers mouth or lock their auld fathers in the cow byre for the night And mebbes they are ecksiteable that perticler day but even if that be so still they only did what they did because they are loyale to ther kinge you see Loyal to the first thing in their godfursaykun lives The first thin they can beleef in and be a part of and the first thin that has put clothes on their back and money in the pockets of ther new fustian wool suits and who knows maybe brought wimmin folk to there door too So you see vishus murderus barberus no good dirty bastids they might be but they only do what they do out of respect and loyalty to the Cragg vale Coiners them fellas what run together in the toughest meanest smartest bestist valley mob the whole wirl ever did see.

But as I say I know nowt about no poor bodger so you best not be askin us any more about it.

An almighty sound split the night, an elemental crack and crash of rock and rubble.

To James Broadbent asleep in his bed it sounded like the gunpowder claps of a worked quarry but he knew no quarryman would be mining in the deep dark witching hours.

Up the hill from his lodgings in Scout Rock wood a great hunk of rock the size of a small outbuilding had peeled away from the jagged cliffs that jutted out above the trees and come tumbling down the slopes. As it fell it smashed and uprooted trees, dragging them in its wake part way down, the splintering echo of their momentum ringing the bell of the three-quarter moon. And then another smaller piece followed, a hundred hands round and as heavy as many dead horses.

Young William Wilcox could not avoid it as he fled stumbling and slipping in the soil of the plateau deep in the centre of the wood where he had hidden the purse of creamed coins that he had been slowly stashing in secret over the past several months. He had been reaching deep into the roots of a tree when the first rock had fallen, and it was as if God himself was smiting him for his transgression with the tumbling of the second one. He had reached deeper still for the purse then, for he was only after two coins to give to his mother to pay for her pease pudding and peat hags. He had pulled it out from the moss and soil and turned and ran, the sound of fear rising up through his throat as God's fearful echo reported back on itself from one valley side to another.

He died in an instant, though not before the fearful shadow of the tumbling rock had grown over and round him, eclipsing everything he had known in his short life as the blackness swallowed him and the cold rock that was as old as anything on earth turned him into a pulped mess of bones and flesh, flattened him between stone and mud, the mashed remains of what was once a hand matted around the bag of stolen golden guineas, whose disappearance, like that of the boy himself, would remain a mystery never to be solved by any man or woman of the valley.

Down the hill James Broadbent sat up in his bed. Several Mytholmroyd residents did. Each waited and listened but there was nothing but the strange silence that comes in the aftermath of movement. It was a silence that was tangible, but when no other noise followed he put it down to his disturbed sleep, and the ale, and the many things that haunted his mind, and then he lay back and closed his eyes.

There was knocking. Bone flesh on stout seasoned bone-dry door.

Fetch that will you, William Deighton said to his wife but then said: wait, no, let me.

He opened it onto a bleary-looking James Broadbent; onto the night.

William Deighton leaned out into Bull Close Lane and when he saw no-one else was out there he said to James Broadbent come in then. He led him into the back kitchen where mugs and plates and knives and forks sat freshly washed and stacked, and the range kicked out some vicious heat that to James Broadbent was welcome.

William Deighton poured him some tea from a pot on the range top and then poured one for himself. He gestured for James Broadbent to sit.

Well?

James Broadbent sipped the tea and then sniffed at it and sipped again. It was not a taste he was familiar with. Hot drinks he rarely took.

You're still after the king?

Of course I am, said William Deighton. You know I am.

You and the other fellow. This Parker one.

Yes. And we have supporters too. We have spoken with magistrates. Men of influence in Bradford. They have vowed their support. The full force of the law is behind us. Now I just need to catch Hartley at it.

So you'll still be needing my help, said James Broadbent through a puzzled scowl.

Your help would surely end this sooner, yes. And you'll have surely heard that three more men sit in chains in York. John Pickles of Wadsworth Law is one. Stephen Marton of Stainland another. James Oldfield of Warley the third.

For what?

You know for what. Being caught with the implements of the trade.

James Broadbent did not look up from his tea.

Does the offer still stand though? he asked.

The offer?

The reward of money, said James Broadbent.

Yes. But you have to fully commit to the right side. The truthful side. Your Martons and Oldfields are all good and well but it is Hartley that will end this. It is he who I want.

The two men fell silent for a moment before James Broadbent spoke.

I have something.

What? What do you have?

Information.

Go on, said William Deighton

There's talk of having you done for, said James Broadbent.

Done for?

Aye.

What do you mean?

There's talk amongst some of the lads of seeing you dead.

What lads?

All the lads.

And how do you know this?

Because I was there to hear it with my own ears.

Where?

At Hartleys. At Bell House.

When was this?

Only a few days back.

William Deighton put down his cup.

And how do they propose to do this. What method?

Method?

Yes. How did they discuss they would kill me?

No way particular, shrugged James Broadbent. They just talked general, like.

Was it Hartley that proposed my killing?

Aye. I think perhaps it was.

Well either it was or it wasn't.

Then it was.

Don't say it was him if it wasn't.

It was, nodded James Broadbent. He called a meeting. Dragged us up there.

How many men were present?

Hard to say.

Try.

Fifteen. Only the best of us.

And he thinks you're one of his best men does he – Hartley I mean?

James Broadbent shrugged.

Must do.

Because I thought that David Hartley said you were as useless as a lame donkey.

He said that?

No, said William Deighton. It's just an assumption.

Because I'd pull the stuffing out of any man with my bare teeth who said that.

Including a passing stranger?

What passing stranger?

They say a man went missing thereabouts, said William Deighton.

What man? asked James Broadbent. Where?

A worker.

A valley man?

No. A travelling man. A man of the woods.

Where?

Between Mytholmroyd and the moor.

That could be a lot of places. The moor is everywhere you go.

He was seen entering Bell Hole.

Travelling men travel, said James Broadbent. It's their nature to be missing.

I think something befell him.

Like what?

William Deighton sipped his tea.

I think he met some men.

What men?

Your men.

I have no men.

You know who I'm driving at, said William Deighton. Fellow clippers. They say he was a bodger out looking for work. A decent fellow. Family minded. Might be that it was round about the time of this meeting that Hartley called.

I know nothing of no bodger, said James Broadbent. And that's the truth of it.

But say there was one.

What of it?

And say he went a-wandering up onto the moor.

It's a free country.

Is it though? wondered William Deighton. Say he crossed some Coiners coming down from Hartleys. And say these men were drunk on the threats of a king suspicious of all-comers. A king talking about killing off me, a man of the crown.

James Broadbent nodded slowly.

It is a possibility.

Then what would you do?

James Broadbent considered this for a moment.

Me? I would question this man. I would ask his family name and what business it was he had being up there where the land

175

meets the sky and strangers do not pass through. I would warn this man.

Just warn him?

Yes. I would warn him with great persuasion. To him I would say this is still the kingdom of the shitneck King David dog-breath Hartley—

I think you would hardly use those words.

I would say what I wanted for I no longer hold my tongue for any man, fake king or real pauper alike.

Go on then, said William Deighton.

Yes, said James Broadbent warming to the subject. I would say this is the kingdom of the bastard King David bastard Hartley and this is no place for a lowly bodger. You'd be minded to watch the bogs that suck you under and the Hartley brothers who will pull the piss from your pecker. I would say watch out for that David Hartley especially, for this man is prone to mad visions and strange reckonings—

William Deighton raised a palm.

Wait. What mad visions?

James Broadbent grinned wolfishly.

Oh yes. They say he sees creatures dancing in his room. They say he does believe that men become animals and animals become men and together they dance like man and wifey in the moonlight. All his life he has talked of these things he sees that no other man does. He is not right in the head, is David Hartley. That's why I'm telling you this: how could I follow the law of a man who sees animals dancing in his bedroom? Such talk will bring trouble to his own door – mark my words. When David Hartley swings the valley will have one less man gone mad with the moorland fever. But for now you must watch your neck Mr. Deighton.

One hundred guineas, said William Deighton. A further one hundred guineas I will give you out of my own pocket if you serve me Hartley.

They'll come after me.

With one hundred guineas you can live well a long way from here, said William Deighton.

James Broadbent stared at his mug. He stared deep into it and at the dregs of leaves clotted in the bottom too, and he nodded. He said: for a further one hundred guineas on top of what is already coming to me I believe I would do most anything.

Wielding a dead hen like a lantern that had been snuffed out, William Hartley strode into the front room of Bell House. He threw it down on the table where his eldest brother was carefully applying a thin film of polish to a pocket watch from a piece of rag wrapped around one finger.

Bad things are afoot, brother.

David Hartley looked at the chicken and then back to his watch.

Look at this time-piece, he said. Who would have imagined owning such a thing? Me, the son of a smelter from the hill tops.

Never mind that and look at this hen.

He glanced at it.

It's dead is that.

I know it's dead, said William Hartley.

They say there is a physician down in that London who advertises he can bring the drowned back to life.

What? said William Hartley.

They say that this physician down that London reckons on bringing the drowned back from the dead by blowing in their mouth. Perhaps you might consider putting your lips to the beak of that cackler and giving it a kiss, my brother.

This is no joking matter, our David.

David Hartley smiled and returned to his watch.

His brother was insistent.

Look at it.

The fox has had it, said David Hartley, his impatience rising. What of it? We need to get the boy to mind the hen hut for a night or two. He's tip-top with that slingshot. I've seen him take moving squirrels from their branches at fifty paces. He'll soon fettle it.

This is the work of no fox.

Well.

There's not a mark on it brother. And they're all like that.

All?

Dead. The chickens. The whole lot of them. Snabbled. That's what I'm saying. And that's not the half of it.

David Hartley set his watch and his waxing rag aside.

He took the bird and held it in his palm. Its neck hung loose. He stroked its feathers and then he parted them. He looked at its feet and eyes. He turned it this way and that. Then he put it down again.

Then we've been struck with ill luck, he said. These chickens have been poxed.

You're not listening, brother. It's not just the chickens. It's all of them.

All of who?

All the animals, said William Hartley. The grunters are dead and the cow is dead. Up top George Wharton's sheep too. They are dead also. They are laid on the moor with their legs pointed to the clouds. Dead they are.

David Hartley pushed his chair back.

Where is that hound of mine? Where is Moidore? This must be his work. Fetch that mutt and I'll give him what for. I'll make a jump rope from his gizzard.

I have not seen the dog. But there are birds too. Birds on the ground. Birds of different varieties. Crows and gulls and spugs. They are dead, as if taken from the sky by your boy's slingshot. Dead birds everywhere. No hound could do that.

How can this be?

William Hartley raised his open palms and shrugged.

It's murrain, he said. We have been stricken brother. That is the only explanation. Bell House and all around us have been stricken by the murrain. It is as if the moor is poisoned and the soil is poisoned and the sky is poisoned. Cursed. All the creatures have fallen over stone dead like this here cackler.

He picked up the chicken.

Burn it, said David Hartley. Burn it now.

William Hartley took the bird and he threw it onto the fire where it turned the flame blue and bristled with the sound of a charred blaze. The fire stripped it of its feathers. It singed them in an instant, then its skin shrank and tightened. Its eyes disappeared. Deep inside it, a fully formed egg cooked and then popped. The hen's burning claws flexed inwards and then soon they too were gone.

David Hartley walked to the window.

What of the stag?

What stag?

Has there been any full-antlered deer found dead up here on these moors?

No brother. None seen.

What about down in the woods?

The lads have not reported seeing any dead deer as yet, said William Hartley. Why do you ask this?

David Hartley touched his jaw. Felt that he needed a shave there. He said nothing.

Also the boy, said William Hartley. He has not been seen either.

What boy? said David Hartley.

Young Wilcox of the woods.

What do you mean not seen?

His mother reports he has been gone for a night or two.

That is not uncommon for a lad of his age. Did we not wander off to spend nights with the owls and fox howls?

That we did, said William Hartley. That we did.

And the fresh air and soil pillows made us strong.

That they did.

179

Because it's good for your bones to know the cold young.

Yes it is.

So are you saying he is to be blamed for all this?

No, said William Hartley. No I am not. I just mean with dead animals and a missing boy perhaps bad luck has befallen us.

Still looking out of the window across Bell Hole woods, David Hartley spoke.

It was the Alchemist, he said quietly.

The Alchemist? said William Hartley. The Alchemist did this? Then I'll murder him for you. I'll bring you his scalp and his teeth and his fingernails for this.

No. There's no call for that. The Alchemist did not bring this murrain about the place – he prophesised it. He saw it in the flames. This plague is a portent.

A portent. Like witchery?

Like a sign of things to come.

David Hartley turned and picked up his watch and held it to his ear then looked at it.

That's what he said to me: *You will wish you had read the signs.* This then must be a sign.

Now you're troubling me, said William Hartley.

And you're right to be troubled. Dead hens is nothing. Birds falling from the sky is nothing. What comes next is what we should be concerned with. It's the two sevens coming is what it is. It's the fall of an empire.

I don't understand.

Neither do I, young blood. But it has been seen in the flames. It has been spoken of. It is beyond even our control.

They sat in the back room of the Sun Inn, a mile or more outside of Bradford, on mismatched chairs and upturned barrels beneath smoked oak beams. The exciseman William Deighton and a man widely known only as Magistrate Leedes. In the corner was a spittoon slick with the sputum of passing men and on the table in front of them sat an ashtray and the abandoned remains of an undercooked spatchcock that they had split and picked at.

This Broadbent, enquired Leedes, not for the first time. Is he trustworthy?

The magistrate looked uncomfortable in his surroundings. He was not a man at ease drinking in a public house where he might encounter those he had sent down. His first ale he had drained in seconds and his second he had made light work of too.

No of course not, said William Deighton. He's as crooked as they come.

So am I expected to sit here all night waiting on a man whose word is worthless?

His word may be worthless and his morals crooked but James Broadbent is driven by something great: greed, Mr. Leedes. Greed is what fuels this man – greed and revenge. The best motivations for a man to do just about anything, I find.

Well that's certainly true in my experience, sniffed Magistrate Leedes. But why isn't your Halifax colleague Robert Parker joining us?

Mr Parker prefers to stay in the shadows.

As do I. As do I. And Broadbent is late.

As I have already explained he has a long way to travel on foot, said William Deighton. Eight miles it is from Halifax and five more before that from his lodgings in Mytholmroyd.

Could he not come by horse or have a companion bring him over by trap?

He has no such friends that I know of.

I thought these forgers were meant to have full pockets yet you say this man comes on foot?

James Broadbent is not a significant man, said William Deighton. His work for the Cragg Vale Coiners is of the dirtiest kind.

Then why do you bring him here?

William Deighton sipped his drink to hide his frustration at the magistrate's impatience and lack of understanding. But before he could reply Magistrate Leedes spoke again.

This man has lost his nerve.

I do believe he will come.

He is close to two hours late.

Though he did not show it, William Deighton was concerned. He stood and went to the door of the inn again. He looked out into the fading day and his spirits rose as he saw two figures ambling up the incline towards him. He recognised the slouched form and ambling gate of James Broadbent and a few paces behind him his father the charcoal burner, Joseph 'Belch' Broadbent. A sorry sight they may have been, but William Deighton felt like rejoicing.

He went out to meet them.

You are late, he said.

That is no way to greet a man, said James Broadbent. You are lucky we are here at all. My father is not a well man and the valley is long and arduous.

Yes, yes, said William Deighton. I have inside with me, as promised, the magistrate. Do you still intend to testify?

Do you still intend to give my boy one hundred guineas?

Joseph Broadbent said this. His voice was a thin, dry rasp.

Yes, said William Deighton. Of course. Now come inside.

After introductions were made and drinks ordered the quartet of the lawman, the exciseman and the two Broadbents retired to a quiet corner of the inn.

Now then, said William Deighton. You just tell the magistrate what it is you told me.

About what? said James Broadbent through a mouthful of broth.

You know what. About David Hartley.

He is a louse.

As he said this broth dribbled down his chin. He wiped it away with the back of his shirt sleeve as Magistrate Leedes,

182

unaccustomed to observing such low company at close quarters, looked on aghast. Beside him his father was wearily hunched over his bowl, his red-rimmed eyes barely open, a hunk of bread dangling into his bowl, food glistening in his wet whiskers.

Tell Mr. Leedes what you have seen him do, said William Deighton.

I have seen him do many things – and none of them good.

Have you seen him forging coins? asked the Magistrate Leedes.

Of course, said James Broadbent. And he's not very good at that neither. Ham-fisted he is, for a man they call the king.

You've seen this on more than one occasion?

Aye. Many times I've seen him.

Tell Mr. Leedes what you saw *exactly*.

James Broadbent folded a piece of bread into his cheek and chewed a moment, then swallowed. He forked a hot buttered potato and lifted it aloft.

I have seen him take guineas and clip them.

Did he say why he was doing that? asked Magistrate Leedes.

Broadbent shrugged.

How do you mean?

Did he express his intentions?

Eh?

He popped the potato into his mouth.

Did he say what he was doing?

It might be he said he would take those guineas and he would strike them, James Broadbent said through his mouthful of food.

Strike them?

Aye. Mill them.

Was anyone else present? asked the magistrate.

Different people at different times. His bastard brothers were usually about.

He means William and Isaac Hartley, interjected William Deighton. Who else?

Oftentimes Thomas Spencer. Tom Clayton too. They're thick that lot. The moor-top boys. They came up together.

Was there anyone else there when Hartley clipped the coins? said William Deighton. We need specific incidents.

James Broadbent spooned more broth.

I do believe James Jagger was there as well.

Jagger? said the Magistrate Leedes.

He's one of Hartley's confidants, said William Deighton as an aside. An odious individual by all accounts.

And you are quite prepared to put this down in writing?

James Broadbent put down his fork. His father looked up from his bowl.

He's not a book learner is James, he croaked.

It was only the second sentence that he had spoken since meeting the magistrate.

I don't understand, said Magistrate Leedes.

And you a man of the education, said James Broadbent as a crooked smile played about his mouth.

I think he means he does not write well, William Deighton said.

He don't write at all, said Joseph Broadbent. Neither do I – and it's never done us no harm either.

Evidently, said William Deighton. Clearly you're thriving.

He and Magistrate Leedes studied the men across the table from them for a moment and then the latter sighed.

Then I shall write it for him, he said.

He reached down beneath the table and brought up a brown leather valise. He opened it up and began removing a congeries of items. A roll of papers. Ink jars. Pens. Nibs. Blotter. A candle stump. A monogrammed sealing stamp.

He took his pipe and carefully tapped it onto the table before packing it with a fresh plug of tobacco, then lit it.

James Broadbent sat back and quietly belched.

My throat is still tight, he said.

William Deighton sighed and then stood.

Two of the same? he asked.

Better make it four, Mr Deighton, said James Broadbent. They say that ale loosens the throat and I do believe that this writing lark does take a man some time and effort.

Oh but I miss my Crag Vayle and the lanes and the woods and the folk what live up there Salt of the earthe folk and sum rite caracturs like Turvin Jim though James Lee was his berth name but we orl called him Gratye Jim The Grass Eater because this man had the belly and appytite of a hog I mean old Turvin Jim could eat throo owt Aside from thirty tankards of ale I've seenum sink over the corse of a day without even seeming drunk Jim The Grass Eater would sumtymes eat a dead sheep or a stillborn calf that had layde in the field from sunup to sundown and even if there were flyes or maggots on it Old Jim wuddent care No Old Turvin Jim would tuck into it raw even with no fyre to cook it on Hens and lambs gone greene as well or a fish thats floaten belly up in the silted ponde he'd think nothing of norrin on it and no sickness was ever cummin Worran appetite that man did have about him A hog he was A real greedy goate.

And what of Henry Wadsworth orlso nowen as Harry O Yems Well Old Harry made his wage by reeleeving weevers and packmen of ther stock as they made ther way over the moor tops from Colne and Marsden and Burnlee for a time Yemmsy was the most feered vagabond since Dicky Turpin and The Long Corsway was his preferred root Yass out past Heptstonstall he'd wayte lingerin in the shadow of a marker stone where thurs nowt but endless nite and boggards and malkins and stagmen for companee and then heed leep out and heed cut their cargo strait off the packhorse backs with a blayde Of corse this was when King David was a sprat for I would never allow such beehayvyor in my valley No that brings much attentshun Forteen year of penal servytude Harry O Yems got Forteen year in a dunjen like this wun in which I sit now the silly bastid A silly bastid for getten himself cort that is.

Wat lads.

Aye good lads of Calderdale and menny more besides orl just tryen to scratch a living from this dank shallow red soil that gives up nowt but trubble and stinken gasses like eggy guffs.

Blisters marked the palm of his hand as the old man clutched at the stirrup and walked as fast as he could without stumbling or breaking into a run that he was certain would kill him.

Beside him the horse's flanks rippled in the snatches of moonlight that found its way through trees that closed in on them on either side, the walls of this dark, knotted corridor appearing to oscillate as they passed through it. But mainly the clouds conspired to keep the moon at bay, and there was only the sound of the reins in William Deighton's hands, the sleek movement of the horse and Joseph Broadbent's breath thin and tight on one side, the steady breathing of his son on the other.

The old man's breath burned and he kept having to hawk up dry clots of phlegm and spit them out, the lung curds appearing silver as they landed on the rough ash, dirt and grit of the packhorse track.

They came back from Bradford over by the farmstead of Shelf and dropped down through wooded vales in the direction of Northowram. Here the trees ended and to their left the land opened out, sweeping away to the south where open pastures were dotted with copses and spiny thicket. They followed a sike through marshlands for a way and the horses struggled, and the old man wheezed. His lungs were on fire; his dry throat spiked with a piercing pain.

Mr. Deighton, he said, but the exciseman did not hear him. He went to speak again but his voice did not come. There was only a rattle in his chest as he gasped and his blistered hand loosened its grip from the leather. He slumped to the ground. The hooves of the departing horse flashed silver. Seeing his father fall James Broadbent tugged on William Deighton's stirrup and said Mr. Deighton, Mr. Deighton, hold up, and only then did the exciseman look down and then back behind him to where the old man lay at the side of the trail like errant cargo. His pale face was drawn, like a skull wrapped in waxed preserving paper. He brought the horse to a standstill and climbed down.

The two men walked to the prone third.

James Broadbent crouched beside his father. William Deighton joined him and offered his flask of water. Joseph Broadbent took it and drank long.

Well what is it, man? said William Deighton.

He's unwell, snapped James Broadbent. Anyone can see that. He's got the fever on him.

We'll soon be back.

Aye – to Halifax. Then it is on to Mytholmroyd that we go. Fifteen or more miles we must have done this evening yet with barely anything in our stomachs.

You should have eaten.

Eaten what? said James Broadbent. Our boots? We've got nothing.

There is ale at my house and food if you want it. You can stop there a while.

It is full rest that my father needs.

Joseph Broadbent nodded in agreement.

Or a ride, he croaked.

A ride?

Aye, said James Broadbent. On your horse.

William Deighton shook his head and clicked his tongue to the roof of his mouth.

This horse belongs to the county of the West Riding, which in turn is funded by the crown itself. This is a king's horse, man. It's not for the likes of you two.

What do you mean by that? said James Broadbent. The likes of us two?

Are you not a member of the Cragg Vale Coiners?

I were, said James Broadbent. You know that and you also know that I'm not anymore, neither. And my father here never was. He burns the charcoal.

But until you have done what it is I have paid you to do you are Coiners, the both of you.

I've given you names.

How do I know you're not still working for Hartley?

Because I said so, snapped James Broadbent. How do I know you're not just some pettifogger who is going to turn me out into the ditch like a tick-bitten dog with the mange? How do I know you're not going to serve me up hog-tied and fire-roasted to David shithouse Hartley and his bleeding brothers?

Because I am a man of my word, said William Deighton. One of the very last by all account.

I am a man of my word too – and mark my word when I say I'll slit the throat of any man that dares to double cross me.

This James Broadbent said with a snarl, his bared teeth bestial in the moonlight.

William Deighton looked at the man crouched across from him, and his father. They were but sorry shapes; two dark blue silhouettes.

Be very careful with those words, forger.

James Broadbent spoke quietly.

These woods are dense and dark, Mr. Deighton.

And the gibbet is strong, Mr. Broadbent.

They are endless.

And you have signed a statement that is already long locked away in a magistrate's chambers have you not?

Between them the old man coughed again.

Listen to him, said James Broadbent. My father is crying cockles. He is not a Coiner.

Saying that twice doesn't make it so. Besides, he spawned one.

He is here for my concern, that is all.

Well then, said William Deighton. We must make haste and get this man to his bed where he needs to be.

By horseback?

By foot, of course.

You would have this man walk the long dark miles rather than let him onto your nag?

To put him on my horse would be against the crown's law that decrees that all horses are only for those in the employ of royal business. I've already told you.

His insides are shot from the charcoaling Mr. Deighton. He is on his last legs. No-one would know.

I would know, said William Deighton. He'll be right. A jug of ale and a good sleep is all this man needs. It's not far now.

The old man looked from his son to William Deighton.

How far mister?

Not far. Only an hour. Two at the most.

Joseph Broadbent coughed and then groaned.

William Deighton turned and walked back to his horse.

I need a pipe, said the old man. Just a couple of toots on a hockle-cutter would see me right. Let me rest a while and have a pipe.

Smoke is not what you need, said William Deighton as he mounted. Think on this instead: imagine what Hartley and his cohorts would say if they saw you two sorry sacks walking through the valley with the dreaded exciseman Deighton on a bright autumn morning. The darkness is your friend. You'd be wise to keep that in mind. The darkness is all that's keeping them from you. The darkness and my knowledge of the best way through it. So let us get moving while the night still favours us.

Raindrops danced around them like diminishing sparks. It spotted across the distant hills in forms that shifted shape – vague apparitions stripping the mottled sky of its stars until rain and night and the scratching of trees around them, and the flexing haunch of the horse upon whom they rested their heads, was all that they knew.

When they finally reached the outskirts of Halifax the old man had to be lifted to the chair by the fire in William

191

Deighton's kitchen by his son. Awoken, Deighton's wife placed the old man's hat back on his head.

They rested and ate and drank and the old man slept and they warmed themselves, and then when the time came James Broadbent helped his father to the door and the cold air that blew in from Bull Close Lane seemed to rouse him for Joseph Broadbent was just about able to stand unaided. He leaned against the doorframe.

At the doorstep his son paused.

It's an ill draught that blows in, said William Deighton.

Aye it is.

The walk and that belly of food will warm you though.

With his back to him, James Broadbent nodded.

Well then, said William Deighton. Be in or out but don't just stand there letting Jack Frost pay us a visit.

The money, said James Broadbent.

What?

I'll be needing them hundred guineas then.

William Deighton shook his head.

I don't keep that sort of money around the house.

James Broadbent turned to him then.

You swore on it.

Indeed I did. Though I believe I swore to deliver one hundred guineas to you from my own pocket for information that leads to the arrest of King David Hartley of the Cragg Vale Coiners.

Well then.

Well then. When he is arrested you will be paid.

This not a fair game that you play Deighton.

And is forgery, corruption, intimidation and violence fair? No it is not. You must wait.

James Broadbent turned to his father.

Do you hear what this so-called man of honour says to me, father – that I must wait for my money?

Joseph Broadbent nodded meekly. He was beyond conversation.

I thank you for your help tonight gentlemen but I would advise you to keep your counsel, said William Deighton, ushering both men out into the street. You'd be wise to remember I have enough on you for capital charges and wiser still to note that if Hartley is not arrested you do not get paid. If he were to hear that you have been collaborating with me, well...

He left the sentence dangling there for a moment.

He is not known for his mercy, now is he? I bid you well.

He shut the door.

For a time the wind was up and it rattled at the stable's shutters but then it dropped and all the night was still. Inside the air was thick with the sweet funk of the horses.

They were never entirely at rest. As one slept another rearranged itself. A third shook its mane for even in October the flies were still gathering around the warm wet fleshy pockets of their eyes, noses and mouths. Horse flies and black flies and stable flies. Some laid their eggs in open sores and others feasted on equine blood. The cold of winter would kill them off but for now they circulated, then settled, then circulated again, locked in a perpetual cycle of irritation for their hosts.

There was the sound of a metal shoe on stone and the slow rustle of the chewing of tufts of hay pulled in greedy clumps from broad summer bales, then the fleshy snort of a sleeping horse deep in a dream of galloping across open meadows, its memory reaching back to somewhere deep as it ran with the herd, thundering through woodlands as around it other horses fell into its stride, their hooves tearing up the soil, the boles of coppiced trees flashing by as if moving around them, and then suddenly bursting as one into a stubbin to rest and breathe and drink water as the sun played upon their steaming necks. It was a dream of experience and sinew intertwined, memories held in muscle. The solid core of something that stretched through thousands of centuries.

In the bluest part of night a slit of light grew broad for a moment and then narrowed again. Expanded and contracted. There were footsteps on the byre stone. There were hushed voices too, then the sound of a candle being lit and the faces of two men caught at the very limit of the flame's reach. They moved the candle around and saw the creatures in their stalls – some were sitting with legs tucked under, others still standing. The light framed the large eye of one horse and its black pupil grew larger still and fearful in the glare of the dancing flame. The men moved on to the next stall. One nodded to the other. He gestured with his chin to the standing horse, whose hide appeared russet coloured in the gloomy elastic night.

That one, he whispered.

The other looked. Blinked. His hot breath hanging in the cold night.

Are you sure?

I know those markings. That horse is yon devil Deighton's.

He raised the candle and ran it around the outline of the horse, tracing its form. He spoke with eyes. His eyes said: go on then.

From his coat his companion pulled out a large pair of cloth shears, their handles worn smooth with years of use, the forged blades blackened by dirt and time. He stepped forward and took the horse's tail but his friend hissed no – not there, higher up, you bloody doylem.

The man raised the scissors; he moved them right up to where the tail met the horse's haunch and holding it there with one hand he hacked through the bunched hair. It was tougher than he thought so he hacked some more. When it did not give and the horse went to rear he paused a moment and then he moved the scissors further down and cut again and this time the thick hairs came away in strands. The horse stirred again and looked back over its shoulder, but it did not buck. Instead it repositioned its feet and looked on with mute indifference.

These shears—

Just get on with it.

He finally stepped away with the tail in hand and held it there before him as if it were a trophy: a legendary pike perhaps, or a leveret freed from a snare or a trapped fox ready to be tossed to a pack of baying terriers. He held it up to the candle and the light showed that the tail hairs were earthy brown in colour, running down to black where they fanned out at the tip. A ragged oversized hedgehog of hair remained on the horse's rump.

Tie it, said the one holding the candle and his friend said what?

Tie it at the top end, he said again.

The man looped the tail. He encircled his fist with it.

He tied it round. Knotted the end.

Held it there again. Aloft. A trophy.

Deighton, he said.

That bastard, said the other.

I'll nail it to his front door.

Aye. Just as was ordered. His scalp will be next.

In the dead of night the wind spun down the tight corridor of the hidden valley-within-a-valley that was Cragg Vale. It sprinted in across the open moors of Blackstone Edge and it screamed and shrieked when it found itself trapped between the steep sides of the shadowed vale that drew it deeper into the cleft of land.

Down through Turvin Clough it blew, and it whipped the waters of Elphin Brook into a fuming white foam then rose to the place where several houses huddled close together by a bridge and a marsh to form a hamlet. It pelted the black face of Cragg Hall with leaves and grit and shale. Rained down upon it. It shifted stones across the packhorse route and even flattened some headstones that marked the beds of the dead in the tiny cemetery. It blew metal buckets in noisy half circles. It tore rushes from the marshy grove and sent scarecrows on the seeded plots skywards, their matted straw stuffing spiralling from the collars and cuffs of old wool coats. It opened gates and then snapped them shut and took anything that was not tethered off into the darkness of the surrounding woods, where branches collected clothes and sacking and string and ribbons, and boots that had been left drying upturned on metal scrapers in stone porches.

Then just when the wind seemed as if it couldn't get any louder the valley shaped the gust into a whistling twister; turned it into a spinning top that ate up the trees that grew densely packed in the narrow coppiced part of this fecund gulch above the village. It took trunks that had grown seventy and eighty years thick and pulled them up like carrots. It yanked tangled roots that had dug seventy or eighty feet deep into soil and tore them out in screaming wrenches. Roots that held amongst them boulders and warrens and setts and dens dug over generations by rabbits and badgers and foxes were now suddenly exposed to a whirlwind that sounded to them as if their very world was ending. Riven like rusted nails from warped wood, four dozen trees were snapped and felled in seconds. Others were split as if stricken by unseen axes that fell from the sky, and then they were upended so that they became distorted images of themselves, their roots now reaching skywards like arthritic fingers.

The storm howled once more and then it was over.

The spinning streak of violent wind had spun itself out, exhausted its dark centre into a nothingness, after which there followed only the creaking of timber and the shifting sound of small runs of mud sliding down the reshaped inclines before they slipped plopping into the stream that was now dammed in several places with the snarled entanglements of branches pressed down into the shallow waters by the weight of the thick trunks rent asunder above them.

The water swelled and by morning it was lapping over the banks and pooling in the lower clefts and channels of the newly cleared leys that had opened up in woods that were once dense, but which now had greatly diminished overnight.

The roosting birds had already left a land they no longer recognised. Great gaps had opened up and what was once a maze of looming wooden columns that obscured any view from one side of the gully to the other was now a place of new spaces and chaotic uneven ground pitted with fresh holes that gaped like open mouths. A wrecked place. A ruined cathedral.

Then finally there was silence. A solemn, still silence.

At the Red Lion. In the barn out the back. The flat black back patch beyond the single street lamp's reach – beyond the watching eyes of anyone who might chance to pass by.

Here the sharp sting of several types of smoke scented the air: the burned leaves of a bonfire, the greasy oil smoke of the hanging lanterns and the narrow plumes from clay pipes that clicked against black and broken teeth.

There was the stiff wet smoke too, ingrained in the wool and leather that the men appeared to wear as a second skin. And cutting through it all the pungent stench of chicken dung from the Red Lion's own prizefighting bantams that were stuffed into their cells in a giant coop out the back, where they were kept mean and hungry.

In the centre sat a makeshift pit. Nothing more than a dug hole, circular, with three steps leading down into it and a sagging rope cordon to keep the men at bay. Only the landlord Piggy Ratchard and his boys – his setter-ons – were allowed down there to fix the spurs and remove the hoods and pick up the lifeless pecked carcasses of the weaker birds.

The pit edge was lined three-deep with men jostling to get a view as the hens were lifted aloft and odds were called.

There were sixteen cocks in the Welch Main contest, and the last one standing was to be declared the winner. It cost two guineas just to be there and much more to wager on a fight. Coins were being buffed and passed and checked and tossed.

197

Pressed into palms in the half-darkness. Clipped coins and true coins, and the faces of the men that took them were halved and quartered by the falling shadow angles of the inn's sharp corners.

There were familiar faces. Tom Clayton and John Tatham. The boy Jack Bentley. William Hailey and Joe Shay. Eli Hoyle. Eli Hill. William Hartley and William Hartley, the elder and younger. Isaac Hartley and David Hartley. James Jagger. Others. Their arms draped around one another, their pint pots slopping. Coins being flipped. A song on their tongues.

It was a time of plenty and together they faced an incoming winter without the usual ache of wanting; this winter there would be logs and ale and meat and oats and coins left over for those rarest of things: luxuries.

One of Piggy Ratchard's setters lifted a bantam aloft and turned in a circle. It was a meagre-looking bird, and already scrap-scarred. More than once it had been bathed in Ratchard's own piss, a practice he believed speeded the healing of the injured. Another was to suck the blood from a cock's head wounds. This would not be this bird's first fight but the odds being called suggested it would more than likely be its last. Another of Ratchard's setters climbed down into the pit and paraded the opponent, making sure to keep its spiked spurs folded away beneath it. The two were then presented at close quarters, eye to eye.

At the back of the crowd Isaac Hartley rested one elbow on his brother's shoulder and said to him: the river runs thick with gold still, my brother. It seems good fortune continues to shine down upon us.

In the pit, in a flurry of feathers, the frantic cocks were released and immediately tore into a clinch, spurred feet first, their heads drawn back.

Fortune or luck has little to do with it, said David Hartley.

Well then. It is good to enjoy the fruits of our endeavours nonetheless.

Isaac Hartley raised his drink and took a long swig. David Hartley said nothing. Around the pit the men jeered as the game birds reared and pecked then reared again. Beer swilled from their tankards onto the dirt floor. The two cocks became one rolling ball of tangled wings and falling feathers and the men cheered them on.

The brothers watched a while before the younger spoke.

They say they fixed the exciseman, the black devil Deighton, said Isaac Hartley.

David Hartley turned to him.

Who did?

A couple of the boys.

Fixed him how?

Just a little frightening.

A little frightening?

I don't know. I believe they did tamper with his prize horse.

David Hartley shook his head and looked away in disgust.

To tamper with a horse is the act of cowards.

They didn't kill it, brother.

Then what?

They sent the bastard a message. That's all.

And this message said—?

Isaac Hartley looked at David Hartley in confusion.

I don't understand.

I'll tell you what this message said. It said: we are cowardly men who would rather harm the horse that carries a man across the moors in innocence than meet the man himself. It said: come and get us, for we are nothing but yahoos full of wind and piss. It said the coining lads of Cragg Vale are nothing but hackums and hectors. Bouncers and merry-begotten bastards ourselves. Dung-dwellers and needy-mizzlers. Laming or branding or mutilating his horse will not deter that black devil William Deighton. It will only fuel his ire. Think on, man.

Brother, you need more ale in you, said Isaac Hartley. You have the look and words of one who has the gallows in his eyes.

I have seen signs.

What signs?

Omens and portents, Isaac.

Isaac Hartley grinned a crooked smile. In the pit one of the bantams had pinned the other to the ground and was pecking furiously at its neck. Around them the men were shouting it on. Tiny flecks of blood dotted the dirt.

Omen and portents brother?

Yes, said David Hartley. Omen and portents – like birds flying backwards and swans born with two necks. Signs of bad things afoot.

This is the talk of old crones and hedgerow-hoppers, David.

Are you denying all those dead animals, brother?

Isaac Hartley considered his answer.

No, he said. No, I do not. That was something I cannot yet explain.

And the storm that split the trees but two nights ago?

That is just nature's way.

David Hartley shook his head.

That evil wind only blew upon the village of Cragg Vale; the vale whose name we Coiners carry. It didn't even reach us up top on the moor. It passed right on by below, not but three hundred paces away. That was no mere hand of nature. That was a message from darker forces; a warning sent to us Hartleys. Yet still you talk of good luck and fortune and rivers running gold.

Are we not lucky not to have had Bell House blown away?

It was a sign I tell you, said David Hartley. They say a tinker went missing too.

He was no tinker.

Then you know about him?

It's just rumour, David. You need not worry about that. Are our pockets not full?

At what cost though?

Isaac Hartley shrugged.

The people of the valley are fed and clothed and understanding happiness for the first time, he said. We all are. The land is ours.

The land is not ours, said David Hartley. Changes are afoot.

What changes?

Great changes. It starts with traitors amongst us.

I've had one beady eye on the Alchemist for some time now, said Isaac Hartley. Perhaps it is he who is responsible for the animals. Shall I fix him, brother?

And then what?

Isaac Hartley pointed to another barn whose sides were quietly thudding with the movement of the three dozen creatures from whom Piggy Ratchard earned his name.

And then feed him to Ratchard's guffies over there.

David Hartley shook his head.

Killing him will bring more trouble. And anyway who will clip then? This magic man is a master of metallurgy.

Isaac Hartley shrugged.

We were clipping before that man was brought on.

And look at the coins we made, said David Hartley. Crooked crowns and dirty guineas refused by half the traders in Jórvíkshire. Shit bits.

But we have those people on our side now. Our might is known. Fear has worked its wonder.

No, said David Hartley. The Alchemist is a man of magic with the metal and fire. So long as the coins keep coming in he is needed. After that – well. But it is not he who brings trouble to our door. I believe there are other forces at work. I'm thinking now perhaps it is time to cease.

Isaac Hartley looked at his brother, aghast.

Stop our clipping?

David Hartley nodded.

The two brothers looked around at the other men swaying and jostling, some of them smiling and singing, others sullen, but all with money in their pockets and meat in their stomachs. They saw their other brother William and their father too, smiling with the warm glaze of liquor in their eyes.

Look at the old man, said Isaac Hartley. At death's door from starvation but two winters back but now given a stay from Old Nick himself. You did that, our David. You've made the Hartley name great. But now you talk about giving that up just as we're getting started?

David Hartley nodded.

Kings don't give up, said Isaac Hartley. Kings get dragged off their throne. They get beheaded or overthrown but they never walk away from their duty.

David Hartley turned to his brother.

What fucking duty? he said in a low tone.

Your duty to this rabble, said Isaac Hartley. And the rest of them. They fucking love you. Without you—

Without me what?

Without you I'm certain this valley will fall fallow. The coining will die off and the men will lose their will to fight because no man will go back to the loom after having the taste of gold on his tongue. And these others you speak of with their plans and their mills and their giant spinning machines, and their weaving machines and their fucking water wheels and their canal boats, they will be the death of all of us. They say they can spin a hundred unbroken yards of yarn in them factories, David. I heard tell of it. I heard that in the Black Country there are already mills the size of cathedrals. Is that right?

I saw one with my own eyes, said David Hartley. Water does the work of a hundred men and it's a mile of unbroken yarn they can spin if they desire it.

Isaac Hartley shook his head.

No good can come of it. These buildings will not last, brother. We'll make sure of that. We'll burn them to cinders.

David Hartley stopped him.

It is too late, he said. Know this: we will not recognise this valley ten years hence. We will not recognise it and there will be no place for the likes of our lot.

But this valley is our valley, said Isaac Hartley. You've said the words enough yourself to the boys. They've sung it in song. A song to ring down the ages. The land is ours and the sky is ours and the moor is ours—

But David Hartley had already turned and walked away. He pushed through the men around the cockpit where one of Piggy Ratchard's setters on was holding a broken ruffled flaccid thing aloft, its eyes gone, beak shattered, its dimpled skin as white as the moon that lit the path that he walked upon, and behind him the men cheered and then cheered again.

It began to rain.

Yes yes I remember the night at Piggee Ratchids well as that nite the moone appeert as if it were a hole in the sky throo witch feerless moths did fly Cold it was too and the cocks kept coming and that pit it did begin to fill with the blood of them what looked black in the moonlite Black as pitch beneath the lanterns old Pigghe had strung from strings out the back of that fine hostillry he keeps that they do call the Red Lione And what it is I wud give now to have just wan or a cupple of jugs of that ayle he serves there Aye Piggy's foamin ayle would set me just rite in the cole darkness of this stone toom they've gorrus in.

Becors here in Yorke assises they do give us naut but pewtreyde water that maykes you weeke as a citten if you tayke it and they saye the fud they give you in the shotbox was allso yoosed to bild the jale itsel They says this stickee shyte is what holds the briccs together and thats eesy to beleeve becors when I squat to scwees one out mornentimes often it is like passen a brick A big thic brick And other times it is like the Rivver Calder itsel is flowern out me erse anin that momunt I says to mysel I says sweet jeesus what a life yoov made for yersel King Daevid What a bleeden life sitting here in your stink with naut but wet straw forra bed and these big fuken nite rats chewing the dead skin off the soles of your sweet stinken feet when yer sleep and nothing to do but rite this memwar for my chillen to reed with pride if they learnit to.

But that nite at the cockpit I had a bad feelun Corl it premmynishun call it omens and potents call it a sense of superstisheen but I do beleev the stagmen was sent to guide us and to warn us and the stagmen that nite they was sayan to us gerrowt Kinge Divaid get out wiile you can They was saying do the peeple not love you for all that you have done for them and will they not sing your praysus up to the heavens for feeden them and clothen them and making the valley a place of plenty even for

just a few short seesuns and fertharmore have you not showern
them a new way and just becors the big men with the big plans
is comern over the horisum with all this talk of takern down the
looms and bildin mills and diggin canals and increasing the cloth
trade a hunnered fold doesunt mean the valley folk have to go
back to sucken stones and mashen oats and eaten docks Heck
no They say this is Gods cuntree so why not live like a God then.

No becors what you did King Dayvid says these voyses that I
did heer was you showed that no man need live to the lors of
another man just becors that other man has welth and whiskers
and land and an educayshun No you have shown that valley folk
belong in the valley becors the valley is thers and the moors is
theres and orl of it is thers and yours too It is in you And Grayce
has your hart and Bell House has your hart an the sky has your
hart an the mooers have your hart and the crags have your hart
and the hetha an the mud and the rain an the milstoene grit an
the spelter stamp an the spyder web an the incummin clowd an
the cawing crow an the mooing cow an the fox an the hawke an
the sow and the priyze winnen bantam an all of it The hole big
Yorkshyre lot of it has your hart becors when you come from a
place you want to stay in a place And you are a place You make
it and it makes you.

But did I lissen to them werds of the Stagmen did I buggeree
Cors if I had I wudna be sat here riten these thorts these peoms
these lassed werds offa grayte man aye but a desprut man to.

He left Bull Close Lane. He strode down Cheapside into Halifax. William Deighton walked briskly towards the centre of it. To George Street. To George Square.

To the guts of the town.

He passed clusters of people. Some singing, others vomiting. He saw a woman squatting in an alley, her skirts hitched, dark piss trickling and steaming in the October night and when he stopped and looked she laughed and pointed as if it were he, a family man in employment and of good standing, who was without shame or dignity.

He turned into Southgate. Here the street narrowed and the sky was blocked out by the shapes of buildings on either side. No stars. Around the back way he went. Into Old Cock Yard. Narrower still. He walked towards the inn on the corner after which the dead-ended street was named. Two hundred years it had stood and two entrances it had, one on the corner with a painted gallows sign swinging on chains above it, and a side entrance. William Deighton knew its history – how the Cock had belonged to the wealthy Saville family and had once housed them, but now was a hostelry that played host to crooks and forgers.

William Deighton walked on. Once more round he went. Round the block. Once more for luck; for security. Once more to check the doorways and alleys for eyeballs, for the shadow forms of the watching.

Then he walked back into Old Cock Yard and he pushed open the street door and he entered the inn.

In the hallway Robert Parker was waiting. He nodded to William Deighton then he tipped his head towards the tap room. William Deighton looked through the glass of the door and saw that it was deep with the bodies of men in coats and shirt sleeves, crowded into the space with their drinks in hand. Fine blue ribbons peeled away from their pipes to join a canopy of smoke that hung above them.

The light from the oil lamps was low, but nevertheless through the room he could see seated sideways at a table in the corner one David Hartley. He was surrounded by men. His men. Seven or eight of them, all clippers, raucous in the drink, their hats discarded and some with their shirts unbuttoned. In their centre David Hartley held court.

William Deighton stepped back into the hallway as two men entered the inn from the same street door. When they saw him they discreetly touched their fingers to their forelocks. Arkle and Baker. They were both burly men. They filled their clothes and their eyes were black beneath furrowed brows. Both bailiffs had been brought over from Huddersfield, hired for no reason but their bulk and availability. To meet muscle with muscle.

William Deighton introduced them to Robert Parker. The men appeared wary and then one of them spoke. Baker.

Two hours or more Hartley has been here, he said in a voice that was surprisingly high for such a squarely built man. We saw him come in ourselves.

He is well on his way, said Arkle. I would not like to interrupt his flow.

That is the last ale King David Hartley of Cragg Vale will drink, said William Deighton.

Beside him Robert Parker solemnly nodded. The bailiffs said nothing but both the exciseman and the solicitor noticed that neither of them could stand still. They fidgeted. They shifted. They appeared as if they were coming undone.

Are you men frit? asked William Deighton.

The bailiffs looked at one another but said nothing.

Come on – speak upon me. Are you scared?

Hartley is with many friends, said Baker.

We'll get him out of here before they know what is happening, just as we discussed, said William Deighton. Him and James Jagger.

James Jagger is not here, said Arkle.

Not here?

He is in the Cross Pipes.

What is he doing there?

The same as he would be doing here. Drinking until his skin can hold no more I would say.

William Deighton shook his head.

Then we will have to move twice as quick lest Jagger hears about Hartley's arrest and makes a run for it. Silver Street is but a minute's sprint from here. We can hit both.

Perhaps we should reconsider, said Robert Parker. Try another night.

No, said William Deighton. It has to be now. It must be this day. Even just being here we will have been seen. Broadbent's testimony will send Jagger to the gibbet. We cannot let him abscond. If he takes to the hills we may never see him again. We must take Hartley tonight. First him, then Jagger.

The four men looked at each other and nodded in agreement.

You will accompany me, said William Deighton to Baker, and then to Arkle he said: and you watch the street entrance as planned. No-one is to enter or leave. Mr. Parker, perhaps you might now want to retire for the evening? For your safety of course.

We'll all be safer when Hartley is in shackles. Not likely Mr. Deighton.

The Cock is a rough house, Mr. Parker. The Coiners will know your face.

As well they should. I'll stay until this business is done.

William Deighton capitulated.

Very well, he said. With God as our witness let us bring the king of the Coiners in.

The hand fell on the shoulder of David Hartley and fingers curled around cloth once woven by his own wife and cut to shape by the best tailor that the town had to offer. The hand clasped and pulled and dragged David Hartley to his feet, his tankard of ale sloshing across his hand and wrist, soaking his unbuttoned cuff. He turned to swing a fist but the bailiff Baker came around the side to clasp his arm and twist it, drawing it up his spine. David Hartley's chair fell backwards and drinks wobbled and slopped on the table as he flailed in the grip of Deighton and Baker. The other men – his men – did not move; they were frozen in the moment.

Only then did David Hartley see it was the exciseman William Deighton who had him. He struggled in what space there was but the bailiff was pressed up too close – so close that he didn't see the irons as they were snapped onto his wrists.

David Hartley looked to his men to see who would strike either his captor or the burly bailiff whose hot breath he felt on his neck.

But still his men were unmoving, torn between fate and consequence. They stood suddenly sober, caught between the passing seconds and a future that they saw suddenly unravelling before them like unspooling yarn. A future of patina-patterned coins turning green in the hidden troughs of fallow fields; of long winter weeks living on nothing but kale broth and chicken bones; of rope and chain; of forgotten pouches tucked into tree roots and tools turned blunt by the seasons; of crumbling cottages and rotting fruit; of sobbing wives and starving children; of farmsteads waterlogged and moss-covered and tumbling; of twisting creaking rope and desperate legs thrashing.

This is what David Hartley saw in the eyes of these men he had grown up with – the closest of whom he knew as well as any man might. Hunched men, scowling men. Mean-eyed men, muscular men, lean men. Men who appeared as if risen from the soil. Tommy Spencer and Wild Willy Clayton. Big John Wilcox and Absolom Butts. Jonas Eastwood.

None moved as they saw before them the ending of something, the collapse of an empire of dirt and clipped metal. They saw the falling of the good times, the death of the era of plenty and the dearth of abundance and freedom.

None moved and David Hartley's struggles ended with a final shirk of one shoulder. The unflinching hands that held him there were the ultimate humiliation.

Deep from his throat he summoned phlegm and spat it to the floor, to the feet of the men whose pockets he had lined. Then John Wilcox turned and pushed his way through the crowd of the other drinkers beyond their immediate circle, who had slowly fallen into silence as one by one they realised who it was that was being arrested. Thomas Spencer put down his drink, picked up his coat and followed him. William Clayton was next. Other men – men on upturned barrels, men warming themselves by the popping fire or leaning on the bar – stood and left too.

William Deighton nodded to the bailiff and then with fingers curled around his biceps they led David Hartley through a corridor of bodies that had appeared in the packed tap room and out along the hallway, where Robert Parker watched as the king of the Coiners was taken out into the square where people were already gathering in a throng of whispers.

Not a single word had been spoken except that which now came from David Hartley himself, hissed with venom through crooked teeth clenched shut as a cloud crossed the autumn moon and a despondent mizzling rain fell, and the night decided that rain was not enough for such an occasion, and it turned the raindrops into a hail shower, the first of the season.

Bastards.

He did not sleep. Instead he sat shivering in wet clothes on the cold stone floor of the small square lock-up by the side of the Duke of Leeds Inn. Outside was a pick-up point for the stagecoaches, and periodically through the night there was the scrape and clatter of wheels and hooves on the cobbles, followed by low murmured voices tired from long rides, and the sweet stench of horse scat and wet hides hanging heavy, tumaceous and steaming close by.

In the early hours the door was unlocked by the landlord of the Duke and the bailiffs Arkle and Baker brought another man in. The door was closed behind him. He was just a shape in the dark. The shape had a voice, dry and cracked. The damp walls held it and flattened it. Muted it.

Now then, King David.

Is that you James Jagger?

It is me.

A pause. The two men looked for each other in the near darkness.

They strong-armed you then? said David Hartley.

Aye, said James Jagger. Dipping my bill alone in the Cross Pipes, I was. They had a written warrant. It was that bastard William Deighton. Clipping and defacing the king's coin he is claiming, to which I said there is only one king I follow and that is King David Hartley of Bell House, Cragg Vale, Erringden Moor, Upper Calder fucking Valley, Yorkshire cunting England. That's what I told him. Thems the very words I used.

And then what happened?

I gave these two big bastards who were with him a clump each and they gave me a dozen more in reply. Bailiffs I reckoned them to be. Blow-ins from Huddersfield. And now a tooth is loose and I think some ribs are cracked. Listen to me wheeze, brother.

David Hartley spoke quietly.

Not one man stepped in when they arrested me.

Not one?

Not one. Between the best of us we could have buried the devil Deighton in the soil by sun-up, and his burly bastard blow-in bailiffs by his side too, and the silence of the inn would have been ours, there's no doubt about that, the town and the valley is on our side, but instead they froze like ice shoggles. They just stood and stared. Gloared at the lawman. They shit it.

David Hartley felt James Jagger move closer and then sit beside him on the cell floor.

Maybe they have a plan.

What plan?

A plan to get us out of here.

There's no fucking plan, said David Hartley. It's me that does all the planning round here. Without me they'll neither be able to lace their boots nor wipe their yellow cowardly backpipes.

They fell quiet for a moment.

What'll become of us? Will they let us out tomorrow?

David Hartley said nothing.

Another long silence followed. The street was empty now, and the inn was shut and no stage coaches had stopped to alight.

I said what will happen to us, King David?

I heard what you said.

What do we do?

We keep our mouths shut.

But they know what we've done, said James Jagger.

They know nothing. They can prove nothing. There's neither of us been caught at the clipping red-handed.

They say a man would hang for forging coins.

David Hartley spoke quietly again.

How many men do you know who have clipped a guinea, James Jagger?

Many. Scores I would say.

Scores in the Upper Calder Valley alone.

Yes.

And how many have swung for it?

None.

Well then. That is what is going to happen.

What?

Nothing.

Nothing, King David?

Nothing. You keep your mouth shut and your teeth clenched, and best keep your fists curled and ready for whatever them bastards bring to us for breakfast because you can be sure it won't be eggs and ham hock. These bastards are out for us but no one keeps this king down. We'll get out fighting if need be. Just bide your time, Jagger. Bide your time.

To the darkness David Hartley said this, and his voice was so calm and steady he almost believed it himself.

At nite now I taykes to singin sum of the old songs The songs that the boys did synge an some they rote themselves Songs they say is good for the mood and I reckon that to be true enuyff because weed always singed when weed worked our fingas to the bone clipping a goode haul Singen too before that when farmen or loomin or bildin and the man had given us good coyne honest coyne then weed filled our skin with ale and slakund ower tungs and be feelin like all ower trubbles had been drowned like rats to the ayle barrel That was wen weed tayke to singing the old songs Aye songs like Sing one sing orl Coiners tayke your hole and steal your sorl or maybe King Daevid king Daevid he is the graytest king that ever warked the earth or maybe weed sing summat like Clip a coyn and fuck the crowne if a lawman comes knocken choppum down.

Or maybe even a vers of Valley boys clip an valley boys sin Valley boys kneel to none but ther Kinge.

Good songs old songs new songs Songs that tell the tayle of me and mine So at nite now I sing them lowd an prowd an that's when the men start showting at us to turn it in Turn it in they says Turn it in you bellowing thundercunt But I jest larfs at this an I gets to singin even lowder and make sure I waken all the silly sossidges soes that I'm sure they orl no about King David because I do this nite after nite Aye nite after nite for weeks on end I sing my good songs and now ther all bangin and moanin but none of them says wat it is theyll do to us if I don't stop my singin becors they knows I is King Daevid of the Crags and to mayke a threat against King Daevid of the crags you mite as well take that hemp rope an not that hemp rope an sling it over the gibbet yersel becors to do that wud be to lose an eye or your tung or wark only on broken bones for ever more or maybe even greet death himsellf Jussed as the cundemt man nose his fayte.

An so I showts out I shout Get a wash yer blacc Lancastreen bastuds becors even tho the most of them is Jórvíkshire men lyke myself its the bestst way to get theyr blud and piss boilin by corlin them black Lancayshite bastids like that and so on and on I sings on with my good song I sings Valley boys clip an valley boys singe and Valley boys bow to none but ther King over and over and sure enuff in time I do beleef my mood now begins to lift just as I thort it would An my hart too it swells beneath my ribs so strong Rite good it is Rite bluddy good.

Away from the eyes of the valley the brothers William Hartley and Isaac Hartley met deep in Bell Hole. They walked down through bosk and spinney to a clearing by the stream. They took circuitous routes, made sure they were unseen. It was a place of their childhood. A place of conspiracy.

Here the water ran down through small falls and spouts and levels. Often when it rained for days the stream flooded the surrounding lea and turned it into a thick dark mire.

They have our brother, said William Hartley, the younger of the pair.

Yes, replied his sibling. But not for long.

Not for long?

No. I don't believe they can hold him, said Isaac Hartley. He'll be out from Halifax gaol by nightfall.

But he is not in Halifax,

Not in Halifax? Where then?

They have already moved him to York Castle. Have you not heard? They say there is a testimony.

What testimony?

That one belonging to the cursed black devil Deighton, said William Hartley. They say he already has a signed testimony that is enough to have our David committed for trial at the assizes. It is a witness statement.

Who would go against the Coiners and bear witness to this lawman? There is no-one in the valley who would have the hide to cross us.

Do not be so sure, brother. I believe someone has turned – just as David predicted.

One of our own?

Perhaps.

But who?

Someone who has seen enough to spill his guts, said William Hartley.

But why would they do this?

William Hartley walked to the stream. He crouched and scooped cold water into his mouth. He looked for fish – a habit of a lifetime – but there were none. This stream ran straight from the moor; none had ever made it this far up.

Choose a reason. Spite or jealousy. Perhaps the devil Deighton has them blackmailed. But most probably it is greed. Wanton greed. An offer of money can turn any man.

Not our men, said Isaac Hartley. They have plenty of money. A river of coins does flow from these moors and down through this valley. Between us we have made sure that them and theirs want for nothing.

A river can always run deeper and wider.

But why ask for more?

Because some men are never satisfied.

Greed then it is, said Isaac Hartley.

Yes. Or power. Perhaps this turncoat fancies the crown of the valley for himself.

You mean one of our own would sell on our brother's soul to the lawman so that he could take over? Anyone that would do that is ready for the asylum. It could never work.

No. It could never work.

From high up in the slopes of the woods William Hartley could hear the raven's croak, dry and throaty. Another one joined it in a slightly higher pitch. A nesting pair. William Hartley stood and searched for their blue-black shapes against the sky but he could not see them. He looked to the tree tops for their bowl-shaped nests lined with mud and bark and roots and softened with snags of deer or sheep fur. He could not see them.

As boys they had climbed these trees here in Bell Hole to seek out such nests and take eggs. Scores they had collected, from the nests of birds of dozens of varieties, David Hartley always scaling the most obscure trees to heights where the branches seemed too thin to hold the weight of an adolescent swaying in the breeze. Cliffs they had climbed too, to find the eyries of falcons and their woody, nut-coloured eggs. Kestrels they hunted down for their clusters of mottled cackleberrys. Owls also, their eggs often as perfectly pure white as the moon.

Such rare finds were kept as treasures or occasionally traded with other valley boys, the brothers' collection set on the beam above the beds where they slept so that their translucent shells were best illuminated by a morning sun that crept over the brow of the moor.

William Hartley turned back to his brother who had lit a pipe and was letting the smoke swirl around his face like the unravelling bandages of a shot-blasted soldier back from the far-flung killing fields of the bloody rebellions.

So what do we do to free him? he asked.

There is only one way.

Tell me.

We must flush out the rat, said Isaac Hartley. He passed the pipe to his brother who took the mossy smoke into his mouth.

And cut strips off him? he said.

No, said Isaac Hartley. We flush out the rat and we get him to change his testimony. Without that, any trial would surely crumble. There's none of us have been caught at it. It's all hearsay, is that. The black devil man Deighton has not seen the clipping, nor does he have the tools of our trade or any evidence save surely for a few coins he has accrued from barmen and butchers here and there. They mean nothing. Anyone could clip a coin. It all rests on this rat. This turncoat.

We must find him.

We must.

And we shall.

James Broadbent felt the warm ale slip down his throat and wished that he had a pipe because although he rarely took one he felt like scorching the anger that was burning in the pit of his stomach. He felt like burning his insides and raging and smashing and breaking all in sight. He felt like punching chunks out of the valley. Great holes into it. He wanted to bite boulders. Burn houses. Slit the throats of calves and daub William Deighton's name in blood across the face of the Halifax clock tower. Of all that he felt capable.

Without the money to drink all day the bitter embers within him were only further fuelled by thoughts of poverty. He ruminated on the work he had done for two opposing sides and the outcome was always the same: neither had given their dues.

He poured his drink down quickly and shouted for Barbara to bring him another. With each swallowed mouthful those one hundred guineas that were owed to him seemed further beyond reach, intangible and nebulous like early morning bog fumes. They were mythical coins now, less real even than those they had milled and stamped and sent back into circulation. Because at least those moidores and shillings and half guineas and pennies had been something to touch and hold and feel and bite with your teeth to confirm they were real. Deighton's guineas had been nothing but a lure. Mythical money. He saw this now. He saw this and he cursed William Deighton and he cursed David Hartley and he cursed himself.

In the early afternoon the day outside spilled into Barbary's and a shaft of autumn sun crossed James Broadbent. He raised an arm to screen his eyes, to block it out, and with it came James Stansfield, looking first to the left where a small huddle of turnpike workers were taking their beer and then to the right where James Broadbent sat slumped, one foot raised onto a stool, eyes squinting into the momentary brightness. He made straight for him.

Have you heard? said James Stansfield. They've got the king.

James Broadbent looked and leered. Sneered. He did not like James Stansfield. Never had. Stansfield was slight and weak and blond. One of the soft ones. Everything about his appearance annoyed him: his small wet mouth, his beardless chin, his girlish blue eyes. Stansfield was under the Hartley brothers' thumb and without the Hartleys he was nothing.

Without the Hartleys most of them were nothing. They could never stand alone; not like him. When the Hartleys swung – and that was surely soon – this lot would go back to being land labourers and weavers and farmers scratching at the soil for vegetables in their shallow, barren plots. They did not have the courage that he, James Broadbent, had. They were as low as field mice that seek the warmth of a man's home in winter; they were nothing but rodents but *he* was the mythical wolf of old England that stalked the woods alone, crunching skulls. By season's end he would be gone.

He said nothing. He just looked at James Stansfield, flush-cheeked and short of breath. James Stansfield stared back and saw a man whose eyes could not focus and a jaw that was slack. The face of a savage in his cups.

The Jagger lad too, said James Stansfield. They got Jagger.

James Broadbent wiped his mouth with the back of his sleeve and then rubbed his neck.

Much money, he said, his words sticking in his throat.

What's that you say?

Many guineas.

Yes, said James Stansfield. Between us we have milled many coins. They say the Alchemist can work magic with metal and fire. But now they say this bastard devil Deighton has pulled in our king and James Jagger on false charges. They say he has sworn statements.

James Broadbent rolled his head around on his neck until it cracked and then he took a drink.

William Deighton is indeed a bastard, he slurred. A bastard of the very worst kind.

James Stansfield saw that the big man's eyes were wet and glassy, his teeth crooked and chipped. He saw the dirt beneath nails that never got scrubbed and the dirt too that coloured the creases of hands too large and cumbersome to ever properly make the working of a loom worth a man's while; hands only good for cleaving, pummelling and pounding. Wasn't that why the Hartleys had taken him on – because James Broadbent had been turned out of the army and had failed at the loom and was too lazy to burn the charcoal like his father, but yet had greater strength and fighting skills than almost any other valley man?

Deighton is as worse a bastard as the bastard David scatmouth Hartley, said James Broadbent.

James Stansfield looked around him then pulled up a chair and sat. He leaned in.

You'd be minded to watch your drunken words, James Broadbent. People will get to talking.

You don't tell me what to do, growled James Broadbent in response. You're nowt but a cunny-thumbed Miss Molly, just like Queen David Hartley, you.

James Stansfield ignored the insult.

Again I warn you to mind that tongue of yours less someone cuts it out.

Beneath lidded eyes James Broadbent stared back.

No sane man would durst to.

They say there is a rat amongst us, said James Stansfield.

And the rat is me.

James Broadbent said this and then began to chuckle quietly to himself. But it was laughter without a smile. James Stansfield saw that it disguised something ugly and damaged; a harlequin's mask worn askance.

Aye, he continued. It was me what put the men in. Hartley and Jagger.

You're ligging, said James Stansfield.

James Broadbent's smile faded. The laughter crumpled in on itself and died in his mouth. He looked away, indignant.

Please yourself.

James Stansfield studied his face.

I think I do believe you, he said.

A wise man would.

Then your life has a limit.

All life has a limit.

Let me test my head handles one more time, said James Stansfield. Are you saying now that you have turned against your own? That it is you that has spoken to the exciseman they call William Deighton of Halifax?

The Coiners aren't my own, said James Broadbent. Your own looks after you, protects you. The Hartleys have done nowt for me. Fuck all.

They've kept you fed and paid and seen you right.

They've given me piss but no pot to put it in. That's all.

You're part of something. This is the brotherhood of the valley.

James Broadbent took a big drink. He drained his cup and felt his head hanging heavy.

Brotherhood bollocks.

They'll come after you.

I'm here.

Not just you either. They'll fix your old man too.

A rogue's move they call it, said James Broadbent. The blackmail.

What do you mean?

The exciseman. He has tricked me and my father, an ill man with the reaper's scythe flashing in his eyes, with threats and promises and lies. But I too can string out a line of lies like a baited wire in the pike pond. Yes. I too can feed ligs to the ligger. You all think I am short on thinking, but I am not.

You swore a statement to the lawman though?

A trough of pig-swill is what that was.

But why? asked James Stansfield.

Fetch me a drink.

I will not.

James Broadbent's head lolled to his chest for a moment as if he were falling asleep.

Fetch me a drink, he said.

Again I will not, said James Stansfield. I do not buy for turncoats. Tell me why you did it.

There was a moment's silence and then James Broadbent raised his head and spoke quickly, as if to beat the sleep that was settling behind his eyes.

You want to know why I fed that devil-cunt Deighton a mouthful of lies about the bitch-born Hartley?

Yes, said James Stansfield.

James Broadbent's head began to dip again. It reminded James Stansfield of a fell shepherd's dog nodding off in front of a roaring fire.

For my freedom. And for money. And because he had threatened to put me over a barrel. It's simple.

I still don't understand.

James Broadbent hiccupped and then sighed and then hiccupped again.

And people say it is I that is dim like a fading candle. Listen doylem: I gave the man what he thought he wanted to hear, but as you say it is of no consequence.

You have done wrong, Broadbent.

We have all done wrong.

You do not strike me as someone with a conscience.

I'm the one they laugh at. I'm the one whose cupboard is empty while the Hartleys get fat.

You must make amends, said James Stansfield. That is what you must do. Reparations.

All is broken.

You must take back your words. Scrap this statement. You must tell Deighton that it was all lies – if that's what it was.

Big hairy bull bollocks to that.

James Broadbent spoke this in a loud voice that caused the turnpike navvies to look over.

You say that now but wait until you're upright and the froth has blown, said James Stansfield.

I'll stay drunk then.

You need to speak to Deighton.

I'll stay in ale forever.

You need to take those words back.

But then he'll have me. He'll have me and the old man.

For what?

For coining.

Has he seen you at it?

No, said James Broadbent. Because I've never wielded a hammer. I've never owned one. Who needs a hammer when you've got these?

He lifted his large hands up and looked at their knotted knuckles and crooked fingers as if they were strange foreign objects.

Well then, said Stansfield. Has he found the spoils of this forging business of ours?

No. I have nothing but the clothes I sleep in.

Well. So. William Deighton has nothing to link you and the Coiners but your own admittance.

James Broadbent shrugged.

Get me a drink, he said. Fetch me a finger of gin.

We need to get you to the Duke of York.

Isaac Hartley?

Of course Isaac Hartley, said James Stansfield. Is there anyone else with that nickname? Listen, there is still time to straighten out these crooked actions of yours. Isaac will know what to do. If your statement is pig-swill then this case cannot stand. If it's a choice between the exciseman and Hartley I know whose side I would want to be on. It's about choosing the better of two enemies now, for you will surely have no friends left.

It's too late for that. It's too late for any of that.

Think with your brain-pan, man. Coining we might be guilty of but neither King David Hartley nor James Jagger will kick the wind because of the greedy foolishness of some born-backwards sot that's been on the rant since he first tasted ale.

Who's this sot? said James Broadbent.

You are.

James Broadbent pushed his chair back and made to stand but his legs gave and he stumbled sideways. James Stansfield grabbed at the larger man and guided him back onto his seat. James Broadbent slumped back and then reached for his cup but only managed to knock it over. It was empty. It rolled to the floor and broke. His chin sank to his chest.

I should slit your throat right now and be the hero of every Coiner for what you've done, said James Stansfield. But what good would that do when our king is rotting in a York cell and you're the only hope for his freedom? So listen to me and I might just save a life.

James Broadbent lifted his head.

Is mine a life worth saving though?

James Stansfield stared back at him with disdain.

It's not your life I'm thinking on.

They corls it hangin in chaynes but really it is not chains at orl but summat more like a rort iyun cayge that they rivet on to the body of the poor hanged man like bones of metal worn on the outside with his head held fassed and his legs held fassed and the arms held fassed And the only acksool chayne is that which dangles the poor godforsaykun bastid in this most fearful and barbrus suit from the gibberd mast And what happens is they leeve the dead man dangling this way for all the four seesuns long Aye for all the valley fowk to see and thur chillum to see too and what happens is the rain it does sile down and the wynde it does blowe strong and the frossed it does frees and the birds they do come a-pecken for a nip and twist of flesh and insex too Great big insex in the summer layern thur eggs in the drippy woonds though they says it is the eye borls that do go first been as they offer the tastiest morsulls to scavengers And then in thyme what was wans a man becomes something else He becomes a dark shadder on the hill as the chayne rusts with the rains and his boddee feeds the beasts of the air and oh how it creaks and oh how it mones laike you wuddent no.

As the brees does turn the cayge and that mans head lolls on his snapped neck and all the crowes and rayvuns and jackodaws gather thicker still and that mans meat it does become a meal for menny more still and they leeve him hangin until the sky is black with clows of screechin birds and that hanged man is carryun now and his flesh is stript away as the birds sit on the mettle bars of his rort iron suit And down the hill at nite the folk of the town can heer the chayne and then there is meet no more and we are down to the corr of it now Down to the bones what first were red and then browne and then grey in culler then after that yeller and then finally they are boans of pure wite and there is nothing left to hold that man together but the idear of him But still the rort iron cayge in whose mettul bayse his parts *gather and in time they will be nout but dussed and the cayge it will further rust and the plump birds swollen will sing sweetlee and hope against hope that another hangd man will be brung up and strung up and suspended like a grate gift to the skye Gods if you go in for all that godly preechin shyte wich as it goes I dunt but still But still I moan his nayme.*

o God.

O god.

Sequestered in their square stone cell, James Jagger finished noisily urinating in the sluice channel that ran down one side of the space then he shook himself off and dropped down into the straw that covered the floor.

It burns when I piss, he said, then he took off one of his clogs and removed a sock. He began to pick at his big toe-nail. He took a piece of straw and scraped a layer of grime that looked like a millipede out from beneath it. He flicked it away.

Stop that, said David Hartley.

What?

That.

This?

James Jagger held the stem of straw aloft.

Aye. Cleaning your fucking wagglers. Stop it.

But it's ailing us. It's sore.

I don't give a tinker's tit for your toe.

I fear it has turned septic. There was juice coming out of it in the night. Yellow water, brother.

David Hartley stared at James Jagger until the latter looked away.

A full minute passed before they spoke again.

This stonejug is full of queans, said James Jagger.

They say gaols can make a man that way.

Not me but. Yesterday in the courtyard some big lump tried to touch me down there. Grabbed at it while passing. I gave him short shrift, don't you worry about that. Like an angry bull I kicked him hard right between the left toe and the right toe. Clang went his sweetbreads. He fell like a flour sack from a cart just like that time you told us about when you were away down there in the forges of the midlands.

What time? said David Hartley wearily.

I mean fancy trying that with a Cragg Vale Coiner. He must be bent in the head to do that. Well, anyroad. He's limping now.

I do believe I've not met anyone who talks as much as you, Jimmy Jagger, said David Hartley.

I thank you.

It wasn't meant in kindness. I never noticed how much you rabbit before.

Our lass says I am a sunny person.

Does she.

She says nothing gets us down.

Not even the hangman's shadow?

No. I have faith.

What faith? said David Hartley. No-one told me you were a bible man.

Give over. I have faith in you, King David. You've steered us to success and now I believe you'll steer us out of these dangerous waters too. Deighton is just a worm in the apple barrel. He can't get at us all. Someone'll burst him first.

A face appeared at the cell door. It was the turnkey Charles Claxton and one of his aides. They unlocked the door and the two men slowly stood.

Bread day, said Charles Claxton as his aide passed David Hartley and James Jagger a six shilling loaf each. They were hard and weighted in their hands. Uniform in size. James Jagger rapped at his with his knuckles and then sniffed it.

What's this made from – wood shavings?

Charles Claxton turned away.

Is that it? said James Jagger.

Until Tuesday.

What happens on Tuesday?

You get another loaf. If you're paid up.

Paid up?

Aye. You didn't reckon on getting owt for nowt did you?

Well, what fucking day is it now?

Friday.

Incredulous, James Jagger glared back.

What I am supposed to scran in the meanwhile?

The turnkey shrugged.

Your socks? he said.

James Jagger raised his voice.

We're the fucking mighty Coiners of Cragg Vale.

Not my concern.

The gaoler's aide spooned water into the empty jug on the floor.

Oh, what I would do for a bowl of something hot, said James Jagger. A dollop of sweetened furmenty would do for me.

Them that pays get fed, said Charles Claxton, dropping his ladle back into his bucket.

I'll be wasting away, said James Jagger again.

Charles Claxton said nothing. Charles Claxton shut the door.

James Broadbent did not wonder what Isaac Hartley was doing in the sodden parrock that lay behind Elphaborough Hall in the fading light of day; instead he accepted only that he was there and that his fate lay in the man's hands.

Already the courage that ale gave him was ebbing away and when he saw the shape of Isaac Hartley in the far corner with his back turned to them he slowed his pace and he said in a low voice this not a good idea but James Stansfield, feeling a reversal of roles, and recognising that his part in the saving of King David Hartley would not go unnoticed or unrewarded, replied: this is the only choice that you have now James Broadbent.

They had trudged across the field that had been churned by horses, and the mud clung to their boots. It added another sole and made the walking heavy.

When they reached somewhere near the centre James Stansfield said: you better wait a while. James Broadbent said what – wait here, in the mud like a bloody donkey? and James Stansfield replied: yes, exactly that – like a donkey, and he strode off across the field.

Again James Broadbent wished he had a clay pipe to clean and fill, to ignite and inhale while he waited in the softening evening light, if only to give purpose to hands that he put in and out of his pockets and then ran through his hair and used to adjust his clothes on his frame. He wanted another drink and he could smell himself as he watched James Stansfield, a queer sot if ever there was – a man that he would never otherwise have call to socialise with, had not the yellow trade brought them together through greed and geography and circumstance – call out to Isaac Hartley.

They walked to one another and conferred for some time. Aware that he suddenly needed to urinate James Broadbent walked to the edge of the field and pissed against the wall and then walked back to the centre. James Stansfield and Isaac

Hartley were deep in conversation and the latter kept looking over at him. He could see anger.

They continued talking and then there was a sudden raised voice and Isaac Hartley pushed James Stansfield aside and walked across the field with purpose. He strode across the ruined furrows and quickened his pace as he approached James Broadbent, who saw the rage on the man's face, yet still nullified from a day's drinking he did not think to move out of the way but merely watched on impassively as Isaac Hartley, the smaller of the two, threw a heavy right hand to his nose, which cracked beneath his fist, nor did he dodge the short, tight jab that dug deep into the soft space beneath his arm-pit. When this second punch landed he felt all the breath being drawn from his body in one swift exhalation; his lungs felt flattened and his stomach lurched with nausea. A howl of distress rang through his entire system as he struggled to take in air. Isaac Hartley ended him with a third button-punch straight through the centre of the man's waistcoat.

James Broadbent bent double and could hear himself wheeze but a well-aimed knee to his temple sent him slipping sideways into the dirt. Pain did battle in three different parts of his body and his pride ached too. He had not been beaten this way since he was a child.

He thought of all the men he had punched and kicked and stamped, and wondered if it had felt like this for them – or worse?

What hurt more was that he knew he could fight this man. On any given day he could mince him but he could not do that now, for that would bring about a whole lot more trouble and trouble he had plenty of as it was.

Get up, said Isaac Hartley.

James Broadbent felt the soft mud beneath them. He saw the old tree at one end of the field, and he saw the rookery of nests that had been constructed in the fork of its branches, and he heard the birds too. The hoarse mocking chorus of them was like cruel laughter; the very sound of autumn itself.

Get up, said Isaac Hartley again, and he grabbed James Broadbent beneath one arm. James Broadbent touched his hand to his broken nose and though there was no blood he could feel his eyes swelling in sympathy on either side of it.

That's for what you've done, he said, and he took a large knife from his pocket and said; and this is for what you have yet to do.

He moved towards James Broadbent and said: turncoat, I'll cut your fucking tongue out.

James Stansfield stepped forward and laid a hand on Isaac Hartley's arm.

Now just one moment, Isaac, just one moment, he said, putting his body between the two of them. This man has already confessed to me his wrong doings but also confessed that his words are worthless. It was not your brother that he wanted to see arrested, but his own skin that he was saving. You see, this bastard William Deighton is cunning and we all know that Broadbent here is more like the blind poxed rabbit that sits in the sun all day long, and yet wonders why he gets his neck snapped. He has been had by Deighton, that is all. He is a drunkard and a ligger too, and he has filled the man's papers with nothing but lies about the business of the Coiners. I do truly believe that there is nothing in there that can be proven and that this man and this man only is the one who can get your brother, our king, freed. And after that – well, then it is up to you and yours to decide what to do next. Cut his tongue out then if you see fit but I imagine by then James here will have made amends and will surely be indebted for life.

Isaac Hartley looked from James Stansfield to James Broadbent.

Well? he said. What say you, turncoat?

James Broadbent dropped his eyes.

I will do whatever it takes to get him freed.

And Jagger?

Yes, Jagger too.

I will cut your tongue and cock off and feed them to my guffies if you do not do this.

I will speak to the man that has wronged me, said James Broadbent quietly. I will speak to the cunt Deighton. I will spend my time in that cell instead of your brother, if that is what must be done.

Aye, not a bad thought, said James Stansfield. You'd be safer there than here.

And you'll swear before the magistrate? said Isaac Hartley.

Yes.

I don't believe you, turncoat.

You have my word.

Your word isn't worth a tagnut on a sheep's scut, said Isaac Hartley.

You have it all the same.

James Broadbent felt the bridge of his nose again.

I thought you were a brawler, said Isaac Hartley. But it seems you're not so solid.

I'll fight any man, me.

I licked you in two punches, turncoat – and you'll get the same twice daily if you don't get yourself to York Castle and beg forgiveness from your king. You're lucky you have someone speaking up for you.

James Broadbent said nothing.

Soon it will be Samhain. Two weeks hence.

James Broadbent shrugged.

The beginning of the darker half, said Isaac Hartley. And them stone holes are no place to be in winter.

Especially for a king, nodded James Stansfield.

The one true king of the north, nodded Isaac Hartley.

James Broadbent looked sullen. He said nothing.

Death awaits you should you fail, turncoat.

I said I would help and I will.

By Samhain eve my brother and James Jagger will be at their fire-sides, giving their wives a tickle. The bastard Deighton's case will have collapsed and you might yet still be alive to see another Calderdale day. That is what will happen.

Perhaps, said James Broadbent.

Isaac Hartley moved closer.

No, not perhaps. That is what will happen. Otherwise every day you will get a beating like this. Mob-handed the Coiners will seek their revenge. Every day a new broken bone.

James Broadbent grunted.

Tomorrow I will travel to Halifax and do this business you ask of me, he said.

Halifax?

That is where the black devil Deighton resides.

At this Isaac Hartley exploded. His face was suddenly animated and his spittle flecked the face of James Broadbent

Fuck the black devil bastard cuntsucking Deighton, he cussed. It's the king's forgiveness you first must find, because without that you're as good as dead and buried.

Fine. Tomorrow I will go—

Isaac Hartley stood as close to James Broadbent as he could. Stared him down. His nose nearly touched the other man's chin.

Tomorrow? My brother rots in the dungeons of York in another county and you talk about tomorrow. Tonight. *Tonight* you go to York and you get down on your knees and you beg for forgiveness. You beg for your life and that of your family.

James Broadbent did not flinch. A small, slight trickle of blood ran from one nostril and settled in the stubble of his upper lip. His tongue darted out to taste it.

And I will go with you, said Isaac Hartley.

You?

Only an imbecile would let you out of their sight when my brother's liberty hangs in the balance. No. I'll fetch us horses.

And what of my father?

What of that mangy dog?

Can he come too?

He is an old man with one foot on death's doorstep – and a fool with it too, said Isaac Hartley. No. He will only slow us down.

Not by horse he won't.

He does not need to come.

I would prefer that he was kept within sight.

Do you think I'll have him killed in your absence?

James Broadbent did not reply. Isaac Hartley gave a knife-wound smile and nodded.

Then you're finally learning how this works, turncoat.

Beneath the shadows of the stone edifice that had darkened under the sheets of rain that fell in the night, David Hartley and James Jagger walked the iron palisade between the right wing that held the debtors and the governor's chamber, and the left which housed the inmates.

Above them loomed the clock turret, the large ticking hands a form of torture to those held without conviction. Below, they paced the quadrangle whose bars looked out directly onto the street. City life was out there, just inches away, as people passed by going about their morning business.

York gaol may have been admired for its architecture and close proximity to the neighbouring court by those visiting dignitaries, writers and clergymen who received tours of the gaol, yet its inmates knew little of this. A fever had killed a quarter of its felons in one cruel month the previous winter and the noise that echoed around the stone dungeon chambers now robbed the inmates of any chance of unbroken sleep. Only in the infirmary did men have the luxury of reclining on rudimentary mattresses – and only ever in their last dying days.

Minor ailments went untreated. Fights were a daily occurrence as old grievances found a new home and inmates included some as young as eight or nine years old, easy prey for the many predators awaiting trial for a litany of transgressions.

The two valley men walked the length of the gaol and then back again as the sky darkened and the fine morning rain danced around them.

As they passed by cells they saw their fellow inmates. Some sleeping, others slumped in their straw. Faces looked out blankly from between their bars, others attempted conversation with acquaintances further along the wing.

They saw one felon crouched over the drain runnel with his trousers around his boots, another huddled naked and covered in drying brown streaks of his own effluence. His eyes wide and white, watching like a cornered animal.

The rain drew down and David Hartley tilted his head to it; he tasted it, let it wash his face. He opened his mouth and tried to catch the elongated droplets. While James Jagger cursed, David Harley let the drizzle mat his hair and soak his shirt until it was so wet that he took it off and draped it around his neck, letting the cold October air tighten his white flesh and bring it out in tiny bumps.

He felt Yorkshire on his skin. Then they were called back in.

The three men rode through the night.

James Broadbent felt his ribs and his nose and his head ache, and his sick stomach moil sour from a lack of food and the hangover that had set in, while alongside him his father coughed and quietly moaned about having to undertake another nocturnal journey. Isaac Hartley, the second of the Hartley brothers, rode with quiet determination, saying little.

At the Kings Arms in Leeds they took drink and food and had the horses fed and watered and then proceeded on to York. For fifty miles they rode through darkness. Twice there were violent downpours that soaked them through and once a badger flashed before them to send the horses skittish.

They entered York in the middle of the night and found a place to tie up the horses, then they climbed a bank of dirt to take shelter in a dark triangle of shadow cast by the old wall that ran around the city. From here they could rest and watch the animals.

James Broadbent and Joseph Broadbent and Isaac Hartley arrived at York Castle in time for the daybreak turn-out of those inmates allowed to slop out their basins and water jugs and stretch themselves with a half hour's exercise in the yard. From the street side they could shout through the bars. Isaac Hartley called to the nearest man. He slowly sauntered over.

I'm looking for the one they call King David.

The prisoner stared at him a moment.

The only king I know is the one that sits on the throne down that London, he said. George I believe they call him. No kings in here though.

I'm talking about the true king of the north – David Hartley the king of the Cragg Vale Coiners of Calderdale. My brother.

Now them I have heard of. The Coiners is the ones that do the clipping.

So they say, said Isaac Hartley.

Clever idea, is that. Is he one of that lot then, your brother?

He is.

In here, is he?

He is.

Well then. He'll not be long for the gallows I expect. They say it's a capital crime is that.

Isaac Hartley reached through the bars and yanked the man towards him. He cracked his forehead on them once and then a second time. The inmate howled in pain. Other men in the yard looked over but no turnkey appeared. They did not care what happened in the yard; whatever went on in the outside air was prisoners' business.

Go and find him.

The man stepped back and scowled, touching his fingers to his brow.

Now, said Isaac Hartley.

Or what?

Or I'll have someone in here slit you from cock-end to bottom lip in your sleep this very night.

A few minutes later David Hartley and James Jagger crossed the yard and greeted Isaac Hartley. They shook hands and grabbed at each other's forearms between the bars. Isaac Hartley pressed a sackcloth parcel through.

There's good food in there, brother, he said. A cooked chicken and apples and boiled eggs and plenty of your Grace's biscuits. Enough for a few days. A jar of stingo too.

And coins for the turnkey?

Of course, brother. Of course. A Coiner without coins is no man at all.

Jagger took the sack and rifled through it. He pulled out an apple and bit into it.

Seeing James Broadbent and his father lurking behind him David Hartley raised a finger and said what's that rat-cunt doing here?

He has some explaining to do.

About what?

You're not going to like it.

To imajun I went back in my sell full of hope that day thinken on that perhaps Jaymes Broadbean cud stop us having to do the Tyburn Frisk and that mebbe he had sumhow been dubble cerossed by the bastid Dyeton which is not summat I woud put past the eggsize man becors remember the bastid Willyam Dieton dus this type of thing for a liven Yes he is payde by the crowne to trick and snare his prey just as the poacher tricks and snares the fesants from the trees at night or russels the stag from under the nose of the growndsmen Not that I wud ever kill a stag haven seen what Ive seen becors I know a stag is more than a meer deer of the wuds and hill and moors No a stag is summat else Aye but hees a crafty bastid all the sayme is Willyam Dieton As crafty as they cum.

But what I didunt reeleyes was that it was Broadbent that was pullen the strokes on us by tellen us he cud get us owt the York hole and if weed have been smart weed have kilt that man stone ded in his bed the very day he confessed in his cups to our Isaak what it was he done That is him becoming turncoat for the tacksman an all that Yes for that we shud have fed him his own borls and the old mans too for by orl accownts the old charcole burner Josuff Belch Broadbent was in on it as well and my own father did say Belch was a yellow belly rat breeder Thems two go back way back to when they was just sprats Spynluss fucks the pear.

Greed it was that oiled there tungs to the man Greed and cowerdyse and a streek of beetrayul.

No I never did truss Broadbent for he was big and stoopit and of cors the mayne thing is he didunt like King Dayvid Hartley His respect I did not have for one reesun or another.

Still it makes me mornful to think that that man walks the vally freely while I sit here lonelee with me pensil stub and paper and not even a tallow candul to lite us as I rite these memwars By jingo I think I woud even tolerate that gobby stinkpot Jaymes Jagga for a half hour or so.

After taking food at an inn by the York fortifications where a mildew pattern had formed on the wall in the shape of cat poised as if ready to launch itself, Isaac Hartley took James Broadbent and Joseph Broadbent on to an attorney called Wickham who held an office up a flight of stairs off Whip-Ma-Whop-Ma-Gate, and whose windows looked over the whipping posts and old stocks that stood in the street below.

Here they sat and stated their case.

Wickham listened impassive and close-faced as James Broadbent lied to the attorney about lying in his statement, and as he did he secretly took pleasure in the fact that no-one but he and his father knew the full truth of the situation, not even Isaac Hartley – especially Isaac Hartley – whose punches from the previous day had turned his nose crooked and blackened both his eyes and caused his breathing to be short. It would, if he got his way, which he fully intended to, come at a very high price to the Hartley brother that they called Duke of York but who in fact was anything but that, for when they walked down the cobbled streets of the old city no-one gave them a double glance, suggesting to James Broadbent that Isaac Hartley was nothing but a braggart like the rest of that clan.

Isaac Hartley didn't even know his way around the city of the nickname bestowed upon him and the humiliation of the beating sat heavy in James Broadbent's sour stomach.

Wickham listened and quietly catalogued what he saw: men of the hills of ill education. He saw black eyes and swollen knuckles. He saw a broken old man who looked set to expire right there in his front office. And he saw through the litany of lies with which James Broadbent was furnishing him. He saw bandits, vagabonds, and forgers out to cut each other's throats at the first opportunity. He saw the jostling throng of Tyburn and the snap of the hangman's trapdoor. He saw a lot of trouble for no money, for hanged men rarely pay their debts.

Isaac Hartley asked Wickham if bail could be secured for the two imprisoned men, to which he sighed and then patiently replied that this would first require William Deighton being called before a magistrate, which was unlikely, and that Broadbent would have to admit perjury before the same magistrate, and even then it would almost certainly be judged that Broadbent had done this of his own volition without solicitation from the exciseman who, these three ragged men from the hills should be aware, had an impeccable record. Not only that, he urged, but they should also note that Deighton was on crown business and, if that week's newspaper reports were to believed, was on the very cusp of ending the biggest financial fraud on English soil that there had ever been. At this the men smirked. A smile even played about the corners of the stone-set mouth of Isaac Hartley

So how do we get my brother, King David Hartley, freed? asked the latter.

You go to trial at the assizes and prove his innocence, said Wickham.

How do we do that?

The same way any man would. You hire an attorney. You refute the evidence. You find others to vouch for your brother's good character and standing. And you have an alibi.

This feckless fucker's statement is all lies, said Isaac Hartley.

Then with God's will the court will recognise this and your brother's liberty will be assured, said the attorney. If he is guilty then it is up to the court to mete out an appropriate punishment; though of course you're no doubt aware such an offence as forging coins brings with it the highest penalty.

Our David is a man of notoriety now, said Isaac Hartley.

Wickham replied.

Yes. I believe I have heard of him.

And this exciseman has it in for us.

For all of you?

Yes.

Now why would that be?

Because.

Wickham frowned.

I find it difficult to believe that one single man in the employment of the crown's own office would persecute dozens of lowly hill farmers and weavers – if that is what you say you are – purely for his own entertainment.

He does not work alone, said Joseph Broadbent. There is a lawman called Parker behind him. A young lad, but wealthy already.

That's as maybe, said Wickham. But William Deighton clearly believes he has a case against both David Hartley and –

Here he paused to thumb through the papers before him.

James Jagger of Turvin, Calderdale, West Yorkshire. And of course a case against the others that he has named as forgers in the newspaper also.

What newspaper?

Wickham reached into a drawer and handed Isaac Hartley a folded copy of the *London Gazette*.

Our David is the book learner, he said quietly, and gave it to James Broadbent, who shrugged and then passed the paper to his father who held it an inch from his face for a moment and then passed it back to the attorney.

Even if I could my eyes is shot, he rasped. All is mist now.

Wickham considered the men.

Well it names at least a dozen men as good as guilty of this foul practice, he said. And I do not believe that all of them are innocent, though they will no doubt protest it just as you protest the charges laid against your brother, Mr. Hartley. Nor do I know this William Deighton in person, though it seems to me he is a true hero of England, a man doing God's work in a valley blighted. Now if you will, gentlemen.

Wickham stood. He did not offer his hand.

Does this mean Hartley's not getting out, said James Broadbent as he slowly stood, pressing a hand to his broken ribs.

It means it is time for you to leave.

Fog filled the valley holes and pockets. It appeared as if it were a living thing – a chimera that stalked the hollows, rising up from a river that was running thin after a mere three dry days in succession. It draped itself over the trees so that only the tips of the tallest branches reached out from this dense vapour like the fingers of a drowning man.

The swirling fog softened everything. It dampened all noise to a muted hush; the frantic chatter of the last roosting birds became restrained and the expansive sky which seemed so often to roar with the last scratches of dying light was now silent, an unseen ceiling.

Through this the men came down from their isolated homes. Again they gathered. Again in Daibary's by night, where secrets could be better shared and strangers sent away, less they overhear something they'd have to be silenced over.

Yet still amongst friends, the eyes of the men would not settle. Restless, they flitted about in case they revealed their suspicion of one another – or worse, a suggestion of their own guilt.

The room too was thick with smoke as if the fog had seeped through the key-hole to bear witness to the conversations that were taking place.

Here were Coiners. Coiners subdued and shaken. Coiners concerned and fearful.

But still Coiners one and all.

They gathered in tight groups of two or three and drank slowly, for this was no celebration time.

There was Abraham Lumb and Absolom Butts.

John Wilcox and Joseph Hanson and Jonathan Bolton.

William Harpur and William Hailey and William Folds.

Jonas Eastwood and Joseph Gelder and James Crabtree.

James Stansfield and Jack O' Matts Bentley.

Thomas Sunderland and Crowther O' Badger and Peter Barker and Aloysius Smith.

Tommy Clayton and Johnny Tatham.

John Parker and James Green.

Benny Sutcliffe and Nat Horsfall.

Eli Hill and Jonas Tilotson and Thomas Spencer and Israel Wilde and Matthew Hepworth and Ely Crossley and Brian Dempsey and Eli Hoyle.

Others.

And then finally Isaac Hartley and William Hartley, the pair known affectionately amongst the men as the Duke of York and the Duke of Edinburgh, who arrived last, making straight for their usual corner table, for they knew a Coiner should always sit with his face to the exit and his back to the wall.

It was the largest gathering of Coiners and clippers and strong-arm men since the previous summer's meeting up at Bell House. This time the mood was as different as the season itself.

Best of order, said Isaac Hartley. You all know why we're here. Not for jokes or riddles or song. Not for ale or skittles or skirt. We're here for our brother, the one they call the king of Calderdale, the true king of these northlands, David Hartley, who dwells in a dungeon in York, rotting away because of one man.

Broadbent, said Joseph Hanson.

Broadbent will pay, said William Folds.

Broadbent will indeed pay, said Isaac Hartley. But this man was outsmarted, tricked, misled by a greater foe, someone who will do or say anything – who will go to any length imaginable – to bring about our downfall. Granted, Broadbent is as dumb as a donkey and will be lucky to see next Lent, but even so he remains a Coiner and he is needed for our brother's freedom. This man Deighton who is a representative of the crown of England would sooner see us starve than live as free, enterprising men. They do not give a fuck about us hill-dwellers in their palaces down in London. They sleep under silk while we have only straw. They eat goose and pheasant while for years we sucked on pebbles. They have five fires blazing while we burn green wood.

Hear, hear, said several voices in agreement. Isaac Hartley continued.

Broadbent fell for the devil Deighton's trickery and so here we are. Make no mistake: William Deighton might live a humble life in Halifax but he is another king's lickspittle. Follow the chain and you will find Robert Parker, a man younger than most of us, yet who is buying up half the hills in the valley, and already deep in talks with these mill men. Don't you see them measuring up their plots to split and share and sell – the land we farm and dwell upon? And behind Robert Parker, others like him. Men of wealth and privilege out to line their own pockets.

What then must be done? asked Eli Hill.

Each and every one of you has answered this question in your heads already, said Isaac Hartley.

Some of the men glanced at one another. Others looked to the floor, to the ceiling. They chewed at thumbnails and callouses. Picked at their noses. Made busy with their pipes.

Fixing is what Deighton needs, said William Folds.

Fixing. He left the word hanging. Open-ended. Fixing.

James Stansfield cleared his throat. He was not used to speaking openly but his role in bringing James Broadbent to account had emboldened him. He cleared his throat a second time.

But who is it that is to do the fixing? he asked.

The men were silent for a moment.

And who is it that will pay them, for a man to do something like this would surely require a reward?

Isaac Hartley spoke.

Payment would not present a problem. William Deighton is the problem. When that is solved everything else will follow.

There are enough valley folk that would put up good coins to see that dog dead.

Crowther O' Badger said this. Then he added:

I know of two lads.

Who would that be then, Crowther? asked Isaac Hartley.

Crowther O' Badger looked around at the faces of his fellow forgers.

Matthew Normanton is one of them, he said. And Robert Thomas is the other.

Thomas of up Wadsworth Banks? asked William Hartley

That's the one.

I know of him, said Isaac Hartley. But who is this Normanton?

He's from Sowerby. They're farm-hands the pair of them – when they're not out stealing or up to skulduggery. They're desperate and merciless with it. They'll do anything for money them two.

They don't clip though.

No. King David would not have them, said Crowther O' Badger. Reckoned on them being a yard too shifty.

William Hartley nodded and addressed his brother.

He's right. I remember the name Normanton now. A right pair they make.

Well I heard that Matthew Normanton did rut a horse, said Thomas Sunderland.

The men laughed.

Rut a horse? said Crowther O' Badger.

Aye.

You're a liar you are.

I'm not though but.

Yes you are. It wasn't a horse.

What were it then?

Crowther O' Badger paused.

It were a donkey.

The men laughed harder at this. Some of them shoved and cajoled him. Slapped him on the back and in turn he enjoyed the attention. It felt good to laugh. That which had gone unspoken had now been intimated, and though the consequences for all men were perilous there was nevertheless a lifting of the tension. The drinks slipped down more quickly now. More rounds were bought and without it being said directly it was decided.

Isaac Hartley picked up a drained jug and brought it down on a table several times.

Enough of this, he said. Thomas Spencer – you know every corner and cranny of this valley.

Indeed I would say that's true.

Then you are to gather the funding. Starting now. Deighton's days are dwindling and the king himself has pledged twenty guineas so dig deep into your cloth pockets, Coiners. Dig deep and think of the mouths of your children, them that have them. Tomorrow you take to the hillside hamlets, Tom Spencer. You need not tell folk what their coins are for, only that they are funding their own futures. That will be enough. The valley is on our side.

And what of Normanton and Thomas? said John Tatham.

If they are as cut-throat as Badger here reckons then they are the men for this job. I will arm them myself. I will arm them and send them off into the savage night.

A Malkin an all I seen malkins stows of times up ont moors A Malkin been the man that's made of shirts stufft with straw to scare the crowes I seenum moving about thrae or for at a time at nite Circlin they were just like the stagmen done circlin And dansin and laffen too Onse I saw a malkin with his feat and hans on fyre On fyre they were And he was runnen Runnen across the moor he was as if to reech a tarn or sluice ditch to save himself from the friteful burnin And I say with my hand on the book I did heer that Malkin man screem becors even though he were maydde of straw and cloth there was life in him too and oh the sound he made it was like no man or annymul yoove ever herd Friteful it was.

Friteful A fritefull site indeed.

Believe me when I say that I seen Scarecrowes dancing and laffen and screaman on more than wan occashun Yes lissen but I say this now as a man what sleepes with deths shadder cast across his face at night A man who lives with deth close by now I say this with nothing to loose but my reputayshun and I only say it now becors men mite reckon I was mad if Id told of the dancing laffen screamun bugaboo with a head made of flour sacks and a besum stick for a back bone before Only now can I tell the hole whirld that the moors is a special place A secrut place where things do occuer beyond any explanayshun Things you must never meddul with No No.

But ah still it sadduns me to think that eyell never get to see the screemun Malkins of the moors or the dansun Stagmen or all them other sites again even if they did put the willies rite up us.

Rite up us I say.

Tom Spencer walked to Horsehold and folk there gave up their coin. Tom Spencer walked to Burnt Stubb and folk there gave up their coin. Tom Spencer walked to Boulder Clough and folk there gave up their coin. Tom Spencer walked to Midgley and folk there gave up their coin. Tom Spencer walked to Luddendenfoot and folk there gave up their coin. Tom Spencer walked to Luddenden Dene and folk there gave up their coin. Tom Spencer walked to Old Town and folk there gave up their coin. Tom Spencer walked to Pecket Well and folk there gave up their coin. Tom Spencer walked to Midgehole and folk there gave up their coin. Tom Spencer walked to Lumb Woods and Slack Top and Tom Spencer walked to Mytholm and Charlestown and Callis Wood and Jumble Hole Clough and Hanging Royd and Eastwood and folk there gave up their coin. Many purses he carried back to Bell Hole, each bulging with grubby money not for clipping but to pay for the head of one William Deighton. This was the payment pot to give to men who would gladly trade a bag of coins for the heart of another with little time for thought, feeling or consequence. The valley closed in. The valley drew together. Folk gave up their coin.

Samhain morning and the early sky was swollen grey. Soon it become too heavy to hold itself and it sagged through the night, finally falling apart in fragments of sleet. Swollen drops of water froze and settled briefly in the form of snowflakes that blew in on the diagonal, blurring the sharp edges of tree lines and the jet-coloured crags that the valley seemed to wear as a crown.

Dawn as was dusk and then the temperature dropped and the sleet flakes hardened into tight little balls of hail that rained and rattled down on slate roofs and brought still ponds to life. They littered the troughs and ditches by the newly dug turnpike.

Then when the downpour eased and the clouds passed over to slowly bank across the open moors in the direction of Haworth, the valley slopes were left with a fresh dusting of white, a patchwork of powdered shapes divided by the black streaks of stone walls that snaked over and around copses, hamlets and the top quarries whose embedded stones had been used to build all the dwellings, byres and barns for ten miles in any direction.

The sun rose then, for it had only skulked like a struck cat at the sight of the incoming storm, but now it yawned and stretched itself in layered lengths of light reaching crossways along the smallholdings of the Calder Valley, each named for the wood or landmark, creature or farm that occupied it: Wadsworth, Red Acre, Daisy Bank.

Old Chamber. Roebucks.

Brearley. Crow Nest.

Sandbed.

The day began, and with it came the first winds of winter, bone-cold and unadorned.

Thomas Spencer heard the dusty sound of a flail whipping the threshing floor as he approached the grain store at the back of the Salter place at Sowerby, where Robert Thomas and Matthew Normanton were hired hands brought in for work that should have been completed weeks ago.

He found the former elbow deep in a grain barrel and the latter raising the flail that loosened the seeds as he struck the corn heads. Their hair was speckled with grain and chaff, their eyes dry with harvest dust. Surrounding them in the store were sacks and sieves. Bushels of wheat were tied and stacked to one side. Despite the day outside, Matthew Normanton was stripped to the waist.

Thomas Spencer saw that the threshing floor was cobbled to help loosen the grain in readiness for winnowing. It gathered there in the crevices. He entered the barn. Matthew Normanton looked at him as he lifted the flail, paused for a moment and brought down the two sticks that were hinged by a metal loop with a violent grunt. The sound ricocheted. He lifted it again and whipped it down, once, twice, three times. Dust danced upwards in puffball spurts.

With a scoop Robert Thomas poured more grain onto the floor and then picked up a flail and joined him. The men swung their sticks with determination, with violence. First Robert Thomas and then Matthew Normanton. They found a rhythm. An alternating pattern. The Coiners' messenger Thomas Spencer watched. He counted twenty alternate cracks before the men straightened together, breathing deeply.

I've a job for you pair, he said.

What job's that then? said Robert Thomas as he wiped his brow with the back of his forearm, his breath shallow in his throat. Collecting grubby coins from the palms of toothless old maids while your leader chokes his chicken to the sound of the gaoler's whistling lament?

Beside him Matthew Normanton grinned at this, but said nothing.

It's not a job to be taken lightly.

Go on, said Robert Thomas.

There's good money for those that do it rightly.

Might this be doing the dirty work of yon David Hartley?

Does that matter? said Thomas Spencer.

Robert Thomas shrugged.

Not if the price is nice, said Matthew Normanton. He folded his threshing stick and held it in his hand. His chest was slowing to its regular breath.

It pays better than the threshing of summer corn on a cold afternoon. I reckon this coming winter to be a long one. Could be that it's cursed with lean times; Samhain today, and we've already seen sleet and hail. The wise men will be holing up already, not out in a barn bashing rocks and waiting for the fever to take them.

Talk on.

It's not my place to say more on the subject, said Thomas Spencer. I am only here to confirm that you are interested.

What queer business this is, friend, Robert Thomas said to Matthew Normanton. I do believe this moor-man speaks in riddles.

Not riddles, replied the Coiner. I speak only with discretion and ask you one more time: do you want to earn good money – enough money to live well for many months – doing a job that few men would dare to; a job that would raise any lawman's hackles?

Yes, said Robert Thomas with little hesitation. I do believe we would.

Then I can tell you that Isaac Hartley wishes to speak to you.

So it is for you coining lot after all. You that have never once extended an invitation to me and my friend here to come in on this yellow trade that they say keeps the valley flowing gold?

That's as maybe, said Thomas Spencer. But we're asking now. And it's a damn sight more than a small coin's cut you'll be getting for your labours here. This is real work for real men with the guts to do it. Isaac will be the one to explain it to you.

When?

Now.

Now? said Matthew Normanton.

Now.

We're threshing.

Surely the grain can wait.

Robert Thomas reached for his shirt.

Aye, he said. I imagine it can.

It was mizzling when the three men walked over the back of Scout Rock and dropped down into the sunken holloway that led to Stake Lane. The Coiner Thomas Spencer led. Robert Thomas and Matthew Normanton followed at their own pace.

As the branches closed in and the track dropped them below the level of land that surrounded them – a long sloping open pasture downhill, a tangle of scrub above them – Matthew Normanton stopped by the mound that held the complex rabbit warren that had a dozen holes or more, each littered with neat clusters of droppings.

What he's doing? said Thomas Spencer. What are you doing?

Matthew Normanton reached into his pocket and pulled out a ball of twine.

Snaring, said Robert Thomas.

Snaring?

Aye, what's it look like? He's snaring for his pot.

We haven't got time for that.

It'll only take us two shakes, said Matthew Normanton over his shoulder. I'll pick us up a coney or two on the way back.

He searched the undergrowth for a branch or twig.

Fuck your rabbits said Thomas Spencer. There's a hundred guineas waiting for you down Hollin Hey Bank if you wriggle. But Isaac Hartley is not a patient man.

Robert Thomas sniffed the air.

Maybe he's right, friend, he said to Matthew Normanton. Might be we'll be bathing in goose fat and picking our teeth with duck bills by Gunpowder Treason Night. I expect the rabbits can wait this one time.

Matthew Normanton put his twine away and the men continued down the tunnel that had been trodden deep into the Yorkshire dirt by hundreds of years of passing men and horses back through the days of Saxons, Normans, Brigantes, Romans, Celts and Vikings.

Isaac Hartley was crouched by a wall on Hollin Hey Bank when he saw them. As they approached he stood. His voice met them first.

You're the boys who are fit for this job then?

Fit we are, said Robert Thomas. But boys we are not.

We be men, said Matthew Normanton.

Men then. Even better for taking down a taxman.

I've told them what's needed, said Thomas Spencer.

Isaac Hartley took the measure of them.

Money is what's needed, said Robert Thomas.

You'll get your money, said Isaac Hartley. I heard you was greedy.

We'll be wanting it now.

You'll be wanting it now I'm sure, but you'll be getting it after the deed is done, he said. One hundred good milled guineas that Tom here has collected rests on the devil Deighton's head. If the exciseman goes on there'll be no living for any of us.

Isaac Hartley reached into his pocket and flipped a guinea first to Robert Thomas and then one to Matthew Normanton.

Get yourselves fed and watered with that. Your pockets will soon be full with plenty more like them.

How do we do him? asked Matthew Normanton.

I'll get some guns to you. Tom here will bring them up.

And when do we do this Deighton?

This night.

Tonight?

He's not hard to find, said Isaac Hartley. Bull Close Lane is where he lives and he takes ale at the corner inn until it shuts. When it's done the money will be with you. Don't come to me. Don't come anywhere near me. Anything else?

Aye, as it happens, said Robert Thomas. How come it's not one of your Coiner boys that's doing the killing? If you lads are as tough as teak and run the valley like everyone round here reckons you do, why is it you're asking me and him here to do it. Has your nerve left you along with this one they call the king?

Which one are you? replied Isaac Hartley.

Thomas.

Well listen, Robert Thomas. A hundred guineas I've promised and a hundred guineas you'll get. That's all there is to it.

That doesn't answer my question, does that.

You're asking why I'm hiring on a couple of simple corn threshers to kill William Deighton?

A man could take your tone as insulting.

Take it any way you like.

We do a lot more than fucking thresh corn, said Matthew Normanton, stiffening his stance.

Yes, said Isaac Hartley. That's what I heard. My ears told me that Robert Thomas and Matthew Normanton are the two most ruthless bastards around. Do anything for money those two – that's what I heard.

The men smiled at this. They nodded with approval.

My boys reckon you'll kill for coins. That's why I asked you. The only reason.

Then I have one more question to ask, said Robert Thomas. What?

How come you never had us coining or collecting for you?

Because you are the two most ruthless bastards around. Do anything for money those two, they said.

So?

So any man who does anything for money is not to be trusted. And that's why you'll get your guineas when Deighton's blood is running cold across the stones and pooling around the shining cobbles. Now trot on.

Through icy rain and lifting wind they walked. Beneath their coats Robert Thomas and Matthew Normanton carried pistols and a twist of gunpowder. Two pieces of guns and slugs to fit. The Coiner Thomas Spencer went with them.

They took the long way back round, through the villages of Sowerby and Sowerby Bridge. Down one side and up the other they walked, crossing swilling waters where foam gathered in swirls, and then passing by still dark pools and hamlets of houses and inns with lights in the window, and the rain began to fall harder. And then they were in trees and the wind blew and it took two long hours to reach the top of King Cross bank where they saw Halifax below them, and suddenly the night was real, and the guns were real and the slugs in their pockets were ready to bring death.

They reached Bull Close Lane and the street was quiet so they took up positions in the shadows of houses, and it was not yet late but the cold came in with a vengeance now.

The sky fattened and the rain fell, and they waited.

Time passed slowly, slower than the clouds across the autumn moon, slower than the dull distant chimes of a midnight bell that came and went, and they shivered wet in their wool layers, sopping right down to their undershirts. Robert Thomas did not have a hat nor Matthew Normanton a light for his pipe and Thomas Spencer watched the men watch Deighton's door from afar until no-one came and the night defeated them, and after several senseless hours spent shivering in silence they departed for their beds, silent still save for the wet squeak of their boots and the rattle of unspent slugs still full of death in their pockets.

Stolen coyns they tork of a lot in here now that many of my fellow poor shackled sods no ecksackly who it is I am and what it is I did For the word on the Crag Vayle Coiners has spread far and wide these passing munths Yes a lejun I am becummin as I sit in the condemmed mans cell awaytin my fate Stolen coyns they say are buried around the Royd and now every day they axe me about it King Dayvid King Dayvid they corl across the eckersise yard or down the airless corrydoor Where is it you hid the ginnys and I shouts back What fucken ginnys and they say The wans your own men stole off you and I shouts No Coyner stoll a fucken penny off me you daft and dirty black Lancastreen bastids and they laff and says Thats not the werd from the valley The werd from the valley is there was so much munny being clipped that there was yung lads what absconded with great bags of it from rite under your greesy nose and they burryed it in the wuds and in the crags and on the moors and they hid it in worls and roots and midden pits and horse byres and now they say that Calderdayle is rich with treshurs so menny treshurs that one day in the fucher men will find it and they will be rich rich rich And to this I bellow back turn it in you silly cunts But that nite as I lie moiling and tossen I carnt help but wunder if its true what they say Meanen wud my men really steel from the mitey King Daevid of Bell Howse becors after all this enterprise got so big so fucken quick hoo can relly say how much munny was clippt and filed and milled and melted Aye becors when orls said and done hoo can reely no owt about owt that goes on.

Green clumps of wet goose scat dotted the flagstone path that cut through the field as the honking birds were driven from cart to fold to pen. Their owners used stripped willow sticks to steer the waddling, hissing creatures to the showing circle where they were paraded in gaggles of a dozen or so.

Every November valley men brought down their best birds for the goose fair. It was a sign of winter incoming, a final chance to trade and gossip and boast before they holed up for the shortest darkest days. Cheese-makers came down too, and bakers with loaves and brewers with fresh furmenty, and a butcher with smoked sides and prime cuts to sell and a great pot of beef water being stirred over a smouldering fire.

Children ran screaming amongst the chaos of birds and people and baskets of wares.

To one side, by the pasture wall, the hired collaborator Robert Thomas and Coiner Thomas Spencer watched as geese were paraded, and they puffed on their pipes and exchanged an occasional word through gritted teeth. When Matthew Normanton arrived he took them to one side, away from the bustle of the birds and their drovers.

He has gone to Bradford now, he said. Deighton has gone to Bradford.

Bradford is no use to us, said his partner Robert Thomas.

No it is not, but tonight he will return.

Then tonight he will be full of slugs.

Thomas Spencer shook his head.

And I will not be joining you.

Has the yellow trade made you a yellow coward now? asked Robert Thomas.

I will not be joining you. Already I have been to Halifax and it is you who are getting paid. I work for the Hartleys, not you two. I'm staying here.

This man is a coward, Robert Thomas said to Matthew Normanton. He'd rather be amongst the goose shit and kiddies games than doing a man's work.

Call it what you will, said Thomas Spencer. But I'm not coming.

This is the work of three people, said Matthew Normanton. One to bide as lookout and for making distractions and two to do the deed.

Thomas Clayton will take my place.

Thomas Clayton the farmer?

And Coiner true. He will be waiting.

Waiting where?

Matthew Normanton asked this.

At your abode, said Thomas Spencer.

When do we go?

Now, Isaac wants it done this night.

Christ, said Matthew Normanton.

He sends another guinea.

Thomas Spencer handed over another coin.

Where's mine? asked Robert Thomas.

That is to split.

To split now, is it?

Yes.

What do you take us for – bloody Coiners with rusted shears? said Robert Thomas.

Nevermind that, said Thomas Spencer.

Is it true about them other missing bits though? asked Matthew Normanton.

What other missing bits?

They say that there's a stash of coins gone missing and been buried somewhere. Somewhere close. They say that folk have been skimming.

I don't know about any of that, said Thomas Spencer. I just run the messages and collate the intake. Only a fool would skim though.

That's right, said Robert Thomas. Folk say that there's Coin-ers got their hauls stashed in tree roots and rock holes. That some of them have been stealing and others have been clipping their own coin on the side and giving nothing to your Hartley brothers.

I don't know, said Thomas Spencer. And I'll not say it a third time.

Because if that's true we'll be the first to find it, isn't that right, Matty?

Rest assured, brother, said Matthew Normanton. I have a nose for gold. And he who finds it keeps it. That's the law of the land, is that.

You'd have to ask Isaac Hartley and I wouldn't advise doing that while his brother sits in the dungeons of York gaol because of the doings of one of his own.

That nugget Broadbent you mean?

Yes, said Thomas Spencer. Broadbent.

Shall we kill him too? said Matthew Normanton through a yawn as he waggled a finger in one ear to dislodge some wax that was stuck there. It'll cost you another hundred guineas but I'd gladly slit that sly bugger like a breached sow.

No, said Thomas Spencer. Broadbent is not your concern. Enough of this talk: you need to go now.

Robert Thomas looked at Matthew Normanton and said: do you have food at your home, my friend?

Barely. I have bread.

And the guns?

The guns are there too. I've put them in a poke out back.

Then let us fetch Thomas Clayton now and we will eat on the way, said Robert Thomas. Then we will go to Fax and kill this devil Deighton and get this business resolved. Then we will live like gods. Not scrawny hill-top, deer-fucking false kings, but gods. True gods of the valley. Come, I'm tired of standing around in the shadows talking to forgers too yellow to clean up their own mess.

He looked at Thomas Spencer for a lingering moment and then turned and left, kicking a goose that blocked his path out of the way as he did. Ruffled, the bird stumbled and then cut a zig-zag path through the crowd.

For several months a John Walton and a James Lord had been in dispute over the purchase of a barn at the end of the village of Cottingley, and the amount of hay contained within it. Twice they had nearly come to blows in the street over the transaction. Lord, as purchaser, had claimed the hay had turned rotten and so reneged on the full payment, and then one night in revenge Walton's brother-in-law attacked the brother of Lord, who was but an adolescent. A blood-feud had developed and now William Deighton had been called upon to take out a warrant on both men over unpaid duties.

Accompanied by a Justice of the Peace, one Colonel Patrick Peasholme, the exciseman travelled the ten miles from Halifax to the village in the Bingley ward of Bradford. This day they took a coach as Cottingley was the far side of Bradford.

Each valley across the West Riding seemed to wear its own weather – those further to the west suffered the clouds that blew in from the Irish Sea and dropped their sheets of rain onto the spine of the Pennines, while those older wapentakes to the east and south had their skies blackened by the clouds of industry blowing over from Bradford and Leeds and all the cotton towns in between. North beyond the Ridings led to miles and miles of nothing but the sheep-rearing Dales and beyond those the coal fields of Durham and slate mines of Westmorland.

It was an evening dusted with sparkling stars as the sky cleared itself of cloud and the temperature dropped further; it was not a night for riding, nor was it a time for Coiners' business.

Afterwards, with the Walton–Lord matter only partially resolved, William Deighton and Colonel Patrick Peasholme took a coach back to Halifax. In the Nag's Head inn they met with an attorney, Tommy Sayer. They talked. They drank. They drew up an agreement that they hoped would settle the matter between the two men, whose idiocy they happily mocked, and Deighton ensured the necessary tax levee and fines for non-payment were to be made to the crown.

He was hungry. He had travelled twenty miles and neither John Walton nor James Lord had thought to offer him a bite nor an ale all day long. He thought now of the meal his wife would have waiting for him. There was always something. Even when he had returned in the middle of the night from the godforsaken Erringden Moor aback Bell House there was a pot on the range or a plate under a cloth. Always something. A serving of stew. Slices of ham and baked eggs maybe. Or chops in the cold store. Cobs. Fruit cake and cheese. The bottle of brandy and his glass beside it. The fire banked and glowing. The log basket never empty. Upstairs his family asleep.

With these in mind he bade farewell to Tommy Sayer and to Colonel Patrick Peasholme, whose company he had found fatuous and condoscending, as so many men with military titles were, and he rose to leave.

William Deighton opened the door and the night came flooding in. It was still and clear and bitterly cold. The stones of the street winked with frost as he walked downhill only slightly unsteadily. Swires Road swayed before him, most of its windows cast in darkness, and the inhabitants of each domestic residence asleep, as his family were, and he soon would be.

Tomorrow he would rise a little later than usual, he decided. Tonight he would drink three fingers of brandy slowly and tomorrow he would not hurry to do his daily tasks. He would raise the glass to King David Hartley and he would smile, knowing that his own belly was full and his bed warm, and his liberty boundless.

He heard his feet. The comforting *clett-clett* of leather on stone.

He turned down Savile Park Road towards Bull Close Lane and the night seemed so cool and clear, the sky so bejewelled, that he felt as if he could chip a piece of it away and mount it on a ring for his dear devoted wife.

* * *

265

They heard the footsteps – expensive shoes pacing the frosted pavement – and like phantasms they rose from the tight shadow by the wall that cornered the meeting of three lanes. Their joints were stiff with the cold. Finger-tips benumbed.

Clett-clett.

Two men. Hired.

Matthew Normanton. Robert Thomas.

Two guns. Loaded.

A third man was on lookout. The farming Coiner Thomas Clayton. Up the hill he waited, his eyes set on the silent street for the past two hours. The night was still but not so beautiful to him; it could not be beautiful when he knew it was shortly to be poisoned.

Clett-clett.

Matthew Normanton became a shifting shape. Matthew Normanton was black liquid. Matthew Normanton was pure silence.

Beside him Robert Thomas was unfolding. Robert Thomas was rising.

Robert Thomas was seeing.

And Thomas Clayton crouched up the hill. Thomas Clayton was looking out and Thomas Clayton was looking on.

Matthew Normanton was a spectre now. Matthew Normanton was a spirit.

Clett-clett.

Leather on stone. He raised his musket. His joints stiff. Finger-tips numb.

He rested the butt on his shoulder. Wood against wool. Wool against flesh. Flesh against the future.

Robert Thomas had a pistol. Robert Thomas had a pistol that was small and snug in his hand, and the trigger was cold as his cold numb finger-tip touched it. Frost rimed the bony barrel.

Clett.

And that was when William Deighton stopped and saw them, off to one side, two shapes hesitating. Two shapes hanging there, draped like dyed-black shalloons drip-drying on a worsted twill man's rack. Two blank phantoms framed by the night; betrayed by it.

He turned to them squarely. And he looked.

He looked deep into the brilliant blue of eternity and the night gave William Deighton that jewel that he thought he had wanted – a gleaming flash of diamond, a final exploding star – and it was in him forever, a jolting powdered flash like a gemstone lifted to the sun between thumb and forefinger. Something dazzling lit the back of his eye and lodged there. The street pitched sideways and the cut stone came to greet him.

A bullet sat in the centre of his skull.

Robert Thomas fired too, his small, snug gun louder still. He felt its power in his wrist and arm and elbow. It recoiled up his shoulder.

The stone was cold and wet to William Deighton's cheek. His breath was short but though one eye was a ruined mess like a blooming flower, the other was blinking clearly, wet and alive with a flinty look of indignation.

The bullet just sat there. He was aware of the path it had taken, and the space it now occupied. He felt it in his core, an icily indifferent intruder.

From further up the street Thomas Clayton watched.

Several short steps brought Robert Thomas to the exciseman first and he did what he always did when death was close by: he met it head on. He stamped William Deighton with his feet. He jumped on his heaving, rasping chest with shoes that had spiked nail soles to provide traction, and he punted the taxman's face and then Matthew Normanton was beside him, fighting to get at the prone body with the butt of his gun. He swung it like he swung the threshing stick, and he felt wood on bone, and heard things crack and split and give and spill, and then they were going through his pockets, the two of them, pulling out coins and a watch and a tin of snuff and a spectacles case and a knife and a roll of papers and a seal and a jar of ink and a notebook and lozenges and matches and a crucifix.

From up the street Thomas Clayton watched as they took William Deighton's cufflinks and they took William Deighton's wedding band. They took William Deighton's wallet and they took William Deighton's life.

Robert Thomas and Matthew Normanton.

They took these things and then they turned and vaulted a wall and ran off into the long night of a million shining flawless crystals.

The guns splashed and then sank in the gelid waters of Mill Dam below the valley bottom village of Luddendenfoot, and in the moonlight they flashed silver like the taut bellies of young darting trout as they fell to the river bed. Robert Thomas and Matthew Normanton followed the guns with rocks and boulders hoisted in the same direction to make sure they were covered and hidden from view.

Then they turned and walked the short way back along the river route to Mytholmroyd.

Oh we have done for yonder black devil tonight, said Robert Thomas.

Indeed we have, said Matthew Normanton. When it is men's work that needs doing it is to men they come. Never again will this Deighton one enter the valley and seek out business that is not his. We fettled him right good, we did.

Is it not true that these Coiners are as soft as tripe in their own ways? They must be if they can't take care of their own grim business.

That is true, Bobbsy.

Then is it not also true that their riches could be our riches, said Robert Thomas. That is – they are there for the taking?

There are many of these Coiners to contend with, said his companion.

The men continued walking briskly into the freezing night.

Indeed there are but their leader is locked up now and they say he will swing for it. These coining men are nothing. They scrape together shavings and they melt them and stamp them and pass them on. That is all. Even then they say there is only one of them who truly knows the art of coining.

But with great success it seems, said Matthew Normanton.

With some success, yes – if you consider your new home address of York gaol a success, as it is now of their leader. No, it is you and I who are the ones with the hearts of killers, brother. Cold blood does not bother us.

Matthew Normanton smiled into the nothingness. Robert Thomas continued.

All we need is the coins – and they are not hard to come by – and, of course, this man that has the knowledge of the fire and metal. An alchemist. They say there are a hundred Coiners or more sharing the profits of this golden venture.

Yes.

Well think on, brother. All that could be ours. Yours and mine. The wealth of one hundred fools and cowards.

No more threshing corn, said Matthew Normanton.

No more threshing corn.

They let their feet guide them through the cold mud. They were quiet for a few moments and then Matthew Normanton spoke again.

Certainly this is worth some thought. But perhaps not on this long night. I am algid and weather-worn.

So too am I.

You can rest at mine – it is closer. And tomorrow we shall go and collect one hundred good milled guineas from that daft cunt Isaac Hartley.

He threw an arm around the shoulder of Robert Thomas.

A hundred golden guineas, he said again. One for every bint we'll fuck.

At Normanton's lodgings they made straight for his room where they peeled off stiff clothes that reeked of sweat and death and they fell into bed together, shivering naked in the night, white skin taut and touching in the eldritch winter dark, both awake under a heap of blankets, both thinking of coins – hundreds of them, thousands of them. Millions. More coins than there were sheep turds in the whole of the crooked valley. Then they slept and in their leaden slumber they dreamt of coins too.

So they say the lore man is ded As ded as moldy blue bread Deightons ded its said Blassed in the phiz with shots of led an stomped abowt the hed The nite street paynted a bluddygud red.

Part V
Winter 1769
Bubblinmeet

Robert Parker received the news at first light on the cold crisp morning from his young clerk: the exciseman William Deighton was dead. Shot twice. Once in the head.

He had been found trampled and bleeding and broken by his daughter, Susannah, and the Deightons' house-maid Mary, his last gasp still on his lips. His final breath ascending out of sight. Much blood.

Gunned down in the street like a dog that's gone foam-mouthed, were the young clerk's precise words. Shot down in the cold clear night, on the slick stone, not thirty paces from his own door-step, his wife now widowed, his children fatherless, two of the boys over the seas, the town a-talk with names of those that might have done it.

I know who has done it, said Robert Parker. But knowing isn't proving. So I will prove it.

The solicitor wasted no time. He first paid a visit to Bull Close Lane to offer his condolences and make a solemn promise that he would see justice was served. He then returned to his chambers where he spent several hours consulting the file that Deighton had accrued on the many suspected forgers: their descriptions, movements and interlinking relationships. Their last known whereabouts. To these Robert Parker added his own notes. It was imperative that a clear chronology was set in order, beginning with Deighton's first encounter with the Coiners, taking in his many reconnaissance missions and verbal threats or acts of intimidation received, and concluding with this diabolical deed that had taken place the night before.

The murderers were from a pool of many, but greed would surely smoke them out like rodents beneath a grain store. The turncoat James Broadbent had proven that greed could make a Coiner talk and Robert Parker knew he was more than capable of avenging William Deighton's death the moral and legal way, just as he had promised – though of course as a practising man of the bar vengeance was not a word he would entertain using. This was about pragmatism and trust in a system. The English way.

The solicitor worked right through luncheon and long into the afternoon, and then he called upon his clerk to receive dictation for a press missive and a series of posters and hand-bills based on the late William Deighton's thorough findings to be printed and distributed immediately.

WANTED FOR CLIPPING, COUNTERFEITING
AND MURDER

UNDER THE HIGHWAYMAN'S ACT OF 1692

Information on the activity and whereabouts of
the following.

Any Person making such Discovery of af'd
(except as before excepted) shall receive a
Reward of forty pounds which is hereby offered
by the Gentlemen and Merchants of the Town
and Parish of Halifax to be paid by the Constables
of Halifax.

THOMAS CLAYTON, late of Turvin in the
township of Sowerby, and Parish of Halifax,
Stuff-Maker, aged about Forty, and about five feet
seven inches high, is slenderly made and round
shouldered, has light-coloured Hair, is thinnish
visaged, and of a fair complexion. He used to wear
brown coloured Cloaths, and was but indifferently
dressed.

BENJAMIN SUTCLIFFE, late of Halifax, Stuff
Weaver (commonly called Benny Nunco) aged
about Sixty, and about five feet four inches High,

is a broad sett Man, and has a reddish pimpled Face, and wears a Brown wig. When he went off he was dressed in Claret coloured Cloaths.

ISAAC DEWHURST, late of Owle Nook, in Luddingden Dean, in the Township of Warley, and Parish of Halifax, about Thirty-Five or Thirty-Six years of age, about five Feet eight Inches high, is a stout broad made Man, wears his own hair, which is black, and is black complexion'd. When he went off he had two Suits of Cloaths, the worst of a light coloured drab Cloath, and the better was of a Sad blue Colour.

NATHAN HORSFALL, late of Saltonstal, in Warley, Butcher, aged about Thirty, and about five feet seven Inches high, is a broad sett Man, wears his own Hair, which is dark, brown and bushy; he is of a fresh Complexion, and much marked with the small Pox.

JOHN TATHAM, late of Wadsworth, in the said Parish of Halifax, Stuff Weaver, aged about Twenty-Four, and about five Feet ten Inches high, is slender made, and active, wears his own Hair, which is Flaxen coloured and curls, is of a fair Complexion, cherry cheek'd and handsome; when he went off he had blue worsted Shag Coat, and a Draw-Boy waistcoat, with mixed colours of blue, white and Scarlet.

JOHN PARKER, late of Shackleton, in Stansfield, Stuff Maker, aged about fifty, and about five feet ten Inches high, is a thin Man, wears his own Hair, which is of a saddish Flaxen Colour, and a little bushy; he is thinnish visaged, and has remarkable thick Lips, wears an old blue Coat and waistcoat, and is shabbily dressed.

JAMES GREEN, late of Halifax, Heald-striker, aged about Twenty-five or Twenty-six, is about five Feet three Inches high, a broad sett man wears his own Hair, which is black and bushy, and is of a blackish Complexion, pale looking and a little mark'd with the Small Pox; he used to wear a Scarlett Stuff waistcoat, and a blue Cloath Coat.

PETER BARKER, late of Stanfield in the Parish of Halifax, Miller (commonly Called Foul Peter) aged 36 years or thereabouts, a broad-set Man, about Five feet seven Inches high, black hair, tyed behind, dark complexion'd, and generall wears light-coloured Cloaths.

WILLIAM CLAYTON, late of Sowerby, in the same Parish, Weaver, aged near 40, about five feet seven inches high, broad-set, flaxen-coloured Hair, which curls a little, is fresh-coloured, and generally wears dark brown Cloaths, sometimes a Crimson Shag Waistcoat.

JOHN IBBOTSON, late of Ovenden, in the same Parish, dealer in wool, about 25 years of age, five feet six inches high, slender made, fair complexion'd, looks pale but very smart, wears his own Hair, which is brown and curls a little.

MATTHEW HEPWORTH, late of Ovenden, in the same Parish, Butcher, about 40 years old, 5ft 7 ins high, rather slender a little pock-broke, wears his own Hair, which is of a reddish Colour, and almost straight.

JOSEPH HANSON, late of Halifax, Innkeeper, broad-set, about 5ft 6 ins high, of a dark Complexion, a Mole upon one Cheek, dark Eyes and Eye-brows, and some Pimples on one Side of his Face, wears a brown Coat and Waistcoat, and a brown Cut or Bob Wig.

ISAAC HARTLEY, late of Erringden, in the Parish of Halifax (commonly called the Duke of York, being younger Brother of David Hartley, usually called King David, now a Prisoner in York Castle) about 35 years old, 5 ft 7 ins high, a dark down-looking man, wears his own Hair, which is black, a little pock-broke, and generally wears light-coloured Cloaths.

JOHN WILCOX, late of Keelliam, in Erringden, in the same Parish, Weaver, about 30 years old, 5ft 7 ins high, broad-set, black complexioned, wears his own Hair, dark-coloured, and generally stripp'd Waistcoat and brown coat.

JOSHUA LISTER, late of Halifax, Innkeeper, about 30 years old, 5ft 4 ins high, round shoulder'd and broad set, a ruddy Complexion, wears his own Hair, which is flaxen-coloured and curls a little; he used to wear a Copper coloured Bath Ruggy Coat and Waistcoat.

JOSEPH GELDER, late of Halifax, Stuff weaver, about 25 years old, of a Dark Complexion, and squints, wears his own Hair, which is of a dark Colour, and curls well; he is about 5ft 7 ins, high: had on when he went off, a light-coloured Drab Coat and Waistcoat.

JOSHUA SHAW, late of Halifax, Innkeeper, about thirty-five years old, five Feet four Inches in. high, well looking, rather pale Complexioned, wears his own Hair, which is of a light brown Colour and curls a little; he used to wear a dark mottle-coloured Coat, and a red Waistcoat.

In small print along the bottom of posters and hand bills was printed:

Other Persons suspected of Coining etc include:
WILLIAM PROCTOR of Maiden Stones
JAMES BROOK of Collingbob
BARTHOLOMEW WALKER of Mytholmroyd
CROWTHER O' BADGER of Sweet Oak
ISRAEL WILDE of Deerplay
GEORGE O' SMITH of Soyland
WILLIAM FOLDS of Callis
RICHARD CLEGG of Turvin
JOHN PICKLES of Wadsworth
THOMAS PICKLES of Wadsworth
PAUL TAYLOR of unknown
BOB ARDELL of Halifax
WILLIAM HARPUR of Lee Bank
STEPHEN MARTON of Elland
WILLIAM SYKES of Waton Mill
JOSIAS SMITH of Bradford
ABRAHAM KERSHAW of Turvin
ANTHONY SUTCLIFFE of Swamp
JOHN RADCLIFFE of Lighthazles
JOHN FEATHER of Roughead
BRIAN DEMPSEY of unknown
THOMAS VARLEY of Warley
JONAS EASTWOOD of Eringden
DAVID GREENWOOD of Hill Top
& others.

Robert Parker dispatched the missives for facsimiles to be printed overnight; by the following afternoon they would be pasted and pinned in every shop and inn across the town and in every one-horse hamlet the length and breadth of the Calder Valley.

Because the voices of the same valley, he was sure, would talk. Not every man was a Coiner and those that were would surely see that with their king caged the days of their forging and laundering were limited. A candle only burns once, and always downwards.

As this dark day darkened still he had his clerk contact the same two bailiffs who had helped with the arrest of Hartley. Arkle and Baker. One was to stand outside the Deighton household in Bull Close Lane and the other outside his own home in The Square. They would remain there until told otherwise. This was now a war, of sorts.

Finally the sky was free of clouds and the stars cut through the night like smashed quartz sprinkled and thrown aloft to stick there. Everything tightened. A crusted hoar of glistening frost formed over rutted scrolls of mud like bull's liver and puddles retracted into plates of white scratched glass. Shards of grass became spines that snapped underfoot, and the prints of nail-soled boots and cloven hooves and clawed feet alike became markers of the nocturnal traffic that passed through the woods and glades and dells of the valley.

The icy air held hot breath as if it were a strange weightless object – the human form expelled into abstractions bigger than any torso that made them; life turned inside out and hung there, solidified, sculpted and suspended.

The sun warmed only the top half of the northern valley slopes now. The rest were kept in a state of permanent shadow, and when the burning ball set it was with one final burst of shattering rays that blazed up from beyond the line where the angular bronze peaks bowed to the salmon sky.

The trees held no leaves. They were skeletal now. When a breeze lifted, their branches played a fidgeting rhythm and the dry stiff leaves that had matted together around their roots stiffly flapped an inch or two but mostly the air was still, as if that too was frozen. As if that too was a solid thing to be chipped away by the indifferent rays of a sun that sat low, malevolent and with little warmth.

The sheep were brought down. The cows brought in. Stray cats took to the woodsheds and found spaces beneath split logs that had hardened with frigid sap, and the birds busied themselves with the gathering of berries and nest-lining. Deep winter circled like a fairytale wolf around a clearing of lost children.

Soon all the valley was first frost and then ice, and then dry flecks of granular snow fell, spiralling like ash coughed back from a blocked chimney, and though it did not settle it began to fall heavier and the ground was so cold the snow had nowhere to go. It piled in windswept drifts. It sat then on the frozen ponds, dusted vegetable patches and gathered in little dry drifts. The dusting became a quilt.

Overnight the river ran thin and then thinner still. It became a rushing streak of water bubbling through shelves of ice on either side that grew jutting from its banks like blades. Everything around it hardened. All became stone. Even the sun appeared solid, a stone wheel suspended, immutable and unyielding.

And the snow moved through the various stages towards an end purpose: first powder dry and ball-like, then young, aerated and playful, and then more complicated flakes fell and linked together like acrobats in the air. There was a panic to their spinning freefall as the plunging temperature drew them in. Settled, they became something else – something vast and powerful.

The morning sun softened the next wave of falling flakes slightly but only enough to alter their form before they too turned into beautiful gems gleaming in the afternoon stillness, stitched to the earth like dress sequins.

The valley was beautiful and blinding. A world of black and white. Of day and night. A world of binaries and oppositions.

Winter.

The window was mottled with a thick frost that appeared to Matthew Normanton to mirror the blemished rippled skin of the woman whose large round rear was pressed up against his morning stiffness. Her untied hair lay tangled across the pillow.

He could not recall her face.

He lifted the blankets and surveyed the rest of her body, saw the bruises on her forearm and the scratch marks upon her waist. The soles of her feet, dirty. A red rash around one wrist. Big hips.

Behind him there was stirring. He rolled over and was face to face with another woman. Her mouth was open and he could smell her stale morning breath: the aftertaste of gin and ale and meat and tobacco. Her front tooth was missing and the breath whistled through the gap. It was June. Her other name he could not recall but he had known her since childhood, and now she worked for Old Rose putting men in her mouth for coins. Last night, his coins. His stick.

Matthew Normanton looked down at the mapwork of veins across her breasts, one pressing down on the other. Her nipples were dark and distended from recent suckling. Her children would go without breakfast this morning.

It was in Old Rose's back room that he lay. He must have paid extra to stay the night. Extra still for sheets and the empty bottle on the bedstand. The fire was dead in the grate and his cock end felt tight. Sore. Shredded.

Someone farted and he wondered what had become of Robert Thomas.

He tried to remember the night that had gone before; he tried to recreate it but all that remained were a few fleeting scenes.

He remembered singing, slipping on ice. A lot of drinking and boasting. Ale and gin and his first ever taste of whisky like a small fire ignited in his stomach and scorching his throat with its rough, woody vapours.

He recalled falling up the stairs, and the sound of coins rolling and laughter too. And then the women undressing him, and the wax-coloured winter moon nearly full and shining down, making something beautiful out of those frost patterns on the window, and the bright moon on their tallow flesh, everyone shivering and laughing and shivering still, and the moon smiling too.

And as the broken night pieced itself together in the aching fog of his gin-hammered head, Old Rose walked into the room and said right you lot, up and out, and Matthew Normanton lay wondering what it was that had been done and said, and again what had become of Robert Thomas.

As it happened Robert Thomas had stopped on his way home on the flat fields by the river at the hamlet of Brearley to take a pipe and sing a victory song to the very same moon, an improvised ditty that bragged of his physical and sexual prowess, and which told the world that he, Bobbsy Thomas, a lowly corn thresher and sometime stuff-making weaver that was born a bastard, had slayed the devil Deighton while David Hartley sat in a cell a broken man, and was therefore in fact the true king of Yorkshire, and wealth and fame and more women were assured, until midway through the sixth verse when he slipped off a rock like an otter into the shallow, fast-running ice cold waters of the River Calder.

Fortunately for Robert Thomas his bellows were heard by a widowed herdsman who grazed cows on the thick lush grasses of the plain and he and his sons came running from their home with lanterns and blankets and a rope that the eldest son used to lasso him as he clung to a semi-submerged log. Only then did Robert Thomas realise that he could in fact stand in the river, yet was too frozen by the shock of the waters to manage even that, so was instead pulled flailing and gasping by the herdsman and his two sons up onto the very same rock from which he had slipped. Here he was swaddled in blankets and led to the house where, in front of a stoked fire, he was stripped naked and given a cup of something strong and clear from an unmarked bottle, the likes of which he had never tasted before but which managed to bring him around.

The alcohol also served to loosen his tongue once more, and Robert Thomas started singing again, this time through chattering teeth that gave his song a new staccato rhythm with percussive enamel accompaniment. The herdsman and his sons looked on and shook their heads and one of them remarked that it seemed like they should have left this cracked cuckoo in yon river.

Only when Robert Thomas managed to rhyme the words frighten and Deighton though did the herdsman raise a hand and say: wait one tick, stranger, is this the exciseman William Deighton you sing of?

At this Robert Thomas raised his head from his chest and lifted the blankets further around his shoulders and said aye, the very same black devil himself, slayed by my own hand not but two nights since so that you good men might be free to carry on with your coining and your clipping and the valley will flow with gold once more. You can thank me in any which way you choose, starting perhaps with another nip of that fiery stingo you've got in that there bottle, friends, and very fine it is too.

In the clearing in the wood, where his blackened metal burner stood, Joseph 'Belch' Broadbent coughed through his pipe and watched as his eldest son lumbered through the frosted trees towards him.

He was speaking before he had stopped walking. His words were flat and breathless. They were devoid of shape or air; forged and flat like the coins he coveted.

285

The taxman William Deighton is done for, father, he said. All the Royd is full of talk about it. Deighton is dead and with him goes our last chance of one hundred guineas.

What happened?

They say he was shot and stamped and then shot again. In the street it was.

By who?

Make a list, father. Make a list of names and any one of them might have done it. One thing is certain though: the Hartleys are behind it.

Joseph Broadbent sat on one of the tree stump seats and removed his pipe from between his teeth. It had gone out so he upturned it and tapped out the black flecks of spent tobacco, then he coughed for a long time. He tapped and coughed.

Well, that's that then, he finally said.

James Broadbent walked to the charcoal burner and pressed his palms to it. He flinched and then pressed them once more.

We have been robbed by ill fortune.

It was a roll of the dice, said the elder Broadbent. Getting involved with the taxman was always a risk and as with any cock fight or badger scrap it was a gamble, a decision for us to make as free men of sound mind. This time it has not paid off. Just be glad it was him that was shot and stamped and not you; be thankful your heart still beats. A man has died but you still walk the valley, my son.

But for how long? And anyway, this was all your stupid idea.

Joseph Broadbent coughed again.

I am old, he said. It's not a time for regrets. I doubt that I'll see this winter through.

James Broadbent dismissed his father.

Don't talk daft.

It's true. Death is in my cage of ribs now. It has moved in. Taken root. Can't you hear it?

It's all this wood burning – that's all, said James Broadbent. You've always suffered for your charcoal.

286

No, James. No. These days are numbered for me now.

You'll be all right once spring comes around. You always get like this. Just wait for the first sign of snowdrops.

Joseph Broadbent spoke quietly.

When the snowdrops come I'll be under them.

James Broadbent turned from the burner and paced.

Never mind your moaning, he said. It's what's occurring now that concerns me.

His father wheezed and spat.

You just keep your beak out of it all, son.

My beak is already in. What if they think that it's me that has done Deighton?

But you didn't, said his father.

I know that. But folk know that Deighton had me over a barrel.

You'd not kill that man – not least because he'd not yet given you the money he promised.

But that's exactly the same reason a man might want to murder him.

There's no proof.

James Broadbent laughed incredulously at this.

Proof? Deighton works for the crown. The crown doesn't need proof, you silly old cunt. When the man decides it's you, then it's you that will be swinging. There's no arguing otherwise. Robert Parker is already gathering men of power, you can be sure of that, and these men from London won't need telling twice. If enough people say my name then it's me they'll collar.

Joseph Broadbent re-packed his pipe.

Then you should find out who has done it in case you're asked about it, he said in a quiet voice. Information is the only thing on your side.

Our side.

This is your business, son. I'll be dead already by the time this is resolved. Mark my words. I'm down to darkening days now. The candle is at its stump and the wick is flickering. My shadow is growing long.

James Broadbent turned and snapped.

Then what are you doing out here mithering in the cold and tending to your stupid burner when you should be at home in bed?

I'll go on doing what I've always done – that which folk know me for. Hard work on the land. My charcoal sacks sits in scores of houses. Folk will be kept warm all this winter because of a full calendar of toiling. I'm thanked for it.

You're a silly old cunt, James Broadbent said again.

That's as maybe, but it's too late to change now.

James Broadbent kicked at the stiff frozen sod.

They say they is offering a reward for any man who has information. Parker has put up bills.

His father looked up.

How much?

Forty pounds.

That's a lot of money, son.

It's not safe for me here.

Forty pounds is worth some thought, said Joseph Broadbent.

The coining shall continue now that the taxman is gone, and I'm no longer to be trusted. I'll be no part of it. There'll never be any place for me here.

Pity will get you nowhere. And you could burn like your old father burns.

James Broadbent scowled.

I'd rather die than live your life.

Then talk to these lawmen who'll soon fill this valley.

I cannot speak against the clipping gang again.

Take that forty pounds for it will surely get you to where you need to be going.

And where is that, father?

Anywhere.

Here is all I know.

Then you'll not know it for much longer. You'll join me in the hereafter pushing up the snowdrops if you don't use that head of yours for something other than butting and filling with beer.

The labourer had been paid for one month's work breaking stones and clearing trees and burning out roots and stumps to make way for the new bridge in the woods down from Colden. The bridge would bring the goods to build the mill that would straddle the waterway. The water would turn the wheels and some men would die and a few others – one or two perhaps – would get wealthy. Here too a chimney would rise above the trees, and a cluster of workers' cottages were already marked out with stakes and ropes on frozen ground. At the first thaw the cellars would be dug in and the foundations laid.

His thirst was great after thirty days of sawing and splitting and smashing and digging, and the walk up from the woods to Heptonstall only made him crave the ale more. He went to the Cross Inn and took the first drink down in three gulps and then put coins on the bar.

Abraham Ingham was his name and Abraham Ingham had made a commitment that day to drinking ale until his head rested on the stone pillow. He had thought of it much during these cold weeks living under crisp canvas and drinking nothing but nettle tea and stream water. He had dreamed of that first taste; the way it would slip down and spread a malty warmness throughout his body.

The second one went down easily and the third he held in his hand as he turned to survey the room.

He saw that the fire was banked and snapping and the inn was quietly busy.

High up on the hill Heptonstall was an isolated place, a rarefied village of houses huddled like black sheep in a moor-top whiteout, all looking inwards as if to form a stone phalanx against invaders – in this case the elements and particularly the wind that whipped around its sharp corners at all times of the year.

The half mile walk down steep slopes to Hebden Bridge might as well have been a thousand times that; Heptonstall was its own world, a cloud land of scratching rain and whirlpool skies.

Abraham Ingham took more ale and by his fifth tankard he was buying drinks for new friends. Men like him, of blood blisters and dirty necks. He had come from Cumbria to work here and everything he had been told about this Pennine valley had so far proven to be true: that it rained constantly. That there was little sun and the moors were a strange and unending place like a dream you never wake from, a landlocked sea to be feared.

But in ale none of that mattered; only the moment. Only this Friday night. And his new friends too, these men of toil and soil and dirty jokes. Their acceptance mattered.

By drink number six he was singing Cumbrian shepherds' songs accompanied by a small dark man with a drum and by drink number seven he was confiding his plans and hopes and secrets, one arm slung around a fellow drinker.

There were Greenwoods and Jaggers drinking in the Cross that night. Sutcliffes and Smiths. There were women too. Wives and sisters and cousins. Wildes and Butts and Barkers.

They listened and they watched as the labourer sang and swore and sloshed his drink. They listened too as he told anyone who cared to listen that he had heard tell of who it was that had filled the Halifax exciseman full of lead shot, and how he had a mind to turn those names over to the men that mattered. It was only right, was that. They heard him slur as he said he would see them men done for, because murder is murder and that man had a wife and children left wanting now.

And besides, he grinned, was there not a generous reward being offered?

They listened and they watched a little longer and then they rose. Not as one, but slowly over a minute or two. Drinks were downed and cups settled. Eyes checked the door. Glances passed between them. No words were exchanged – just a look here and there. A look was all it took. The twitch of an eyebrow across the room. A dipping of a head. The contents of a pipe tapped out onto a table. A cough. Conversations reduced to murmurs.

There were Butts and Barkers and Bentleys in there.

Tathams and Tilotsons. Harpurs and Hills.

The Wilcox boy.

And a Hartley too. The son of the brothers' cousin, with a girl he was courting by his side. Here were the tangled roots of valley families who had lost good men to the cells because of the turncoat rat James Broadbent and the devil bastard William Deighton and some snotnose young town cunt called Robert Parker.

Men stood and Abraham Ingham didn't even notice the tightening of the room; didn't register the movement or the hush that settled or the bar-girl who put down her towel and left. The fire was snapping with the crack and hiss of a pyramid of split logs collapsing in on itself. A man bent to prod and rake it and then he left the tongs there in the white heart of it.

Another gently dropped the latch on the door.

Abraham Ingham, labourer, stone breaker and beer-drinker, was deep into his drink now and like a man swimming in ale he was repeating what he had said already, but speaking it as if for the first time, and louder still: *and is there not a reward being offered?*

Shadows lengthened then and boots scuffed the floorboards and hands were upon him. Two, three, four pairs. For a moment he thought it was a prank, a local ritual or the initiation of an outsider into the inn. He even laughed but then his feet were kicked away with force and he fell forward. Hands held him at collar and cuff and belt.

The fire popped and blue flames danced as Abraham Ingham was lifted and thrust towards it like a ram for battering. No words were spoken. Not one. The fire grew large and he was held there. He felt the wall of its heat. He saw as a hand reached for the tongs that were glowing incandescent orange and smoking as they were lifted from the florid grate.

Still no words were spoken as he was pushed and shoved and kicked and booted into the fireplace and the heat screamed at him then, and he screamed with it, and as hockle bubbled at his mouth it felt like the end of the world as an inferno raged around him and his legs thrashed, and his hair was gone in seconds, the smell of it acrid and bitter in the nostrils of all around him, and then the tongs closed around his neck like a noose of pure white heat and someone squeezed them tight as if he were a piece of metal being forged. And he was held there as his flesh blistered and burned and all was fire and everything was flame and he became the fire.

And even then no words were spoken as glowing coals were shovelled from the grate and dropped down his loosened trousers, his legs twitching and his burnt blackened head slumping into the raging chaos of wood and coal and the ash that fell gently like snowflakes down into the ass-hoil pan below, and the hot coals burnt and melted the flesh of his buttocks and back and genitals and thighs. They singed through his clothes and fell smoking to the inn floor. His skull was stripped in the blaze and left as a charred shape in the fire, as if placed there like a peat hag or a sawn green willow stump that was only good for slow-burning. The labourer Abraham Ingham was dead.

And then Sutcliffes and Smiths and Butts and Barkers and Bentleys and Harpurs and Hills and the young Hartley boy too turned back to their tables and their drinks and their talk and their troubles, and Abraham Ingham was left smouldering, a spent match in human form, his head and neck a scorched mess of bone and sizzling sinew and stubborn fat, of burnt blood and bubbling meat.

Turncoat ratts get what is cummen to them but just imajun what a burnded head popping must have sounded like Madd fucken thort that The sent of it All that bubblinmeet Chryst.

Rats is everwhere and jussed like the stagmen and the scaringcrows of the moors rats are following your King David Heartlee Yes now jussed yesterday the piss runnel of this prisson did get backed up and blocked up and the sells were fludded with piss and our straw beds did get soppen with the stink of it and what it was rite it was the drayne beneath our dunjan homes did get blocked up somthen rotten.

So the man came jangling and lets a couple of the lads out King David incloodid and says Rite then one of you barbrus vermin can get down them steps and get the drayne unblocked and he pointed down a deep dark well that was sploshing knee deep with the shyte and piss of menny men and the lads says No fucken way cleen your own fucken scat and dribble and the man says Theres meat and ale and coyne and a brass from the hoor house to give a gobbil to any man what will do it so we all think on it for a minnut and neebody says owt and then I goes Go on then Aye ayell do it Thurs naught but death awaiting us anyway Deth and eaturnetty Becors king Dayvids a gayme cock never lerrut be sed Oh yass gayme as fuck this wan.

So I took off my britches and shirt sleyves and I climbed down into the stink of it and it wassunt so bad I poked around in the murky worter until it mite be that my fingus did touch upon some thynge down there Something soffed and slimey to the touch And big aswell as big as a bread baskit but it weren't no bred baskit it was like a big borl all wet and soft in the middule but harder and hairy further owt and whatever it was it had blockt the drayne like a bastid.

293

I dug in deep then becors the lads were going Wor is it King David Becors they all corl us King since the black devil Dighton got filled with led Wor is it they says and I was in up to me elbows and I bent I lifted this wet soft stinking mass of slyme and fur with both me arms and I cradled it there like a baybee and only then could I see there in the drayne that it was a grayte big borl of rats A duzzen of them if not more and all their tayles were tangulled and like notted together and they must have drownit that way and I swear it was the most horribullest thing a man ever did see so horribull it did give me the fear but I cuddent show that to the lads becors sum of them silly sods wership the ground the King warks on so I grunted and I lifted and I heaved the hole lot up and out the drayne with the most oarful skwelchen noise and it flopped there in front of them all and I goes.

I goes Narthen looker it's King Rat himself it's Jaymes fucking Brordbent And that's when they started yellen an pewking an runnen backwards like a wifee thats seen a field mouse in the pantryee the big fucken cunny thummed arse fuckers.

Now lissen now though Lissen the point here is in lyfe there are sines everywhere Sumtimes they appear in diffren forms and as diffren creachurs but they are sines orl the same and you got to watch out forum at all times This one said the rat Broadbent had gorrus gud and proper Guddan proper I saye and that's ther true laingth offit.

Robert Parker, Solicitor
Parker Esq. The Square, Halifax
November 7th 1769

To: Lord Wentworth, Lord of the Treasury

My Lord,

I write with grave news of the callous murder of Supervisor William Deighton near his home in Bull Lane Close in the town of Halifax where I hold practice.

It is of my opinion that this deed was committed by members of a gang of Counterfeiters and forgers of the King's crown widely known as the Cragg Vale Coiners and others times as the Turvin Clippers, on account of the remote township where their leader David Hartley does dwell.

As previously written, I had of late been assisting Mr. Dighton, a family man of good standing, in his endeavours to bring these Forgers to account and in this we had successfully made the Arrest of the aforementioned David Hartley, who resides in York Castle where he is awaiting his Punishment which is more than likely to be execution. It is also of my Opinion that members of his family or their gang are responsible for the murder of Mr Deighton.

I request that this case be taken on by you in your position as Lord Treasury, and seek your humble advice on the direction in which to proceed.

I am, humbly yours, &c,
Robert Parker
Solicitor, Court of the King's bench.

Last Friday morning, (10th inst.), betwixt Twelve and One o'Clock, as Mr Dighton, Supervisor at Halifax, who lived about Half a Mile from that Place, was going towards Home, when he had got within a Hundred Yards of his own door, some desperate Villains, who, it is supposed, had planted themselves for that Purpose, fired at him, and the Ball, entering his Head, he instantly expired; after which, the hardened Wretches took about Ten Guineas out of his pockets, and, from the Marks upon the Body, are supposed to have stamped upon and otherwise abused it. As Mr. Dighton has been extremely active in unkenelling and bringing to Justice the Clippers, Coiners, &c, it is generally believed some of that infamous Gang have perpetrated this inhuman Murder. One Person, we hear, is already apprehended, and the strictest Search is making after others.

Mr Dighton's Death is greatly lamented; he has left a Wife and seven Children, which, we doubt not, will be well provided for. A few Days ago George Thompson, belonging to this part of Yorkshire, was apprehended in Pilgrim Street, Newcastle, for clipping and diminishing the Gold Coin of this Kingdom; and on Tuesday he was committed to Newgate in that Town, by the right Worshipful the Mayor.

Leeds Mercury. November 14th 1769

Lord Weymouth, Lord Of The Treasury.
St. James's, Nov 14th 1769

To: Charles Watson-Wentworth, former Prime Minister,
Second Marquess Of Rockingham and Vice Admiral Of
Yorkshire.

My Lord,

It having been represented to me that a gang of Villains
near Hallifax have for some years past made a practice
of diminishing the coin, and of late years of coining
Portugese Pieces, that the practice was become so
common that it put the merchants under great difficulties
with regard to their payments: that prosecutions were set
on foot last summer, and that by the activity of Dighton,
Supervisor of the Excise, seven or eight of the gang have
been taken and committed to York Castle, but that others
of this gang, suspecting what was likely to be their Fate,
repeatedly vowed revenge against Mr. Deighton and
waylaid him on the 9th inst, and shot him dead, near
his own house. I laid the state of this matter before the
King, and by his Majesty's Commands have inserted in
the *Gazette* an advertisement for a reward of £100 for
discovering the person or persons concerned in this
murder, and offered the King's pardon to all except the
Principal Offender.

I am further commanded to recommend this matter
to your Lordship, not doubting but that your Lordship
will take such steps as you shall think most likely to put
a stop to a practice so very dangerous to a trading town,
and of course that will exert yourself in such measures as
will bring the guilty to condign punishment, and thereby

restore security to that part of the country where some of the inhabitants are so much alarmed that they talk of being obliged to leave it.

I am, with great respect &c.,

Lord Weymouth

Lord Of The Treasury.

Notice: Whereas, It hath been humbly represented to the King that Mr. Dighton, one of His Majesty's Supervisors of the Excise at Halifax, in the county of York, was, in the night of the 9th instant, inhumanly shot and murdered within a few yards of his own house by some malicious person or persons unknown, his Majesty for the better discovering and bringing to justice the person or persons concerned in the said murder, is hereby pleased to promise his most gracious pardon to any one (except the person who actually shot the said Mr. Dighton) who shall discover his or her accomplice or accomplices theirin, so that he, or she, or they may be apprehended and convicted thereof.

And, as a further encouragement, his Majesty is hereby pleased to promise a reward of one hundred pounds to any one of them (except as before excepted) who shall make such discovery as aforesaid, the said reward to be paid by the right Right Honourable the Lords Commissioners of his Majesty's Treasury, upon conviction of any one or more of the offenders.

– Weymouth, Lord Of the Treasury.
London Gazette. November 14th 1769

James Broadbent was dragged from his bed. Snatched at sunrise, shivering beneath his coarse wool blanket, he was taken over to Halifax in a carriage cornered by four of the sheriff's bailiffs.

The solicitor Robert Parker was awaiting him in his chambers. This time he was not as hospitable as when he had first received the large and awkward man in his home. Nor did he sit on ceremony. He dismissed the bailiffs and gestured to James Broadbent to take a chair.

We know you are implicated in the murder of William Deighton, he said curtly. And damnation will see you pay.

That's fresh pig scat is that, snapped James Broadbent. That's just plain ligging. I never shot no black devil.

I didn't say anything about him being shot.

James Broadbent scowled.

Everyone knows he had a head full of balls. The voices of the valley have spoken.

Indeed they have, said Robert Parker. And the voices say that you, as usual, are involved.

I'm no blabber.

But it is already long established that you are.

I'd rather hang.

Then hang you shall because there are five dozen Coiners who will put you there in Bull Lane with your eye staring down the barrel at that poor man.

James Broadbent remained indignant.

I never shot no Deighton. I knew him.

Precisely. You knew him and he owed you money. So in the eyes of the law you are the most likely culprit.

Me and one thousand others.

You're the only one they're naming

James Broadbent shook his head.

That's not right, is that.

You have no friends, felon. Only me.

Ballcocks, spat James Broadbent. You're no fucking friend.

Perhaps not, but I brought you here.

So?

I brought you here when I could have handed you straight to the sheriff. Or, worse, to Rockingham.

Who the fuck is Rockingham?

He is your former Prime Minister, said Robert Parker, making no attempt to hide a mixture of bemusement and contempt for James Broadbent's ignorance.

I've never heard of him.

Nevertheless, continued the solicitor. He is a man so powerful he could have you strung up by your innards right out there in the street – and be thanked by his people for doing it. The Marquess of Rockingham occupies a world that you could never imagine. He has the ear of the King, who himself now demands that prosecutions for the senseless slaying of my friend and colleague William Deighton are to be brought with no public expense spared.

James Broadbent was confused.

King David?

Robert Parker smiled gently. He shook his head.

The King of England, you fool; the man who wants Deighton's killers brought to account. And as a representative of the King's bar here in Halifax that is exactly what I intend to do. Looking at the evidence presented to me to date it's as likely that you as anyone pulled the trigger.

That's not just.

No, you are right. And I am ultimately a man of law. So I intend to see justice served.

James Broadbent looked down. His gnarled and knotted hands were clasped together in his lap. For the first time before the solicitor he looked defeated. He spoke quietly.

If I give you names will I be spared prosecution for this crime I did not commit?

That depends whether they are those of the killers, said Robert Parker. Or just the latest monikers plucked from your fanciful imagination.

I'm done for anyway.

Not necessarily.

Isaac Hartley, said James Broadbent without hesitation. It was he who raised the finger on the shooting of the devil Deighton.

Isaac Hartley shot him?

No. Not shot him. It was he who paid the lads to do it.

What lads?

James Broadbent looked at Robert Parker. He blinked.

Well? said the attorney.

They're two rum bastards who work over Sowerby way. One lives up Wadsworth and that's all I know. Dogs, they are.

Their names, said Robert Parker. I need names or descriptions at the very least.

Two right mean-eyed beasts they are, said James Broadbent. Not Coiners either.

Not Coiners?

No. Outsiders.

Why?

James Broadbent shrugged.

Because the Hartleys are all sack and no balls, that's why. And because these two men would as soon as kill for a handful of coins as comb their hair.

Their names then.

James Broadbent sniffed.

Their names, said Robert Parker again. I'll not repeat myself.

Robert Thomas is the name of one. Matthew Normanton is the other.

Robert Parker nodded.

James Broadbent looked to the door.

Can I go then?

Yes, said Robert Parker. You can go to York Castle, where your old friend David Hartley is in residence. The sheriff has

302

a warrant on you for counterfeiting, forgery, violence and complicity to murder. His men are waiting outside.

James Broadbent stood so quickly his chair fell backwards.

You son of a tip rat, he said. You chissum gargler.

Robert Parker whistled and the bailiffs entered.

You can see to the turncoat's transportation to York now.

James Broadbent's curses were muffled by the hand of a bailiff as he was manhandled out of the room.

Employed by the solicitor, the sheriff's officers and his bailiffs moved quickly upon Robert Parker's instructions to bring in the killers.

Robert Thomas was sitting on a stool outside his house high up Wadsworth banks changing his shoes when the men emerged from the cluster of trees that blocked the craggy skyline behind his one-room dwelling.

On his feet he was wearing clogs made of wood and leather and beside him were shoes with broadheaded nails driven into the soles. The men formed a semi-circle around Robert Thomas as the sheriff's officer stooped and picked up one of his shoes. He examined the spikes. He touched a finger to them.

Are you just coming or going? asked the sheriff's officer.

Robert Thomas shrugged and reached into his breast pocket for his pipe. All the men could see that his hands were shaking. He took a twig and busied himself with cleaning the bowl.

Where were you last night?

Robert Thomas cleared his throat. He squinted up at the man.

I was with one of Old Rose's shagbags, he said. Two of them in fact. You can ask them yourself.

And where were you the night before?

Same.

One of the bailiffs laughed, but a glance from the sheriff's officer silenced him.

The officer turned and surveyed the valley.

It is a nice view from up here.

I don't notice it, said Robert Thomas.

You can see all the way across to Bell House.

I don't know it.

You don't know the house of your king?

He's not my fucking king.

Yet you know which king I'm speaking of. The one whose dirty deeds you do.

I'm no coin clipper, said Robert Thomas, if that's what you're saying.

The officer turned back to face him. He reached into his coat.

Let's not turn this into a jamboree. I've a warrant with your name inked on it.

I've no cause to learn the reading.

Well you do now. I'm here to take you in.

Then you should take me in.

Is that all that you have to say?

Robert Thomas put the pipe between his teeth but the sheriff's officer stepped forward and swiped it out of his mouth. It fell to the ground and the stem broke.

Don't you want to know the charge?

Robert Thomas squinted at him again. He clasped one of his shaking hands in the other.

I'm not so curious.

The sheriff's officer sneered at the murderer's arrogance.

A barbarous and stone-hearted bloody murder of a good innocent man is the accusation.

He raised Robert Thomas's shoe.

And this fits the description of the weapon used in the deed.

It's a queer-looking gun is that, said Robert Thomas.

The sheriff's officer shook his head.

You won't be laughing when you hang.

I'm not laughing now.

I see you don't deny the accusation.

I can't deny what I don't know.

Deighton, said the sheriff's officer. The taxman William Deighton is the one you murdered.

With a shoe?

Yes, with a shoe. And guns and fists. There's a man down Brearley who says you made a confession.

Robert Thomas hesitated. His left eyelid fluttered.

No, not I, he said. It must be another Bob Thomas.

See how he pales, said the officer to his men. It's as if someone has driven a spigot into him and drained his blood.

If you and a man down Brearley say it is so, then it must be so, said Robert Thomas. I am but a humble grain thresher—

And a killer.

—but you are a man of law and he is a man down Brearley.

That I am, said the officer. That I am. You'll miss this view, I expect.

When you've seen valley rain once you've seen it a thousand times. I'm pig-sick of it, I am.

You'd rather the rope than a drop of rain?

Rope or rain or a day threshing grain, said Robert Thomas. I take each as it comes.

On Saturday last the Man who was taken up on suspicion of murdering Mr Deighton, Supervisor through the reward offered by his Majesty, and the Persuasions of the Gentlemen of Halifax, impeached other persons, supposed to have been connected with the above Murder, who was apprehended on Sunday at a place called Wadsworth Banks, about five miles from Halifax, and as they were to be examined yesterday, it is expected they will be very soon committed to York Castle.

One of the Persons had on a Pair of very strong Shoes, and Nails, with large Heads, drove into them; on which he was interrogated whether it was with them he stamped upon Mr Deighton's Body; but he refused to give answer to that, as well as to several other Questions which were put to him.

Leeds Mercury. November 21st 1769.

James Broadbent, Robert Thomas and Matthew Normanton, the persons taken up on Suspicion of murdering
Mr. Dighton, as mentioned, in our last, were brought
to this Town, and on Thursday Morning moved to York
Castle.

Broadbent, who was first taken up and informed
against the Others, fixes the Murder upon Thomas,
and, to strengthen his Evidence says: that being all Men
upon the Watch, he was stationed about the Length of
a field from the rest; that at the time the murder was
actually committed he was asleep, and that the Report
of the Blunderbuss awaked him; whereupon he got up,
and soon after Thomas coming to him said *I have done
for him, &c.* Thomas and Normanton, while they were in
this Town, seemed much cast down, and seldom spoke,
except that Thomas was observed to ask Broadbent, in a
low Tone, what he thought of himself by accusing him,
when he knew he was innocent of the Matter.

Leeds Mercury. November 28th 1769.

307

Oh but I laffed when I did see the ratt man himself Jamyes Brordbent brung up to York and not only Broadbent but some other men whose faces I new but naymes I did not but soon disccuvvered were Tommas and Normytunne The two men who it was said did for the devil Deighton with guns and his feet Them boyes what our Isaac did pay good ginnys too to bring that man down but them been big stiff idjuts they soon got themselves cort by the collar of the law the fuckern donkeys Me eyed have made shoo no cunt cortus.

Brordbent you rat I'll skin you alive I spits through the bars of my cell as the rat bastid skulked pass that first morning Broadbent you yellor dog I'll stitch your scut hole shut and feed you moldy parsnips all day long And he flinched when he saw us Achulay he shatter his britches as right he shud And he goes King David and I says Dunt say a word ratman fat use you turned out to be well its the sells for you now and a lifetime of me on your back and that's a promis I tell thee And he says Its all a mistayke King David that black bastid Dighton had me but now he's done for and I am an innersent man as are you so I reckon to thinken that all will be well wans this missunnerstandin is cleared up like And I shake my head and point my grubby finger and I goes Broadbaint you are indeed a worm and like a worm I'm going to chop you in half and then half again and wans more still you skwirming turd you.

Sir,

The late violent outrage committed at Hallifax, and the great Height to which the dangerous and villainous practice of clipping and coining is now risen, requires in every consideration that the utmost attention should be shewn in order to detect the guilty, and to put a stop to a practice so ruinous and detrimental to Trade and Credit, and so injurious to the public in general.

Great Zeal and Activity have already been shewn in Hallifax and that neighbourhood; and it appearing to me that on such an occasion the Exertion of the Civil Power and the Diligence and Activity of the Justices of the peace in all the neighbouring places (where there may already be too much reason to suspect the practice of clipping, coining and uttering coin so adulterated may extend) should not only be encouraged, but also supported by all the Gentlemen and considerable Persons of the neighbourhood.

I must therefore take the Liberty to desire, that you meet me at Halifax on Tuesday morning.

As the time is so short, I hope you will excuse me addressing you in a circular letter, which I mean to send to all the gentlemen now *Acting*, and also to those whose names are in and who have not as yet Acted in the Commision of the Peace for the West Riding in the neighbourhood of Halifax, Leeds, Wakefield and Bradford.

My object in addressing those Gentlemen who have not as yet acted is with some hope that on this very interesting public Occasion some of them might be inclined to act, if it was only for a few months, during the present situation; and even if that idea did not succeed, yet the very appearance of many considerable Gentlemen, concurring in the Proceedings of those who do Act, would have, most probably, at this juncture, a very good effect.

I have the honour to be, Sir, with great truth and regard.

Your most Obt. Humble Servt.

Rockingham

From across the county in carriages they came. From sprawling rural retreats and town dwellings; from churches and chambers, from working farms and landscaped estates with lakes and follies and ornamental gardens. They came from north and east and south; from Beverley and Bradford. From Richmond and Harrogate and Tadcaster. From Penistone and Pocklington and Bedale and Cottingham. From Malton and Ripon and Skipton. Whitby and Wharfedale.

Men of standing.

Lord Viscount Irwin from Temple Newsam. Sir James Ibbetson of Denton Park.

Sir Lionel Pilkington.

Colonel Henry Wickham and Mr. Richard Wilson.

One a Justice of the Peace, the other the Recorder of Leeds.

The Right Rev. Alexander Leigh.

Mr. Robert Parker and Mr. Thomas Sayer, the Halifax solicitors.

Mr. John Caygill and Mr. Michael Wainhouse.

Mr. John Edwards and Mr. William Prescott and Mr. Christopher Rawson and Mr. Samuel Waterhouse.

Across the ridings they rode, summoned by a letter.

Others too.

Lords and clergy and doctors and solicitors.

Mr. Robert Charlesworth and Mr. John Cookson.

Mr. Charles Swain Booth Sharp and Mr. William Crowle and Mr. William Buck and Mr. Samuel Harper and Mr. Marmaduke Ferris and Mr. Timothy Puxton and Mr. Thomas Ramsden.

Law-makers and politicians and mill owners and landowners and mine operators and exporters and men of many interests, investments and enterprises.

Up they came and over they came and through they came. These noble Yorkshire gentlemen.

They were wealthy men, endowed with family names

deep-rooted and double-tied to time and place; names of purpose and profession and location and meaning. A roll-call of northern wealth and power.

Mr. James Wetherherd and Mr. Samuel Waterhouse.

Mr. Thomas Woolrick and Mr. Benjamin Ferrand.

Mr. John Blayds and Mr. Thomas Hardcastle and Mr. Richard Mawhood and Mr. Christoper Rawson.

And Charles Watson-Wentworth, Second Marquess of Rockingham and former Prime Minister in the Whig administration. Graduate of Eton and St. John's College, Cambridge, proprietor of Wentworth Woodhouse, the largest private residence in England.

From across the moors they came to heed his call; from all horizons.

They travelled along uneven carriageways and through pollarded woods. Some journeyed by night along strange darkening lands towards a far-flung town unfamiliar to most. To Rockingham's call they came, these merchant men of trade and travel.

Men of honour and titles and entitlement. Men of land and law and power. Of family mottos.

Those who resided in the West Ridings set out before dawn, while others took lodgings in the town of Halifax whose economy, they had heard, was on the verge of collapse. They brought with them footmen and secretaries and valets, all of whom were dismissed for the morning's meeting.

As former Prime Minister, Rockingham's arrival was greeted by a peal of bells rung in his honour, and he was welcomed as the guest of wool merchant John Royds at his newly built opulent home, Somerset House in George Street, a stone's throw from the Old Cock Inn, where David Hartley had been apprehended. As well as schooling, the two gentlemen also shared an architect – just the previous year Royds had welcomed King Christian VII of Denmark to view his new home during the monarch's grand tour.

Up the hill and out of town towards Illingworth, at the Talbot Inn they gathered. At Rockingham's request Robert Parker had engaged the services of a half dozen trusted bailiffs to patrol the area.

Inside there was an air of anticipation as old acquaintances greeted one another and libations were shared. In the corner a table laid with drab food went largely untouched; most of the men had brought their own crates and hampers and, in a couple of cases, their own cooks.

In his cold dark room Joseph 'Belch' Broadbent's fire was unlit; the stone floor dotted with mucus and strings of blackened blood. There were congealed clots of it on the hearth and clots on the rug too, and a small pool of spittle connecting the old man's mouth and chin to the floor of millstone grit cut squarely into slabs a century earlier. His nearest neighbour would later swear to her husband that she could see old Joe's last cough hanging in the air above him like pipe-smoke, although perhaps it was pipe-smoke indeed, for although the fire grate was full of unlit dried kindling that had been folded in there, his flint and steel and tinder box on the crooked mantle trunk above it, his pipe was on the ground, a small heap of tobacco curls smouldering beside him, a silent glowing reminder of a life spent in smoke and fire.

Hip-hip.

As Rockingham entered the inn the gathered men put down their cups and brushed aside their plates, then stood to attention out of respect. All had received missives from the man, and some had received him at their homes previously too, but several knew the Marquess only by a reputation as one of the most honourable men in England.

Hip-hip, he said again to hush those few still talking. These are Godless times, gentlemen.

With short economical movements he removed a cape

coloured a mottled azure blue and hung it, then removed his hat and patted hair that was gently curled at its tips down back into place. The men saw that the Marquess's centre-parting was as straight and true as a gate-post and that the back of his cape displayed an elaborate family crest.

He waited until the men had settled and then he continued.

Men without God are men without respect for their crown, their country and even themselves. Men without God are those whose existences are at odds with the very tenets of this empire of ours. And here in the Yorkshire that we all know and adore – the Yorkshire that they say is God's own country, in fact – there is, as you are all now aware, a scourge of men who have been forging the King's currency for their own gain. These are men of greed and violence who would rather kill another, in this instance a Tax Supervisor named…

Here Rockingham paused for a moment then leaned over to the nearest man, who happened to be Robert Parker, and conferred with him.

Yes, continued Rockingham, William Deighton is his name. These felons would rather make the wife of William Deighton a widow than cease this evil, godless practice. Not five miles from here in the dale of the Calder these beasts reside, and to you I say their days must now be numbered.

He let the words settle. The men nodded in agreement. They spoke among themselves.

Let us first commend ourselves for the public-spiritedness we have shown by being here today. For it is up to us, England's noblemen, to tame these savages.

Hear, hear, said a voice and others joined it.

A man who dares to call himself 'King' David Hartley now resides in York Castle where his future is bleak, continued Rockingham. This individual and his minions are responsible for not only plunging the local economy into chaos – many of you, I know, have seen your enterprises adversely affected – and undermining the King's treasury and mint, but also for cutting down all those right-minded colleagues who have challenged their behaviour. Deighton is one of them; his callous murder, I have been reliably informed, committed by two or more of Hartley's own, possibly his brothers, who are known amongst their acolytes as the Duke of Edinburgh and the Duke of York.

These are common men taking titles of standing, said one Sir James Ibbetson. Hill-top farmers parading as dukes – it is an insult and it should not be allowed.

Hear, hear, replied a chorus of voices.

Rockingham continued.

I agree. Therefore I call upon you all today as men of power and sound moral judgement to solemnly swear to support the civil magistracy in bringing these men to account, safe in the knowledge that doing so will help restore the reputation of this corner of Yorkshire which has been otherwise sullied and besmirched by these ditch-dwelling felons. The King himself has spoken upon the matter. Justice will be served.

You can count on me, my lord.

Colonel Henry Wickham said this, and promptly received several pats on the back.

Other men immediately pledged their support.

Rockingham spoke again.

I also propose that subscriptions be sent on foot in the otherwise thriving towns of the West Riding for the discovering and apprehending of all Coiners, forgers and corrupters of coins, with immediate effect. It is imagined that there are between one and two hundred persons concerned in the clipping or uttering of false or diminished coins in Calderdale alone. Thirdly, I ask of your support in petitioning that the widow of Mr Deighton be recommended as an object of His Majesty's Royal Bounty in recognition of her late husband's brave and devoted attempts to – with the aid of the honourable Mr Robert Parker here – bring about the downfall of this gang who are known both locally and now nationally as the Cragg Vale Coiners. Parker here is a good chap who tells me that only the charitable and liberal donations of several persons have met the widow's immediate financial necessity.

At this Marmaduke Ferris cleared his throat and raised his cup.

And may I propose a toast to both you, my lord, Charles Watson-Wentworth, Second Marquess of Rockingham, and to the only King there is, our monarch, the King of England.

To Rockingham, said a chorus of voices. To the King. *Huzzah.*

To think that all them men gathered from across auld Jórvíkshire and beyond to disguss King David and his gang of clippers Well it bends the mind and warms the stomach and makes my stones twitch knowing that I the bestest Kinge of the North brought all them men to the valley The very same men who have plans to carve it up and dig it up and yoke the folk as if they were oxen and work them into the grownd in ther mills for a pittans of coin.

And this Rockenham carracter who they say was wans the Pry Minnyster of grayte Brittun and whose house they also say is the biggest in the land and whose garden has lakes and fountains and mayzes and stone sculpchurs and swans and herons and peacock fowls brought over from Injur on the spice boats It was this Rockenham that was to see the Coiners done for once and for all Yes the black bastard Dyeton and yes the yellow ratt Broadbent are to blayme but it was this Rockenham what had the ear of the King himself and I don't mean King bloody Dayvid I mean George the bloody bastid the thyrd Yes reely it was this Rockenham who brort your humble host down from his moorland pallas and onto this long slow wark up to the gallows jibberd that awaits me now But who also withowt reeleyesing it took the name of the Crag Vayle Coiners to the world and made the name of me David Hartlee a ledgend.

Becors a stone thrown in that dark corner noen as Cragg Vale has rippled orl the way up to the English throne my frends Orl the fucken way.

The three children played in the patch of purpling heather that was their pen. David Hartley the younger was old enough to walk and talk and know his own mind. As many remarked, he had the very same flinty eyes as his father. Mary Hartley was learning the ways of the world by following in her brother's footsteps, while Isaac Hartley the younger had just turned one, and was still discovering newness in everything he touched and heard and tasted.

Though the air was cut through by a cold sharp edge, they were dressed in good wool, their thick jerkins warm against the winter, and the smallest swaddled in a blanket gifted to Grace Hartley by a grateful brogger whose merchants' route passed across the moor close by, and who had been guaranteed safe passage by her husband's men in exchange for goods and coins.

Only the eldest child knew that his father was gone, but the concept of forever was impossible to grasp in an imagination that knew only moors and sky and the innocence of play.

The sky was turning grey to white with the promise of a storm on tomorrow's wind but for now David Hartley and Mary Hartley and Isaac Hartley rolled and dug and danced and wrestled and sang and chattered in a land of make believe.

They made figures from twigs and housed them in homes of moss; they fashioned crowns from sprigs and wore them on their young heads, then snatched them from their scalps and threw them spinning off into the air, then fell tumbling to the ground.

They conversed with worms and mimicked the calls of birds and they built kingdoms there down on the ground, from leaves and wool and feathers and pebbles, just as their father had built a kingdom from what he had to hand.

The baby tried to put a small fist of soft moor-top dirt into a mouth that was starting to show the first row of teeth, and his sister reached out to stop him. After the third or fourth attempt the baby succeeded though, and chewed on the mud, black drool running down his chin until his brother and sister pointed and laughed, and the baby laughed too, grit and peat on his gums and tongue.

Young David Hartley stood and ran around, laugh-screaming through the stiff roots of the heather, and his sister joined him to do the same, both gulping mouthfuls of a breeze that filled their lungs and inflated their imaginations, and the baby gurgled dirt, and above them crows circled, familiar shadow forms briefly reflecting the movements of the hill-top children before scattering.

From Bell House Grace Hartley watched, her face at the window, pale and drawn, as the eldest boy bent and picked something from the ground. He examined it for a moment and she saw that it was a jagged two-pronged branch, large in his little hands. He lifted it to his head and, turning into profile, he held the branch there, mounted in his thick curls, and then he tipped back his head and let out a bellow. It was such a strange roar, one that she did not imagine a child could ever produce from his young lungs, a sound almost inhuman, and then she realised that there were no trees up here on the moor, and it was not a branch that he held.

Grains of morning sleet blew down the chimney and hissed in the roaring fire. An ice storm was blowing in off the moor.

Isaac Hartley, William Hartley, their father William Hartley Sr and Grace Hartley were at the table in Bell House. Spread before them was a newspaper.

The previous night, as on that same night every year in December, the sky had screeched with the sound of what was said to be spectral hounds believed to stalk the firmament, and the distant portentous rumble of the giant unseen huntsmen who were said to pursue them. It was the night of the wild hunt; a time for staying close to the warmth and light and safety of the flickering fire. Little sleep was ever had on this night. Instead the valley dwellers preferred to sit up until first light, sharing stories and drinking hot ale until the chase receded and the sky was free of these great snarling, unseen beasts that split the sky with their animalistic howls of rage.

Protecting Grace during the wild hunt was the Hartley men's pretext for choosing this night to congregate around the hearth of Bell House to discuss their predicament.

See how they are set to turn the valley against us, griped Isaac Hartley. He pointed at the page.

You know I cannot make this out, said his father William Hartley the elder.

They've already turned one of us against David, said Grace Hartley.

Broadbent?

Yes. You should have silenced him when you could.

Isaac frowned.

Well. He's in the gaol now. I'm sure our brother has welcomed him well. It'll be buggery for breakfast from the boys for Broadbent.

His brother leaned in and slowly underscored the words with a finger.

What does it say? asked his father.

A lot of squit.

Read it to me, my son.

That'll take all day, father, said William Hartley. But here is the part that matters. It is a proclamation by one Mr Chamberlayne, solicitor to his majesty's mint, and some posh cunt called the Marquess of Rockingham. It is dated this very week, December, and written in the Talbot Inn, Halifax.

I know it well, said their father. I was put out on my ear once.

It says that by an Act of Parliament in the seventh year of the reign of his late majesty King William the Third, any person guilty of coining, clipping or diminishing the current coin of the realm, who shall afterwards discover two or more persons who have committed either of the said crimes, and give information thereof to any one of his majesty's justices of the peace, for as two or more be convicted of the crime, is thereby entitled to his majesty's pardon for all his said crimes which he may have committed before such discovery.

Well what the dusty fuck does that mean? said the old man.

It means that any man caught clipping will be pardoned so long as he gives up two or more of his fellow Coiners, said Isaac Hartley.

No Cragg Vale clipper would durst do such a thing, said their father.

It is already happening, said William Hartley the younger.

It is true, said Grace Hartley. The valley has already turned for the worse. People are talking.

There's more, said William Hartley as he continued to read the advertisement. It says here that if such a person be an apprentice, he is thereby declared to be a freeman, and hath thereby liberty to exercise any lawful trade, profession or mystery, with all liberties and privileges, and in as full and ample manner as if he had served the full time of his apprenticeship, and is moreover by the said act entitled to the reward of forty pounds for every person convicted.

He paused. There was nothing but the sound of the sleet lashing at the window. The cough and sigh of the fire.

These are just words, said their father. And long-winded ones at that.

No, said Isaac. These are more than words. Don't you see? This is a challenge to any man, woman or child, Coiner or otherwise, to become turncoat and speak out on this yellow trade of ours. Look, there is a footnote to this declaration: the towns of Halifax, Leeds and Bradford have offered a reward of ten guineas for every person convicted, over and above the reward allowed by Act of Parliament.

The elder William Hartley stood. He raised his voice.

Who is this Chamberlayne? Who is this Rockingham? You should chop them both down.

Isaac Hartley shook his head. He spoke in a low voice barely audible over the thrash and rattle of the windows.

Not this time.

Why not? No government man has brought us down yet. Coiners bow to no monarch but their own.

There's too many men, father, said William Hartley. We can't shoot or stab or stamp every man into the moorland dirt who pries into our enterprise. If we kill one, two more will replace them.

He's right, said Grace Hartley. My husband is done for and now the real King of England's men are coaxing cowards out of their stone hiding holes. People will surely talk when the crown is on their side.

Then the tongues of those that do will be cut out and shoved up their arseholes, said the old man. Isn't that right Isaac? It is up to you now.

Isaac took the paper and screwed it into a ball and threw it into the fire. It burned briefly and brightly, a blue flower unfolding into the flames.

Grace is the one who is right, he said quietly. Informers are already informing.

Again I ask: who would durst to? said their father.

Many. Not everyone is a friend. We have enemies too. There are those whose businesses have suffered.

Only the greedy and the wealthy. Them that deserve sufferance.

It is the greedy and the wealthy who wield the power, father, said Isaac Hartley. There is much talk of this Rockingham, whose intention it is to end the coining once and for all.

Coining will never end, said the elder William Hartley. He snorted and then continued. It has been done in the valley for years; we were the ones who got organised. That's all. Clipping is in our blood. Don't they say on certain days the valley rivers flow gold?

Things are changing, said Isaac Hartley.

Well change them back. We've got a fucking army out there.

Isaac walked over to the window. The sleet was coming in on a diagonal now.

You're an old man, he said.

Yes. And I'm tougher than the lot of you, the way you're talking.

I do believe you are. But it's a different world that's coming.

Listen to Isaac, agreed William Hartley.

More sleet came down the chimney. The wind picked up and rattled the panes again. Outside a basket was upturned and it tumbled across the grass before snagging on the bean poles of the vegetable plot that was little more than a sad patchwork of winter decay now.

I'm old enough to know that the world stays much the same, continued their father. Rain falls and puddles gather. Puddles become streams and streams become rivers. Leaves grow and leaves fall and the sun always sets westwards. The moor is the moor and the wind always blows.

I'll say it again, said Isaac Hartley. You are an old man and your eyesight is failing in more ways than one. There's none of us can see into the future but I have glimpsed it, and so has our David. All this clipping was his last chance – our last chance – to protect our little corner of the world and profit from it. To have our name writ in stone. Because the future of this valley is not for the likes of you and me. We are born free men; we are not to be enslaved, for that is what surely beckons when the wheels of industry do grind onwards.

You're talking dotty now, said his father, then turning to William said: our Isaac's nerve has gone.

Listen to him father, said William Hartley again. He's speaking the truth. If only we'd put more coins aside when we could we'd have enough to leave this world behind, the all of us.

The sky-line is thick with factory smoke now, said Isaac Hartley. The land is being sold off. They say there are mills the size of cathedrals in Lancashire. They're putting up great chimneys of stone that are twice as tall as any tree and there are machines that do the work of a hundred men, and it takes mountains of coal to feed them. They're sinking mines just to get the dusky diamonds from the ground to fuel the mills. Children are in their employment now. Children the age of your grandchildren. The hand-loom is over. The smallholdings are being bought off and people are turning each other over just to make a coin anyway they can. It's every man working for themselves now, father. There are men who are said to be making fortunes far greater than anything we can imagine. We're fucked. The weaving is finished and the farming is finished and the clipping is finished and we are finished. Fucked, I say.

I refuse to believe it, said the old man.

Perhaps it is better that way, said Grace Hartley. Hope it is that keeps a heart beating.

I'd rather die than be owned.

Die then, said Isaac Hartley. For our days of clipping coin and wandering the moor unmolested are over.

Christmastide morning and along the length of the valley houses were rich with the scents of the season – of stew pots full with broth flavoured thick with spice and dried fruit that had been bubbling overnight, and mulled ale, and plum cakes lifted steaming from side-ovens.

For many it had been a better year than most; the Coiners had made it so. Those who had clipped but were still free were licking their lips at the thought of the plump turkeys or geese or the fowl pies they had baked, some for the first time.

Yet for others their businesses had suffered with the devaluing of the coin. Those who had laboured all year and chosen not to join the Coiners' enterprise found their wives and children wanting. The economy was bent out of shape; supply had swamped demand and the innocent were paying a high price for it.

The valley had turned. With David Hartley facing the rope they now spoke, these victims of the valley. The slighted and the godly. Small unheard voices were heard now.

Already there was a child-like rhyme in circulation about the coming fate of King David and his motley Cragg Vale crew. That Christmas evening, as children played games of frog-loup outside, the King David song was as popular as any traditional feast-day ditty:

> *The hangman sings,*
> *as Hartley swings –*
> *a-yip, a-yip-yay,*
> *God give him wings.*

Not all the valley homes had their menfolk to carve the meat, nor those in Halifax either. For many of the men were absent: some now in seclusion at York, but others called upon to do their civic duty by the sheriff's officer who had the full support of Parker who, in turn, was backed by Rockingham and others all the way up the chain. Volunteers were called upon this day of all days, and all added to the payroll and promised Christmastide bonuses.

For this was the biggest mobilisation of co-ordinated authoritarian force the town had seen, and any non-coining man deemed physically strong and of good standing was welcomed. Some bore grudges for the downturn their enterprises had seen, others volunteered for theological and moral reasons. Some men had nowhere else to be on the twenty-fifth day of December. All were united in their disgust for these rogues.

At first light there was a knock at the door. At first light there were many knocks at many doors.

In clusters of three or four, and armed with guns and clubs and cudgels and knives, these new bailiffs arrived at the hillside homes of those identified as defacers of the crown's coinage, or of distributing the newly forged coins, or of acting as go-betweens for the Hartley gang. Every man deemed a suspect received a visit from these state-sanctioned militia.

They knocked on the doors of John Bates and William Varley. Of Peter Barker and John Sutcliffe and John Dewhurst.

Of Crowther O' Badger and James Crabtree and John Cockroft and Eli Hoyle.

They forced their way across the thresholds of Brian Dempsey and David Greenwood and Daniel Greenwood and Thomas Varley and James Oldfield.

They cornered Joseph Gelder and William Harpur and Jonas Tilotson and Paul Taylor and Thomas Sutcliffe and Thomas Stansfield and James Stansfield and John Pickles and Abraham Lumb.

They seized these men and had their wrists in chains right before their crying children. All were presented with warrants for their arrest for the diminishing of the crown's coin.

Some went fighting – Brian Dempsey bit the tit right off one of the bailiffs who had tried to drag him away from his family and his fire. Paul Taylor ran into a nearby field and when cornered fought three of the hired men for ten long minutes in the frozen ruts of mud until one of them struck him cold with a rock to the temple.

It was not yet light when William Hartley, who had chosen to sleep late, heard the metallic tinkle of bells of his rigged alarm system. He was already opening his bedroom window when the string was pulled at his front door and the sneck band quietly lifted.

He was hanging from the stone sill before the foot of the first bailiff reached the bottom stair, and then dropped down onto frosted ground, barefooted, his night shirt flapping up to reveal his nakedness before the same bailiff reached the landing, the soles of William Hartley's feet feeling every brittle blade and every scratched cluster of heather as he turned and ran, and men piled into his bedroom to find only tangled blankets where once a man had slept.

He looked back and when he did the younger William Hartley saw the shadows of men growing tall across his bedroom wall, their lamps swinging so that it appeared that those shadows were locked momentarily in a frenzied dance. Then the shadows came to rest as one of the bailiffs bent and touched the straw-stuffed sheets and said: the impression's warm.

Another bailiff said: this one they call the Duke of Edinburgh must have been as quick as a jackrabbit.

A third said: these hill-folk are born into different ways, they're half-animal this lot, feral beasts they are. Then the bailiffs crowded the window but all they could see was endless miles of rumbling sky shot through with the first streaks of daylight, and through it William Hartley ran, into the moor's dark interior where he knew he could lose them, and himself.

In York Castle cells James Broadbent could not sleep. James Broadbent could not eat. James Broadbent had been beaten and burgled. James Broadbent had been spat at. James Broadbent had been stabbed in the leg and he had had piss pots thrown in his face. James Broadbent had wet bedding and then he had no bedding at all. James Broadbent was forcibly fellated and made to do the same in turn. James Broadbent had live rats and burning rags of excrement fed through the bars of his cell door. James Broadbent was beaten by guards who had been given money. James Broadbent was set upon by different men every day and he was violated and he was humiliated. James Broadbent could not sleep. James Broadbent could not eat. James Broadbent was the key witness for the prosecution in the forthcoming spring trial concerning the murder of excise officer William Deighton. These were his twelve days of Christmastide.

Part VI
Spring 1770
Windkicker

The night came in like a bruise of purples and blues and then finally gripped so tight that the sky was black and broken by the weight of time impressing upon it. Dawn would melt the night in fading yellows but for now the sun seemed like an impossibility; a dead concept. A foreign country.

Geese flew in a V flight down through the centre of it, the chevron following the hollow cleft of the valley and the black and silver waters of the River Calder below.

The noise they made was a music of sorts: the measured rhythmic honk of the lead bird was like an unoiled gate in the rising wind that signals the coming of a storm, and the fine feathered sound of seven sets of wings pistoning in perfect precision a symbol of their stamina and streamlining. Their beautiful grey blades sliced the air and sheared the sky as they crossed a large Imbolc moon. And the moment of silence that followed in their wake created a brief window in the night, a space soon to be filled by the rustling of leaves, the clicking of branches, the snittering of tumbling young badgers at play and the lone distant scream of a fox in search of a mate.

The night was not eternal though. It was shortening, and at first light fresh snowdrops quivered like rung bells, the peal of dawn birdsong their accompanying soundtrack. Their delicate, oversized white crowns hung heavy on thin green stems like the heads of newborn babies, then as the sun rose and spread its rejuvenating rays across the valley base, the snowdrops moved with it, slowly tilting their chins skywards to drink in the warmth. They turned and lifted as one, nested chicks in search of sustenance, and found it there in the Yorkshire sky.

Spring.

Dear reeder I rite this with shaken hand in neer darkness with deths breth on my collar for to day was the day I reseeved my sentuns of deth by hanging of the neck until dead for the crime of coinen after a trial wich wud be comickal in all ways were it not my lyfe at stake.

Let me tell you about this tryal lest the hisstree books rite it down rong This tryal was a jesters farce This tryal was wayted agaysnt King David before it even began This tryal was what is known as a foghorn concollusion as if my fate was alreddy rit in the stars.

The ratt Broadbent who cud barely stand in the cort room he was so battered and bandy leggd after four months in the York cassel with the boys was the mayne witness and he did tell the cort that he had seen Me King Daevid clip four ginnees with a pair of sissers and that poor Jimmy Jagger did hold a peece of paper to reseeve the clippens and that I King David said I would go and smelt and strike them golden shards in a speshul secret place made out of stone out back of Bell Howse on the moor of Eringden.

Well wat a lot of shyte.

Then they brung another witness one Joshuar Stancliffe now let me tell you I dunt know no fucken Joshuar Stannliffe from Adam espeshelly not this one who they said was a watch maker from Hallifax who stood up and said that some time before the devil Dyetun became cold meat Our Isaak did go into his shop and declare that the devil Dyetun would find hisself murdered very soon and furthermore that if Dieghtun could not be waylayd in the street he would instead be kilt in his bed rather than live to give evvydence against me King David.

Well wat another barrer load of shyte As if our Isacc would do such a thynge Honestly a jesters farce all this Lyars cummin out the woodwork like scuttling slaters.

This Joshua Stancliffe did then produce a letter which was read out in cort and which I include a copy of bellow for possterrytee and whose hand I know not by which it was ritten but I do no it was not mine This letter it was left on the inside shutters of the mans shop and it seems to me now that the cort saw this as further proof of my bastidly dastidly ways even though I've been in this place for months now with no way of riting anything but these scribbuld hidden confesshuns They sed this letter proved a thret was on his lyfe from the lads but so what if it was Thats not my business if folk want to go round killen folk for speaken out So what I says So fucken what.

Allso they did say that this Stancliffe was reedin from a staytment that was in the handritin of this Roberd Parker I've heard tell of He is the one behind all this The one who along with the taxman planned to bryng us all down and bryng us down he did They say he has the ear of the Kynge but every man knows there is only wan kynge round here Yes King David you cunts.

Anyroad this day April Sickth I was sentunsed as I say to death and me never even haven kilt a man least not that devil Willyam Dyeton Bastids the lot of them Heartless bleeden bastids.

Heres the cursed letter.

Halifax, 12th April 1770

Joshua,

An affair happened on Friday night last which is of the utmost consequence to you. Pray God grant that you may take this friendly warning; otherwise you will be an undone man. It's a matter of no less moment than the preservation of your life. To speak plain with you, there is an agreement entered upon by very near a dozen to take your life, if David Hartley suffers. I durst not say anything against it, as they avowed that whoever dissented in that company should undergo – you may guess what. They all sworn upon the Bible to stand true; besides they affirm that you deserve shooting for some others thing which little becomes one of your profession.

I am shocked at the Thoughts of this affair, and was resolved to take this secret method to warn you of your eminent danger. I could not with safety do it any other way, as I would certainly have been discovered and my life placed in danger as well as yours, for it's resolved and sworn as above to stand true to one another, etc; and, if you cannot be catched out of doors at nights, it's resolved upon to take a shorter method. My hand trembles while I write.

Wishing that God may give you grace to take warning, and in time of this desperate affair, so I am,

Yours
Unknown

Well now yoov red it with your own eyes Har har don't make me laff As if a Clipper could rite so well as this Everyone knows Clippers might be good with tongs an sheers an fyting an drinken beers an good at weaven and farmen an fucken but riten is not any of thur strengths eggsept perhaps for this grate poet me David Hartley as this dogument will surely testify.

An one other thynge no Coiner would ishyou a warnen of murder A true Coiner wud just do it and it's no use asken for God's grace nyethur God's grace is beyond us all Espeshelly me

Oh I am tyred So bluddy tyred but how can a man sleep when he nose his days are numbad.

The hills beyond the hills shimmered in a haze that lightened each layer of landscape in colour and softened their shape. It was the clearest of days: so clear that when Grace Hartley stepped out of her door to feed the chickens and retrieve their eggs and clip kale for broth and check the snares around the vegetable patch, and give the dog his scraps and fresh water and then untether him, she saw a new world stretching way behind her usual horizon. The sky was perfectly blue and cloudless as if it were a mottled mirror reflecting the bluebells that now carpeted Bell Hole woods and turned them into a dream-like wonderland.

Soon it would be May and the sky was a doorway onto a new world that reached beyond the valley. Perspective extended and for the first time in a long time Grace Hartley did not feel the weight of the grey ceiling pushing down upon her, nor the need to wrap herself in blankets or dry herself by the fire, or turn her back to the moor.

She had not left the valley in a long time. Many months or more. The children had never gone beyond the old packhorse bridge a mile or so down through the woods in Mytholmroyd.

The ground was dry and the wild grasses that fringed the moor perfectly still. She straightened and stood with a bucket in one hand and egg basket in the other and she listened. She heard the shrill exchange of birds and then when they fell silent she heard nothing but endless space.

She thought of her husband. She thought of David Hartley in a cell, the man she would never see again unless his execution was stayed and two days away that was now unlikely.

His swinging body she would not see. A man of glory choked like a chicken – no. Such an image would haunt her for all days. She knew she would stay away.

She thought of her husband's brother, William Hartley the

younger, now gone. Last witnessed fleeing to the moors like those scarecrows and dancing creatures that were part-deer and part-man that her husband had once drunkenly confided in her to having seen. She thought of their other brother Isaac Hartley, gone. Whereabouts unknown. Lynched and dead in the turnpike ditch for all she knew. She thought of their father, William the elder, as old as the hills, also gone. Last heard of in the Colne Valley four months since, when the snow was still on the ground.

She thought of all the other men, gone. Locked up and shipped out. Or in hiding, gone to ground, like cowardly creatures. Some, like the one they knew only as the Alchemist, was now little more than an apparition that stalked recent memory, nameless and faceless and so vague it was as if he had never been there at all.

All that was left in their wake was the house and the children. The moor. No-one had been round since the arrests; no men had visited to pay respect or offer a tribute. They stayed away now. They were gone now. Invisible now. A full season she had spent with no-one but three children under the age of four: Mary, David and the little bawling baby Isaac, already the image of his father. Her husband had wanted to replicate his generation by · siring a fourth that they would name William. His seed would spill no more now though.

Yes. A full season it was that had passed, of hungry mouths, soiled blankets and a frost that had lingered beyond Easter. And all with little to eat but that which she could produce or procure: oats, eggs, potatoes, bread. Breast milk.

She could not venture down the hill. Would not. No. Not with David facing the rope. Not with the valley crawling with the unfamiliar faces of new law enforcers and sheriff's officers and bailiffs and well-dressed gentlemen and newspaper writers from places as far away as Rotherham and Hull and Newcastle, all here to see the hills that spawned the Cragg Vale Coiners; not, too, with the surveyors and labourers and mill men scattered across the hillsides with ropes and stakes and spyglasses and maps.

These men presented the biggest threat.

With the king of the Coiners deposed and his army defeated it was now open season in Calderdale. David Hartley had been wrong about many things but not this. Isaac Hartley too. The great hellish cathedrals of toil were indeed coming. There were new turnpikes and talk of a canal; new houses and furnace chimneys. New folk from beyond the valley – from beyond Yorkshire – were flooding their world.

No. With David facing the rope Grace Hartley would not face them. She would have him brought home. She would see him correctly buried in the soil of his birth. And then...

And then.

A voice echoed down the stone palisade. A lone cry of protest. It sang singularly for a few strained moments before another joined it. Then a third, to create a tuneless song of anger and excitement, of violence and a declaration of triumph too. More voices joined in; the voices of men, starved and shackled, chained and beaten. The voices of men unwell and illiterate and perverted and corrupted, all forming a chorus that reverberated around the bowels of the gaol. The voices were joined by a clattering of cups – hollow tin on cold stone. Then the soles of stout boots stamped the floor. They kicked at heavy doors, leather on wood, and they rattled at their chains, iron on flesh, and scraped their bait-boxes and clanged their bed-pots. Their stiff wool blankets were twisted and whipped and flayed, the straw beneath them scattered. The voices grew stronger, louder, more indignant, more furious. The entire building came alive with the noise of scraping and banging and howling and rattling and smashing and singing and shouting and braying and grinding and grating and crashing and clobbering and splintering and cleaving and burning and wresting and splashing and beating and clawing and shredding and shouting and splitting and screaming.

It was the strangest of eulogies for a person not yet dead; a symphony of destruction for a condemned man played by an orchestra of stone and bone and meat and metal and fists and feet and blood. That man was David Hartley and in the morning that man would hang.

Close to the banks of the River Calder the wives of William Clayton, Thomas Spencer, John Wilcox and Jonas Eastwood met to gather in the nettles. The virulent plants had come up thick this spring and were already swaying at waist height. The women pulled up their dresses and tied their coats and waded into the thick patches. Here by the waters on the dirt path trampled smooth, the weeds grew deepest. Each woman had a practised way of clasping and twisting the leaves away without getting stung, and within minutes their baskets were brimming with large ash-green leaves, the fine barbed hairs of their stalks glinting in the late April early morning sunshine.

They picked sorrel too, and garlic leaves.

Nearby, the copper water edged noisily over shale and river stone down to a slow-flowing pool that sat beneath a tangled overhang of tree roots where occasionally a fish rose to gulp at a fly that had settled on its surface. Once or twice they leapt, twisting like brilliant spindles. Glinting like something forged and buffed.

The women did not speak of their husbands.

To speak of them was not the thing to be done when they were all locked away awaiting their outcomes. That these men would have been beaten, maltreated and starved was a given. In time perhaps some of their husbands would be released, others gaoled under lengthy sentences. Some could be sent away or, worse, transported to overseas penal colonies never to be seen again, and perhaps some would yet swing.

And didn't they have enough weighing on their minds, with mouths to feed and the memories of the previous year or two of an abundance of food and drink, and money for clothes and housekeeping, and even gifts from their men already fading? The coining had given them that. The yellow trade had offered them a glimpse of better times.

But now the guineas and pennies and moidores were gone – or hidden or buried or stashed or stolen or spent – and the days of coining in the Upper Calder Valley were few. Only one man had truly done it well enough and his true name went unknown. The Alchemist. His whereabouts, also, were unknown.

No. To talk of their men now would be to tempt fate and to admit their fears and loneliness.

Instead the four women took to the little inlet shore of the river where they crouched and brushed their nettle stems through the water. They dipped their baskets and lifted them dripping. Swilled them. Cleaned the leaves in the rusted runs.

They walked slowly back to Mytholmroyd speaking only of the weather and what the summer might bring. At the wooden bridge they parted ways with strained smiles, each heading to homes where the nettles would be chopped and mixed with oatmeal and onion, with the sorrel and garlic leaves, and then the mix shaped into clumps and dropped into a pan of bacon fat if there was any, but of course there wasn't, so a finger of lard would be used instead. These pudding slices would feed their families for days, and until their men were freed to earn once again they would carry on living off nettles and sorrel and dock and oats and eggs, and each night they prayed in silence that their husbands might be spared, and that one day the valley would flow with gold again, and better days may yet return.

It was a bright morning. Clear. The sun streamed into the yard and even in their stone dungeons the men of York Castle could hear birdsong and smell summer on the breeze. They heard too the carillon of the city's bells, a reminder that life was going on close by just through the castle's entrance, over which there sat an escutcheon featuring crossed swords and a motto in Latin that none of them would or could ever hope to read.

340

They were two days off May Day, and though imprisonment had robbed them of the seasonal signs and prompts that were the mechanics of these countrymen's internal calendars, history had nevertheless shaped them to feel the annual upsurge in seasonal energy.

In his room David Hartley paced. He wished his head had never once hit a cushion or pillow in his life and that he had savoured every waking moment instead of spending all those hours prostrate in a dream-state. Time was a commodity now, more coveted than any gold coin.

He wished too that he had used those extra hours to make more coins, gain more power, and to have built a great big wall around the valley flanks to keep out incomers.

He also wished he had thrown more fucks his wife's way than he had. He wished he had spawned ten children. A hundred children. He wished for many things.

The castle was strangely silent, but from the streets of York he could hear the thrum and chatter of a city unsettled. It sounded busier than usual out there and the cadence of their combined voices was one of nervous excitement.

He paced, then he bent and ripped up the sacking of his bed and he flung it to one side and then he grabbed fistfuls of the straw and he stuffed it into the open drain, blocking it.

David Hartley looked around the room but there was nothing else but his roll of papers and the stub of pencil within it, the bait box that his meals were served in and his tin cup which he flung against the wall, and then stamped with his foot until it was nearly flat. He picked it up and turned it over in his hand. He crouched and placed it underfoot again and bent and folded it over into a triangular shape, then began frantically scraping the narrowed end of it on the floor. He had never needed a weapon before in here; his reputation had been enough.

He was furiously scraping and sharpening the useless shards of tin when the door was unlocked and the turnkey Charles Claxton stood there flanked by several men.

You'll not be needing that now, King David Hartley, he said.

David Hartley noted the mark of respect by which the gaoler had addressed him.

I'll go down fighting.

It's not worth it, Hartley, so put it down.

Or what will happen?

He clenched his fists.

You can either cast that thing aside or we'll rush you and beat you senseless, then you'll be dragged to your end bleeding and wearing the torn clothes of a broken man. You don't want to look like a broken man, do you now?

Before David Hartley could answer Charles Claxton continued: because a man who is called a king should at least walk to his death with grace and dignity.

There's no dignity in what it is you're doing, said David Hartley.

That's a fair judgement but why go out looking like a pauper?

David Hartley slowly stood.

You can go out your own way, said Charles Claxton. Dick Turpin did it with dignity.

How would you know? Turpin were thirty year ago.

David Hartley threw down the piece of tin nonetheless.

There were plenty of witnesses. And I tell you what else: there's even more for you out there today. More than Turpin if the old-timers' stories are to be believed.

David Hartley looked at him. He stood taller. Blinked.

For me?

Yes. For you. There's bloody hundreds of folk out there to see the king of the Coiners and I'd wager there'll be hundreds more waiting for you when you're taken back home over the moors. Thousands. It's like fucking feast day. There's folk making good money selling chestnuts and beef water out there.

David Hartley stood for a moment, breathing slowly. By his side he unclenched his fists.

Then it is time, he said. The people shall feast.

He went to leave but he stopped and turned. He reached for his roll of papers. He picked them up and thrust them towards Charles Claxton.

You will keep the promise of my final request?

Yes, said Charles Claxton. I will see the safe delivery of your papers to your wife.

Grant me that, said David Hartley.

It is granted.

Faces were at the bars of the cells. David Hartley saw eyes blinking in the darkness. Arms dangled or fingers curled around cold metal bars as he was brought up from the stuffy stone corridor.

In the yard he was lifted up onto the cart. Hands grabbed him and hoisted him. His hands were tied. Fresh air flooded him.

A coffin fit for a king, someone shouted from one of the cells. Farewell to the true king of the northlands.

David Hartley nodded and lifted his bound hands. Raised a thumb.

Clip a coin and fuck the crown, shouted another, though after the previous night's catharsis the voices were muted now. The inevitability of the death act was on the minds of all the felons.

Only then did he see the coffin laid behind him: an unadorned rectangular box of the cheapest construction. Open and ready. His home for eternity. Waiting.

Gaolers joined him on the cart, the reins were yanked and they left for Tyburn.

In past days it could have been to other gallows in other York parishes that he might have been led. Burton Stone Lane perhaps. Or that area known as Horsefair, down at the junction of Haxby Road and Wigginton Road. Fossgate. There used to be gallows at Garrow Hill too.

But today it was towards the most famous that they turned.

They passed beneath the arches of the gateway and David Hartley was into the city streets for the first time in nearly half a year. Already there were folk waiting and watching. Even here. Just standing and staring, saying nothing. Young and old, visibly rich and odorously poor. Side by side they stood to see the last journey of a doomed man.

The cart rocked and David Hartley nodded to those who dared to meet his eye.

They crossed the Ouse by the only bridge to connect the two sides of the city. David Hartley looked down into the flowing waters and wondered if he could make the leap from the cart across the railings and down into the water, fifty feet or so below, and then he considered whether death by drowning was worse than hanging, and then they had crossed the bridge onto Ousegate and were heading up the slope of Micklegate, and it was too late for a watery ending.

Micklegate Bar led to Blossom Street.

Blossom Street to The Mount.

He knew the route. He had done the journey every night in his mind for weeks. He had walked the city streets and he had followed his footpaths of the Calder Valley too. Each night he had revisited his favourite places: the moor-top hollows and the wooded slopes above Cragg Vale. The vegetable garden at Bell House and the view from Daisy Bank over to Hebden Bridge. He had walked the length of Heights track and scaled Scout Rocks. He had lain in the bluebells with Grace.

He had seen the stagmen dance again.

And each morning when he awoke to the stench of hundreds of men, he felt a sliding feeling somewhere deep inside of him; a scream of abject horror contained by his ribs and flesh and organs. In was death within him, seeding there. It was rooted.

Many people lined the way. In places the crowds stood five deep. Some shouted his name and waved, and to these David Hartley signalled back, while others stared in silence.

They left the city walls behind them as the cart creaked towards the open land of the Knavesmire and the Tyburn gallows. David Hartley tried to steady his breathing. As he did so the gaoler next to him turned and spoke.

Hundreds have hung here before you David Hartley, he said.

He said nothing in reply.

And hundreds more will follow no doubt.

Without looking at him David Hartley spoke.

You have a mouth as baggy as an old nag's guit.

Perhaps. But it's a mouth that won't be gasping its last any time soon.

David Hartley sneered.

At The Mount the turnpike turned into Tadcaster Road and they moved along it now. The green expanse of the Knavesmire opened up to their left.

Yes, the gaoler said breezily. Hundreds before and hundreds more to come.

Then I hope their crimes will be worthwhile ones.

Were yours?

David Hartley looked at the residents of York. They were town people, not country folk. Not valley faces. Yet still they had turned out to bid him goodbye. All knew his name, his story. They had heard of the gang known as both the Cragg Vale Coiners and the Turvin Clippers. They had eyes, they had newspapers. They had read of the yellow trade. They had surely read of the murder of William Deighton too, and most of them at least knew it wasn't his finger on the trigger or his boot on the exciseman's face, even if the devil deserved it. They knew too how most of their wealth had been given away and those coins – his coins – had fed the starving of the Calder Valley for over two years; no widow or child or old-timer without work was left wanting. They had been clothed and fed and given hope, and that was more than any landowner or dignitary or law-maker or mill-owner had done. It was more too than the King of England himself had offered.

David Hartley turned to the gaoler. He squinted at him even though their heads were only a foot apart.

I don't know your name, he said. Neither do any of these people, of which there are many thousands – not mere hundreds. *Thousands.* More people than I ever did see gathered in one place.

Now it was the gaoler who was puzzled.

So?

So they all know my name, cunt. They will carry it on their tongues for their rest of their lives and then their children will carry it too. And their children's children will one day talk of the day their grandparents saw David Hartley paraded through the streets of the city like a king.

You leave behind a wife.

David Hartley inched closer to the gaoler.

Do not speak of my wife at this time, he said, then he added: you will leave behind nothing. You are naught but a key-turner. Your life has no meaning whereas mine has been one of enterprise and greatness and I would sooner bow out now with my name planted in the ground of my Jórvíkshire and left to grow there for centuries than be nothing more than two words scratched onto a headstone that casts a shadow over a lonely weeded plot. That surely is the destiny of you, brother – and all the other men who choose authority over freedom. You, my friend, will die old and worthless in a pool of piss and shit while I will be young and strong and handsome forever. Now shut your flapping mouth and let me have my moment. I've still got enough vinegar in my piss to kick the living fuck right out of you.

Did I say lassed confayshun becors eyell be a Dutchman if you thinke King David Heartly is going to whittle when the hangmans got his neckweed around his scrag Hell no any learnit man nose a confayshun is what a man maykes when rong it is that he has done Confayshun is when he wants to make his pease with God and is seeking penans for them sins that he has cermitted And I tell you now with hand on both hart and borls it is no sin I have cermitted except those that any man cermitts over the cors of his lifetime.

Dippin my bill dippin my wick and slakin my bacon on occashun and breakun some bones and putting the feer in men onlee as and when nessassuree Thees are my crimes Maybe some blastfeemin But steelin from the needy or the hurten of chillum or the beatin of wimmen No none of this did I do My crimes were agaynst only those who could afford to lose a little.

So when it is they leed me from this sell and out into the sitty where it is the fowke will gather and whisper to ther nippers Looker its King David its King Dayvid of the Crag Vayle Coiners King of the Turvin Clippers lookit that man and remember his face see how he warks with dignutty and pryde becors that is a man who fed his famlee and the famlees of others that is a man who lucked after menny that is a man of the people a man who can wark with his headup That is a man who brort magic to the valley of the Calder people Who brort magic to England Becors that man is the troo king of Jorvikshyre Thass what theyull say and I will no I have only dun my bestest.

There are thynges I will miss when I'm gone like a nice jugg of stingo and Grayces throddy boddee and the smiles of my children and a thick slice of greesy dock pudden fresh from a wite hot skillet but the boys in here dun give me a rite gud send off it fair brung a tear to my peepers and anyroad when yor gone yor gone so whats to miss anyway.

Of cors therll be those hool be bendin ther elbows and raisin a cup and glad to see me go but these are not my lot No they have never nown suffrin and hunger and this is why I rite these werds down for you now becors historee is only ever remembud by the powerfull and the welthy the booke lerners in the big howses with thur fancy kwills and ink blotters And to these I say no No I say to these I say this is my story not my confeshun My story as I sor it These are not the werds of a man turned sower with regret and if I had another chance Id do it all the sayme again but bigger and better and I'd forge coynes of marigolde an yool all know when that noose is tytund and David Hartlee is left kicking the wind all you will hear is the sownd of crying cockulls All yool hear is the choken sounds of a man hoos life itself was liyved like a pome Hoos every thort and ackshun was poetry And who rose to graytnuss and his final ritten words and his lassed dyin breath Well that was poetry too.

As they skirted the wide open space of the boggy Knavesmire David Hartley thought he saw a familiar face in the crowd. A man gesturing for his attention amongst the hundreds of others. He stood.

Isaac, he shouted. Brother, is that you?

But hands were upon him again, pushing down on his shoulders and pulling him by his shirt-tail so that he stumbled backwards and knocked the lid from his own coffin.

He looked back and shouted one more time: *Isaac.*

But the horses kept walking and the cart kept moving and the hands of the gaolers held him tight and the past, like the pale faces of the people that stood on either side of the street, slipped away behind him.

And then the crowd thickened into a bottleneck as the cart turned onto turf and David Hartley was being manhandled down, and he felt soft damp ground beneath his feet. Behind him the crowd closed in to block the road.

Ahead of him stood the gallows, and then everything felt unreal.

He was led to the Three-Legged Mare, a wooden triangle standing on three wooden pillars. Three weathered beams were supported by three weathered uprights. It was happening too fast. It was all happening too fast.

In the shadow of the gallows Jack Ketch was waiting.

David Hartley turned to the gaoler and said what is the hangman's name? but the gaoler just shrugged as he helped in bundling him towards the wooden structure upon which the hangman now stood.

David Hartley saw the steps and David Hartley saw the rope and David Hartley saw the door they called The Drop.

And then his feet were on the steps and the crowd was getting louder and everything seemed to be moving in double time: clouds flitting low across the Knavesmire; a dog far beyond the crowd that was running across the grass, followed at some distance by its owner, oblivious to or uninterested in the spectacle of death that was about to occur; Jack Ketch turning to him and putting a hood over his head and David Hartley crying out no, but the words not leaving his body. Instead they remained trapped inside him like a kitten down a well, a tiny desperate voice heard by no-one. Eternity's loneliest echo.

There was no offer of a chance to say any last words as the noose was placed over his head. It sat there loose; The Drop would take care of the rest, which it did as the floor fell away, quickly, too quickly, and it was really happening, and the crowd were roaring and only now was David Hartley aware that his life had a limit like everyone else's.

When the rope jerked and tightened he felt nothing for a moment and then his head seemed to swarm with an unfamiliar warmth, a not unpleasurable feeling of hot blood coursing. He heard it in his ears. A crackle then a snapping. A popping. The noise of the crowd became distant and calming, like the wind in the trees of a copse. It had no individual voice but was instead a rhythm driven by a form of lust, hunger and sexual excitement.

But then that blood kept coursing and it felt as if it was engulfing him, like he was drowning in himself. His head swelled in an instant, or so it felt, and David Hartley thought of the times he had swum in the river and dived down too deep and the mute water had pressed down on his chest and then stolen his breath, and he had come up gasping just at the final moment that the water was beginning to fill his mouth, and he rose, gasping and spitting and coughing, all the sounds of the world gushing back at him, his senses enlightened, everything amplified, everything brightened. His head pounding to the heart source. To the life force.

But now he could not do any of that and his breath was being squeezed out of him and blood was everywhere. It was pushing at the back of his eyes and filling his lips and twisting at his tongue. His head raged and screamed with a pain that he felt in every muscle, bone, hair, organ and sinew. And in every memory. Every desperate memory.

He was flooded with blood, black blood, hot in his every urgent thought, so much of it that there was no room for anything else; only a scorched and roaring sensation of everything accelerating at once towards a finite redness, a deep roaring screaming to a place beyond pain and on into a poetic silence.

And he welcomed it.

On, Saturday, 28th April, about half-past two in the afternoon, David Hartley, commonly known as King David, under sentence of death for coining and diminishing Gold Coin, was executed at Tyburn, near York. At the fatal tree he behaved every way suitable to his unhappy circumstances, though we do not hear that he said anything by way of a confession. The report of him having had a reprieve was not true, the Judge having left a discretionary power with the High Sheriff to put off the Execution.

Leeds Mercury. May 1st 1770.

The casket shifted as the hearse wheels rolled over uneven stones and crested the Northowram bank to descend into Halifax. Twice on the journey over from York they had stopped the cortège and opened the casket to secure David Hartley with ropes to stop his body sliding around, and a third to reinforce the casket's lagging on the carriage.

Here Grace Hartley joined the procession from the cart of a neighbouring farmer.

She called him to stop and wait, and then she climbed up onto his carriage where they lifted the lid for her one more time.

Down the hill Halifax spread out before them.

She saw her husband's bloodless face staring upwards to an equally bloodless sky, his lips blue and eyes grey. He seemed so much smaller in death, she thought, than he had in that large, large life; it was difficult now to imagine the ideas and power and potential that his body once carried. It looked so helpless now.

Like a tiny bird that had fallen from its nest.

Well husband there it is then, she said. The town that brought you down and strung you up. One last time you'll get to see it. One last time and then no more the Lord will anoint you and I with the oil of gladness. Husband, you are dead now and to your grave in the soil that spawned you we shall go, to bury you like the king that you are, for it is the king that they called you.

She wrapped a scarf around a neck swollen to twice its size to cover the rope burns and bruising. Then the lid was pressed down again. She walked back to the farmer's cart.

The cortège resumed its journey.

On the street corners of Halifax there gathered people. Bodies with faces pale and curious. Wool workers and weavers and traders and pen men from the offices and meat men and dray men on their carts, and street-walking ginnell lurkers and mothers with their children and navvies passing through, all now drawn to the growing crowd like flies to something fallen and rotting.

The name King David Hartley was on their lips, just as he had predicted.

A voice said here he comes, and the people jostled to see the carriage that carried the casket that carried the man whose brutality had put the fear in many and whose wicked practices had damaged the trade of the common man, but whose efforts had rewarded the brave too, and whose rumoured generosity had put clothes on the backs and food on the tables of the starved communities of the upper moorlands when everyone else had failed them.

At the passing of his carriage one or two spat or cursed quietly but no-one laughed and no-one threw fruit because everyone was aware that other Hartleys still stalked the valley and who knew where the rest of the coining gang were; for surely not all of them resided in York Castle.

The Coiners still had sons and sisters and brothers and cousins and eyes and ears in every back room and trading floor the length and breadth of Calderdale. They had borne witness to what had happened to those that had gone against them. Hot coals and tongues removed, some said. Fingernails pulled out and eyes gouged and balls stamped. People buried not yet dead. Some said their enemies had been made to drink mercury; others claimed Coiners fed turncoats to their pigs with their hearts still beating. There were stories of rats and cages, of river dunkings, of a hollow far up on the moor, where unspeakable things happened by firelight. A hooded man. Inexplicable reckonings.

The procession left Halifax and moved deeper into the valley. It followed the new turnpike's curve and soon the town was behind them, and the green slopes of spring flowed down to meet them on either side, and the people gathered by the road in smaller clusters.

These were true valley folk, down from the hamlets and farmsteads. They had walked from the hills to greet their king.

From Warley and Friendly.

Hathershelf and Luddendenfoot.

Boulderclough, Brearley and Banksfield.

The tone was different now. Here they threw flowers and wreaths and garlands and daisy chains onto the carriage and they shouted words of praise and lines like *valley boys clip and valley boys sing, valley boys kneel to none but their king* and *clip a coin and melt the crown, if a lawman comes knocking, chop him down.*

They approached the meeting of the two waters at Mytholmroyd. High off in the far distance to the west, where Bell Hole woods led up to Cragg Vale, unseen from the turnpike, sat above it all Bell House, a tiny dot shimmering in the haze of the first day of May on the moor's lip. From its chimney there plumed a thick green smoke.

The crowd deepened. The men, women and children of the village watched as dead David Hartley made his last journey. They lifted their hats and raised their hands, and others muttered silent prayers. Children stepped forward to place loaves or potatoes on the carriage. Cups of ale and plugs of tobacco, too. There were more flowers, more garlands, more wreaths. Sprigs of heather. Many were thinking of their own brothers and husbands and sons and cousins and fathers locked away, facing, perhaps, a similar fate.

The procession followed the River Calder for a mile to the town of Hebden Bridge, and here too many more lined the streets. The walls of the valley squeezed in.

Their destination was Heptonstall, perched up on that spur of land between two densely wooded gorges, a stone island of the sky. The only way up was via The Buttress, a paved packhorse track that took the shortest route straight up the hill, a steep climb of five hundred feet.

At its foot was the Hole In't Wall Inn, the last building at the town's far boundary.

Here the cortège paused and the drivers of the carriages and their men climbed down and entered the inn. They quickly drank an ale each and then returned to their carts where a crowd had gathered outside in silence. Grace Hartley did not join them; she was not invited to.

Instead of taking their seats the men led the horses up the hill by hand.

Grace Hartley walked on foot behind them. She was joined by the familiar faces of friends and distant relatives.

The hearse-bearing horse struggled with its load as its shod feet struggled to gain a purchase on the stones. People stepped forward from the quiet crowd then to lend a hand. Men got behind the carriage and put their shoulders to it, King David Hartley's coffin dead in the centre as they heaved and pushed and sweated and puffed.

The cart creaked up the bottom half of the hill and then turned onto the track that cut a final diagonal stretch to Hepstonstall village with its soot-blackened frontages, and then moved along the main street, Town Gate, a tight passage of squat houses with dimly lit windows like eyes squinting into a storm, that ended abruptly where the flagstones met the turf, and after which nothing but miles of moors lay beyond.

They reached the churchyard of St Thomas a Becket. The men untied the coffin. They shouldered it and lifted it down.

They carried it to the hole that sat in the rich red soil like an open wound, glistening in the Yorkshire sunshine.

They held it there.

Epilogue
1775

Five hundred and sixty pounds in circular discs of grubby metal takes up a lot of space. At a quarter ounce a coin, it weighs heavy in the hand too. One hundred and fifteen ounces of metal in all.

She has the boy hoist it across the moortops for her. There is no need to fear thieves or highwaymen up here, for he carries the family name and that still means something up on the moor.

Her oldest boy is growing. He will be bigger than his father. Stronger and taller. He is filling out young, and already Mary and Isaac the younger look up to their older brother David, born the year after his father returned from the Black Country.

He knows the moors well. He has a feel for every porous bog and calamitous fissure. He knows the archipelago of remote farmsteads, and those that live there; he knows whether their owners had been a friend or foe to the Coiners and his late father whose face he no longer remembers.

His uncles have told him so. Schooled him. Old grudges have been carried over and vendettas remembered, but most profited well enough from what the King had done for them. A martyr, some call his father now. The Martyr Hartley. A gentleman. One of their own.

And they show gratitude still. His father's headstone is never bereft of phlox flowerheads and ale bottles both full and emptied, or yarn balls and sprigs of summer heather. Apples in the autumn, the occasional coin from those that can spare it. And once a stag skull sliced at the scalp, its young antlers flowering like coral, the dark ridges of its twisted bone stems stained dark by the Pennine peat.

357

Only a handful talk ill of his father, and even then they are words whispered behind closed doors amongst trusted company. The fear is still there because the stories still circulate: of burnt heads and broken bones. Hot pokers and musket sparks.

There are those treacherous bastard traitors who have fallen in with the mill men at the first opportunity, of course: those valley folk that sold up and let the money men take their soil and fence off their streams to sink water-wheels there, and build these great stone monstrosities in which boys like him were made to work for fourteen hours a day.

Many of his friends were in the mills now. Some had lost fingers, hands and limbs. One was blinded by the backlash of a snapped spinning belt, another left shrunken from lack of food and light and sleep, a half-formed boy kept small by industry.

The turnpike has brought noise and offcumdens and now there is talk of sinking another fresh stretch of canal through the heart of the valley too, as if a river wasn't enough. It wouldn't work. His mother said so and his uncles said so and all the men who paid a visit to Bell House with food and drink and clothes and clogs said so. All this was a passing fad, they said. Hand-looms were still the best way; any right-minded valley man or woman knew that. A hand-loom in a wool loft never killed a child. Only the men from the cities with their stone cathedrals of mass production killed children.

Down in the vale below there were already new mills. Not just for the cotton, but paper too. Mills brought people, families. Chimneys had grown from the ground as if born out of spring snowdrop bulbs, and Cragg Road was paved with slabs now. There were new cottages in the trees. Three had gone up in Hollin Hey Wood last summer, three more in the spring. Spa Wood echoed to the sound of more building; another mill. Whams Wood and Sandy Pickle Wood were shrinking; great gaps had appeared in their silent centres to make way for buildings to house dye vats and storage barns, combing racks and foremen's quarters.

There was a constant procession of stone and timber passing through these days, and the sound of the workers' voices rang up to the moor tops. Noise carries here. Always has. Couldn't the cough of a coming lawman be heard a mile off?

Yes. It was only a matter of time before the trees of Bell Hole would feel the bite of the forester's axe too. Mills needed fuel and it was all around them. Already David Hartley the younger pined for the old times when men with courage and initiative could control their turf. He finds himself nostalgic for a time he has never known.

He carries the coins right across the moor's interior now, where a flat dullness gives an impression of eternity until finally after a hard hour he drops down to an obscure valley called Sandbeds above the hamlet of Eastwood, and Lodge Farm, their new home, perched high and alone.

The dog goes with him. It trots alongside and then bounds ahead, stout chest puffed, short muscular legs flexing. It is still strong despite the advancing years, and the dog's blood runs on in many offspring it has spawned across the valley and beyond now. He has sired several similarly stubborn little dogs of the moors.

He whistles. Calls the dog's name. *Moidore.* The beast turns and runs back to him, tongue lolling, ears flapping.

The farmer is waiting for him when young David Hartley arrives. He has a sheaf of papers for the boy to take back. Once signed, the house and outbuildings will be theirs. The Hartleys' new home. Paid for in cash once stashed. This was his mother's foresight and good thinking, as these coins have been brought up from the soil, raised like ghosts. From beneath twisted roots. From holes in walls. From boxes buried. From beneath boulders. Some even tethered in purses deep in slow-flowing stream beds. Coins going green and mouldy, coins battered and bent but all perfectly milled and perfectly kept.

Tomorrow with their uncles' help they will hitch up the cart with their chairs and beds and tables and lanterns and rugs and plates and pots and their father's tools, and his mother and his brother and his sister and the dog and he will trek across the moor and move into the new house on the far edge of the moor.

And they will begin again.

Postscript

David Hartley was hanged at Tyburn in York on April 28th 1770 for forgery and diminishing the coin. He is buried in the hill-top graveyard at Heptonstall, West Yorkshire, England.

After a trial in which conflicting evidence was presented, much of it by James Broadbent whose numerous witness statements varied wildly, both Matthew Normanton and Robert Thomas were acquitted of the murder of William Deighton.

Coining continued in and around Calderdale sporadically over the next decade. The Coiner Thomas Clayton was arrested for counterfeiting in 1773, escaped in chains in 1774 and was then re-arrested in Liverpool while seeking passage to America. He offered a witness statement that implicated Normanton and Thomas in the attack on the exciseman.

Normanton and Thomas were charged again, this time with the highway robbery of William Deighton. Robert Thomas was convicted and sentenced to death but the case against Matthew Normanton was dropped. Clayton was also cleared of any involvement in the attack on Deighton, as was Thomas Spencer.

For his part Robert Thomas was executed in York in August 1774 and his body then hung in chains on Beacon Hill, Halifax, despite fervent opposition from the inhabitants of the town who gathered in protest against such gratuitous barbarity.

The following year Normanton was tried yet again, pleaded guilty and was convicted of the murder of William Deighton. He too was sentenced to death and executed in York in April 1775. His body was also hung in chains beside the weathered corpse of his friend, this time in the middle of the night so as to avoid further public protest.

The night before their respective executions both Normanton and Thomas gave written confessions for the murder of the exciseman.

Thanks to his collusion with the authorities, James Broadbent escaped prosecution for his involvement both in coining and the murder of William Deighton. His life beyond the trial is unknown.

The last recorded execution for coining was that of one Robert Iredale of Southowram, a village above Beacon Hill, in 1776, though the aforementioned acquitted Coiner Thomas Spencer was later executed in 1783 for leading a starving mob on a series of riotous raids on a Halifax corn grain store and several grain wagons during a period of civil unrest. Locally he was martyred as a man who had tried to feed the hungry, and was buried close to David Hartley.

William Hartley Sr. lived until 1773. During the downfall of the Coiners, the last sighting of his youngest son, William Hartley Jr, also known as the Duke of Edinburgh, was of him fleeing in his nightshirt. He later resurfaced, escaped any prosecution and lived until 1789. The middle brother Isaac Hartley, known as the Duke of York, was also never prosecuted for any offence and died what witnesses described as a slow and painful death at his home in Midgely near Mytholmroyd in 1815 at the age of eighty-three.

The solicitor Robert Parker, who brought about the downfall and prosecutions against the Coiners, enjoyed a successful legal career. He established the Halifax County Court and generated substantial outside financial investment for both the town and the Calder Valley during the burgeoning Industrial Revolution. Some of the money was used to build new turnpike roads, install a clean water supply and construct a canal, which is still in use today. Some historians and literary scholars believe that Robert Parker, admired for his integrity, was the inspiration for the character of Heathcliff in Emily Brontë's *Wuthering Heights*, written ten miles away in Haworth, West Yorkshire, and published in 1847.

Four years after her husband's execution Grace Hartley moved a mile or so across the moor to Lodge Farm. She paid £560 for her new home – in cash.

She died in 1802.

In June 2016, shortly after the completion of this book, the original fireplace in which the labourer Abraham Ingham was tortured and killed was uncovered in the Cross Inn, Heptonstall. A neighbouring pub, the White Lion, and the Heptonstall Museum both host several original Coiners artefacts.

Today many descendants of the Cragg Vale Coiners and their associates still reside in Mytholmroyd, West Yorkshire, and its surrounding areas.

Sources & Inspirations

The following books, publications, websites, films and recordings proved helpful in the writing of this book. I am especially indebted to *Clip a Bright Guinea: The Yorkshire Coiners of the Eighteenth Century* by J. Bright and *The Yorkshire Coiners 1767–1783 & Notes on Old and Prehistoric Halifax* by Henry Ling Roth, both of which contained several letters, news items and bill posters that I have replicated as accurately as possible. Most names featured in this telling of this story are those of real people.

Alexander, M. *British Folklore, Myths & Legends*. Sutton Publishing, 2002.

Bright, J. *Clip a Bright Guinea: The Yorkshire Coiners of the Eighteenth Century*. Robert Hale Ltd, 1971.

Bull, M. (Ed). *www.calderdalecompanion.co.uk*

Carey, P. *True History of the Kelly Gang*. Faber & Faber, 2000.

Cooper, D. *The Horn Fellow*. Faber & Faber, 1987.

Davison, D. (Ed). *The Penguin Book of Eighteenth-Century English Verse*. Penguin, 1973.

Defoe, D. *A Tour Through the Whole Island of Great Britain* by Daniel Defoe. Penguin, 1724–26 edition.

Drake, M & D. *Early Trackways in the South Pennines*. Pennine Heritage Network, 1982.

Ely, S. *Englaland*. Smokestack, 2015.

Foss, M. *Folk Tales of the British Isles*. Books Club Associates, 1977

Garner, A. *Strandloper*. Harvill Press, 1996.

Gaskill, M. *Crime Mentalities in Early Modern England*. Cambridge University Press, 2000.

Green, J. *Slang Down the Ages: The Historical Development of Slang*. Klye Cathie, 1993.

Grose, F. *1811 Dictionary of the Vulgar Tongue: A Dictionary of Buckish Slang, University Wit and Pickpocket Eloquence*. Digest Books, 1971.

Hartley, S. *Yorkshire Coiners*. Unpublished.

Hartley, S. (Ed). *www.yorkshirecoiners.com*

Here's a Health to the Barley Mow: A Century of Folk Customs and Ancient Rural Games. BFI, 2011.

Hughes, T. *Crow*. Faber, 1972.

Hughes, T & Godwin, F. *Elmet*. Faber, 1994.

Kershaw, P & Danks, V. *The Last Coiner*. Duchy Parade Films, 2006.

King, Ian 'Shedrock'. 'Yorkshire Coiners' from the album *Outlaws of England*. Released 2012.

Kingsnorth, P. *The Wake*. Unbound, 2014.

Ling Roth, H. *The Yorkshire Coiners 1767–1783 & Notes on Old and Prehistoric Halifax*. Kessinger Legacy Reprints, 1906.

Lupton, H. Glossary notes from *The Ballad of John Clare*. Dedalus, 2010.

Macfarlane, R. *Landmarks*. Hamish Hamilton, 2015.

Mills, A. D. *A Dictionary of British Place Names*. Oxford University Press, 2011.

Murty, S. *Summat A' Nowt: The History of Saxokakaurhs, A Long Forgotten Settlement*. Self-published, 2009.

Northern Earth magazine. Various issues. Billingsley, J. (Ed).

Odetta (Odetta Holmes). 'The Gallows Pole' (traditional) from *Odetta and the Blues*. Hallmark, 2013.

Ondaatje, M. *The Collected Works of Billy the Kid*. Picador, 1981.

Pegg, Bob. 'The Man From Luddenden Dean' from *The Last Wolf*. Rhiannon Music, 1998.

Requiem for a Village. Directed by David Gladwell. BFI, 1976.

Stripe, A. *Dark Corners of the Land*. Blackheath Books, 2012.

Tilston, S. 'King of the Coiners' from *Ziggurat*. Hubris Records, 2008.

Valley Life magazine (various issues) West, G. (Ed). LGB Media, Hebden Bridge.

Various. 'Hanging Johnny'. *Shanties & Sea Songs*. Crocodile Records, 2009.

Welsh, S. *Cragg Vale: A Pennine Valley*. Pennine Desktop publishing, 1993.

Whone, H. *Essential West Riding*. Smith Settle, 1987.

Whalley, B. *Protest Walks*. Unpublished.

Winstanley. Directed by Brownlow, K. and Mollo, A. 1975.

The original publisher of *The Gallows Pole* was the independent publishing house Bluemoose Books, based in Hebden Bridge, West Yorkshire.

For more information about their books please visit www.bluemoosebooks.com

Acknowledgements

Thank you Kevin Duffy, Hetha Duffy, my editors Leonora Rustamova and Lin Webb and all at Bluemoose Books who first brought this book to life, and saw it through many print-runs. To Delaney Jae at Artonix for the cover design.

For their support and input I wish to thank my agent Jessica Woollard and all at David Higham Associates: Alice Howe, Clare Israel, Penelope Killick. To Alexa von Hirschberg for the leap of faith, and all at Bloomsbury: Ros Ellis, Marigold Atkey, Jasmine Horsey. Ben Swank and Chet Weise and all at Third Man Books.

I extend gratitude to the Royal Society of Literature whose Brookleaze Grant enabled the undertaking of valuable research time. I am also extremely grateful to the Society of Authors' Roger Deakin Award, of which this book was the recipient, and which facilitated the completion of this work.

Thanks also to Steve Hartley, great, great, great, great, great grandson of King David Hartley. Steve has kept the Hartley story alive and his website www.yorkshirecoiners.com is a key resource for anyone who wishes to read more on the subject. The story of the Coiners lives on the lips of generations, and in the descendants of those on both sides of the law, so a broader thank you is extended to friends, neighbours and passing strangers in Calderdale, West Yorkshire who have imparted information, stories or opinions on the subject, and who have supported the book since its initial publication in 2017.

The Cragg Vale Coiners' Walk, a map to accompany the novel, has been designed by cartographer Christopher Goddard and is available from his website: www.christophergoddard.net.

Thanks also to Carol Gorner, and Richard Clegg at the Gordon Burn Trust. Robert and Jenny Dutson at The Workshop in Hebden Bridge for the practical coining advice. Claire Malcolm, Anna Disley and everyone at New Writing North. Jeff Barrett and all at *Caught by the River*. Thank you to Boff Whalley for sending me extracts from his book *Protest Walks*. Steve Ely. John Billingsley at Northern Earth magazine. All at The Book Case in Hebden Bridge and The Book Corner in Halifax. Mal Campbell and the Trades Club. Richard and Elizbeth Buccleuch and everyone at the Walter Scott Prize.

To friends old at new: David Atkinson and Anna Barker. The Shining Levels, who have recorded an album of music inspired by *The Gallows Pole*. Anthony Luke. Lisa Cradduck. Katy, Matt and Iris Calveley. Ian Stripe. Michael Curran at Tangerine Press. Sam Jordison and Eloise Millar at Galley Beggar Press. Nick and Candice Small. Alan the Ex-Postman. Mary Anne Hobbs and Elizabeth Alker at 6Music. Stephen May and Sarah Crown at Arts Council England. Rob St John and Emma Cardwell. Amy Liptrot. Jenn Ashworth. Thanks also to Richard Dawson and his vile stuff.

I reserve special gratitude to my parents, family and to my wife Adelle Stripe, who first suggested that perhaps this story needed telling.

Benjamin Myers
Upper Calder Valley
AD2019.

ALSO AVAILABLE BY BENJAMIN MYERS

BEASTINGS

Winner of the Portico Prize for Literature and the Northern Writers' Award

'A brilliant, brutal novel' Robert Macfarlane

A girl and a baby. A priest and a poacher. A savage pursuit through the landscape of a changing rural England.

When a teenage girl leaves the workhouse and abducts a child placed in her care, the local priest is called upon to retrieve them. Chased through the Cumbrian mountains of a distant past, the girl fights starvation and the elements, encountering the hermits, farmers and hunters who occupy the remote hillside communities. An American Southern Gothic tale set against the violent beauty of Northern England, *Beastings* is a sparse and poetic novel about morality, motherhood and corruption.

'Intimate and elemental . . . Myers has the potential to become a true tragedian of the fells'
GUARDIAN

'Bitter, alarming, occasionally visionary'
NEW STATESMAN

'Myers is quite simply an excellent and already accomplished writer. His prose is taut, confident, professionally polished but at the same time maintaining a sense of rustic and unrefined authenticity, that which is truly hewn'
SARAH HALL

ORDER YOUR COPY:

BY PHONE: +44 (0) 1256 302 699; **BY EMAIL:** DIRECT@MACMILLAN.CO.UK
DELIVERY IS USUALLY 3–5 WORKING DAYS. FREE POSTAGE AND PACKAGING FOR ORDERS OVER £20.
ONLINE: WWW.BLOOMSBURY.COM/BOOKSHOP
PRICES AND AVAILABILITY SUBJECT TO CHANGE WITHOUT NOTICE.*

WWW.BLOOMSBURY.COM/AUTHOR/BENJAMIN-MYERS-68131/

BLOOMSBURY PUBLISHING

PIG IRON

Winner of the Gordon Burn Prize

'One of my best reads this year . . . A deeply rural story, a book full of passion for the English countryside and centred on the conflict between the travelling and the settled community' Melvin Burgess

John-John wants to escape his past. But the legacy of brutality left by his boxer father, King of the Gypsies, Mac Wisdom, overshadows his life. His new job as an ice cream man should offer freedom, but instead pulls him into the dark recesses of a northern town where his family name is mud. When he attempts to trade prejudice and parole officers for the solace of the rural landscape, Mac's bloody downfall threatens John-John's very survival.

'His poetic vernacular brims with that quality most sadly lost – humanity'
GUARDIAN

'A staggeringly powerful book. It held me page by page, totally took me over. If I had to opt for a single word to encompass the experience of reading the book, I'd settle for "ferocious"' Dominic Cooper, author of *The Dead Winter* and *Sunrise*

'Authentic characterisation, a monstrously compelling plot, and frequent humour . . . *Pig Iron* deserves to find itself on many a reading list, if not the National Curriculum'
3: AM

ORDER YOUR COPY:

BY PHONE: +44 (0) 1256 302 699; BY EMAIL: DIRECT@MACMILLAN.CO.UK
DELIVERY IS USUALLY 3–5 WORKING DAYS. FREE POSTAGE AND PACKAGING FOR ORDERS OVER £20.
ONLINE: WWW.BLOOMSBURY.COM/BOOKSHOP
PRICES AND AVAILABILITY SUBJECT TO CHANGE WITHOUT NOTICE.

WWW.BLOOMSBURY.COM/AUTHOR/BENJAMIN-MYERS-68131/

BLOOMSBURY PUBLISHING